the Summer of Lost things

the Summer of Lost things

a novel

Jenn Bennett

An Imprint of HarperCollinsPublishers

hc.com

FIRST EDITION

Interior text design by Diahann Sturge-Campbell

Library of Congress Cataloging-in-Publication Data

Names: Bennett, Jenn author
Title: The summer of lost things : a novel / Jenn Bennett.
Description: New York : HarperCollins, 2026.
Identifiers: LCCN 2025030433 | ISBN 9780063452237 trade paperback | ISBN 9780063452220 ebook
Subjects: LCSH: Treasure troves—Fiction | LCGFT: Romance fiction | Novels
Classification: LCC PS3602.E46867 S86 2026 | DDC 813/.6—dc23/eng/
    20250905
LC record available at https://lccn.loc.gov/2025030433

ISBN 978-0-06-345223-7

26 27 28 29 30 LBC 5 4 3 2 1

For Gina

Chapter 1

The afternoon I flew back to Michigan after my freshman year at Harvard, no one was there to pick me up from the airport.

It's not as though I expected a shower of confetti to welcome me home, but having a friendly face to greet me would've been a comfort, which was something I hadn't had much of lately. This past week alone, (a) I found out my financial aid was in serious danger of being stripped away, and (b) I was forced to give up my spot on a once-in-a-lifetime field study trip to Europe.

Not exactly how I expected my school year to end.

Or how I wanted my summer to start.

Jazmine Neely, I said to myself, staring at our recent texts as I slid into the back seat of a rideshare outside Ford International Airport in Grand Rapids, Michigan. *What's the real reason you didn't pick me up?* I'd sweated in baggage claim for half an hour before she texted apologies for why she couldn't make it, blaming a vague work emergency. Jaz and I hadn't seen each other since I flew east to Massachusetts for college last fall, and I was *almost* positive she was lying about the work emergency. But, even though I was supposed to be the big brain of our childhood friend group, I couldn't for the life of me figure out why.

"Hi there." A cheerful, ginger-haired rideshare driver smiled at me from the front seat of his sedan, unaware that he was my second choice for the hour-plus drive from Grand Rapids to my small hometown on the shore of Lake Michigan. "It's Paige, right?"

"That's me," I assured him from the back seat while zipping an outer pocket on my carry-on.

"And today we're going all the way to Lake Michigan, huh? Haven Beach?"

"Yep."

Eyes in the rearview mirror scanned me from top to bottom. My dark hair was wound into a messy bun, and I'd made a rash decision the previous night to cut my own bangs in my dorm—I wanted a change before flying home. I followed an online tutorial, but they were fringier than I wanted and a little too long, which made me briefly self-conscious under the driver's gaze. But it wasn't just that. My academically challenged skin hadn't seen much sun lately. Arm and leg muscles, once toned from swimming and dock-jumping into the lake, had weakened. I felt like a hermit emerging from a cave after months of solitude.

I was *not* summer-ready.

The driver's roving gaze finally stopped on my crimson Harvard T-shirt before he pulled away from the airport curb, merging with other cars. "Harvard, huh? You an Ivy League girl?"

I nodded.

"Cool. That's out in Massachusetts, isn't it?"

"Yeah, Cambridge."

"Is this your first time here, or . . . ?"

"No, I just go to college out east," I told him. "Haven Beach is my hometown."

The car curved around an exit ramp as we left the airport.

"Cool, okay. That's one sweet strip of sand. At least, in the summer."

"Definitely better than anything I saw out east."

"Nice," he confirmed. "You do a lot of boating in Haven?"

My family hadn't owned a boat since my father ditched us. "Paddleboarding."

He glanced at me in the mirror again as if he were trying to picture me on a board. "For real? That's dope."

It was the one thing I was looking forward to doing while I was home.

The driver's phone buzzed, and he excused himself to take a personal phone call. I popped in earbuds, lazily slouching in the back seat, and watched through my window as the glass-and-steel buildings of Grand Rapids changed to highway and flat green land. The one-hour drive to the coast seemed to take longer than my flight from Boston, especially with late-afternoon sun making me feel sleepy. I tried not to think about Jazmine avoiding me, or the daunting task that I needed to brave this summer: facing my estranged father for the first time in several years.

Talk about annoyances. My father was Public Annoyance Number One.

If it weren't for him, I'd be with the rest of my small academic department, who were all getting ready to fly to Italy for a special summer "excursion seminar," touring museums and studying art masterworks. Being the all-around overachiever that I am—Jazmine's words, not mine—I was pursuing a concentration in history of art and architecture. I'd always loved history, and my nana was a painter, so I grew up surrounded by art. Getting into Harvard's art history program was a dream come true . . . until the person who both inspired the dream and raised me died unexpectedly last summer, just a few weeks before my first semester in Cambridge was due to begin.

In fact, it was Nana Malone's beach cottage where I was heading right now, where I'd lived since I was six, after my mother died. Nana raised me by herself—my father was already long gone by that time—and she left me the cottage in her will.

She didn't leave me much else.

The Malones *used* to be prominent Haven residents, until my asshole father changed all of that. Just by existing, he'd taken away everything I'd worked for over the past year and snatched away my trip overseas. And if I couldn't get through to him this summer, I couldn't afford to return to Harvard in the fall.

Just thinking about it made my stomach hurt.

The scenery changed as we drove through rural towns, and as the sun began approaching its race to golden hour, I spotted a sign that gave me butterflies.

WELCOME TO HAVEN BEACH

WHERE THE LITTLE RIVER MEETS AMERICA'S THIRD COAST

Feeling excited and panicky all at once, I took out my earbuds and leaned my forehead against the glass of the window to greedily soak in the sights. The road hugged the southern bank of the Little River as we drove through Haven's downtown—where a kaleidoscope of colorful shops and restaurants called to tourists and locals. After a few blocks of bustling sidewalks and shops hawking T-shirts, the river flowed into Haven Harbor, and finally into Lake Michigan. We made the turn onto Shoreline Drive, and after nine months away, I gazed at the slow-rolling waves that crashed on its beachy shore.

My ocean. That's what I used to call it when I was a kid. Everyone who visits here for the first time is amazed by the size of it.

How could all this blue water be a lake when you can't see the opposite shore? Milwaukee was two and half hours across the water from us by ferry. Chicago was the same distance southwest. But you couldn't see either one from Michigan.

Nothing but endless blue water.

"Captain Wyrd Jack's pirate ship," the driver said, squinting into the distance, where an old packet steamer was moored on the harbor, outside a museum.

Wyrd Jack was one of the town's big tourism draws, the only man to be officially arrested and charged with piracy on the Great Lakes, back in 1929. He captained a ship that hauled mail to Chicago until he decided he could make a better living by hijacking cargo on Lake Michigan, stealing lumber from the government and alcohol from gangsters . . . Any boat on the lake was fair game for hijacking. When he finally got caught, he wrote a poem from jail that was said to contain all the information needed to find his most valuable stolen treasure: the priceless lost antiquity known as the Golden Venus, a standing marble sculpture covered in gold. It was found off the coast of Italy in the 1500s, claimed by Charles V, Holy Roman emperor, then it went missing for hundreds of years . . . until Wyrd Jack stole it off another smuggling boat passing through the Great Lakes. He conspired with his pregnant wife, Mabel, to hide the golden statue, leaving nothing but his prison poem to point at its location.

Thousands of treasure hunters had shown up here from around the world to find the Golden Venus. No one had gotten lucky yet. At least, not when it came to the statue; it wasn't the only thing Wyrd Jack had smuggled over the years.

"Did you hear someone in your town found a single bar of gold in a sewer drain a few weeks ago? Been speculation on the local news over whether it was a part of a bigger cache of gold buried by Wyrd Jack back in the day."

Jazmine had texted me the news story last month.

"Believe it or not, I'm descended from him—Wyrd Jack," I told the driver. "He was my great-great-grandfather."

"No lie? That's crazy. You know where the rest of the gold is? Or maybe where the mother lode is buried, that priceless Roman statue that Wyrd Jack smuggled—some ancient goddess of love?"

"Afraid I don't." Not for lack of trying. The gold bar that had recently been found was a fluke. Golden Venus was the real treasure. Everyone in my family had looked for it. When I was a kid, I spent most of my summers combing the beaches, chasing down clues to its existence with a group of four friends. We called ourselves the Wags—short for Scallywags—and growing up, we sometimes pretended to be pirates ourselves and hid our own "treasures."

I was Wag number one. Jazmine, the person who *should* be giving me a ride home, she was a Wag, too. Another old friend, Benny, was Wag three. But it was the fourth Wag who truly matched my own zeal for treasure hunting back in the day, my oldest friend in town, a towheaded kid named Seb Jansen.

When we were young, Seb and I were inseparable, daring to go places that the others wouldn't, in search of the gold. He had a big personality and tons of energy to explore and see new things. My nana encouraged our adventures and even gave me and Seb a matching pair of Blackbeard decoder rings from a 1940s radio show about pirates. I still wore it on a chain around my neck, along with a ring that belonged to my deceased mother. And as I gazed out the window in the back of the rideshare, I couldn't help but run my fingers over the decoder ring's warm metal and wonder what Seb was doing with his life.

No telling. Seb left both me and the Wags behind years ago.

The driver turned onto the main drag that ran perpendicular to the public beach. I caught a glimpse of a Slushie-red lighthouse as we traveled south along the coast, where sleek resorts and lake homes faced the water. Toward the end of all the newer developments were smaller beach cottages that had been around since the late 1800s, perched on the edge of the sand and surrounded by wild grass. As the car slowed, I spotted my nana's house, painted various jewel-like shades of blue and surrounded by a white picket fence.

Heron Cottage.

Two tiny bedrooms, one tiny bath. Named after the great blue herons that lived around the lake. Females often made nests in our trees. I remembered nearly running into one of the big birds on the beach the last time I was at the cottage—I'd been walking around in a fog, tying up loose ends after Nana's funeral. My heart squeezed at the thought of her, and it was all I could do to endure a fresh wave of grief that washed over me as I hefted my luggage out of the car.

"Right on the water, *noice*," the driver said, making a half-concerted effort to help me with my bags as he looked around. "You ever rent this? You could make a ton of cash."

"It's a private home."

"Shame."

I thanked him for the ride and tipped him on the rideshare app to get him to go away, sighing when the wheels of his car briefly spun in the sandy gravel of the driveway. Then I quickly took stock of the cottage while digging out my old keys.

All the plantings around the front of the home were overgrown and spilling across the stony walkway, spiky sedge and butterfly milkweed. We didn't have much grass, but what we *did* have should've been mown. Our family lawyer handled most of the probating of my nana's will and was supposed to have hired lawn care services.

Guess I'd be doing it myself.

Even the cottage's mailbox was overflowing. "What the hell am I paying you for, Mr. Kimbell?" I whispered to myself. I supposed I'd add "book a meeting with the attorney" to my to-do list.

At least I'd made it here. I stuck my key in the front door and inhaled familiar scents before I even stepped inside. Old wood and my grandmother's oil paints, the smell of my childhood. For a fraction of a moment, some sort of internal autopilot kicked in: I was home, which meant Nana was just there, inside, waiting for me. A strange, disconcerting feeling followed when my sluggish brain remembered she'd never welcome me home again. I paused at the door as grief crept out of the corners of my heart and ambushed me with hurt.

Oh, Nana. I don't think I can do this . . .

I swiped at my eyes before tears could fall and exhaled a shaky breath. Then I steadied myself and swung the front door open. When I did, shock hit me like a punch in the gut.

My family home was not in the state I'd left it last fall.

Furniture lay broken. Beer bottles were strewn everywhere. Books scattered. And a pane of glass in the back living room window had been smashed.

The beach cottage had been trashed. Utterly.

"What the . . . ?" Dazed, I parked my rolling luggage near Nana's old rocking chair, the spines of which were busted, as if someone had kicked them. And when I took tentative steps across the old wood floor, my sneakers crunched broken glass.

Books *everywhere*.

Pizza boxes littered the kitchenette.

My nana's painting easel lay on its side.

A warm breeze blew through the smashed window as I crossed the small living area to the narrow hallway that contained the bath and bedrooms. Nana's mattress had been pushed off the bed. The drawers of her dresser were pulled out, as if someone had been searching for something. But last summer, before I left for Harvard, I'd packed up all her stuff and taken it down to the basement. So there was nothing in her room to find. Nothing but her paintings—all signed with her name, *Kitty Malone*—which had been taken off the wall and stood in a stack. One was slashed down the middle.

"What the hell . . . ?"

My mind snapped to the news story that my driver had mentioned, the one about the gold bar being found in a sewer last month. If that renewed the public's interest in Wyrd Jack's treasure, people might be coming out of the woodwork. Professional treasure hunters, and not-so-professional. Had one discovered that I was related to him? Broken into the cottage to look for more gold bars?

Distressed, I stepped out of Nana's old bedroom and opened the bathroom door. All my toiletries and towels were dumped in a heap inside the bathtub.

But it wasn't until I entered my old bedroom that my shock shifted to anger.

It was the only room in the house that wasn't completely trashed. But that was the least of my worries.

My paddleboard was missing from the pegs on my wall. Paddleboard, paddle, leash—all my equipment, gone. And that wasn't all . . .

Someone has been sleeping in my bed.

Wrinkled sheets formed the shape of a stranger's body. A small bedside pottery tray—one that normally held jewelry I'd remove at night—was being used as an ashtray for joints and empty disposable weed vapes. When I stepped farther into the room, I glanced at my old chest of drawers and found myself staring at two more surprises.

The first was a spotted sandpiper, lazily nesting inside my open underwear drawer.

The second was a silver key chain sitting behind the sandpiper.

Not my key chain, not my keys.

"Scram, beach chicken," I shouted at the bird, shooing it out of my drawer.

It made a lot of noise, and for a moment, I thought it might even attack me. But when it finally left the room in a flurry of feathers and headed out the broken window, I was able to pick up the key chain.

That's when I spotted the vintage brass decoder ring, dangling with the rest of the keys.

Shocked, my hand flew to the matching ring that hung on a chain around my neck.

A coldness spread through my core.

All at once, I knew who'd been squatting here and had trashed my nana's cottage like the world was about to end.

Seb Jansen, erstwhile fourth Wag and the biggest deadbeat in town. My former childhood best friend.

Way former.

He'd just made himself my new enemy.

Chapter 2

It took forever to clean up the mess. I filled three garbage bags with trash, clogged up the vacuum, and scraped dried paint off the floor. Tossed a bag of dog kibble—I'd never owned a dog in my life—and filled up the washing machine. There wasn't anything I could do about the broken window today, so I did my best to cover it with cardboard and tape.

When I sat down on the sofa to rest, despite all my hard work, all I could see was my nana's kind eyes staring back at me from a photo on the table, and I knew she'd be utterly upset if she walked in here and saw things in this state. What if I hadn't come home this summer? Would this place even be standing by the end of the year? I felt violated on Nana's behalf, but instead of indignation, I just felt empty. And sad.

Bits of memories surfaced . . . Nana cooking stew in the kitchen. Swaying me in the rocking chair, which was now broken. Laughing with joy when I got into Harvard. All the grief I'd been keeping in check suddenly breached my defenses, and I held my face in my hands and sobbed.

How can I be in this house without you?

I worried coming back home would be hard, but I was wholly unprepared. Because for a long time that afternoon, while I wallowed on the sofa, it felt like the past year in Cambridge had been a fantasy to distract me from my loss. My heart broke all over again.

When I finally pulled myself together, I surveyed the remaining damage in the cottage.

All of this was Seb's fault.

I swear to God, I'm going to kill that boy.

Seb Jansen was a walking, talking tornado. An absolute disaster. At least, he used to be. I hadn't laid eyes on him for . . . two years? Since we were seventeen—Seb's seventeenth birthday, in fact. He got sent off to a military boot camp for troubled teens that day, right before our senior year was about to begin, and he hadn't been back since. Not that I'd heard, anyway.

My friendship with Seb soured long before boot camp, when he decided he'd rather spend his days stirring up trouble with the local criminal element, the Vanderburg boys, than hanging out with the Wags.

I was surprised he was in town now.

Trashing a cottage is something the old Seb might do, but not *this* cottage. Not my grandma's house. Nana loved Seb, and he loved her. He'd spent half his childhood here.

Why would he do this to me?

I dreaded confronting him, but there was no way I was letting this slide.

Other than knocking on his father's door, I had no idea how to track him down. Wiping the remaining tears from my cheeks, I lost my mind and left a voicemail for Jazmine that I instantly knew I should've deleted, angrily asking if she knew about the state of the cottage. Then I left another one, apologizing for the first. And when the sun began setting, I realized that I hadn't had anything to eat all day except dry airplane cookies and a Coke.

So I gave up on cleaning, slipped on my favorite old pair of cutoff jeans, and headed out the back door.

Everything looked okay outside, thankfully. A wide porch was attached to the back of the house, with steps leading down to the beach, and at the bottom of them, the trunk of a long-dead tree that had been carved into a great blue heron. When I was a kid, all my friends called it "Mr. Legs" because they seemed to go on forever. Mr. Legs stood as sentry to the porch, and sometimes people walking down the beach would stop and take photos of him.

Heron Cottage is about a quarter mile from civilization in either direction down the beach. To the south were a couple other cottages that I could see from my narrow back porch, if I peeked around Nana's giant porch swing. But when I hiked down the steps onto sand, and walked in the opposite direction for five minutes, past a hill blocking the view of the town, I ended up at Neely Marina, where all the rich folks docked their boats.

Owned by Jazmine Neely's parents.

I'd spent more than my fair share of my childhood running the marina's maze of docks and piers with Jazmine and the other Wags. But it wasn't where I was headed now. Right outside the marina's entrance was a small ring of food trucks surrounding a dozen picnic tables. A smattering of tourists and locals dined on burgers and fish tacos under strings of white lights while a jangly classic rock song played over speakers.

I followed the scent of sweet cornmeal batter toward the mustard-yellow food truck parked at the far end of the circle, Patty's Pups. It was owned by Jazmine's older sister, who, despite being in her late twenties, looked so much like my old friend that the sight of her made me both happy and hurt. I *still* hadn't heard back from Jazmine.

"Well, what do we have here?" Patty grinned down at me from the open window of the food truck, splotchy freckles smattering her light brown skin. A bandanna that matched the yellow of the truck was tied tight around her head, binding springy curls. "The big brain is back from Princeton, and she's got bangs."

"Harvard," I corrected, smiling back at her as I fiddled with my bangs. "And I'm not sure about them yet."

"They're different."

High praise—typical Patty. "Still serving up the best corn dogs in Michigan, I see. Thought I was hungry before, but now I *really* am. Smells like home!"

Patty's mouth lifted into a pleased smile for a moment. Then she frowned. "Nuh-uh, I keep telling you guys, this is *not* your personal kitchen. I'll let you have three on the house this sum-mer," she said, holding up fingers. "After that, you're paying—I've got the same deal with Jazmine. This isn't gonna be a repeat of last summer."

No Malone in my family tree would dare turn down free food. "Fine. I'll take one now, extra mustard."

Patty nodded, and while she dunked a hot dog into cornmeal batter, I grabbed several napkins from the metal counter. "Speak-ing of, I've been trying to get in touch with Jaz all day. Is she at the marina? She was supposed to pick me up from the airport . . ."

One brow shot up. "And she didn't?"

I shook my head. "She isn't mad at me, is she?" Honestly, I couldn't understand why she would be. We kept in semi-regular touch over the past year. Texting. Commenting on socials. A few phone calls. When I told her my summer plans were changed at the last minute to come home, she seemed so excited.

Her sister squinted at me with a little suspicion. Was I missing something?

"Not that I'm aware," Patty finally said, using tongs to lower the battered corn dog into hot fat. "However, Jaz has been, shall we say, struggling a little lately."

"Struggling?" That alarmed me. Jazmine hadn't said anything to me about this. I knew we weren't as involved with each other's daily grind like we were before I left for Harvard, but she was still my best friend. I would've liked to feel confident that she'd reach out to me if she needed anything. But now I wasn't so sure.

"You didn't hear that from me. If she wants to share, she will . . ."

I nodded. "Of course."

Patty shrugged lightly and clapped her tongs together. "She rarely comes down to the food truck anymore, unless our parents threaten her with death. However, if you don't need to get in touch with her tonight, she should be at work tomorrow, bright and early."

"Thanks," I told her, when a flash of light caught our attention farther up the beach. A bonfire roared to life, and a crowd of people cheered. "I thought the mayor put a stop to bonfires inside city limits?"

Patty signaled for a waiting customer to approach the counter. "Dock bros don't care about rules."

Dock bros were Haven's version of a beach bum. Their beach bonfires were legendary—not for parties, but as beacons that drew crowds to their version of a non-secret Fight Club. Most of the crowd that ran with these guys were rowdy high school dropouts who liked to pretend they were the next MMA champions. Some of them were scumbags with serious police records. The highest in the food chain were the Vanderburg boys—a family who lived on a compound outside of town. Daddy Vanderburg, otherwise known as Big Burg around town, was a "prepper," one of those end-of-the-world, let's-amass-guns-in-the-woods, fuck-society types. If there was an illegal way to make money, he took part in it.

The Vanderburgs were not good and decent folk.

"Big Burg's doing house arrest for manslaughter. Not sure if you heard."

"Jaz told me a few months ago."

"And Big Burg's oldest, Paul? He got hauled off to jail a few days ago for drunk and disorderly," Patty informed me, and then added, "fighting your boy."

She didn't have to say his name. I knew from the way she arched a brow that she meant Seb. Who else did I know in this town who would be fighting on the beach? None of my *actual* friends, that's for sure.

"He hasn't been 'my' boy for years," I complained when she set the freshly fried corn dog into a paper food tray and slid it across the metal counter. "Last I heard, Seb was practically Paul Vanderburg's shadow. Are they on the outs now?" To be fair, I hadn't heard much of anything about Seb since he got sent away to boot camp two years ago.

"Apparently. Not sure what Seb did to piss off that crowd, but they don't seem to be friendly anymore. Bet you a million bucks he's over there at that bonfire right now, about to get his ass beat again. If he keeps taunting the Vanderburgs, he's going to end up in jail," Patty said, shaking her head. "Dammit, got a line forming. See you around, Paige."

"Appreciate you," I told her, holding up the corn dog in thanks, but she was too busy to notice. I cast my gaze toward the bonfire and begrudgingly headed in that direction, burning my tongue on the fried crust while I woofed down my free supper. As I got closer, I surveyed the group of people—mostly male—who gathered around a flaming pile of wood scraps and cardboard boxes. It appeared that Patty was right: a fight was about to go down. The crowd was watching a couple of shirtless, tanned white guys who were circling each other and shouting out taunts.

The fighters were both lean and muscular. One had a military-short buzz cut, and as I got closer, my pulse pounded inside my temples and my anxiety spiked. When Seb first got sent away to military school up north, he mailed me a handwritten letter that included a printed photo of him with his new buzz cut—his one-and-only attempt to contact me. Now I was recalling that photo and struggling to match the face I once knew with the buzz cut in the middle of this impromptu fighting ring.

A loud barking dog tore me out of my thoughts. I swiveled to find the ugliest, shaggiest husky I'd ever laid eyes on—no leash, no apparent owner—barking madly at me. I flinched and backed up. Me and dogs? We didn't get along. I was bitten by a Doberman when I was a young child, and I'd never gotten over the fear.

This dog was no Doberman, but it was certainly big enough to scare me.

Those ice-blue husky eyes, so otherworldly . . .

When I backed away, the other fighter inside the bonfire ring turned to glance at the dog, squinting and pushing blond hair away from his face to reveal one blackened eye. I immediately knew I'd been mistaken about the other fighter.

This was Seb.

It just wasn't the Seb I knew.

Loose blond waves swooped over his forehead. A pair of board shorts hung from his hips, threatening to fall off. Bronzed muscles glistened in the firelight.

Had it been only two years since we'd laid eyes on each other? In that time, the sweet, skinny boy I once knew had gone from gangly to utterly *ripped* and now looked like a full-grown man.

His eyes widened. "Paige?"

Anger rose, swift and hot. "You're dead to me, Sebastian Jansen!" I shouted.

The buzz-cut fighter laughed, turning toward me to reveal the face of a male model . . . if that model's face had been covered in burns and scars. I knew him, too, unfortunately. "Pretty Paul." That's what people called him. His real name was Paul Vanderburg, the proverbial king of the dock bros. He'd graduated two years before us.

The devil of Haven Beach.

"Looks like we have a new contender," he called out. "Think you can hold your own against a doughy girl instead of me? I'd love to watch that, Jansen."

Doughy? God, I hate him.

Seb replied, but I couldn't hear it for all the damned barking. Or maybe I was just too busy being spellbound by the sight of Seb after so long. The way he looked at me, with eyes bigger than the moon, caused a chaotic flurry of emotions.

I wanted to hug him.

To ask him a thousand questions.

Then push his face into the sand.

Make him hurt like he'd hurt me.

But a couple dozen faces were staring and whispering about

me—"That's the Malone girl, the family that owned the cherry farm outside of town"—and then I heard someone else in the crowd say my grandmother's name.

That was my tipping point. Fresh grief welled up, and everything suddenly felt as if it were closing in on me. The fighting ring. The barking dog. The wild faces watching . . .

I can't do this.

I turned on my heel and walked away from the bonfire before I did something regrettable like breaking down in front of all these dumb boys. My chest was tight as I trudged across the sand, ignoring whistles and taunts and the dog's barking, which seemed to follow me, no matter how fast I walked. Then I felt heavy footfalls coming up fast from behind.

"Paige! Hold up!"

I swung around to find both the husky and Seb racing toward me. Seb gripped a T-shirt in one hand. His racing slowed to a jog until he caught up with me. The black dog stopped behind him and continued barking.

"For the love of Christ, shut it, Punkin!" Seb told the ugly husky, breathless. "Nobody's fighting, okay? No barking!"

Punkin . . . ?

The dog quit barking and politely sat, panting.

"She's a retired sled dog from up north. Got her off a musher . . . it's a long story. Anyway, she hates fighting," he explained, almost sheepish but not quite.

"And you hate dogs," I said, remembering the mystery bag of kibble that I threw away inside the cottage when I was cleaning up. "Since when did that change?"

He chuckled and tugged his T-shirt over his head, one that had the Neely Marina logo on the front. "No, *you* hate dogs. I only went along with that out of solidarity after you had to have a rabies shot, princess."

"Don't call me that."

"Why? You still have the crown."

Before my father ruined our family, the Malones owned one of the best cherry orchards in western Michigan. We lived in a stunning turreted Victorian near the harbor on the "good" side of town. Even after we lost the farm, I entered the Little Miss Cherry Princess contest during the town's annual Cherry Festival when I was seven years old and won a plastic crown.

Seb has never let me forget it.

He exhaled, curious eyes flicking over me. "Bangs, huh?"

Jesus. Never cutting my own hair again, that was for sure. *Stupid influencers and their dumb videos . . .*

"I just can't believe it," he said. "You look so different. But also, the same . . . ?"

So did he, now that I wasn't forced to avoid staring at his bare chest. "You look like a homeless surfer who got clocked by his board."

He wrinkled his nose and gingerly touched the skin around his black eye. "Clocked by Pretty Paul Vanderburg, but yeah. I've been doing a little surfing. What about you? I thought you were going to Europe for the summer. Surprised to see you back home."

How would he even know about Europe? And he didn't look all that surprised, frankly. Were he and Jazmine talking again? She hadn't mentioned him.

Police lights flashed on Harbor Drive, the main drag that curved along the lake.

"Shit," Seb said. "We should probably . . ."

He didn't have to tell me. The last thing I needed today was getting questioned by the local Haven Beach cops, who all seemed to be a horrible mix of dumb, power-hungry, and bored. Seb whistled at his dog and set off after me as I headed past the food truck park, praying that Patty didn't see me with Seb.

"Christ, Paige! Slow down. Thought you were studying art history, not track and field."

"And I thought I could leave this town for two measly semesters and come back to find my own home intact." I halted long enough to dig his key ring out of my pocket and threw it at him, missing by a mile. "Don't even tell me it wasn't you who trashed the cottage."

"But it wasn't!" He bent low to search for his keys in the sand, shoving blond waves out of his eyes. "Paige, come on—"

"Don't, okay? Just don't. Your lies may work on the rest of the people in this town, but they don't work on me anymore."

I continued trudging across the sand, leaving him behind as he dropped a dozen f-bombs while searching for his keys. For a few minutes, I occasionally glanced back at him and the dog, wondering if he'd just give up and leave. But after I rounded the little hill that harbored my grandmother's cottage and made it to the back porch, I felt him running up behind me again.

"I found 'em," he announced, like I cared.

"Next time I'll throw them in the lake. See that?" I said, pointing toward the window I'd secured with tape and cardboard. "You're paying for that."

"Me?" he said, sounding like the bewildered boy I once knew. And I suppose it was the proverbial straw that broke the camel's back, because all the grief and hurt I'd been feeling earlier while cleaning up the cottage now came back in a rush of anger.

"How *dare* you," I said, stopping at the bottom of the cottage's back porch. "Nana would have been so disappointed. Would've broken her heart that you did this to our home. She took care of you when your dad was working—washed your clothes, fed you. Gave you presents."

"Paige—"

"And to pay her back, you break into the cottage—"

"I didn't break in!" He pulled out his sandy key ring and jangled it in my face. "I still have a fucking key!"

That honestly surprised me. "You've been letting yourself into my house?"

His eyes flicked everywhere but my face as he tried to come up with a story. But I knew him too well, knew that fight-or-flight look on his face and the nervous laugh that followed. "Okay, I may have, once or twice, crashed here—but only when I didn't have any other options. I had the old spare house key—"

"And that gives you the right to host ragers here and tear up my stuff? Nana nursed my mother in that rocking chair! It's been in our family for decades. But if you didn't care about that, I thought for sure you'd respect Nana's paintings. Four of them were so damaged, I don't think they can be saved. What the hell is wrong with you?"

He looked wired and exasperated. Defensive. "I didn't break the chair or the paintings, Paige. You've gotta believe—"

"I don't 'gotta' do nothing," I said, unable to stop my eyes from brimming with tears. "Why should I believe anything you say? You made it clear that you didn't want anything to do with me or any of your other friends years ago when you all but abandoned the Wags for those fucking Vanderburg dirtbags!"

"I got sent off to boot camp!" he shouted, throwing up his arms while his dog started barking at us again.

"And we all tried to get you out of that place! You know we did, even though you barely spoke to us the year before you got sent away. We still wanted to help you. You know this! After Nana got in a fight with your dad when she tried to intervene, and you sent me that letter and told me to leave you alone—"

"Because helping me was pointless, all right? I was fucked, and I'd done it to myself, and I just had to get through the punishment. That letter, by the way, was supposed to be me riding off into the sunset. You're spoiling my dramatic goodbye right this minute, you know." He said this as if he were joking, but I heard hurt beneath his easy words.

"I left you alone, just like you asked, Seb. I didn't write you back. I didn't call. And I didn't visit. I did what you asked, only to have you waltz back into my life with a sledgehammer!"

"I don't know how many times I need to say this, but I did not wreck the cottage, Paige. I mean, sure, I'm no domestic goddess and may have *occasionally* left the cottage a mess when I *occasionally* crashed there while you were away at Harvard—"

"She's dead," I blurted, angry and confrontational. "Nana is dead. She's been dead for almost an entire year."

Seb opened his mouth to say something and then shut it. He stood still, a little frozen, as if he had no idea how to respond.

"Cut the shit," I said. "You wouldn't dare break into here if she were still alive. And I know Benny told you about the funeral because I asked him to call you last summer when it happened, seeing how he was the only Wag you stayed in touch with," I said, accusatory, then a fresh wave of grief washed over me, and I felt my shoulders sag with the weight of it. When I spoke again, my voice was small and broken. "You didn't come, Seb. She practically raised you, and you couldn't even bother to show up at her funeral—not for her, and not even for me."

I would not cry in front of him, I just wouldn't. When tears brimmed, I turned my face away and climbed the porch steps past the Mr. Legs tree-trunk sculpture, rushing to swing the screen door open so that I could get the cottage unlocked before I lost control.

Chapter 3

Wild emotions pinwheeled inside my chest, and I hated that Seb could make me feel like this within minutes of seeing him again. I couldn't think straight. The dog's barking continued to echo around the beach as I struggled with my keys, and just when I was about to scream at the dog, Seb circled the screen door, ducking his head to get in my face.

"Paige. Please listen—"

"Stop it! Don't touch me!"

He held up both hands in surrender. "Not touching, just trying to talk."

"I said everything I wanted to say. Just go!" My trembling fingers finally got the door unlocked. I pushed it open and stepped inside, about to slam it in his face when he finally gave me a real answer.

"I didn't come to Nana Malone's funeral because I wasn't in town, okay? I was in another state. I couldn't."

"I don't believe you."

"Fine, I was also too fucking scared to come," he said gruffly from the other side of the screen door.

That I believed.

"I was scared," he repeated, "and I didn't know how to re-connect with you after everything. It was spineless and selfish, and I've regretted it. Paige, listen to me. I'm sorry I was a such a fuckup. I know how this looks right now, with the state of the cottage and that bonfire fight back there—I get it, okay? I've been a coward, and I'm just really sorry."

I stood in the cottage, staring back out at him. Part of me wanted to tell him that his absence made Nana's death so much worse for me. That I was so alone last summer, and even until the moment the funeral ended, I kept looking to see if he'd come.

But I didn't say any of that.

"Goddammit, Punkin!" he shouted at the black dog, who had nudged her snout between the wooden screen door and the doorframe and was pushing her way inside the cottage. Seb tried to grab her, but she wriggled away. "You can't go inside right now! Son of a . . ."

Apparently, she could, and she was familiar enough with the cottage to make a beeline for the sofa.

"Punkin, you're in big trouble." Seb stepped into the house to coax her back outside, but she wasn't budging.

"I vacuumed up a metric shit ton of sand from the cushions today," I complained, grateful to have a distraction from old wounds. "No wonder it smelled so bad."

"I'm trying to train her not to jump on furniture, but . . ."

"Next thing you'll be telling me is that *she* broke the rocking chair and paintings."

His head sagged, and he sighed dramatically. "Paige, will you *please* just listen? I caught a couple of guys here last night. They were trashing your place, looking for something. I chased them away. I was planning on getting back here before you came home to clean up, but, you know. Shit happens."

"*What?* You chased off a couple of guys . . . ?"

"Well," he admitted. "Punkin chased them off. No one survives her barking attack."

"Did the police catch them?"

"Police?"

I frowned. "You didn't call the police."

One brow arched as if he were incredulous that I'd even ask. "You're joking, right?"

I supposed squatters weren't exactly eager to call cops. "Fine, then who was it that broke in? Was it the Vanderburgs?"

He shook his head and shoved loose tendrils of hair out away from his face. "Nah, it wasn't Paul, but I couldn't get a good look at 'em. It was dark, and they were wearing ski masks. One was pretty big, all muscle. The other guy was small. When Punkin and I showed up, they scattered and took off on a pair of motorcycles."

I blinked at him and looked around. Ski masks? Was this a Seb-sized lie? By the look on his face, he was telling the truth—I always knew. Well, *almost* always.

Who would try to rob me? If any of the so-called dock bros decided to break in, the ones who worship Pretty Paul, they'd just stumble over here in a drunken haze. Criminal masterminds they were not. Silly to even try to break in because there wasn't much of anything of value in the cottage. And there wasn't anything stolen, except . . .

"My paddleboard! Wait. They rode off with it?" I tried to picture it being carted away on a motorcycle. God knew it wasn't worth *that* much. "Who breaks in a house just to steal a paddleboard?"

Seb squinted one eye shut. "Actually, no, that wasn't them. Jaz borrowed it last week for work. I let her take it because she said you wouldn't mind."

I didn't. But why wouldn't she tell me that?

And how did he know that she was at the cottage last week?

"Seb Jansen," I said, pointing an accusatory finger at his chest. "You haven't been 'occasionally' crashing at my cottage. You've been living in it!"

Now he looked embarrassed. "Not *living*, exactly. Just . . ." He sighed heavily. "It's just that Dad and I don't have much to do with each other. It's not like it was between us before, but . . ." He scrubbed the top of his head. "It's just been a little shitty around here lately, okay? So I've been crashing wherever."

"Like my cottage? You've been sleeping in my bed, Seb. What else have you been doing?"

"In your bed? Quite a lot, I'm afraid. Don't worry, I thought of you every time."

My cheeks warmed. "You're vile. You know that, right?"

"But honest."

"Ha! Now *that* truly is funny." I shook my head, looking anywhere but his face. "I can't believe you've been living here. Jesus, Seb. No wonder the utility bill has gone up!"

"Hey, you should be thanking me. A house needs to be maintained. If you don't maintain it, nature claims it. Or robbers. So, you know, you're welcome. For all the maintaining."

"Maintaining?" I threw up my arms in frustration. "I can't even . . . What's wrong with you? Did you get hit on the head when we were in high school? Because I cannot for the life of me understand how my sweet, loyal friend turned into prince of the fucking delinquents."

"Look, I'm not here *every* night. I stay at Benny's, too. Sometimes I crash in houseboats in the marina."

"Are you serious? Jazmine's parents are going to murder you."

"They don't know, okay? I've been working for Mr. Neely since last fall, and he's been really cool. So please don't blow this for me."

I squeezed my eyes shut, trying to understand it all. "Hold on. *You're* working at the marina? The boy who said his future career plans were to retire at eighteen? What in the world do you do for Mr. Neely?" I couldn't picture him working . . . ever.

"Pump gas, mostly. Engine repair, oil changes. Sometimes I help with valet boat launching."

"Wow."

His brow lowered. "Fine, judge me. I guess when you get a free ride to Harvard, you've earned the right. I may be a lowly gas attendant, but at least I'm bringing in cash."

"Well, for your information, my financial aid is being stripped because some jackass told my resident dean that my estranged ex-father was worth millions."

"Why would that matter? You haven't seen him since you were a kid, and he doesn't support you. You don't even have his surname."

I made the same arguments in the financial aid department. "It matters because the only way I can afford to attend school in Cambridge is thanks to need-based financial aid. People whose families make under a certain amount don't have to pay tuition.

"But if my father can afford to pay tuition, then the school says I'm not below that need-based threshold anymore. I asked the family attorney to send me old legal documents that show Nana had guardianship of me, but that wasn't good enough. So now I've got to resubmit all my financial paperwork with his salary included—or get him to sign a form stating that he's not legally responsible for me. And *that* is why I'm here this summer instead of studying in Europe."

A long silence stretched between us.

"Yikes," Seb finally whispered, squinching up his face. "I don't know what to say, Paige. Have you seen your dad yet? He's a big shot commercial real estate agent in Grand Rapids. Wins awards and shit."

I scrubbed my face. "Yeah, I heard. I just got in town today." Reintroducing myself to the man who ruined my family and begging him to sign paperwork to help me was not something I looked forward to doing. "I can't . . . handle him yet."

"Too busy getting robbed," Seb agreed blithely.

I glared at him. "These so-called robbers had time to drink a thousand bottles of Haven Beach Ale? Because I spent most of my time cleaning up those, along with all your weed."

"You threw my weed away? Dang, Paige. That preroll sale only happens a couple times a year. Please tell me you're joking."

"You care more about that than this cottage—so typical! Nothing has changed. What's wrong with you?"

"Haven't you heard? I'm a waste of space who'll amount to nothing."

"If you're angling for sympathy, it might do you good to remember that I gave you *plenty* of that when you started pulling away from the Wags, and what did it get me? You left your friends high and dry so that you could run around the beach like you were in some stupid gang."

His brow lowered. "At least I was living. All you wanted to do was polish your golden transcript so that you could fit in with an Ivy League crowd and pretend like your family was still rich!"

In that moment, it felt like I'd traveled back in time to when we were both fifteen and having this exact same argument. I remembered fighting with him in the cottage's front yard and Nana racing out to get between us and stop us from killing each other.

She wasn't here now.

Anger rose, hot and fast. I shoved him with both my hands. *Hard.*

Caught off guard, he stumbled sideways into the wall, straight into one of my grandmother's landscape paintings—one that hadn't been damaged by the robbery. I winced internally when it fell off its nail and hit the floor with a terrible *bang*. A corner of the wooden frame chipped off.

"Shit! Paige, I didn't mean to do . . ." He cocked his head as he stared at the fallen painting, and my eyes followed his as he bent down.

A piece of paper had fallen on the floor. He picked it up while setting the painting against the wall. "I think this fell out of the painting . . . maybe from the back?"

Still angry, I snatched the paper out of his fingers and unfolded it to find a very old document.

Certificate of Marriage

This is to certify that Robert "Jack" T. Malone

and

Mabel Elizabeth Springsteen

Were united by me in holy matrimony

on June 2, 1918

in Haven Beach, Michigan

"Holy shit," Seb said softly, reading over my shoulder. "Is that Captain Wyrd Jack's wedding certificate?"

It looked authentic. "Why was this inside Nana's painting?"

"Maybe she put it there. Can I . . . ?"

I begrudgingly handed him the certificate while shuffling around him to inspect the painting, see if there was anything else hidden on the backside. None that I could find.

"This looks real, Paige. It should probably be in the Wyrd Jack museum in the harbor. Wait, what's this?"

Seb flipped over the certificate and made a small noise. I was so curious that I stepped beside him to see what he'd found.

Tiny dots circled the edges of the old paper. They'd been penciled in, like a doodled border you might draw if you were bored and daydreaming. But I quickly realized that the dots weren't random.

Seb realized it, too. "Are you seeing this? Dots and dashes."

"Morse code," I whispered, and as my anger at Seb faded into the background, something I hadn't felt in a long time stirred inside my chest. Something I'd buried deep down, along with so many childhood memories.

The thrill of the chase.

My heart sped as I stared at the shapes lining the paper's edges. Seb and I both knew the old telecommunications language by heart. Nana taught us when we were kids. Even our matching Blackbeard decoder rings had dials that paired letters with Morse code dots and dashes. We used to write each other secret messages.

Seb and I moved toward the reading light near the sofa to see better.

"Weird. Is it . . . all numbers . . . ?" Seb scanned the document while blindly perching on the sofa next to Punkin. "Yeah, I think these are all numbers. Is this just doodling? Like, someone practicing Morse?"

"On the back of a precious document?"

We both knew that couldn't be true.

Blue eyes flicked to mine. "Holy shit, Paige," he whispered. "Did you know someone found a gold bar in a sewer downtown last month?"

"I heard."

"The town went insane for a couple weeks, with people scouring downtown for more gold."

"Maybe that's who broke in here," I said.

"Maybe. People said it might be Wyrd Jack's gold. I thought they were all idiots, but now I'm wondering . . . Do you think this might be an *actual* clue to Wyrd Jack's treasure?"

Waves of excitement rippled through me. I hadn't thought too much about the Golden Venus in a long time. Not like I used to think about it when I was younger—obsessively. "Might just be nothing," I said, trying to temper my own expectations.

"Usually is . . ."

"If Nana had a clue to the treasure, she wouldn't keep it from us." Would she? Maybe it didn't matter. "Hold on," I said, getting up to jog to the kitchen counter and quickly returning with a pen and an old bill envelope. "You sure you remember Morse code?"

"Like the back of my hand," he said, a little proud. "You?"

"Never forgot it." I sat on the living room rug, on the other side of the coffee table. "You read it off, I'll write it down."

He glanced up from the certificate to arch a brow at me. "Like old times."

"Just read," I said, a little frustrated with myself that I was so pumped about digging up an old treasure-hunting clue that it momentarily eclipsed my anger for Seb. Maybe he felt the same way because he began reading the code out to me in an excited voice.

"Three. Eighteen. Nine . . . ?"

"Nine?"

"Hold on, that's just a smudge. *Seven*. Then twenty. Five. Thirteen . . ."

I scribbled down everything he read from the edges of the certificate, rotating the page when he finished with one edge. He was right: there was nothing in the code but a series of numbers. I sneaked glances at Seb while he studied the paper, looking at his black eye. The way his jaw cut . . .

Blue eyes looked up at me. "What?"

I was still blown away by how much he'd changed. "You look so different. It's like, I don't know . . . Owning a tiny yellow chick as a pet, then the chick being taken away and you don't see it again until it's a gigantic rooster."

Seb snorted a little laugh. "Cock-a-doodle-doo."

"Just translate the code," I said, feeling my face grow warm.

"Fine. Twenty-eight. Five. Fourteen . . ."

It took him a couple minutes to call out all the dots and dashes that were penciled on the certificate. Once he'd finished, I'd filled up the back of my envelope with numbers. Seventy-two of them. "What are we looking at here, do you think?"

"Fuck if I know. Map coordinates?"

"Too many," I said.

"*Several* map coordinates?"

I rolled my eyes. "Come on, think."

"That's your specialty, Mensa, not mine."

"Haven't heard that in a hot minute."

Seb doled out nicknames like they were going out of style. At least *that* hadn't changed.

"Are all the students at Harvard brain trusts? I've often wondered if you felt like a little fish in a big pond, or if you could go toe-to-toe with rich smarties."

"You often wonder about me, do you?"

He chuckled softly. "Probably more than you wonder about me."

His eyes found mine, and my mouth went dry, completely thrown by his blurted sincerity. It occurred to me how close we were, leaning over the table, knuckles almost touching. And then Seb shook his head, like jolting himself out of a stupor.

"Come on, Paige. We got a piece of paper filled with numbers. What do you see? What's the pattern?"

I sighed heavily and stared at the envelope. "Hold on . . . Were there any pauses in the dots? Breaks?"

He picked up the certificate and studied it. "Hard to tell since it was handwritten God-knows-when. Wait, wait, wait . . ." He held up a hand, staring at the paper. "How many numbers did I read off?"

"Seventy-two."

Seb did some not-so-quick math inside his head, then got frustrated and demanded the envelope. He started counting the numbers with one finger and then looked at me, wide-eyed. "Holy shit. Is this a book cipher?"

Was it? *Impossible.*

If someone wanted to send coded text, they might find all the words they want to use in their secret message inside a book. Like, let's say *Webster's Dictionary*. If the word "asshole" is needed for the secret message, and that word is on page twenty, on the seventh line, and it is the first word on that line, the cipher code would be 20/7/1. When the recipient gets the message, it will look like a string of numbers grouped into threes. They take out their *Webster's Dictionary*, find page twenty, line seven, first word, and bingo! They would know that the sender is calling them an asshole.

The numbers we'd just deciphered might be a book cipher.

Might.

"Only one problem," I said. "If it's a book cipher, we'd need to know the exact book that was used to write the message." Both the sender and recipient of a book cipher would need to agree on a book to use for coding and decoding.

"Yeah, that's a problem, all right. Maybe it's not even a book cipher. It might be something else, like an A1Z26 cipher, or some kind of Caesar shift variant with numbers."

"True . . ."

He pulled his phone out of his pocket when it dinged, squeezing his eyes closed briefly. "Shit. Sorry, Paige. Gotta go."

"What? *Now?*" Was he not as excited as I was about this discovery? How could he leave right in the middle of it? "Is it an emergency, or something? Your father?"

Seb patted his dog, encouraging her to get off the sofa with him. "Fortunately, no. Things have calmed down between me and my pops these days . . . as long as we stay out of each other's way. If he doesn't see me, then he doesn't ask where I've been."

"So you're avoiding each other."

He shrugged. "Hey, you call it a tomato, I call it 'getting to keep my head on my shoulders.' Which I'd like to continue doing because I've grown pretty fond of this head."

Seb's father was a Coast Guard captain—decorated, a local

hero. He was also incredibly strict. Two years ago, when the man sent Seb away, it wasn't a big surprise to any of us. Seb's mother left both of them when Seb was nine; one day she woke up and decided she didn't want to be a wife or mother, so she abandoned her life here and moved out east. Pretty much just disappeared from their lives. I don't think Captain Jansen ever got over it, and he certainly didn't know how to raise a rambunctious boy on his own. But that was no excuse for why he lorded over Seb.

I'd never been a Captain Jansen fan.

"You can't leave now," I told Seb. "What about the cipher?"

He took a picture of the numbers I'd scrawled on the envelope. "Promise I'll take a look at the code later and let you know if anything comes to mind."

"Okay?" I replied, sounding as unsure as I felt.

He gave me a little smile, cocked to one side like he was hiding a thrilling secret. And for the first time since I'd laid eyes on him at the bonfire, two boyish dimples appeared, indenting his cheeks.

I always loved those dimples.

That was the boy I used to know, with a smile that could charm the scales off a snake.

"Okay, well, obviously I won't be crashing here, now that you're back. But are you going to be okay here alone tonight?" He gave me a questioning look. "You could stay with Jazmine, you know."

Could I? She still hadn't gotten in contact with me since I left that voicemail earlier. "I'll be fine," I told him. "I'll keep the porch lights on and the doors locked."

He nodded as if he weren't completely sure but didn't know what to do about it.

Maybe I didn't, either.

"Come on, Punkin," he told the dog as they headed out the back door. "It was nice catching up with you, Paige. Really sorry about your house again. Maybe you should consider installing some extra locks or at least put up some kind of cheap wireless security camera."

"I'll consider it."

He nodded and gave me a loose salute. "See ya around the lake."

Without another word, he left the cottage just as he had any other day, back when our lives were still small and uncomplicated.

If I pretended they still were, maybe we could be friends again. Maybe.

Chapter 4

Funnily enough, working on the Morse code cipher wasn't as exciting alone. After Seb left, I moved some of the numbers around, played with it, and even wondered if maybe I'd been wrong and all these dashes and dots on the certificate *were* merely distracted doodles of Wyrd Jack or his wife, or even someone else in the family who inherited the certificate after Wyrd Jack died.

No way of knowing. Whatever we'd uncovered in this string of numbers, I couldn't concentrate on it for long. I kept replaying my conversation with Seb, trying to sort out all my old, wounded feelings about him. And the new feelings about why he chose to crash at my place. If he truly did chase away robbers, then I supposed I should've been grateful. But I still couldn't fathom why anyone would choose to break in here.

What were they looking for? More gold bars? Or perhaps this very marriage certificate? If so, why didn't they find it? They certainly broke the frames of several other paintings. Maybe Seb scared them away before they could get their hands on it.

Would they come back?

I listened for strange sounds. Peered out blinds. But after the fear wore off, I realized how different life was out here. Lake life in the summer was sweet and slow. Back in Cambridge, I stuck to a routine with precious little downtime.

Study. Class. Eat. Sleep.

Lather, rinse, repeat.

That routine kept me from falling apart after Nana died. A loop.

But now that I was out of that loop, mundane worries crowded my thoughts. Things like ordering new glass cut for the broken window and buying some groceries. Finding out what was going on with Jazmine. Trying to get Nana's old car running, which hadn't been cranked in almost a year. Washing the sheets on which Seb had been sleeping—and doing God knew what else . . .

And then there was the worst task on my to-do list: figuring out when and how I was going to approach a father I hadn't talked to in over a decade and convince him to help me keep my financial aid.

Considering everything that had just fallen into my lap, I could probably take a couple days to figure out how I was going to approach him. Or even find him.

Even so, I spent a restless night thinking about both him and the day's events. The Morse code cipher on the back of Wyrd Jack's wedding certificate. My interactions with Seb . . . But the next morning, my head was a little clearer, and I decided the most pressing thing was tracking down Jazmine at her job.

After taking the hottest, most luxurious shower I'd had since moving into the freshman dorms at Harvard—thank God for good water pressure—I brushed my damp hair into a ponytail, tugged on my favorite T-shirt, and went outside to unlock the old freestanding garage that stood a couple yards from the cottage. At least it was intact, no signs of break-in. Nana never kept a spare key to the cottage out here, but she *did* keep a spare to the garage. It was hidden in a bohemian collection of vintage aluminum signs that hung on the side of the garage. I nabbed the key that was tucked away behind an old Texaco sign and opened the garage.

My nana's 1965 Danube-blue Chevy Corvair sat safely inside beneath its dustcover. After pulling the canvas off the car, I unlocked it and slid into the front seat, bittersweetly savoring the musty scent of the interior that reminded me of Nana. For a moment, I felt grief tugging me down into dark waters again but was able to pull myself back. *Nana wouldn't want me crying over a dumb car.* Though, to be fair, it was a very pretty car, built right here in Michigan, and she'd taken good care of it.

And despite the model's bad reputation—"Unsafe at Any Speed" was what it used to be called—it took me only four tries to crank.

"Still got it," I told the Corvair, patting the hood while I gave it time to warm up.

Once I was fairly hopeful that I wouldn't break down, after taking a quick test drive down the street, I headed into town, past the marina and last night's bonfire, and drove a couple miles to Haven's main public beach, where Jazmine worked.

Jazmine had been a part-time paddleboard instructor since we were sixteen. Unlike me, who only futzed about on the board for fun, she was a serious athlete who was a member of the International Surfing Association, ISA. Jaz dreamed of competing in the Olympics, and I wouldn't be surprised to see her there one day, if the Olympics committee could ever get around to adding stand-up paddleboarding to their events. She'd gotten into University of Michigan in Ann Arbor—a great school, one of the top ranked in the nation—but was taking a gap year before starting this upcoming fall.

After parking in one of the beach's public lots, I walked past a few closed shops, too early to be open, and made my way down to the sand, where I spotted Jazmine's first paddleboard class of the day doing warm-up exercises on the beach. Bright sun glinted off the lake, dazzling me for a moment. When I held up my hand to block the light, I spotted her.

Tall and brown-skinned, Jazmine Neely stood in the sand wearing a shirt that read *Instructor* in big letters. Red bikini strings peeked from under the shirt, along with more muscle than half the dock bros. Her natural brown-and-dark-honey curls were pulled up into a high puffy ponytail, and much like her older sister, a galaxy of freckles covered her nose and cheeks.

Her left arm was bound in an elastic bandage and cradled inside a black sling.

She's hurt her arm . . . ?

"Hold up. There's only eight of you," she was telling the class. "Someone's missing. Where's Sheila? Did she get locked in the changing room again? You kids are about to test my last nerve. Who knows something?"

Several children shrugged their shoulders in answer. One of the kids pointed in my direction.

Jazmine turned around, and her face lit up. She beamed at me before her smile faltered—just slightly, just for a moment. But I caught it. *What is going on?*

"Paige!" she called out, running toward me. "Oh my God, look at you!"

Frustrations forgotten, I embraced Jazmine while trying to avoid the arm in the sling, inhaling the familiar scent of her favorite sweet almond lotion. "Missed you so much."

"Missed you more," she said, pulling back to smile at me. "When did you get bangs?"

"Ugh, I cut them in a moment of weakness, don't ask."

"Why? I like them."

Crazy that her approval made me feel a little better, but when she smiled at me, I smiled back. I gestured toward her arm. "And when did you do *that*? What happened?"

"Sprained it," she said, deflating a little as she held the arm against her body. "Was racing out at Harbor Point and my foot slipped. Fell wrong, hit the board . . ." She shrugged.

"Racing? Who?"

She sighed heavily, lifting her warm face to the sun. "Fine. I wasn't racing. It happened a couple mornings ago. I was hungover at work after a long night of trying to outdrink Bill Chesney. I was showing off for those brats over there, trying to impress them—which is impossible, just for the record. My ankle twisted, and I fell off the board."

I winced. Now that *did* sound like her. Jazmine was highly competitive at anything physical, even partying. I flicked a look at the brown bandage wrapped around her ankle, then leaned to the side to glance around her and found the kids staring back at us.

"Tough class this summer?"

"The absolute worst," she whispered.

"So sorry, Jaz. Are you in pain?"

She shook her head, looking sheepish. "It aches, but nowhere near as a bad as it did when it happened. You know what the doc told me? 'Take some Tylenol.' I nearly strangled him."

"I'll bet." I smiled.

"Anyway, hopefully I'll have to be in the sling for only a week or so. Then I'll be able to get back on the board."

I nodded encouragingly, then after a moment, dared to say,

"So, hey. I really missed seeing you at the airport. Is everything okay?"

"Yeah, it's fine. Just was in a little pain, and my boss called me in to talk about my performance, and I thought I was getting fired—I'm really sorry, Paige. I know it was shitty, but I just couldn't make the drive to Grand Rapids yesterday."

"Oh God, of course. I wouldn't expect you to drive all the way there with one arm . . ." It was just that . . . "Why didn't you just tell me?"

Her shoulders dropped. "I don't know. I guess I was embarrassed. Silly, huh?"

"Ridiculously silly. I thought you were mad at me, or something."

"Then I guess that explains those voice messages you left . . ."

"Sorry, Jaz. I was upset. I'd just flown in and found the cottage trashed, then I ran into Seb down the beach at a bonfire."

Her eyes widened. "You saw Seb?"

I nodded. "Apparently he's been crashing at the cottage. Did you know about this?"

She gritted her teeth and made a face. "I knew he was doing a little couch surfing lately, but I thought it was temporary—thought he would've cleared out of the beach cottage by now. He mostly stays at Benny's, I believe. I had *no idea* he was trashing the cottage, Paige. I swear."

I nodded, scratching my nose. "Might've at least told me that he was back in town."

"Hey. *You* told me if any of us mentioned his name ever again you'd poison them in their sleep, so I didn't think you'd want to know. He came back last fall, after . . ."

After Nana's funeral. She didn't have to say it.

"And apparently, he's working for your dad at the marina? Seriously?"

"Oh. That? My parents feel sorry for him, that's all. So, what was it like? Seeing him again after all that time?"

"Strange," I admitted. "He really grew up, huh?"

"The glow-up of all glow-ups."

"I mean, what the hell . . . ?"

Jazmine laughed. "Should've seen him last fall when he first came back. You wouldn't have recognized him, all quiet and dead-eyed. At least he looks a little more like himself now." She sighed heavily. "God, I can't believe he trashed your place."

"Actually, turns out he may have caught a couple guys breaking in and scared them off."

Her eyes widened. "What? Who?"

"Seb said it was two men on motorcycles. They didn't take anything. Just broke a lot of stuff." I'd already given her a rundown of the broken things when I left her the frantic voicemail. "So, anyway. Feels great to come home and be on edge in my own house."

"So fucking sorry," she said, slinging her good arm around my shoulders. Which felt nice. Reassuring. Like old times. "If they were local, we'll find them. What can I do to help?"

There was nothing to be done, but everything seemed fractionally better now that I'd shared it with her and knew that the two of us were okay. I still had Wyrd Jack's wedding certificate cipher on the brain and started to tell her about it, but one of the boys in her class waved at her. "Ms. Neely? Are we going out in the water today? If not, I'm calling my mama to pick me up."

"Fuck," Jazmine whispered. "I gotta go, Paige. I can't have these demons reporting me to their parents again."

I sure was glad this was her job and not mine. "Call me later, okay? I've got something intriguing that might be of interest to a former Wag."

"Wag business? All right, then. For sure," she assured me, eyes brightening. "Speaking of, we really do need a proper Wags catch-up. Benny wants to see you, too."

I hadn't seen Benny since the funeral. Back when we were kids, hunting for Wyrd Jack's treasure, it had been Benny's idea to call us the Scallywags before we shortened it to the Wags. Him, Seb, Jazmine, and I spent every summer together until Seb began pulling away. However, Benny and Seb continued talking—long after Jaz and I had given up on Seb. In fact, if Benny hadn't been with Seb on his seventeenth birthday, Seb might've never been sent away to boot camp.

That was then, and this is now. I really hadn't thought much about Benny when I was at Harvard this year, but it would be nice to see him again.

Maybe he and Jaz would like a crack at deciphering the Morse code numbers . . .

After leaving Jazmine and her class on the beach, I walked back up to the parking lot and got the Corvair started again— only two tries!—so I went ahead and drove across town to the grocery store locals used, an ancient Meijer that always smelled of boiled shrimp. But its prices were a billion times better than the Haven Gourmet Market, where all the tourists bought overpriced cheese and wine. I picked up the basics: toilet paper, Cokes, and sandwich-making stuff. Then I went through the Grind-and-Shine Coffee Hut drive-through and got my favorite order since I'd been ten years old, and the most iconic drink in town: iced white chocolate mocha. I like mine with a splash of coconut milk.

Taking long, pleasurable sips from an oversized cup, I got back on Harbor Drive, intending to cruise through town at my own pace, see what I could see. Maybe go inspect the area downtown where the gold bar was found in the sewer.

But I only made it to the next red light when white smoke started seeping out from beneath the Corvair's hood. "Shit! Shit!" I said.

The car had done this once before, a couple years ago, but I hadn't paid much attention to the cause. Nana simply took it into a repair shop and got it fixed.

I didn't have auto-repair money left in the bank account. I *barely* had iced-white-chocolate-mocha money. And I needed to make what little I did have stretch through the next school year.

The only thing I remembered about the last time this happened was that Nana drove the car like this for a couple days. So, not knowing what else to do, I drove the smoking car back to the cottage, utterly embarrassed that everyone I passed gave me dirty looks. When I finally got it parked and the engine shut off, the smoke was so thick, I had to wave it away to find my way out of the garage.

That could not be good.

"Dammit!" I coughed outside the garage as a strange car pulled into the driveway.

An ugly brown Ford Bronco with fat roll bars on the top and a big rusted dent in the driver's door. It was possibly the dirtiest car I'd ever seen, with giant wheels covered in dried mud.

The dented door swung open, and Seb jumped out, followed by his dog.

"Hey!" Dressed in khaki shorts and a bright aqua polo shirt with *Neely Marina* embroidered on the front, Seb waved away smoke as he approached. "Was coming out here and spotted you driving past McDonald's. What's going on?"

I was honestly relieved to see him. "Started smoking when I was in town to see Jazmine. No idea why, but this happened once before but I don't remember the cause. What causes white smoke?"

"Could be a lot of things: a seal, or a gasket. Based on where the smoke was coming from when I was driving behind you, I'd guess it was the O-rings."

He'd always been good with cars. "Is that O-expensive?"

"Not if you do it yourself," he said with a little smile. "Would take three or four hours, probably. I could try if you want?"

It was hard to be mad at him when he was being so nice. "Are you serious? God, Seb. I can't thank you enough."

"Can't guarantee that's your issue until I get under the hood. Could look at it tomorrow, maybe? I've got to work today," he said, gesturing toward his marina polo.

"Of course, yes. Tomorrow is perfect." I already felt the relief of my panic subsiding, but it was mixed with other feelings I couldn't quite identify. I guess it was just strange to rely on Seb, of all people, for something I needed.

He glanced at his phone. "Speaking of work . . . Only got a few minutes."

"Your eye is looking a little purple around the edges today," I noted. "No broken nose, so I guess that means you didn't return to the bonfire fight."

"This right here," he said, waving his hand in front of his face, "is called superior healing genes. Besides, Pretty Paul is a prick. I don't need to fight him again."

"Why were you fighting him to begin with?" *The boy you aban-*

doned all your friends for, so you could run around town together, wreaking havoc. "I thought you were best of buds."

"You and I were best of buds, once," he pointed out. "Things change."

Yes, they certainly did. "Sometimes a *bud* gets tired of helping another bud who is intent on following a path of self-destruction, especially when he's trying to take her down with him and doesn't care if he lives or dies."

He nodded slowly, crossing his arms over his chest. "Completely understandable. Especially when she's smart enough to have whatever future she wants, and he has . . . none."

I didn't know how to respond to that. He'd always had a way of pretending like he wasn't feeling sorry for himself while low-key wallowing in self-pity.

I'd done plenty of my own wallowing over the years. When he left his friends for the company of Paul, I thought I'd never get over it and felt his absence like a phantom limb. I had to tell myself the same thing every day for months and months: my boy was gone, and he wasn't coming back.

Guess I was wrong, because here he was, standing next to me like the past few years had just been a terrible fever dream.

"Anyway, the past is the past, dusty and forgotten," he said, waving dismissively. "I only care about the present, and presently Pretty Paul is under the impression that I'm to blame for his bad luck because he lost something that he wrongly assumed belonged to him."

"And might that be because you *stole* something that belongs to him?" If it wasn't nailed down, he would take it, just because. Dollar store candy. Silverware from restaurants. Cars.

Seb put the "maniac" in "klepto."

"Maybe. What really is property, anyway? Can one human being really own anything?" he mused, giving me a lopsided smile.
"Anyway, Paul and I haven't been on friendly terms since I got
back. Guess our overall life philosophies don't jibe so well anymore." He shrugged as if he couldn't care less.

There was probably more to that story. Always was, when Seb
was involved. Maybe I should be wondering if Pretty Paul Vanderburg and his gang of misfits were involved in my cottage break-
in. When I found Seb on the beach at the bonfire and mentioned
the Vanderburgs, Seb didn't seem to think they had anything to
do with it.

Is he lying?

"Why are you here, anyway?" I asked as his dog snuffled its
nose under my hand. Apparently no one gave Punkin the notice
that I don't get along with her kind. I pulled my hand back and
grimaced.

"So you can thank me."

I arched a brow. "For all the ten-cent recycling deposits I'm
going to collect when I take your empty glass beer bottles down
to the grocery store?"

"Hey, don't knock free money," he said with a little wink. "But
this might be a little better."

"What might be?"

"Solved the cipher."

My heart picked up speed. "What? How? You can't solve a
book cipher without the key text, and we don't know what the
key text is."

"Don't we?"

Oh, the way he lit up. He could barely contain himself, rocking
on his toes.

"Seb Jansen, if you don't spill it, I'm going to strangle you slowly."

"Promises, promises." He gestured with his hand, urging me to follow him to the cottage's front window, where he tapped on the glass and pointed. "Was right there the whole time."

I peered through the glass to see where he was pointing.

A copy of Wyrd Jack's "Prison Poem" had been written in fine calligraphy by one of Nana's old friends and was framed under glass, hanging on the wall near the living room fireplace.

"Oh my God," I whispered. "You're lying—there's no way."

"Keep telling yourself that. Sometimes this mind of mine isn't completely useless."

I rushed to unlock the cottage, and when I got inside, pulling out the envelope scrawled with numbers, I could hear Seb and Punkin come in behind me as I made a beeline for the framed poem.

"Okay, so three numbers in the cipher coordinate to—"

"Line number, word number, letter number," he supplied helpfully.

The first numbers I'd written down last night were three, eighteen, and four. I found the third line, eighteenth word, fourth letter.

"'D,'" I said excitedly. "Oh wow, okay, okay. I probably should write this down."

"Don't bother. 'Drop anchor at Pinemoon Cave.'"

I swung around. "What?"

"The cipher. 'Drop anchor at Pinemoon Cave.' Sorry to spoil your fun, but I gotta get to work."

Pinemoon Cave? Childhood memories flooded my head. That cave was on a tiny island in the middle of the Little River. Where the Wags treasure-hunting crew would meet up when we were kids.

The only way there was by water. Back in the day, the Wags would use canoes to get there.

He stuck his hand in his pocket and jingled coins. "I see the wheels turning, Professor Paige. If you're thinking about finding a way to get out to the cave alone, you should know that I've already talked to Benny. He's getting the canoes out of storage."

Dammit.

"I'll swing by here tomorrow morning in my trusty Speed Buggy and pick you up," he told me, gesturing out the front window toward his dented Bronco. "You might want to tell Jazmine to come along. If she finds out we've been hunting treasure without her, she'll be pissed that we didn't call."

"But—"

"See you tomorrow, Paige. I'll take a look at your car then, too."

He saluted me, winking, and exited through the front door with his dog.

Leaving me astonished, with more questions than answers.

Chapter 5

It took me a long time to calm down after Seb left. I didn't know whether I was pissed that he'd cracked the cipher first or excited about the discovery. Maybe both.

But I double-checked his work, and it was exactly right: *Drop anchor at Pinemoon Cave.*

For all we knew, this Morse code message was written by Wyrd Jack a hundred years ago in reference to something else—stolen cargo, a rendezvous. Without Nana here to tell me why it was hidden in her painting, I couldn't say. However, I couldn't help but think that Nana really *had* been keeping secrets about the treasure, that she'd known more than she let on. After all, she was the one who first told us how to find Pinemoon Cave and encouraged the Wags to use it as their official hideout.

What even is this, Nana? I thought, staring at an old photo of her on the wall. If only she could've answered.

* * *

THE NEXT MORNING, I was showered and dressed before eight. I found some recently expired coffee in the cupboard and was able to brew it in the Mr. Coffee that had been sitting in the same spot on the same kitchen counter since long before I was born. But just when I was about to take my coffee out to the back porch, I heard a vehicle enter the driveway. Two car doors opened and shut, and I started to get up when I heard muffled voices.

"Just saying, before we go in there, you need to promise me that you won't say anything. Not even a joke."

That's Jazmine, no doubt about it.

"And *I'm* just saying that you should just fess up before she hears it around town."

Seb? What were they talking about? A terrible paranoia swept through me.

Their shoes crunched on the sandy gravel in front of the cottage, so I scrambled up from the porch swing and rushed inside to hear them knocking. I took a moment to compose myself, then I opened the door to find Seb leaning against the doorframe in a pair of shorts, blue hoodie, and dark sunglasses pushed up into his blond waves.

"Mornin', valedictorian," he said, giving me a little flash of dimple as his black dog squirmed past his legs into the house. "Dammit, Punkin. Don't give me grief today . . ."

The dog made a beeline for the kitchen, then stood there and looked back at us, disappointed.

"Do you mind . . . ?" Seb asked, sliding past me. "She needs water. I think she doesn't understand why her water bowl is gone."

"My nana's vintage mixing bowl? I picked that up when I was cleaning that first night. Thought it was just part of the wreckage."

Far too comfortable in my house, Seb went straight for the kitchen cabinet that held the vintage bowl, filled it up with water, and offered it to his panting dog. "There we are."

A noise drew my attention outside, and when I leaned through the open doorway, I spotted Jazmine, setting down my paddle-board next to the side of the garage.

"Hey, Paige," she called out. "Bringing back your property. Stashing behind the bushes in case your robbers come back."

"Thanks," I said. "Why did you even need it to begin with?" The board was nice, but nowhere near as good as any of hers.

"I took Benny and his new girlfriend out by Eagle Pointe. She didn't have a board."

"Benny has a girlfriend?"

"He does." Walking back to the open doorway, Seb squeezed one eye shut while making a face. "Lulu. She's . . . quite something."

"She's not coming with us today, right?" Jazmine asked Seb after tossing my paddle next to the board. "*Please* tell me she's not."

Seb shrugged. "Not a Wag, so she wasn't invited. Doubt she'd be interested, anyway. Lulu isn't exactly a lover of the great outdoors." He put his fingers inside his mouth and whistled at his dog, who trotted through my house, dripping water from her shaggy maw, but obediently went outside. Seb turned to me. "Ready to find some treasure?"

Was I? I squinted at him, searching his face for a clue to what he and Jazmine had been talking about when they arrived. When he cocked his head at me, puzzled, I dropped my eyes. Either I confronted them about what I'd heard, or I kept the card close to my chest while I observed them.

"Ready," I said, deciding on the latter. No need to start any drama right now.

"All right." Seb clapped his hands together. "We'll go in the Speed Buggy, since you don't have transportation. I'll take a look at your car when we get back. Sound good?"

I nodded.

"Okay, Wags," he said. "Let's load up."

It was strange but nice to hear him call us Wags. Jazmine gave me a little side hug with her good arm before we piled into Seb's Bronco—me on the passenger's side of the long front bench seat, while Jaz and Punkin got in the back. Seb started the noisy engine, dropped his shades over his eyes, and backed out of my driveway.

A calming male voice was talking through the car's speakers about a train ride through Switzerland. "What is this?" I asked.

"Rick motherfucking Steves, that's who."

"Oh God, here we go . . ." Jaz muttered from the back seat.

His head briefly turned toward me, gauging my reaction. "Just one of the greatest living travel writers. He's the dude with the PBS show about traveling in Europe. Seriously? Little Miss Smarty-Pants doesn't know Rick Steves?"

"Is this . . . an audiobook?" I asked.

"It's all he listens to in the car. Audiobooks about nature, animals, and travel. It's like driving around with someone's eighty-year-old hermit uncle."

"Look," he said, defensive, "audiobooks are free to check out from the library, and they're just like reading real books."

"Of course," I said. "They *are* 'real' books."

"Yeah, no one's arguing that, weirdo," Jaz added.

I smiled at Seb, pleased to hear about this new interest of his. But my smile didn't last long, because looking around at my surroundings, I realized the inside of the Bronco was almost worse than the outside. "What's that smell?"

"Weed?" Jazmine said. "It always smells like a discount dispensary up in here."

"That may be, but this is a storm car," Seb said, turning down his audiobook. "It was damaged in that mega blizzard in the Yoop two years ago."

The "Yoop" was another name for the U.P., the Upper Peninsula of Michigan, which contained a third of the land in our state but only, like, 3 percent of the population. I'd never been much farther north than Traverse City, and neither had Jazmine, so we often referred to the Yoop as the North Pole.

Seb went to boot camp in the Yoop.

"Anyway," he said. "What you're smelling is some massive, massive water damage that happened after its former owner left the window rolled down in a blizzard. Snow filled the truck, then melted, and water sat inside the cab for weeks. You can still see the waterline on the doors, look."

"Charming," I said.

His head turned toward me for a moment. "So you're saying that boys who drive you around campus back in Cambridge don't own fine, restored vehicles such as this?"

I ignored that. "Surprised the state of Michigan will even let you buy a car after the Ferrari incident."

Seb's fingers twitched as they rested on top of the steering wheel. Maybe I'd just pushed his button. I wished I could tell what was going through his head, but I couldn't see his eyes behind his dark sunglasses.

"Yeah, well, that was Juvenile Seb. You're riding with Adult Seb now, and I don't want to hear any more Speed Buggy *or* Rick Steves slander."

Was that true? Had Seb grown up? Changed? Or was he still bad news? Would Nana be disappointed that I gave him another chance to be friends? Or disappointed if I didn't?

I didn't know the answers to any of those questions. But I wanted to find out, and that was a start, I supposed.

Both Seb and Jaz were remarkably quiet for the remainder of the quick drive across town while I allowed memories of when we were seventeen to roll through my mind, still wondering about the conversation I'd overheard this morning.

Maybe we were all thinking about the same thing.

Whatever that might be.

We headed through town and took the bridge across the Little River into Northside. Years ago, that bridge was a dividing line in town. South of the bridge, where the marina and Heron Cottage both were, was the blue-collar side of town. North of the bridge was where the Haves lived. Old money, old Michigan. The Pink House—a big Victorian that Wyrd Jack built at the turn of the century that used to be my family home before my father caused all our money problems—was on this side of town, on a bluff overlooking the lake, now owned by a company that rented luxury estates to rich tourists.

If you turned to the right immediately after crossing the bridge, as Seb was doing now, and drove a block down River Street, you'd find a small residential neighborhood with contemporary mansions that backed up to the river. The first one was the home of Benito "Benny" Morales, the fourth and final Wag.

Benny's family was from Argentina, and both his parents were surgeons. All things equal, Benny should have been the one at Harvard, not me. He was definitely smart enough: his SAT scores were better than mine, even, and he was a minor tech genius, able to write code for just about anything. But Harvard has a 3 percent acceptance rate, and Benny's grades back in high school went downhill after Seb went away to boot camp. So he ended up enrolling in a tech program down the road at Western Michigan University in Kalamazoo.

When Seb pulled into the circular driveway and parked beneath a sleek, covered entrance next to a Land Rover, forgotten memories resurfaced of all four of us meeting up here back in our peak Wag days, and I was suddenly eager to see Benny again. To be reunited.

Punkin jumped out of the Speed Buggy as if she were just as familiar with Benny's house as she was with mine. As she trotted across the lawn, the mansion's front door swung open and two people emerged. I recognized the first immediately.

With the hood of his black sweatshirt covering his bowed head, Benny took his time strolling toward us, briefly pausing to lean down and scratch Punkin behind the ear. He was just as willowy as he'd been in school—Ichabod Crane, Seb used to call him. And he wore the same uniform: all black, from his hoodie to his shorts to the old-school Vans on his feet.

Less *tech bro*, more *fatalistic goth*.

Benny stopped in front of me and pulled back his hood, revealing a dark, low-fade haircut that was stylishly moppy on top, and a perpetually long face that sported a thick new beard.

"Paige," he said in a deep monotone. "Good to see you."

"Nice beard. Very hot and manly," I said, unable to stop myself from smiling when he grunted in response. He brightened a little as he looked me over, and when he bent his head to kiss me casually on the cheek in greeting, I reached up and hugged him, catching him off guard. The distinct scent of weed wafted. But he embraced me back, and it felt genuine, which was nice; as a rule, Benny didn't express a lot of emotion.

I pulled back and smiled at him. "Been a minute, huh?"

"Yeah. Sort of surreal for us all to be standing in the same place, don't you think?" Striking brown eyes—always his best feature—blinked at me with curiosity. "I've been back only about a week, and it's wild to drive around town after being gone for so long."

The first thing to know about Benny is that he's genuinely a genius when it comes to computer programming and coding. The second thing is that he's possibly the worst driver in Haven Beach, having racked up at least seven accidents while totaling two expensive cars—that I knew of. Last I'd heard, his driver's license had been suspended, so it was surprising to hear him talking casually about "driving" around town.

But I didn't want to kill the vibe, bringing any of this up. "Still studying at WMU, right?" I asked, thinking how it was only an hour and a half down the road. "Have you not been back home at all this year?"

"Nah," he said, scratching the back of his head. "I thought about spending the summer somewhere else, but my folks are down in Buenos Aires, staying with my Aunt Renata—helping her with my new nephew for a couple months."

"Ah," I said. "Got the house to yourself this summer?"

He nearly smiled in response. *Nearly.* "Yeah, so I haven't really been alone . . ." He trailed off because a tiny white girl with a bleached-blond pixie haircut stepped between us.

"Hi there! You must be Paige. I'm Lulu Lambert." She spoke in a Disney voice, confident and peppy, flashing me a big smile as she stuck out her hand to shake. "Benny and I met at WMU and started talking because I'm from a town not far from here—small world, right? Mr. and Mrs. Morales have kindly given permission for me to stay in their pool house." The girl touched my arm. "So, Paige . . . Harvard, huh?"

Wow. Way too much talking, way too fast. The girl's billion-watt, cheerleader energy was a total one-eighty from Benny's. And as she spoke, Seb did a silly imitation of her behind her back.

"Nice to meet you, Lulu," I said, trying to ignore Seb. "How long have you two been together?"

"Two weeks?" she said, thinking. "Wait, three."

"It feels longer, though, doesn't it?" Benny said, kissing her forehead awkwardly.

"When you know, you know!" Lulu said.

"Trust me, we *all* know," Seb said dryly, retrieving a backpack from his car while Punkin peed on the perfectly mowed lawn.

"Seb stays in the pool house sometimes, too," Lulu said.

He threw up a hand like a stop sign. "Not in the same room," he corrected, glancing in my direction.

Not my business, I supposed. But I did find it strange that he'd been crashing at my place when he had a perfectly ritzy crash pad here with Benny, whose parents employed a housekeeper and a gardener. This was a thousand times better than Heron Cottage.

"Look, it's been nice chatting, Lulu," Seb said. "But I gotta steal your boy away for some top secret adventure."

"No need. I'm coming along!" she announced with glee. "We already took out the canoes from storage this morning. This way, out back."

Lulu raced away, with Punkin galloping after her. I glanced at Seb and Jaz, who were both frowning at each other. I felt the same way. This was supposed to be a Wags-only event. What if we *did* find the Golden Venus today—highly unlikely, sure, but what if? Would she get credit for the find? I didn't even know this person.

But I guess I didn't have a choice. Benny stalked after Lulu and the dog, trailing them like a dark shadow. She was part of the team today, and that was that.

Jazmine stared daggers at Lulu's back. "Want to strangle that little hobgoblin," she whispered.

"Not if I strangle her first," Seb said.

"She's not a Wag," I insisted.

"I know," he said, sounding as disappointed as I felt. "Then again, I guess if one of us was dating someone—like, say, if you'd brought your Harvard beau home for the summer, then he'd be here, too."

I wrinkled my nose. "A 'beau'?"

"Bae? Boo? Daddy? Whatever you call him," Seb said, slipping his shades down over his eyes as he hoisted his backpack onto a shoulder.

"Daddy? Gross." I rolled my eyes. "He doesn't exist, so I don't call him anything."

The corners of Seb's mouth curled upward. Just slightly. "Interesting. You know, it's totally okay if you're still hung up on me," he said, walking across the side lawn after Benny and Lulu. "I'm a hard act to follow."

He was joking, of course. I was never "hung up" on him. I mean, sure, maybe I developed a schoolgirl crush on him in our early teens before he abandoned us Wags for the Vanderburgs, but it went nowhere because I never told him. Sure, we may have talked *around* the subject of being more than friends once or twice. And by that, I mean that when we were fourteen, Seb would occasionally joke that we try hooking up and lose our virginity together, and I would suggest he take a leap off the pier. But nothing had ever come of it—and I do mean *n-o-t-h-i-n-g*.

I was so surprised by his words that I couldn't think of a witty comeback and just blurted out, "Whatever."

Ugh. Say something smarter, for the love of God!

Seb tossed me a victorious look over his shoulder.

Nothing but dimples.

Chapter 6

The Moraleses' mansion enjoyed an expansive green lawn that extended from the house to the banks of the Little River. Benny and Lulu were already at those banks by the time the three of us hiked our way back to the double-decker dock sitting over the river. A small motorboat was moored on one side, a couple of rope hammocks on the other. And at the front, two canoes had been lowered into the water.

"Are these the same canoes we used back in the day to go to the cave?" I asked Benny when we walked out onto the dock.

"Yup," he replied, tossing paddles into the long, sleek boats. "They both seat three, as you may remember. I figured Lulu and I could take the red one, and you three can follow in the green one, since you're down a paddle, with ol' One Arm over there," he said, gesturing loosely to Jazmine.

"Only need one finger to show you how I feel," she joked, flipping him the bird.

Benny snorted a soft laugh. "Everyone ready?"

"Ready and steady," Seb said, quickly stepping into the red canoe before Benny could enter and dropping his backpack onto the canoe's belly.

"Dude!" Benny complained.

"We're taking this one, Goth Boy," Seb said, sitting on the canoe's back bench. "Because *you* may remember that the green one has a slow leak, and I'd prefer to keep my shoes dry."

"You're such an asshole sometimes," Benny complained, unserious.

"If you're gonna do something, might as well do it well," Seb replied with a breezy smile. "No time to waste. Let's load up. Punkin, come on girl."

Jazmine took the front seat of the canoe, letting Punkin sit between her feet, and I dropped onto the middle bench while waiting for Seb to untie us. Then he stepped behind me, tilting the canoe with his weight. When I gripped the sides of the boat to steady myself, I glanced over my shoulder and found myself staring at the fine blond hairs on his bare legs. As far as male legs went, they were pretty nice, golden from the sun and muscular.

What was wrong with me? Since when did I look at men's legs?

"Problem?" he asked, squeezing into the space behind me to sit on the canoe's back bench. "Or are you just checking me out?"

Oh God. I was, wasn't I?

"Ha ha—so funny," I said, trying to play it off. "I just don't remember this canoe being this small. Since when did your legs, like, double in length?"

A battered Converse sneaker appeared under my seat when he stretched out one of those legs. "Do you need me to explain the finer points of puberty?"

I stepped on the toe of his sneaker repeatedly until he laughed and withdrew into the designated area behind me. When he did, I could feel his knees brush against my back.

"Stop rocking the canoe," Jazmine called out.

"I'm not taking any of your shit today."

"Sorry, Mom."

"Ha!" Benny called out from the other canoe as it floated past. "I forgot we used to call you that, Jaz."

So had I, frankly. Jazmine had always been the voice of reason in the group when the rest of us were too giddy with harebrained ideas to stop and think of the consequences.

"Mother, may I hunt for treasure?" Seb said to Jazmine over the top of my head.

"You may," she answered, laughing. "As long as when we find it, I get my fair cut."

"Let's do this, then! Come on, Wags. Follow that clue!"

Silly, I know, but his words gave me a thrill. Just as it was when we were kids, the prospect of finding hidden treasure still felt wildly exhilarating. Seb used his paddle to push away from the docks, and we glided across the water. It was disorientating, being crammed in the canoe with him, so close that his knees eventually settled against my back and the scent of his soap wafted when the breeze blew. *Is he staring at the back of my neck?*

My nerves jangled at that thought, so I distracted myself by concentrating on paddling. With Jazmine's arm in a sling, all she could do was hold on to Punkin, who was remarkably calm in a boat. Maybe calmer than me. It took a while to get into the rhythm of paddling with a partner, but then it all came back. And other than Seb whistling random unidentifiable tunes, a companionable silence settled over all three of us as Seb and I pulled the canoe through the water, squinting into warm sunlight.

The scenery on this stretch of the Little River was beautiful, green banks dappled with morning sun shining through pines that dotted the banks. A dozen private docks extended on either side, but we didn't see anyone outside this early.

At a sharp turn in the river, the McMansions disappeared and we headed into wilder territory. Blueberry bushes lined one bank, train tracks on the other. And at the point those tracks turned away from the river, we paddled past downtown—the back of it, anyway. Three blocks of old brick buildings sat along the river with their fronts facing the road and their backsides lining the banks. A couple of businesses had small river docks, but for the most part, bramble and underbrush blocked our view of downtown. We paddled past it, listening to morning traffic for several minutes. But downtown wasn't big, and eventually the traffic noises faded away. We passed a motorboat speeding in the opposite direction, and after that, it got much quieter.

Jazmine continually glanced back at the other canoe, first with curiosity, then with daggers in her eyes. I rotated on my bench to see what was bothering her so much. Benny and Lulu were now lagging a little behind us. Benny was doing all the paddling, clearly trying to impress his new girlfriend, who was dragging her hand through the water and laughing.

"Go faster, Benny-boo-boo," Seb said in a high-pitched, breathy voice behind me, imitating Lulu. "You're so strong, my favorite oarsman."

"Just don't understand what he sees in her," Jazmine said, unable to stop watching the couple.

"Not that hard, Jaz," Seb replied. "She worships him. Simple as that."

"Is that what you want, Seb?" I asked, tossing a look behind. "To be worshipped?"

Pale blue eyes blinked back at me. "By you? Hell, Paige. It's all I've ever wanted."

I quickly faced the front of the canoe, feeling thunderstruck, until I realized that he was just giving me grief. Naturally. It's what Seb did. He teased. He used words as weapons while playing dumb, like some verbal agent of chaos. But even though I knew this, I was caught off guard by long-dormant, unidentifiable feelings that now gripped my chest.

Maybe somewhere deep down I wanted what he'd said to be true.

Or maybe my brain was overloaded with everything that had happened since I'd gotten home, and I just needed rest. Whatever it was, I tried my best to ignore Seb's chaotic energy behind me and leaned forward in my seat to prevent bumping into him again.

See? Problem solved. You're just tired.

"Look, guys. Not far now," Jaz said, pointing with her paddle. "There's the big hill."

Seb chuckled. "Remember when I tumbled down that hill and nearly fell into the water?"

"Never knew Old Man Keller could run that fast," I said, smiling. "Thought there was a real chance he might kill you for stealing all that meat."

"I'll never understand people who leave hundreds of dollars of food in a carport freezer, right in the open, where any criminal can walk up and stock up."

"*You* were that criminal," I pointed out.

"Still am. We should hit up Keller's freezer after we're done. I could use a steak."

Jaz laughed from the seat in front of me. "All those steaks you stole the first time ended up in the river anyway. If you dive, you might still find 'em."

"I was ten at the time," Seb argued. "What was I going to do with an armful of steaks? I couldn't even boil water. It was the thrill of being able to nab them, that's all. Hey, there's the final twist in the river. Almost there. Aww, lookie—a little duck family."

While he whistled at a mama mallard duck and several ducklings that glided near the riverbank, our canoe rounded the final bend in the river. I spotted our tiny island, along with the small sandy area near the cave where we used to park our canoes.

My heart fluttered. It had been so long since I'd been out to the island, but nothing had changed. The tiny island wasn't even big enough to have a proper name—what with it being uninhabited, about an acre in size, and mostly covered in trees. But we never cared about that, because what it *did* have was Pinemoon Cave, the perfect hideout for four adventure-loving kids.

"Land ho!" Seb called out, one hand cupped around his mouth.

We paddled toward the stretch of sand and guided our boat onto land. We jumped out, Jaz grabbing the front of the canoe while Punkin splashed onto shore, then we all hauled the boat onto the little island "beach" and waited for Benny and Lulu to do the same.

"Dammit," Benny said, stepping out of the canoe and shaking off his expensive white sneakers. "Fucking leak. Sorry, Lu."

"I'm wearing flip-flops, silly," she said, booping him on the nose with one finger and following that up with a kiss in the same place. "It's all good. Let's have a beautiful day, okay?"

"Yes, let's," Jaz said sourly.

I squinted at her while she looked back at the happy couple with a mixture of pain and longing on her face, and like a bolt from the blue, it suddenly all made sense to me. She was jealous of Lulu.

Did Jazmine have a thing for Benny?

Was *that* what she and Seb were whispering about this morning?

I continued watching her, but the more I did, the more I wondered if I'd gotten it wrong. After all, she hadn't said but a couple words about him the entire time I'd been at Harvard. Maybe she just hated Lulu, or maybe there was some beef with Benny that I didn't know about.

Why didn't I know what was going on with my best friend anymore?

Seb pulled me out of my thoughts when his shoulder lightly bumped mine as he passed. "Sorry," he said with a quick glance from beneath long, pale lashes. I couldn't say why, but I was almost positive he'd bumped into me on purpose. He and Punkin headed up a barely noticeable dirt path leading away from the sandy strip into the woods, and I followed, with Jazmine behind and Benny and Lulu eventually catching up.

Our destination was barely a two-minute walk from where we beached the canoes, up a twisting path through white pines and beech trees. When the ground started getting rocky, the cave suddenly came into view—just a round, black hole in a foothill.

"Pinemoon Cave, how I've missed you," Seb said, lugging the backpack off his shoulder. Inside were two old flashlights, one LED headlamp, and one camping lantern. "Didn't know we'd have Lulu with us, so Benny, you'll have to share with her."

"Cool lantern," she said, snagging it for her and Benny. Jaz took the headlamp, and Seb and I grabbed the flashlights. One by one, we each ducked beneath dangling vines to enter the cave.

The drop in temperature was always startling. I inhaled earthy, cool air as I straightened and swung my flashlight around.

"Damn. Exactly the same as we left it," Benny appraised.

Pinemoon Cave wasn't big. It consisted of two areas. The main one, where we stood, was the size of a small house, and the secondary cavern was long and narrow. Here in the main section, there was a dip in the middle of the stone floor that we'd used as a firepit because a tunnel-shaped hole in the ceiling allowed rising smoke to escape. Apparently we weren't the last to use it, either: there was old, burnt wood in the pit and a fair amount of empty beer cans and some plastic water bottles strewn around.

"Someone's been using our cave as a party spot," Seb said in singsong voice as his dog trotted around, exploring the cavern with her nose.

Benny snorted softly. "Why didn't we think of that?"

"Because the only alcohol we could get our hands on back then was that dusty bottle of cooking sherry in your mom's kitchen," Seb pointed out.

"My parents don't drink," Benny argued. "How is that my fault?"

"Is that why you're such a lightweight?" Lulu said, poking Benny in the stomach with a teasing finger.

"Guilty as charged," he said, flashing her a goofy smile that I'd never seen on his face. "Your man cannot hold his liquor."

"But he can sure hold me," she answered, snuggling up to him.

I mimed gagging at Jazmine and continued past the canoodling couple.

A climbable rocky ledge sat along the back wall. At the far side of it, you could access a smaller cavern behind this one that had a small stream of water running through it.

"It's so much smaller than I remembered," Seb said, kicking one of the empty beer cans. "Wasn't it bigger?"

"I think we just were smaller back then," Jazmine said. "Hey, look over there—is that our flag?"

We crossed the front of the cavern to a small nook, where

tattered, drooping fabric hung from the wall. The summer after fifth grade, we'd painted a sheet with big block letters that read *WAGS*, four swords, and some shoddy Latin for our motto: *Thesaurus nos coniungit.* United by treasure. Once we discovered "thesaurus" meant "treasure" in Latin, we used it as a code word.

On top of our childhood artwork, someone had spray-painted a penis. Several more were painted on the wall beside it.

"Would you look at this shit . . . ?" Jazmine said, shaking her head.

"Guess Banksy has finally run out of ideas," I said.

"Why is it always dicks, do you think?" Seb mused. "Dicks and peace symbols are the only graffiti you ever see in Haven Beach."

"Maybe it's because of that hippie sex cult living in that abandoned mill out past the harbor," Benny said.

When we all quizzically looked at him, he shrugged.

"Hank Johnson told me about it yesterday. Apparently everyone's seen lights out there late at night the past few weeks. People have been telling stories about finding human remains and wondering if there were cannibals squatting out there—"

"Eww," Lulu said, making a face.

"Hank took a crew of guys out to the mill last weekend to find out," Benny reported, "but they just got chased off."

"By cannibals?" I asked.

Benny shook his head. "Just some weirdos wearing a lot of tie-dye."

Jazmine shone her flashlight below her chin and spoke in a spooky voice. "And those weirdoes are now holed up inside this very cave. Hello? Sex hippies?" she called out, voice echoing around the cavern.

"Sex hippie *cannibals*," Seb corrected.

Benny snorted a soft laugh. "Hope they ate one another before they found our treasure."

"So, the treasure . . . What are we even supposed to be looking for?" Jazmine said, adjusting the ponytail holder that was keeping her corkscrew curls constrained. "I mean, over the years, we've probably spent hundreds of hours in here. If Wyrd Jack hid the Venus here, we would've found it. I mean, it is a life-sized gold sculpture of a naked goddess."

"Good point, good question," Seb said.

"I suppose we're looking for something we missed?" I said.

"Like more gold bars," Lulu said enthusiastically.

"Don't hold your breath," I informed her. "There really isn't any proof Jack hid any gold. Mostly just artwork, liquor, a whole lot of lumber, and guns. You know, the American dream."

"By the way, if we *do* find Wyrd Jack's sculpture," Benny said, detaching himself from Lulu, "how are we splitting the profit? I assume we'll sell it, so whatever cash we get, we divide five ways, right?"

"Already picked out your new Italian sports car?" I said.

"So funny," he said. "No, someone back at school gave me an idea for an app."

Benny had built several useless apps. A name generator for alternative pets. Another one that tracked the distance you scroll on your phone. A dating app that paired couples by song listens.

"And what is this new idea?" I asked. "Or is it top secret?"

He hesitated, then gave in. "Think Uber for local babysitters. If someone needs a babysitter, they'll be able to browse for one nearby who's been vetted."

"Yeah, a group of girls in the eighties created that. It's called the Baby-Sitters Club," Jazmine said. "Patty had the entire book series."

Benny frowned.

"Or, you know, people could just ask their next-door neighbor's kid to babysit, like they've been doing for generations," Seb said. "Let's just take a look around here first before you go spending what we don't even have yet on babysitting."

"Hey, it's an untapped market . . ."

Was it really? That seemed unlikely, but what did I know?

I left the boys while they argued and began searching the cavern on my own, pointing my flashlight at the floor and walls. Jazmine went in the opposite direction, and soon there were beams of light roving over the stone like a laser show in a planetarium. I truly didn't know what I was looking for—some kind of hidden button that unlocked a hidden cache? A giant treasure chest buried behind one of the stalagmites? Secret writing on the walls?

"Guys? Hippie cannibal cult strikes again—check it out," Jazmine announced from the other side of the cavern. "Used condom."

And it might be the only treasure here.

As the group laughed over Jazmine's discovery, I climbed onto the ledge at the back, steadied myself, and then carefully picked my way along the stone until I got to the end, where there was a small tunnel leading into the second room.

When we were young, I could duckwalk through the short tunnel, but now I had to crawl, and that made me nervous. But it took me only seconds, and before I could get too panicked, the tunnel ended, and I was standing inside the back cavern, bouncing my flashlight's cone of light around the stone walls.

There was no treasure in the front cavern. Was there something back here?

Chapter 7

The back cavern was cozier than the main area, with a ceiling that was, at best, seven feet high. The curving stream that cut through the ground was shaped like an "S," narrow enough to step over and trickling dark liquid.

"Ugh, what the—shit."

I swung around to put a spotlight on Seb as he crawled out of the tunnel. When he stood to full height, he banged his flashlight against his palm. It was dead. "Seriously?"

"Maybe it needs new batteries? When's the last time they were changed?"

"I dunno, when we were twelve? What do these take, C batteries? Christ, who keeps those on hand?" He banged on his flashlight again several times before giving up and shoving it in the pocket of his shorts. "Okay, this back cavern has definitely shrunk, right? Smells just like it used to, though."

It did: very clean and crisp. Not the same musty smell that pervaded the main cavern. "Remember when you drank water from the stream and pretended you'd been poisoned?"

He chuckled. "I remember you crying."

"I don't, but I *do* remember slugging you when I found out you were tricking us—and I remember *you* crying."

He laughed. "Okay, okay. Maybe I got it a little wrong," he

said, tracking my flashlight's beam with his eyes. "Funny that there's no trash back here. The main cavern is filled with junk."

"It took us almost a year to figure out that this area even existed. Can't really see it unless you climb the ledge." I shrugged. "I'm guessing no one comes back here much. Not even cannibals."

"Which would make it a good hiding spot for treasure," he said, stepping over the stream. "So why does it feel so empty back here?"

Empty and still, yes. Also small, so there wasn't really much of anything to explore. Seb knocked the butt of his flashlight against a small alcove, testing it like he was hunting for a stud in a wall. "No secret doors or traps here. What about that spot over there? Here, move to this side of the stream so I can get over there. Hey, wait—"

As I stepped over to swap places with him, my foot slipped on the wet rock. I nearly fell, but Seb tried to grab my arm. As he reached for me, I dropped my flashlight into the water. And before I could retrieve it, the light flickered and went out.

Darkness enveloped us.

Not like the dark of a bedroom at night, either. Utter and complete darkness. Without a visual anchor to keep me steady, I wobbled on the slick rocks and started to go down again. "Shit!"

Seb managed to grab my upper arm, his grip firm. "I gotcha, I gotcha."

I teetered on the ball of my foot for a moment, but his hand didn't let go of my arm. When I finally steadied myself, I felt his other hand patting me, testing . . . trying to find my other shoulder. And missing by a mile.

Warm fingers grazed my breast.

I froze in place, expecting his hand to move and surprised when it hesitated.

Um . . . ? Why wasn't he moving his hand? Why wasn't I moving it for him? He must've not been aware of where it was. Purely accidental. The way my heart thudded, you'd think I was privately wishing that it wasn't.

My clothes suddenly felt too tight.

"Shit. I—" He suddenly withdrew his hand. "Nope. That was not your shoulder. That was . . ."

Embarrassment warmed my cheeks, and I was temporarily glad we were in the dark so he couldn't see me blushing. *Of course, it was a mistake.* He wasn't trying to feel me up. Why did I even think for a moment that he was? *Get it together, woman!*

I flinched when I felt him roughly patting around my shoulder, where he finally ended up gripping me. "There you are, whew. Really sorry about . . ." He chuckled. "You know." He sounded embarrassed, but he also sounded like he was smiling.

Play cool. Make a joke of it. "It's fine. I mean, surely we've all found ourselves in a dark cave, getting handsy."

He made a strangled noise that was caught somewhere between surprise and laughter. "Hey, you're the one who dropped your flashlight, and that handsy business was purely accidental. It was *not* a grope."

"Sure, that's what they all say. This is my third cave grope this year."

"Goddammit, I *knew* Harvard was full of perverts."

"It's a feature, not a bug."

Seb snickered, and I smiled at him in the dark, feeling warm and elated. Secretly I loved a good verbal sparring with Seb. Always had. But he didn't have a comeback this time. An awkward quiet settled between us. Just for a moment. Then he lightly squeezed my arms in a very non-sexy way.

"Hey, for real, though," he said in a low voice. "Not hurt are you?"

"I'm okay," I assured him, sobering up. I cleared my throat. "I don't know where the flashlight is now, but it definitely rolled away. Maybe you can reach it?"

Seb let go of me, and I hated that he did. Not because I wanted his hands on me. He was my childhood friend, for God's sake. The black sheep of our weird little Wag family. Sure, he was nice on the eyes these days, but that didn't mean I wanted to hook up with him. I just . . . hated being alone in the dark.

Really hated it. "Seb? Where are you?"

"Here."

Water splashed. I couldn't see anything, but I assumed he was hunting the flashlight in the stream.

"Fuck! Where is it? We need the other Wags in here with their lights. We'll . . . Huh. Are you seeing that? Look down. Look at the stream, Paige."

I couldn't see anything but black, but I did my best to look where the stream should be and still saw nothing. *Wait, hold on . . .*

Something faintly glowed in the center of the cavern floor. Glow-in-the-dark speckles. And—hold on. The speckles weren't random. They followed a pattern.

"Is that . . . ? Seb, tell me you're not seeing Morse code."

"Where are you?" His reaching fingers found my arm again.

No boob-grazing this time, which was probably a good thing. *Of course it's a good thing. Stop thinking about it.*

"Stay with me," he said. "Walk toward the speckles, that's it. Can't quite tell— Oh, shit. Welp, so much for dry shoes."

I took wobbly steps, moving where Seb was leading. Two more steps, and we were standing over the phosphorescent speckles.

Most *definitely* Morse code.

Tiny dots and dashes had been painted into a sort of half circle:

- . . . . .-. --- .--

"Below," Seb said. "It says 'below.' Below what?"

Excitement blazed through me. "*Jaz!*" I called loudly, voice reverberating around the cavern. "Get in here!"

Muffled voices in the distance began moving toward us. Punkin barked. After a minute, scraping sounds came from the tunnel, and a tiny, bouncing light appeared—instantly making me feel better.

"Are you guys okay?" Jaz said, emerging from the tunnel with her headlamp. "Hey. Why are you standing around in the dark?"

"Look!" Seb and I both said excitedly together.

But the Morse code was no longer there.

"What am I looking at?" Jaz said as the sounds of Lulu giggling echoed inside the tunnel.

"Glow-in-the dark," I said to Seb. "We only saw it because the lights were off. Come stand over here with us, Jaz, and switch off your headlamp for a sec."

When she did, the Morse code reappeared. "No way!" she said, flicking her headlamp on and off a couple of times to see the glow-in-the-dark effect. "Is it paint? Did Wyrd Jack have access to that back then?"

"Radium was used in paint in the early twentieth century," I said, a little excited that my art education at Harvard was already coming in handy. "We probably shouldn't handle it too much, in case that's what it is."

"What does it say?" Jazmine asked. "I know you nerds still remember how to read it."

"It says 'below,'" Seb told her as Lulu's laughter emerged from the tunnel. "Hold on. Look."

I got closer to see what Seb was inspecting. The code was written around the edges of a flat, round rock that looked a little bit like a manhole cover. Seb began digging his fingers around it, brushing dirt away.

"Help me lift it," he said before Lulu and Benny's lantern light filled the small cavern and Punkin rushed in, barking once to announce her presence.

"What's going on up here?" Benny asked as he brushed dirt off the front of his shirt.

"Dude! We found a code. Get over here!" I told him.

Jazmine and I both kneeled on the floor and dug our own fingers under the edge of the round rock. A moment later, Benny crouched along with us. The four of us lifted, and the rock moved. *Just* slightly.

"Lift!" Seb shouted, and we all complied.

The rock was heavy, but once it came away from the floor, we were able to shift it to one side. Dust billowed.

Seb coughed and waved it away. "Light—shine it here."

Benny stepped over the stream, and his lantern shone brighter than Jaz's flashlight. We all looked down into a black hole in the floor.

"What is it?" Lulu asked, craning her neck to see.

"Let me get a better look. Give me your headlamp, would ya?" he said to Jazmine. "My flashlight bit the dust."

Seb lay on the floor, belly down, and stuck his head into the hole along with Jazmine's headlamp. His voice sounded like it was coming from the bottom of a well. "Oh. Seriously? Wags, there's another cavern down below this one. It's flooded."

"Flooded?" I tapped Seb, quietly requesting the headlamp as I lay on the floor next to him. "Let me see."

I slipped the band of the headlamp over my forehead and dared to stick my head inside the hole. At first, I couldn't really see anything. Then my eyes adjusted and I saw what Seb had described—a small cavern about the same size as this one, but halfway down was a waterline.

Definitely was flooded down there. Disappointment rose, but I pushed it away and quickly ran through possibilities.

"We're elevated in this secondary cave," I said, peering down into the hole, "so I'm betting down there it's probably level with the main cavern. If it is, then it can't be that deep. A few feet?"

Seb pulled me back from the hole. "And if it's not? How the hell would we get back up?"

"Maybe with that?" Benny said.

When I pushed back from the hole, I spotted what he was pointing toward: something poked out from beneath a nearby rock. Seb tugged on it, and a length of thick, braided rope emerged, tied with several fat knots.

Seb whistled. "Wild, absolutely wild."

The rope was anchored to a nearby stalagmite and looked reasonably stable, especially when Seb tossed it into the hole, and we could all see that the frayed bottom of the last knot skimmed the waterline. Theoretically, if someone dropped down into the hole, even if the water was deep, they could reach the rope and climb back up.

Everyone started to talk at once. Punkin barked.

Jazmine shouted over the din. "Everyone, hold up! Let's think about this for a minute. We don't know what's in the water down there, and we aren't kids anymore. It could be seriously fucking dangerous, all right? God knows I can't go down there with my sprained arm. And what if whatever's down there has already been found?"

As much as I hated to think about it, she might be right. We all sat around the hole, taking peeks inside, considering the logistics of dropping into it. None of this was sensible. Jazmine was right: we weren't kids anymore. But somewhere in the depths of my being, where all my pain and grief and loneliness hid, I realized suddenly that I *needed* this.

Needed to feel the rush of danger. To reconnect with my past. To feel . . .

Alive.

"I'm going down," I told everyone. As soon as the words were out, excitement and fear spread through me. I'd already said it aloud, though. No backing down now.

"Absolutely not," Seb said. "You could drown or get hurt. If anyone's going, it's me."

"What was that motto you were always spouting back in the day, when we were kids? Oh, that's right. 'Don't think,'" I quoted, teasing.

"That motto is only for dumb shits like me, not for the big brains."

"Just be ready to pull me back up."

"Paige—*Paige!*"

I didn't think. I didn't hesitate, either. After tightening the strap on the headlamp, I put my feet in the hole, took a deep breath, and jumped.

My stomach lurched as I plunged into darkness.

I immediately regretted my decision. I mean, what was I thinking? I was a walking billboard for a stereotypical pasty academic—not Lara Croft.

But then my feet hit the water, and I knifed beneath the surface. The water was shockingly cold and tasted dank. Even with the headlamp, it was too chaotic to see anything, so I shut my eyes and descended. Down, down . . .

Until I hit the bottom.

My landing stirred up detritus in the water that obscured my vision, even with the headlamp. Yellow lights floated above—the Wags' flashlights. They were useless down here, just bobbing yellow circles. I hadn't considered that I wouldn't be able to navigate well, but now I feared what I couldn't see.

What's down here?

As the sediment settled, I was able to get my bearings. The cavern wasn't big—half the size of the small one above, maybe. And it didn't look like there was much of anything down here. I dared to swim, using a modified breaststroke while keeping close to the floor, and all it did was churn up more dirt and small particles that muddied everything.

However, when I turned in the water, something glinted on the rocky floor in the light of my headlamp. My eyes stung from keeping them open underwater, but I was able to swim toward the glint. What is that? I reached between a couple stalagmites growing from the floor, stretching out my fingers until they touched something cold and smooth.

A key!

A skeleton key.

I grabbed it and started to turn around and swim back up, but I wasn't moving.

Stuck. The rubber bottom of my sneaker had gotten wedged between the stalagmites. I jerked my leg, trying to free it, but it only seemed to make it worse.

Couldn't get my shoe unstuck. Couldn't get my foot out of my shoe.

Panic rushed through me. I was running out of breath, so I shoved the key into the little pocket of my cutoffs and tried to work my shoe out of the rocks. But the more I tugged, the worse I became stuck.

My foot wasn't budging. When I struggled harder, my head-lamp slipped off and fell out of sight, and the sudden darkness made everything so much worse.

My lungs tightened painfully.

This can't be real. It only happens in movies. Why did I come down here?

I couldn't hold my breath any longer, lungs nearly bursting. My vision darkened around the edges. I was going to die inside this cave—that much was clear to me. Best to just give in and let it happen.

Hey, at least I wouldn't have to face my estranged father.

And the financial aid office back at Harvard.

No regrets, right?

Well, maybe a few. The only one I could think of in the moment, though, was that I desperately regretted Seb hadn't felt me up on purpose.

Hey, at least I could admit that now that I was dying.

When the world began slipping away, I felt the water shift. Something was moving. Fast. Somewhere in the back of my drowning brain, I vaguely wondered if I'd discovered a long-lost cave creature, Haven's very own Loch Ness Monster. But a second later, I felt human hands on my leg, jerking me painfully until my shoe popped, and I was free.

An arm made of steel wrapped around my waist, pulling me upward.

Through the dark water.

Until our heads broke the surface, and I gasped and coughed, and gasped some more while light danced and concerned voices shouted. The knotted rope was being lowered.

"You're all right," a rough voice was saying in my ear as we bobbed in the water. "I've got you. I've got you . . ."

I coughed up water and turned my head to see Seb's blue eyes blinking down at me as he held me against him.

Like I was a precious thing.

The most important thing in the world.

<h1 style="text-align:center">Chapter 8</h1>

We barely made it back up the rope. It took all my remaining strength to climb, even with Seb's help. By the time I made it to where the gang could haul me up, my hands were stinging, and my ankle was giving out.

"Don't move!" Jazmine commanded when we were both safely in the back cavern, dripping wet and exhausted. "Are you hurt?"

Seb shook his head as he caught his breath, gesturing loosely toward my leg. "Check her ankle."

My shoe was still mostly intact. The rubber sole was breaking away from the shoe, which was streaked with green algae and mud. My ankle was red and scraped up, hurting, but I hadn't broken it.

"I'm okay," I told Jazmine grumpily when she tried to remove my wet shoe. "Just leave it."

"Holy shit," Lulu said, holding her face in her hands. "I can't believe you guys went down there. You're both nuts. You almost died!"

She wasn't wrong. I couldn't stop coughing.

Wet clothes sticking to every line of his body, Seb lay on his back on the cave floor, sprawling, with one arm draped over his face as he huffed out hard breaths. "Wags . . . not for . . . the faint of heart, Lulu."

"Jesus, Paige. You all right?" Benny asked, squatting over me as I wrung out my hair. "I seriously thought you were going to drown. You were down there for well over a minute before Seb went in—I checked the time on my phone."

I'd always had good lungs. "Yeah, that was dumb, huh?" I glanced at Seb. "Can't believe you came down after me."

"Red Cross lifeguard certification finally paid off," he joked.

I'd forgotten he had that. I shook my head, feeling stunned.

"Never again," Jazmine said. "You really scared me, Paige. This treasure hunt is officially not happening. We end it today. No one is going back down, you hear me?"

"Don't need to." I summoned the strength to fish the skeleton key out of my pocket and held it up. "Found this . . . at the bottom."

"A key?" Benny asked, big eyes blinking. "Wonder what it unlocks."

Everyone stared at it for a moment before Seb snatched it up. The key itself was dark and rusted, but it was strung on a single ring next to an oval brass tag. That must've been what glinted in the water.

Seb polished the tag on the bottom of his shirt and inspected it closely. "Fuuuck," he said in awe. "We've got more code, folks."

"Are you kidding?" Jazmine squinted at Seb's hands.

I leaned closer. "Seb? What does it say? Is it more numbers that we need to decipher with the 'Prison Poem' text?"

He squinted at it, moving his lips in silence. "Letters, not numbers. Starts with 'N.'" Seb continued calling out letters as he interpreted the dots and dashes. "'N . . . O . . . S . . . E . . . S.'"

"Noses?" Benny squatted down to look at it in the light.

Seb polished the brass tag once more, then flipped it over.

"'U . . . N . . . D . . . E . . . R . . . T . . .' Wait, there's spacing here. 'Under' is one word. Then, 'T . . . H . . . E . . . I . . . R.'"

I blinked at Seb. "Under their noses."

"'Under their noses,'" he repeated, nodding as a smile ghosted over his face. "It's the next clue, people. Fuck yes!"

"But what does it mean?" Benny said, taking the key from Seb. "No noses in this cave but ours."

"Let me see," Lulu said eagerly. "This looks really old. Nothing inside this cave that it would fit into, right?"

"The first clue got us here, to Pinemoon Cave," I pointed out. "Maybe this clue takes us somewhere else."

"Where?" Jazmine asked, snatching the key from Lulu's fingers. "To another place where you can jump in some weird water? We don't even know who left these clues, or where they lead. Probably to you drowning again!"

"No one drowned," I pointed out. "We *almost* drowned."

Seb snickered, which only further irritated Jazmine.

"Both of you could be dead right now, you know?" she said, sounding agitated. "And Benny has a point. Whose noses? This could mean anything. I mean, come on. Get real. We didn't really come here today thinking we'd *actually* find treasure. Do we really believe that Nana Malone has been hanging on to this all her life—the solution to one of the biggest lost treasures in the US? And that it was passed down through the family from Wyrd Jack himself? Not to mention that it's a terrible clue."

"All clues are terrible until you figure them out," Seb said, taking the key back from Jazmine. "Why are you getting so worked up about this?"

"Maybe because I thought you idiots were going to die and I

couldn't do a damn thing to help you," she said, tucking her hurt arm tight against her side.

"Jaz—"

"The Wags were nothing but an excuse to do stupid things when we were younger," she argued. "Think about it. When's the last time we were out here? Oh, wait. I remember. It was the week before two idiots drove a stolen car off a pier."

"Which idiots?" Lulu asked brightly.

Benny groaned.

"You haven't told her, Ben? Don't blame you," Jazmine said. "If I'd stolen a Ferrari from one of the biggest assholes in town as a joke—"

"How many times do I have to say that we didn't 'steal' the Ferrari," Benny insisted, getting agitated. "It was just a prank. A joy ride!"

Jazmine's eyes narrowed. "Were you experiencing joy when you couldn't distinguish forward from reverse and backed that Ferrari off a pier?"

"Jesus, Jaz," Benny said, darting a nervous glance at Lulu. "Can you not do this now?"

"Why?" she asked. "Are you embarrassed that you let one of your oldest friends take the fall for the stunt, even though he wasn't the one driving? People who have important parents in this town can't do jail time. And who cares if Seb gets sent away to boot camp, right? Everyone just assumed he was a loser anyway."

"To be fair, I kind of was . . ." Seb said.

"Benny?" Lulu asked, squinching up her face at him. "What is she talking about?"

"Don't take this out on him," Seb told Jaz. "You guys always give Benny shit for the Ferrari incident, but it took two to tango, you know? Benny wouldn't have even dreamed of taking the Ferrari on his own."

That much I believed was true. After Seb and I stopped speaking in high school and the Wags fell apart, Jaz and I got closer while Seb started hanging with Benny again . . . something we weren't made aware of until we saw them goofing around in front of a fancy steak house along the harbor front, both in uniform, working as valets part-time after school.

The boys were on duty the night the Ferrari rolled up to their valet stand. Whose idea was it to take the car for a spin around the block? That was up for debate. But thanks to some panicked driving on Benny's part, putting it in reverse instead of forward, that's when everything went so wrong.

"None of this matters," Seb insisted, "because it's *in the past*."

Jazmine turned on Seb. "Then leave it there! Stop doing dangerous shit! I came here today wanting to have a good time and reconnect with old friends, not drive them to the ER."

"I think we all did, Jaz," I said, hoping to calm her down. She was so upset. "No one's going to the ER. My ankle's sore, that's all."

"Every time we did these treasure hunts, someone got hurt," Jazmine insisted. "Even when we're not hunting treasure, the Wags attract disaster—like that dumb Ferrari stunt. Nothing was the same for all of us after that happened, you know that, right?"

"I know," Seb said very seriously. "Trust me, Jaz. I know."

"So do I," Benny said, eyes pleading. "If I could take it all back, I would. I've regretted it every day the past two years. Spending a month in the hospital with a collapsed lung was not my greatest moment, okay? Not saying I had it worse than Seb—"

"Stop comparing," Seb said. "It's oranges to apples."

Jazmine shook her head. "Idiots. Both of you should understand why I'm not going to sit around and watch my friends almost die. I'm going back to town. Stay out here if you want. This place is a grave."

"Jazmine, wait!" I called out. Was she truly this upset over what we'd just done? Or was this outburst caused by something else, like maybe her being hung up on Benny? I hated that I didn't know. "Please, Jaz. Stay and talk this out."

"Not in a talking mood," she answered. She tried to stomp away, but she had to stop and duck into the tunnel, ruining the impact, especially when Punkin came through after her.

Dammit. This was not how I wanted this trip to end. Now I was anxious about Jazmine and hating that she was upset enough to leave.

Across the cavern, Lulu argued with Benny. I tried to listen to what they were saying but couldn't concentrate because it was all I could do to stand, with my ankle beginning to swell. Seb pocketed the rusty key and offered a hand to help me up.

"Whoa, whoa, whoa," he said, helping to brace me up while I hobbled on one foot. "Hate to tell you, but that's going to suck later when it really starts hurting."

"We need to go after Jaz."

"Give her some time to blow off steam. Can't paddle a canoe with one arm," he pointed out. "She ain't goin' nowhere without us."

Oh. Right.

"I just don't understand why she's so upset . . ."

Seb lifted his eyes to me. "No one likes to feel powerless. Especially Jaz."

Why did she feel powerless? Her sprained arm? Maybe. I just

couldn't help thinking about that conversation I'd overheard when the two of them showed up at the cottage this morning. Did *that* have anything to do with her mood?

I didn't get a chance to find out, not while everyone was squabbling. I focused on hobbling my way out of the cave without re-injuring myself. We found Punkin guarding Jazmine, who was outside by the canoes, sullen and not interested in talking to any of us, which hurt my feelings. But I gave her space, and we paddled our way back down the Little River to the party dock in Benny's backyard. And once there, everything fizzled out pretty fast. If I thought the Wags would be spending a nice day, hanging out together, I was wrong. Benny was busy with Lulu, and Jazmine's mood hadn't improved. To all our surprise, her sister, Patty, was waiting for her when we docked because Jazmine had texted her to come pick her up.

Patty gave me a little wave from her truck, and I waved back, feeling ineffective and concerned.

"Seriously, just let her cool off. She'll come around," Seb told me. "Let's get you back home before we both freeze to death in these wet clothes."

I nodded, and after saying goodbye to Benny and promising to meet up again to discuss the key I'd found, we loaded into Seb's Bronco, and he sped the entire way back to Heron Cottage. We barely said two words the entire way, both lost in our own thoughts as the gentle narrator on Seb's audiobook talked soothingly about visiting castles in Spain.

But after pulling into my driveaway, Seb sighed deeply, shut off the engine, and looked at me. "Well, that was . . . something," he said, tugging his wet shorts away from where they stuck to his thighs. "I know I told you I'd poke around under the hood of your car today. But I need some clean clothes and a shower, so I better go do that first. God only knows what kind of bacteria were growing in that cave water. We probably contracted Legionnaires' disease." He shivered violently. "Fuck me! Why are wet clothes so cold?"

"Just . . ." I sighed and pushed open the passenger door. "Take a shower here."

One brow shot up. "Seriously?"

"Probably have fresh clothes of yours in the cottage—I assume their yours. They were all over the floor of my room, and for some dumb reason, I didn't burn them all."

Seb's face went from surprised to happy. "That would be great." He jumped out of the Bronco, with Punkin following. "Really hope you've got my *Bun in the Oven* T-shirt. People always ask me how far along my wife is when I wear it."

I groaned and let us inside the cottage, where Punkin raced to the water bowl in the kitchen. "You can take the shower first. I'll dig out some clothes and leave them outside the bathroom door."

"Thanks, Paige. I really appreciate it. Seriously."

He headed to the bathroom while I went to my bedroom and dug out a trash bag from my closet that contained his clothes— mostly T-shirts and shorts. A pair of boxers with a Christmas tree print. Several mismatched socks. I pulled out some things and quickly changed out of my own wet clothes, feeling relieved to slip into an old fuzzy housecoat.

And also anxious. *Seb is getting naked two walls away.* Was that a normal thing that old friends did, let them shower in your house while you parade around in a housecoat? I briefly worried Nana would disapprove. Then again, this was sort of an emergency, one might say, so maybe it was totally fine.

By the time I'd placed Seb's clothes next to the bathroom door, I heard the water in the shower shutting off and knocked on the door. "Hey. Your stuff is sitting here, and I let your dog out through the back because she was barking."

The door unexpectedly opened, and Seb's wet head poked out. Soap and shampoo wafted from him as he towel-dried his hair. "That's fine. She won't jump the fence. What'd you say before that?"

There was too much glistening skin on display. And also not enough, because my animal brain was curious to see what was hidden behind the door. I guess all it took was one accidental boob graze for me to turn into a maniac.

I dropped my eyes to where his clothes sat in a neat pile. "There," I said, gesturing toward the floor. "Hope that's good."

"Sweet! Thank you." He started to reach for it but hesitated when he couldn't do so without exposing himself. "Could you just . . . ?"

"Towel around the waist is customary," I pointed out.

"This is the only one in here," he argued, shaking the towel he used to dry his hair. "You need to do laundry."

"Sorry, been too busy spelunking."

"Is that what the kids are calling it these days?"

I rolled my eyes and picked up his clothes. "For the love of God, just . . . there, take them," I said, shoving them toward him while averting my gaze.

"Damn, Paige. My eyes are up here, you know."

I glanced up—I couldn't help it—and as my eyes lifted, I caught the smallest glimpse of his bare hip, just a sliver of skin peeking out from behind the door. He shifted farther inside the bathroom, and that sliver disappeared. But I saw it. Hip. *Side hip.* Was that a thing?

My face warmed before words finally came. "I wasn't looking at anything."

"It's a pretty good view, I've been told." He gripped the edge of the door, offering to open it. "If you want to look, I wouldn't blame you."

My face was on fire. An oven. A forge. The heat from a million dying stars. "Starting to think you really *were* trying to cop a feel in the cave," I managed to say.

"Paige, I swear on Wyrd Jack's 'Prison Poem' that I really didn't mean to do that. Come on. If I really wanted to touch you, you'd know it."

"Oh?" I wished I didn't sound so breathless, but I could feel my pulse in my swollen ankle, and the pain wasn't helping my nerves. "Is that right?"

He tapped the edge of the door several times, then blue eyes flicked toward mine, and he stared at me with an intense, dangerous look I'd never once seen on his face in all the years I'd known him. "You'd have to want me to. That's the first thing."

Warm chills raced over my skin. Was he suggesting I give him permission . . . ? A riot of panic-adjacent emotions broke out inside my chest. Maybe I was confused again. He was only running his mouth, and I was more shaken by that flooded cavern than I'd previously thought.

"Get dressed, asshole," I said, turning away from the bathroom.

"If you insist," he called behind me as I hobbled back to my room.

I didn't respond. I just stood against the wall in my bedroom—

the same wall that separated me from the bathroom, exhaling a shaky breath.

Everything was fine.

I was not thirsting for my childhood friend.

Even if I had to tell myself that a thousand times before it sank in.

Chapter 9

I heard Seb banging around in the bathroom for a bit while he got ready, then he shouted at me again, "Hey, while you're in the shower, I'll head outside and take a look at the Corvair. Is the key to the garage still behind the tin Texaco sign?"

"Surprised you remembered," I called back, hoping my voice sounded normal.

"Mind like a bear trap."

"Mind like a bear caught in a bear trap."

"Just because some of us didn't get into Ivy Leagues doesn't mean we're all dummies, you know. At the very least, I'm smarter than my dog. Usually."

"Speaking of," I called out, sitting on the edge of my bed to dig inside my chest of drawers for a change of clothes. "Where does Punkin stay when you're at work, or whatever?"

"Different places. Sometimes at Mandy's Dog Rescue."

"Your dad won't let her stay at the house?"

"*I* don't stay at the house. My dad doesn't know about her." The bathroom door hinges squealed, and Seb stepped out into the hall, pulling the T-shirt I gave him over his head while pausing in front of my bedroom door. When his face emerged from the cotton, his gaze flicked over my fuzzy robe, but he didn't make any comments.

I sidled my way around him to get to the bathroom. "I thought you said things were better between you."

"They're civil, which is better. But the only reason we're not at each other's throats is because . . ." He shook his head. "I let him see what he wants to see, and I hide the stuff that pisses him off. If he knew I'd adopted Punkin, he'd say it was a 'waste of resources,'" Seb said, making air quotes. "Lucky me, he's got his hands full these days. He's . . . distracted. I haven't seen him in weeks."

"Wow, okay."

He wasn't eager to elaborate so I changed the subject.

"Hey, what do you think the cipher means? Ideas?"

He shook his head. "Anything could be 'under their noses.' My first thought was the Wyrd Jack statue outside the harbor museum, because I was trying to think of anything with a nose in town, and that's our only statue."

"But it says 'under *their* noses,' not 'under *my* nose,' or whatever. Plus, the statue was built in the 1950s, long after he wrote the 'Prison Poem.' His treasure had been hidden for thirty years, and he was dead."

"Point taken. What about you? Any ideas?"

"Not yet." I hesitated. "Hey, what's with Jaz going nuclear back at the cave? Is something going on with her that I don't know about?"

"Not sure. What don't you know about?"

"If I knew, I wouldn't be asking."

But he already knew that. I could see humor behind his eyes, but I wished he'd be serious for once.

"Look, Patty told me Jaz has been struggling, but she wouldn't say why. Jaz has been acting a little weird around me . . ." I didn't want to admit that I've overheard their conversation this morning, so I left it and said, "Only thing I've noticed that's different is that it feels like Jaz's hatred of Lulu is a little personal. She hasn't told me anything, but clearly there's something going on there."

He hesitated then gave in. "This year was kind of tough for Jaz. You'd have to ask her for specifics, but, for example, I know she missed Benny while he was in Kalamazoo, and they made a lot of plans this summer that got wrecked when Lulu showed up. But, you know, she missed you, too. A lot, actually. Patty's right—Jaz has been struggling. I think . . ."

"What?"

"I don't know. Maybe she needed . . . all of us?"

"The Wags?"

He nodded. "You should ask her. Talk to her. For real."

It was strange for him to advise *me* to talk to my best friend. I wasn't the one who left her behind when I chose juvenile delinquency over friendship. But I wasn't in the mood to bring that up again.

We stood together, silent and awkward, not quite looking at each other.

"I'm just going to . . ." I gestured behind me, toward the shower.

"Right, right. I'll be out in the garage." He took a step back but didn't turn around. "Get as naked as you want to. I won't be peeking."

"Oh, thank you," I said with heavy sarcasm. "Thank you for allowing me to be naked in my own home, which I already do every single day."

"God, stop *flirting* with me!"

I slammed the bathroom door shut and melted against it as my nerves went wild. He was only being obnoxious for the laughs, and I just wasn't used to being teased that way—definitely not back at Harvard. No one there knew how to push my buttons.

Classic Seb Jansen.

I did my best to erase it all from my thoughts while taking a shower and instead concentrated on the skeleton key cipher. But like Seb, I couldn't think of any obvious place in town that had to do with noses. The more I thought about it, the more frustrated I became.

After dressing, I put our wet clothes in the washer. Then I rummaged around until I found a decades-old Ace bandage under the bathroom sink—the metal fastener long gone and replaced by a safety pin—and wrapped it around my tender ankle. I hobbled my way outside and entered the garage, where Seb was already shutting the hood of the Corvair.

"What's the verdict?" I asked.

"Don't see anything weird under the hood, so I'm going to assume it's your O-rings and push rods."

"Push rods? Are you making that up?"

He briefly flashed me his dimples while wiping his hands on a shop towel. "I'd need to get into the engine, and to do that, I'd need to bring some tools—a jack, car stands—so I can get under to work. I can borrow those from the marina."

"Seb."

"No, I mean on the up-and-up. Mr. Neely's cool. I'll also need a few things from the auto shop, but it shouldn't cost more than fifty bucks, maybe? If you've got that."

I nodded. "How long will it take?"

"A few hours. I'm off again day after tomorrow. I can get the supplies and swing by here in the morning. Maybe we can put our heads together and figure out the new cipher then, too."

"Yeah, that sounds really good." I crossed my arms, looking at the car.

"How's the ankle?"

I glanced down at the Ace bandage. "Stiff and sore. I took some Tylenol."

He whistled. "Let's not go nuts, okay?"

I stuck out my tongue at him, and after he chuckled, I cleared my throat. "So, um, hey. Thank you for helping with the car. And also for diving into the hole back at the cave. You literally saved my life."

He waved a hand dismissively. "You would've freed yourself."

"No," I whispered, shaking my head. "I don't think I would have."

Seb scrubbed the back of his neck. "Of course I jumped in. It was you."

Seb's gaze met mine, and we looked at each other for . . . far too long. Long enough for big emotions to rise from the battlefield of my heart, which held tenderness for an old friend and an equal amount of hurt for how he treated me when he left the Wags.

And behind all that, another feeling blossomed. Something that I didn't want to feel, because it had disappointed me my entire life.

Hope.

Seb finally looked away and dug out his phone when it dinged. "I hate to run off, but this thing has been blowing up since I came out to the garage. I gotta take care of something."

"Your dad?"

He shook his head. "Sort of wish it was. Which is saying a lot." Pocketing his phone, he gave me a tight smile. No dimples. He was stressed. Was it Pretty Paul Vanderburg calling Seb back for another pseudo-macho bonfire fight? Or something worse? Whatever it was, the rigid way Seb held his body made it clear that he was in no mood to discuss it with me. "Anyway, I'll come in the morning on Wednesday. If you need a ride anywhere before then, give me a ring."

"I don't have your number."

"That's right," he said. "Here, swap. I'll put mine in if you put in yours."

It sounded like a joke, but he seemed distracted, so I didn't comment. We exchanged phones and typed our numbers into our contacts.

Then he strolled out of the garage, whistling loudly for his dog as he opened a gate in the fence. Punkin came running and jumped in the Bronco along with him. "See you on Wednesday, Malone," he called out from his open window before starting up the engine.

I stepped onto the front drive to watch him leave. At the last moment, when he shifted the Bronco in reverse, and Punkin was hanging out the passenger window, I called out, "Bring that dumb dog of yours again when you come back on Wednesday. She can stay here if she doesn't cause me any headaches. I mean, I don't know about overnight, but if you need to bring her here while you work, or whatever . . ."

He cocked his head to one side. "For real?"

"If you're going to rescue a dog, do it properly—don't take it back to the rescue, for the love of Pete." I scrunched up my face in the bright midday sunlight. "But she's absolutely not allowed on my bed."

"Perish the thought. I'll give her a stern talking to," he said, strapping on his seat belt. "She won't put a single paw inside your room."

"Deal. BYODF."

He arched a brow.

"Bring your own dog food."

Laughter floated from the driver's window over the Bronco's noisy engine. "Got it. You're a real human being, you know that, Paige?"

I'd heard that a lot when we were kids. His highest praise. It made me feel warm inside.

"We'll see you Wednesday," he shouted, pulling out of the driveway.

God help me, but I was already looking forward to it.

Chapter 10

Hopefully whatever called Seb away wasn't serious enough to get him another black eye. My worries about him bled into worries for Jazmine, so I texted her a couple of times before she finally answered, later that night: I'm fine, just tired. Sorry I blew up. My arm's bothering me. Going to take a pain pill and go to bed. Talk soon? Xoxo

Pain did make a person grumpy and irrational, I supposed, and maybe she truly did need some rest and space for the time being. But now that Seb had confirmed my suspicions about Jaz's feelings for Benny, I was hurt she hadn't confided in me and made mental plans to try to get her to open up.

The next day, I babied my hurt ankle and laid out on the beach behind the cottage with a book—one about women in modern art, written by a Harvard professor who'd be teaching a class in the fall that I'd already registered for. It was a dry, academic text, but that only made concentrating on it a challenge that I enjoyed. Mainly because it distracted me from the fact that to actually *attend* this professor's class, I'd have to eventually face my father.

I poked around online and found him. At least, I found his place of business. Mr. Rufus Lee was "Grand Rapids' leading commercial real estate broker." He sold office buildings. Entire floors of skyscrapers. Stadiums. And Seb had been right: he'd won a bunch of sales awards. If I had a working car, I could drive the hour to Grand Rapids and walk into his real estate offices. Though, even *thinking* about doing that made my stomach cramp.

However, this was not an optional task if I wanted to get my degree from Harvard, and I knew it. So I took the coward's way out and filled out the contact form on his business's website, R. Lee and Associates:

Dear Mr. Lee,

I have some legal paperwork that needs your signature and was hoping to find a time when we could meet in person. I'm at the lake for the summer and can meet you in Grand Rapids. Let me know where and when is good for you.

Regards,
Paige Malone, your former daughter

I added my phone number and a postscript instructing him to feel free to text me for more information, then I sent it and felt the biggest sense of relief, and right behind that, a prickling anxiety. Because now I had to wait for a reply. I refreshed my email a gazillion times the first hour, then I gave up and tried not to think about it.

He'd respond eventually, I assumed. I knew businesses sometimes took a while to respond to inquiries, so I figured I'd just wait. And for the time being, I had plenty of other things to occupy my time and thoughts.

By the time Wednesday morning rolled around, there was still no reply; however, I'd woken with an idea about our treasure hunt that I couldn't get out of my head. So when Seb drove up in the Speed Buggy, I met him out front.

"Mornin'," he said, blue eyes glittering in the sun. When he opened his door, Punkin jumped over him from the passenger seat and leaped outside. "Dammit, Punkin! Mud on my shorts?"

Punkin wasn't paying him any attention. She barked at me once and wagged her tail. Her teeth were snaggled, and her tongue hung out goofily.

"Why is she just staring at me?"

"She's wishing that you'll succumb to her seductions and pet her," Seb said, hauling an enormous bag of dog food out of the back of his Bronco. There were a lot of tools back there now, too.

"You know what they say, Punkin. Wish in one hand . . ."

"Ignore the mean lady," he told the dog, slinging the dog food bag over one shoulder. "She doesn't want what I brought her this morning on the dash."

While Seb carried the dog food inside, whistling for Punkin to follow, I looked inside the front of the car and spotted a pair of plastic coffee cups topped with pink straws, sitting in a paper holder from Grind-and-Shine. The orders were written on the side of the cups: iced white chocolate mochas. One had added coconut milk.

He remembered?

I smiled to myself for a moment, feeling happier about that than I probably should have, then schooled my face to remain neutral and carried the cups inside. Seb was in the kitchen, already filling up a bowl on the floor with kibble. I'd never seen a tail wag so hard. Punkin stuck her entire big head inside Nana's old bread-dough bowl and woofed it down.

"Slow down, girl. You're embarrassing us, acting like I never feed you," Seb said, looking up as I approached. "Ah, you found our morning fuel."

I handed him one of the heavy plastic cups. "Can't believe you remembered."

"Mind like a bear trap."

I chuckled and picked up my coffee, running a finger across the side to clear away beads of moisture that had sweated onto the cup. The cottage grew quiet, and a strained awkwardness hung in the air. Did he not want to be here? Maybe he'd sobered up after our cavern adventure. Maybe he regretted it.

It was getting weird. *Say something.*

"Hey," I started. "So, um . . . I was thinking about the cipher—"

"'Under their noses'?" He acted as relieved as I felt to have something safe to talk about.

"Yeah," I said, nodding and stirring the ice inside my drink with the straw. "And I was thinking about how you first thought about it being connected to the statue of Wyrd Jack."

"But we already decided it can't be the statue."

I held up a finger. "I'm wondering if the museum itself might inspire a solution. I can't stop thinking about how that phrase means to do something bad right out in the open and no one suspects, right? The museum is inside the old jail where he was held."

"Treasure hunters have scoured the museum for decades, though."

"But they didn't have this," I said, pulling the skeleton key out of my jeans pocket. "Is there something still there, something they missed? Like . . ." I shook my head and shrugged. "I don't know."

Seb filled another bowl with water. "Hmm."

"Maybe I'm just spinning my wheels."

"Maybe. But I'm getting that tingly feeling—you know the one."

"You should really have that checked by a doctor."

He leaned against the counter while Punkin plowed into her food. "Let me get the Corvair jacked up. Then we'll take a trip to the harbor, see what we can see. After, we'll come back here and I'll start tearing down your engine."

A little thrill went through me. This was good. No more awkwardness. We were just two old friends, reconnecting.

Seb went out to the garage, while I let Punkin out back after Seb reminded me that she didn't need babysitting and was perfectly content to sleep on the back porch swing, which would explain the mud accumulating on the swing's palm-tree printed cushion.

It didn't take long for Seb to get the car jacked up on one side—enough that he could slide under and dismantle part of the engine from below. Once he'd secured the wheels, he cleaned up and checked on the dog—and left her dozing on the back porch swing—we piled into the Bronco and headed out.

The drive was less than ten minutes, and with his travelogue audiobook turned down low in the background, we talked about things that had changed along the route. A new sub shop opened. An old laundromat closed. The city was rebuilding our former middle school. After we crossed the river, heading into the nicer part of town, we turned away from Benny's neighborhood and drove into the heart of Haven Beach: the Harbor District.

We didn't have a big harbor, but it stayed busy with tourists in the summer. A wooden boardwalk curved around the water and was lined with quirky shops, street performers, and several hotels. At the far tip of the harbor stood our cherry-red lighthouse—no longer working, just a tourist spot now. Halfway between it and where we stood, a late-nineteenth-century wooden mail-delivery ship was moored along the boardwalk.

Devil's Revenge.

Wyrd Jack's "pirate" ship.

Tourists were already paying for tickets at a nearby booth to tour the ship. We found a lucky parking space right next to the stone statue of Wyrd Jack—a fierce-looking man with a big beard and a corncob pipe dangling from this mouth, dressed in a heavy coat and a fisherman's hat.

"Still looks like you," Seb joked when we hopped out of the Bronco.

"I'm trying to grow my beard back in. Hey, you don't think we should call Jaz and Benny before we go in here, do you? I mean, what if we actually find something?"

"Nah. Chances are low that we'd find the treasure inside there. Best we can hope for is another clue. Besides, you and me are the primary Wags. Always have been. If we find anything, we'll loop them back in."

I supposed that was sensible. I shielded my eyes from the sun glinting off the water and looked around. It was really nice here. Flowers bloomed in window boxes of an old-fashioned ice cream parlor, and pretty trees shaded a cobbled walk that had been there a hundred years. Birds sang. Tourists smiled. And I sighed to my-self in pleasure as nostalgic feelings surfaced . . . until I saw the sign outside the museum.

"Holy shit, they doubled ticket prices," I said. "Ten dollars a person? It used to be five!"

"No worries, I gotcha," Seb said as we walked up to the mu-seum's ticket window. "Those of us who are gainfully employed, see, we have a paycheck—unlike you freeloading students. Two, please," he said to the ticket seller.

"You're fixing my car. I can't let you pay," I told him, digging out cash from my purse.

When I handed it to him, he pushed my hand down and looked around, feigning paranoia. "Not here. I don't want to get picked up for prostitution." He winked at the attendant who handed him tickets. I waited until he entered the museum door then tucked two fives in his back pocket, causing him to jump and make a *yip* noise, like I'd tickled him.

"Christ, you're stubborn. That hasn't changed," he said good-naturedly.

I shoved his shoulder playfully, and he pushed me back, and for a moment, we were kids again, laughing and being silly. A woman gave us a dirty look, so I cleared my throat and stopped as we got in line.

"Jeez, Malone. You're almost as embarrassing as Punkin," Seb whispered playfully. "What're they teaching you out in Massachusetts?"

In good spirits, we waited for the attendant to take our tickets before moving past a red rope into the museum proper, into the town's former police station lobby, where it was substantially darker. Polished wood and brick made up the bones of the space, where a jaunty sailing tune played on a loop over the museum's speakers.

"Well, here we are again," Seb said, glancing around. "Been a few years. Guess this isn't the kind of museum you were planning on visiting in Europe this summer, huh?"

"Not quite," I admitted.

The museum itself was once Haven Beach's only police station, jail, and courthouse and had been built before the turn of the century. We strolled past interactive displays: "Pirates of the Great Lakes," a map that tracked routes of various ne'er-do-wells who regularly stole lumber and booze from ships all across Lakes Michigan, Superior, and Erie. And: "Lawmen of Michigan," which allowed patrons to match up old turn-of-the-century black-and-white photographs of police detectives and special agents in the coast guard who tracked down criminal vessels on the lake.

Seb stopped in front of the display and gazed at the photo in the middle. "There he is, Boatswain Nicholas Jansen. The man who caught Wyrd Jack Malone."

This is why we were always the "primary Wags," as Seb put it. My great-great-grandfather was Wyrd Jack, and Seb's great-great-grandfather was the coast guard detective who took him down.

"Holy crap, Seb. You're beginning to look a hell of a lot more like him than I do Wyrd Jack."

It was the dimples.

"Maybe I should take up the mantle of my ancestors and become a cop. Think they drug test?"

"The Haven Beach cops are so crooked, you'd probably fit right in. We need to concentrate. We're looking for something that fits this key or another clue. 'Under their noses' . . ."

"There's nothing old out here. Let's go farther in and try the offices."

We wandered through families with rambunctious kids and a lot of white-haired seniors who must've been on some kind of group tour, and entered an arched doorway that led into the detective offices.

This part of the old police station was set up as a living history museum. Historically costumed volunteers roamed the original offices, which were re-created to look as they did in the 1920s, when Wyrd Jack was incarcerated here. In the police chief's office, a newspaper and a china teacup sat on the desk alongside a vintage black candlestick phone and old photos of the real police officers who worked here, back in the day. Visitors could walk through each office as long as they adhered to the gold-plated signs that read: HISTORICAL DISPLAY, DO NOT TOUCH.

"'Under their noses' . . ." Seb mused as we stepped around the police chief's desk. When the other visitors in the room with us exited, Seb ducked behind the desk to inspect the drawers. "Only one with a lock, but it takes a tiny desk key, not that big ol' skeleton key."

"The cameras are new," I said, glancing at one in the corner. "Don't want to get kicked out. Let's not touch anything."

Seb touched the desk with one finger. "They have to catch me first."

I rolled my eyes and exited the chief's office to head next door into Deputy Canter's office. This one wasn't as fancy—no china teacups—but it had a chalkboard with lists of crimes that were being investigated in 1929. Rum-running. Gangs. Stolen lumber. Chicken theft.

"Don't think we'll find any locks in Barney Fife's office. None of his desk drawers require keys, and the only thing else in here that would are those metal lockers," Seb said, gesturing toward the back corner. "And those give me the heebie-jeebies because they remind me of boot camp." He shivered and made a cross with his fingers.

Much like the chief's desk in the room next door, the lockers required a different kind of key. Still, I waited until a family of three left the office, then quickly tried to open the locker while looking around for cameras. The locker squealed open, but there was nothing in it—nor the one next to it.

"You know, we've never talked about it, really. What was it like?" I asked Seb. "Marquette Troubled Teens Boot Camp."

He shrugged. "About what you'd imagine. There was a rule for everything, even blowing your fucking nose. You either obeyed or got kicked out."

"The Seb I used to know would never obey."

"Well, the man you see before you now has been screamed at, shoved into mud, slapped, and gone without dinner so many times that I finally decided obeying was the easiest way."

That sounded awful. "We looked up stuff about the camp when you got sent away. Reviews were solidly in the one-star range. Lots of complaints about abuse."

"I'm not sure if you'd call what I went through abuse, but some of the other kids had it worse. The people running the camp did a superior job at making all of us believe that if we didn't adhere to their routine, we'd end up dying on the street. One kid killed himself."

"Oh God," I said. "Were you friends?"

He shook his head. "Camp wasn't a bonding experience. We were all there to survive and get the hell out in one piece."

"Did you tell your dad?"

"Ironside Captain Jansen? Come on. You know he applauded their methods. I was stuck, and there was no way forward but through. So I just hunkered down and did what they asked."

A tense silence hung between us.

"What about classes?" I asked. "Did they actually teach? You graduated, or . . . ?"

He nodded. "Graduated top of my class, if you can believe it.

Not sure why Harvard rejected my application. Guess 'being tortured by retired army drill sergeants' wasn't on their list of acceptable extracurriculars."

His words opened up a hollow space in my chest that ached for him. I may not have known the *new* Seb all that well, but I still recognized the core of him. And I knew from the way he avoided my eyes that he wasn't lashing out at me. He was putting himself down, trying to make me believe he was jaded. And could I really blame him if he were? God knew I'd be if I had to endure what he had.

But I couldn't help but think that the boy I once knew wasn't cynical. A smart-ass, yes. But he'd always looked toward the brighter side of things.

"I'm so sorry you had to go through all that," I told him very seriously.

"Hey," he said softly. "I'm okay, for real. That's all in the past."

"*We* were in the past, you and I, but look at us now, solving ciphers together. Some things don't stay in the past."

"Want to know a secret?" he asked in a low voice. "Being separated from all of you was the worst part of boot camp. Not any of that other stuff."

This surprised me. "But we weren't even speaking at the time."

He nodded. "I know. I guess it was sort of a wake-up for me. Camp finally gave me time to think about everything—about Pretty Paul and the Vanderburgs. The Wags. All the mistakes I'd made . . . I just wanted my friends back, that's all."

His revelation caught me by surprise, and I felt a tenderness toward him that I hadn't in years.

"Oh, Seb," I whispered. "Why didn't you tell us?"

"Coward, I guess."

I shook my head. He was a lot of things, but not a coward.

His hand hesitantly reached for mine. I looked down between us as our fingers intertwined. One thumb made a single, slow stroke down the back of my hand, causing a riot of pleasurable tingles to rush across my skin.

Uh-oh. Not again.

His hand squeezed mine briefly, then he released me. And I was left speechless and a little afraid of my own feelings.

"No need to spoil our day thinking about depressing shit when we have treasure to find. Come on," he said, brightening as he headed out of the office. As if his thoughts couldn't be further from mine. "Miles to go before we sleep. Let's check out the jail cells."

I schooled my features to relax. The last thing I needed was him teasing me about having schoolgirl feelings toward him after all this time.

Seb poked his head into the office across the hallway, but there was a small group of people inside. He shook his head at me, and we continued through the old police station, stopping in an evidence room lined with wooden crates that were all staged to look like confiscated goods and stolen property from the 1920s. A lot of generic rum and plastic tommy guns. It was the least exciting part of the museum, merely a recreation. But I also spent my time sneaking looks at Seb instead of paying attention to our surroundings. And while we were walking through, I began to feel as though the other museum patrons were staring at us.

Or maybe I was still ruffled by Seb's confession. I tried my best to put it out of my mind.

At the end of the hall were the holding cells. All of them were re-created scenes, much like the evidence room. The cell at the end was where Wyrd Jack was held while he awaited trial and transfer to the state prison, and inside was the same small bed in the other cells, same toilet and sink. But the walls were lined with various drawings, bizarre notes, and photos cut from magazines. They were all bolted to the wall under plexiglass because some treasure hunter from Ohio tried to steal them in the late 1970s.

Hanging above the bed was the original copy of "Prison Poem." A camera pointed down at it. Several people gawked into the cell from the hallway while a couple others crammed themselves into the cell to inspect it up close and personal.

"Nothing's changed here," Seb noted quietly. And when the woman in front of him moved forward, he took out the skeleton key from his pocket and discreetly stuck it inside the jail cell door. "Whomp, whomp," he said softly. "Not even remotely the right size."

"Hmm." As we wandered away from the prison cell, I got the funny feeling that someone was watching us. But when I looked around, I didn't see anyone suspicious.

"You okay?" Seb asked.

I shook away the feeling of eyes on my back. "It's nothing." Just a little good ol'-fashioned paranoia. "But you know, I was just thinking about the logistics of Wyrd Jack's wife helping him hide the Golden Venus while he sat inside that cell . . ."

"So chances are the lock for this key is a million miles from here," Seb finished, understanding what I was getting at. "They wouldn't have hidden it in the police station. This would qualify as 'under their noses,' but it doesn't make sense, logically. What would she do, bring a locked box into the station and hide it while a dozen cops roamed the halls? Even if she managed it, people would've found something like that years ago, when the station was being turned into a museum."

I glanced at a framed photo of Wyrd Jack's ship, the *Devil's Revenge*. Hmm. "Uh, Seb? She might not have been able to hide something in here, but what about there?"

He blinked at the framed photo. "His ship? That's . . . a better possibility. All the stuff in the cargo hold, maybe. Or . . ."

We both looked at each other and spoke at the same time. "Captain's quarters."

Somewhere in the back of my thoughts, the logical part of my brain was trying to remind me that hundreds of treasure hunters from all over the world had scoured every inch of that ship. But the thrill of the chase was too seductive. The way Seb grinned at me, I knew he felt the same.

Besides, none of those treasure hunters had our key.

Making a beeline for the museum lobby, we headed back outside, ignoring the attendant telling us that we'd need our hands stamped to get back in the museum once we'd left. It was bright and sunny outside, warming up, and dozens of tourists milled around the docked, out-of-commission ship—taking photos with their children, pointing up at the rigging and the re-creation of Wyrd Jack's black "pirate" flag, blowing in a warm breeze that swept in from the lake.

The entrance fee for the ship was higher than the museum, which I started to complain about when Seb placed a hand on my back and urged me forward so that we could blend in with a large family that had purchased a tour package. "Go, go, go!" Seb whispered near the top of my head, and for a moment I was overwhelmed by his warm hand on me, his breath tickling my hair. But we soon slipped past the cordoned entrance to the ship and the attendant who guarded it, and Seb released me.

"Ahoy, maties!" a perky tour guide called out to our group,

gathered on the ship's main deck, surrounded by fat rigging rope and polished pine. "You are standing on the *Devil's Revenge*, one of the most infamous ships to ever sail the Great Lakes. This ship carried bootleg liquor, stolen federal timber, and even an infamous passenger. The gangster, Bugs Moran, was rumored to have been ferried into Chicago by Wyrd Jack before his men were gunned down by Al Capone's gang in the St. Valentine's Day Massacre . . ."

We'd both heard a version of this tour many times. When the guide asked the tour group to climb steps that led to the helm, Seb and I broke away and sneaked toward the door tucked under those steps, the captain's quarters.

"Booyah!" Seb said when we slipped through the open doorway and found ourselves alone in the cabin, which was preserved much as it was when the ship was confiscated in 1929.

We stood in a small, dark room with paned windows that provided a nice view of the harbor. A large japanned pedestal desk sat in the center of the room, the front of which was ornately carved with swirling dragons and tree branches. Two visitors' seats were parked in front of it, and tucked behind, where the captain himself would've sat, was a padded chair that looked a little like a throne. An unlit fireplace stood along the right wall, and a rather big bed occupied the left wall. Rugs crisscrossed the old wooden floorboards.

"Look for a keyhole," Seb whispered loudly. "We've only got a few minutes before the tour makes its way down here and maybe less than that if someone's monitoring that camera above the fireplace."

My nerves hummed. I'd been in this room a dozen times. The memory of it had lived in my head since I was a child, visiting the ship with Nana, who knew Wyrd Jack's history better than any tour guide here. But now that I stood in the dim chamber, which was lit by battery-operated lanterns and fake candles, I couldn't think of any lock that would fit our skeleton key.

"Okay, let's be smart about this. The obvious lock is the hidden cabinet," I said as we both inspected an open cabinet that was designed to hide valuables, hidden within the wall's wooden paneling. A framed sign described what the police had found there when the ship was seized—several thousand dollars in cash and a box filled with stolen jewelry. It stood open for visitors to inspect, making our skeleton key unnecessary.

"Too obvious," Seb said, shaking his head. "There's the grandfather clock in the corner . . ."

Our key was too big for that, but we inspected the clock with our hands, feeling around for any kind of secret lock and finding nothing.

Above our heads, boards squealed with the weight of footfalls. *The touring group.* Seb looked up and hurried his movements. "There's the trunk at the foot of the bed, but there's no way it hasn't been opened yet—"

I bent in front of the trunk to check it and was surprised that the top swung open. Unlocked. Nothing but dust bunnies inside.

"Dammit!" Seb complained. "I thought for sure we might find something—anything!"

I checked two smaller boxes: one on a built-in bookshelf and one that sat upon the big desk. Both had locks too small for our key. "Is there something we're not seeing?"

Seb plopped down in one of the two wooden visitor's chairs that sat neatly in front of the captain's desk. "'Under their noses' . . . What noses? Maybe he meant literal noses, like in a painting of people's faces? That's where we found the first clue, a painting . . ." Seb rotated his neck to glance around the room at several oil paintings and black-and-white photographs that lined the cabin's walls. They were all landscapes. A framed watercolor of this very ship hung above the fireplace. I slipped my hand around the frame, but it had been secured to the wall with screws.

"There are no noses in this room," I said, taking the seat next to him in defeat. The tour group would be here any minute. I could hear them coming down the nearby stairs.

Seb hung his head and stared at the desk in front of us while I looked over it, toward the slanted windows.

"'Under their noses,' 'under their noses' . . ." he repeated. "Huh."

"What?"

He gestured at the front of the desk, where two stylized dragons stared at each other, their curving tails intertwined. "Dragons have noses," he noted.

We looked at each other for a moment before pushing out of the chairs to squat on the rug in front of the desk. It was made of walnut in the late 1800s by a Parisian furniture maker and was easily the most valuable thing on the ship.

"Keyhole," Seb said excitedly, getting out the skeleton key. "Look for a keyhole."

"Maybe it's under the rug, something in the floorboar—" I stopped talking as my eyes focused on a roselike emblem between the two dragon heads. Right under their noses.

The rose was about the size of a golf ball, and its petals were individually carved. I ran my finger around it as my pulse pounded in my temples. There was something off about it. Something different. At least I *thought* there was as I felt around the rose, hunting for anything at all.

Just when I was ready to give up, my fingertip moved one of the rose petals. Just barely. The play of movement was so slight, I thought for a moment I'd imagined it. But when I wiggled it with my finger and then used the tip of my nail, it definitely moved.

And something snicked open.

"Holy shit . . ." Seb said.

The rose freely rotated. I pushed it to the left, and it rotated enough to reveal a lock beneath it.

"Oh my God!" I whispered. "Is this for real? It can't be . . ."

"Right under the dragon's noses," Seb said with wonder in his voice as he set the end of the skeleton key to the lock's black hole.

It slipped right in.

Not too big, not too small.

Just right.

Seb turned the key in the lock. It clicked, and a small panel at the front of the desk popped open. And as noise from the approaching tour made my pulse spike, we peered into darkness together and spied something twinkling inside.

A lone gold locket.

Chapter 11

Seb and I barely made it out of the captain's quarters before the tour group entered. We didn't inspect what we'd found until we rushed back to the Bronco.

"Hurry!" I said excitedly. "Open it!"

Seb cracked open the gold locket, and we huddled together to see what was inside.

A pair of black-and-white photos, man and woman, dressed in turn-of-the-century clothing and wearing serious faces.

"Wyrd Jack and Mabel," I said as my heart raced. Mabel Malone was my ancestor's devoted wife, a plain-faced woman who'd garnered attention all over the Midwest as a famed spiritualist. She claimed to communicate with the dead, and local legends said she used this esoteric information to lead Wyrd Jack to big cargo hauls. There were even several instances of recorded testimony from the townsfolk claiming she was distraught the day before her husband was nabbed by police out on the lake because "the spirits" had told her he was sailing into tragedy.

Pretty much everyone assumed she hid the Golden Venus herself, and that she worked with her husband while he was jailed to hide all the clues leading to it.

Many believed that Mabel was the brains behind Wyrd Jack's brawn.

"Are these their wedding photos?" Seb asked.

"No. She's not wearing a veil." The museum had an entire room dedicated to Mabel, but it was mostly interactive displays and framed photographs, so we'd skipped it.

"There's no Morse code," Seb noted, turning the locket around in his fingers to inspect it closely. "Nothing engraved. Nothing on the chain . . ."

"Back of photos?"

With the tip of my fingernail, I carefully pried them out while tourists strolled past the Bronco. Neither photo had writing on the back.

No engraving beneath where they sat, either.

"Got the feeling this isn't going to be easy," Seb said, a little disappointment in his voice that I was also feeling as the initial thrill of finding the locket faded. It was one thing to find a clue. A whole other thing to solve it.

The boardwalk was becoming crowded with people, and it wasn't doing us any good to sit here in exasperation, trying to find something on the locket that just wasn't there. So we headed back to Heron Cottage, occasionally sharing ideas.

Like:

"Maybe there's code somewhere on it, but we need a magnifying glass."

And:

"Maybe we need to find an important location that matches up with the locket."

And:

"Maybe we need to reread the Wyrd Jack biography and see if the locket's mentioned."

All ideas were valid, but they'd take time to run through, and

Seb had only a few hours to work on my car. He had plans later in the afternoon that he couldn't get out of.

"I committed to this a few days ago, before I knew we'd be trying to figure out treasure clues," he told me.

"Hot date, huh?" I said.

He arched a brow and gave me a sly smile that caused panicky feelings. *Was* he actually dating someone in town? *Why do you care? Stop being nosy.* I looked away, frustrated that something so small would make me upset.

"Nah."

"What?" I asked.

"Not dating anyone. Just family shit."

"Oh?" My heart soared. I wished it hadn't, but it did. Some part of me was happy he was single. "Hot date with your dad, then?"

"Something like that."

He didn't offer details, and I didn't ask. Punkin greeted him enthusiastically, and afterward, Seb was eager to get started on my car. So I left him in the garage after we agreed to keep the locket stashed away with the other clues, marriage license and key, in a shoebox that we stashed behind the dryer. "Just in case," he said. "You *have* had a break-in, after all."

The afternoon flew by. He worked under my car with the garage door open, blasting the Stooges and MC5. When he took a break, I made sandwiches, and we ate on the back porch, staring out at the shore and talking about various people around town. And, of course, the locket.

We texted Benny and Jazmine photos of it, and ended up talking to them both on FaceTime to show them what we'd found and tell them the entire story. No one mentioned Jazmine blowing up at all of us in the cave, and she appeared to be in good spirits—which was a relief. We agreed to ponder the locket's significance and meet up later in the week to compare theories.

Late in the afternoon, I heard the Corvair rumble to life and raced out to find Seb smeared with grease but grinning ear to ear, leaning over the engine.

"Smoke-free," he proudly proclaimed.

"You fixed it?" I looked the car over. "Oh my God, Seb. You're brilliant. Absolutely brilliant. I owe you big-time."

He slammed the hood down. "I'll start dreaming up ways you can pay me back."

It didn't take him long to gather all his tools and wash his hands. Then he gave the Corvair a quick test drive and gave it a thumbs-up. He whistled for his dog, and when they were both inside the Bronco, he reconfirmed plans we'd discussed on the porch during lunch.

"I'll come over tomorrow night after work to brainstorm. If anyone figures anything out before then, they'll let the group know."

"Sounds good. Hey, Seb? Seriously, thank you. I don't know what I would've done without you."

His cheeks colored ever so slightly, and he looked pleased but brushed away my thanks. "It's nothing. I mean, what are friends for?"

I smiled at him. "I'm glad we are. Friends. Again."

"Same." The rest of his reply was so quiet, I almost didn't catch it over the roar of the Bronco's engine. "Haven't been this glad about anything in a long time."

He drove away, leaving me with a jumble of emotions. But even if I couldn't completely decide how I felt about Seb, I felt good about what we'd accomplished. We'd found the locket today, and I was no longer a prisoner in my own home. That was worth everything to me.

So I did a few things around the house before joyfully settling into the Corvair and taking it into town. It drove better now, or maybe that was my imagination, and I wasn't dogged by a trail of white smoke. What more could I want?

I drove through town, crossed the Little River bridge into Northside, and cruised along Shoreline Drive while the sun was setting, coloring the lake's horizon a pleasant ombré of magenta and orange. After a few miles, I turned around and headed back across the river, turning away from the Harbor District, with the silhouette of the Devil's Revenge looming against the sky, and instead headed down Main Street into our downtown area.

Restaurant patios were filling up and music thumped from cruising cars. Downtown was nice in the summer, a less sanitized area of town than the harbor. When I was a teen, I spent a lot of time walking the wide sidewalks that ran up and down the three short blocks containing most of the downtown businesses. Shops. Bars. Cafés. And a two-story brick building on the corner that was beloved by everyone in town.

Bean's.

Short for Bean's Trading Post.

Back when Michigan was just swampland, this was one of the first buildings in what would later become Haven Beach, where French Canadian fur traders and members of various Chippawa tribes stopped to do business. They used canoes on the Little River to reach it, much like the Wags had used it to reach our cave. At some point before I was born, the old store was bought by a man named Bean Dooley, who turned it into the greatest corner shop in western Michigan. Everyone who lived in Haven Beach had walked its aisles.

As the sun was setting, I snagged a nearby parking space. A faded sign—TRADING POST—had been painted on the side of the brick during Wyrd Jack's time and remained to this day. I walked past it and headed inside, into a long, cavernous shop that smelled of caramel corn and hot meat. Depending on how hungry you were, those scents could be magical or disgusting. Right now, I was leaning toward magic.

Massive wooden beams stretched over wide oak floorboards lined with aisles of goods. Being a general store, Bean's carried just about anything you could want and a few things you didn't. Needed milk and bread? They had it. Magazines from around the world? Yep. Discount ammo and stinky fish bait? That was at the back counter, near the clothing section—which was basically a lot of camo and weird novelty tees.

Dozens of patrons wandered the aisles while Prince played over loudspeakers. Navigating around all the chatting townspeople who were clogging up the aisles wasn't easy. I spotted faces I vaguely knew—faces that once knew Nana—and had a moment of panic when one of them waved at me. I didn't want to make polite conversation with everyone in town. *Yes, I've been away at college. Yes, I've been managing all right since Nana died. No, I don't need anything, but if you keep poking my wounds, I'm going to have a breakdown in the middle of the potato chip aisle, and no one wants to see that.*

Head down, I avoided the stares and made a beeline for the hot-meat scent, which was wafting from a countertop glass food display case filled with three shelves of freshly baked goodness and a sign that read: HOT DUTCH SAUSAGE ROLLS. Basically, puff pastry pies stuffed with sausage and half-melted cheese that would burn the roof of your mouth if you weren't patient, the hallmark of any good food.

I stood in line, continuing to avoid people's eyes, and purchased a kielbasa-and-cheddar sausage roll. It was wrapped in wax paper and smelled like heaven—if heaven smelled of home and memories, anyway—but was way too hot to eat. I browsed a nearby selection of imported candy and nearly dropped my sausage roll when a female voice squealed in my ear.

I swung around to find myself face-to-face with Benny's girlfriend, Lulu.

"Hey, you!" she said cheerfully, pushing a pair of heart-shaped sunglasses up her nose and then running a finger along the front edges of her blond pixie cut to smooth it in place. She clutched a Saint Laurent handbag worth thousands that was popular on campus back at Harvard. Maybe I shouldn't have been surprised; she was dating Benny the Rich Boy, after all.

"Small world, huh?" she said. "If you need the bathroom key, be prepared to wait. If it doesn't open up soon, I'm going to have to drive over to McDonald's and use theirs."

"Good luck," I said, and started to leave, but she wasn't having it.

"How the heck are you? Ankle healed up?"

"Little sore but okay."

She glanced around to see if anyone was listening before moving closer and whispering, "Any breakthroughs regarding the locket? Benny told me already. So exciting!"

Are you fucking kidding me? Benny, I'm going to beat your ass.

"Uh, no. Nothing. Might be a dead end," I told her.

"You can't give up that easily! Do you have it with you? I could take it back with me to the Moraleses' house, and Benito and I could have a crack at it."

Over my dead body. "I don't have it on me, Lulu. And it's probably safer to keep it in one spot."

"At your beach cottage?"

Now *I* was getting paranoid, glancing over my shoulder when a couple of high school boys ducked into the aisle. "It's in a safe place," I whispered.

The two boys squeezed past, hunting candy. When they did, I glanced down the aisle at the man striding toward us in jeans and big black boots.

My chest tightened. Pretty Paul Vanderburg.

He spotted me and did a double take, hesitating mid-step as he ran a hand over his blond buzz cut. For a long moment, it was as if neither one of us wanted to run into each other, but he finally dropped his eyes and continued walking toward me.

"Malone," he said, lifting his chin in greeting.

I'd forgotten just how badly his face was scarred, looking at it up close and personal. It made him look more menacing than he already was. At least he was currently wearing a shirt—unlike the last time I'd seen him, at that bonfire with Seb. I gave him a tight smile and tried not to stare at his face. But then he asked me the most bizarre question.

"Hey. Is Jaz with you?"

Now I looked at his face again, puzzled. "Jaz . . . ? Jazmine Neely?" Why on earth would he be looking for her? They weren't on speaking terms. Heck, if Seb was being honest about the current state of his relationship with Paul, then *none* of the Wags should be on speaking terms with Paul Vanderburg. On principle, at the very least. He lured Seb away from us. He was the enemy.

"Don't get your panties in a twist," he complained. "I just needed to ask her something. Saw you and thought maybe you might . . ."

"I haven't seen her today."

Was that disappointment behind his eyes? I couldn't fathom what sort of question he had for Jaz, but he wasn't eager to share more. He just gave Lulu a look, then continued down the aisle, tossing out a mumbled "Fine. Later."

I stared at his broad back as he walked away, and part of me wanted to chase him back down and demand that he tell me what he needed to ask Jaz.

"Breakups are always rough," Lulu mused.

I glanced at her. "Pardon?"

"You know. All the drama, all the feelings. They're rough."

"*Whose* breakup?"

Pretty Paul broke up with someone? What did that have to do with Jazmine?

Lulu blinked at me, looking genuinely unsure about answering. But she eventually said, "Um, Paul and Jaz?"

All my muscles turned stony as shock washed over me. Lulu was wrong. She didn't know what she was talking about. Paul was bad news. Scum of the earth. We hated him. Jaz . . .

She would *never* date Paul. That was absurd.

But the way Lulu looked at me—biting her bottom lip like she was waiting for the truth to dawn on me—made me realize that maybe it wasn't so absurd after all.

Holy shit.

This was what she'd been keeping secret? This was what she whispered about with Seb at the cottage when she thought I couldn't hear.

My thoughts felt as if they were buzzing inside my head, and that buzzing was getting louder and louder . . .

I couldn't stand there another second. Mumbling goodbye, I rushed past Lulu to the parked Corvair, fumbling my keys with shaky hands until I forced myself to focus. All I knew was that I had to get out of there. I barely saw Lulu looking dejected on the sidewalk as the Corvair screeched away from the curb.

My best friend had dated the absolute worst person in town? And hadn't said a word about it to me? I just couldn't make it make sense in my head.

But.

Something *was* wrong with Jaz. She wasn't her normal, confident, happy self. And she had been keeping something from me.

I felt sick to my stomach. I sped through town, far too fast—I knew it, but I couldn't stop myself, even after I swerved enough to scare myself while patting down the seat to find my phone. I was *this* close to calling Seb to ask him for a confirmation or denial when I remembered his advice to me about Jazmine:

You should ask her. Talk to her.

He was right, of course. I knew that now. Instead of continuing through the traffic light and going home to the cottage, I made a last-minute sharp turn into the marina.

If Jazmine was going to lie to me about who she was seeing, she could do it to my face.

Chapter 12

The Neelys lived at the edge of the marina inside a two-story, bright blue building. Administrative offices for the marina were on the first floor, and their home was above it. I parked in one of the visitor spots and took a moment to wipe my face and fix my makeup, wishing I didn't smell like my uneaten sausage roll, which was currently dripping grease onto the front seat.

Screwing up my courage, I headed around the side of the building, where a set of steps hugged the wall and ended on a little deck. The Neelys' front door was here, and when I stepped into the porch light, I heard muffled laughter and music inside. I rang the doorbell.

You can do this . . . You must do this.

After a few moments, the door swung open and Jaz's sister, Patty, blinked at me.

"Paige," she said, smiling big. "This is a surprise. What are you doing here?"

I could've asked the same question of her. "Did you move back in, or something?"

Patty lived with her wife in a beach cottage about a mile down the coast from mine.

"Nah," she said with a shake of her head. "Just a little family dinner. Come on in."

I stepped inside a small foyer. Pale Scandinavian wood dominated from floor to ceiling, brightened by a patchwork of modern paintings, including one by Nana. The Neelys weren't rich by a long shot, not like Benny's folks, but they were doing better than the rest of us, and it showed in their tasteful furnishings and marble-topped kitchen counters. That's where Patty was leading me, to the kitchen, where heavenly smells lingered and the upbeat tempo of snappy jazz that played over stereo speakers was punctuated by the clink of dishes and soft laughter.

Mr. Neely loaded the dishwasher. A big man in both size and reputation, he was one of the most respected marina managers around. With his shaved head and massive beard, and being the approximate size of a quarterback, he could be mistaken for intimidating. But Mr. Neely was the biggest teddy bear I'd ever known.

His wife sat across the kitchen island from him, sipping wine in a flowing house dress. Blond, tall, and curvy, Mrs. Neely was a former opera singer from Norway who damaged her vocal cords when she was in her twenties. She came to the US to find herself and ended up finding Mr. Neely instead. They were one of those rare couples who seemed to be utterly in love, no matter how much time passed. Their lovey-dovey relationship used to embarrass me when I was a kid, but now it felt like a goal.

"Paige!" they said together with smiling faces.

Then Mr. Neely said, "Get your butt over here, young lady." He held out his arms like Jazmine had a few days ago when I first saw her on the beach with her class, and I didn't hesitate to hug him. He smelled like dishwashing soap and smoke from the grill, and all at once, I realized how much I'd missed the Neelys.

My eyes brimmed with emotion, and I nearly started crying.

But Mrs. Neely signaled for me to come around the island to embrace her, too, gesturing with her arms.

"Come here, third daughter," she said in a melodic voice that still held remnants of her first language. "Let me see you."

"Hey, Mrs. Neely." I hugged her from the side while she sat on her stool. The next thing I knew, they were both peppering me with questions: How was I doing? Why hadn't I come by sooner? Had I had dinner yet? Did the cottage really get broken into?

I answered the best I could and tried to keep my emotions in check, assuring them several times that I wasn't hungry. "No, seriously. I really just need to talk with Jaz, if she's here."

"Of course," Mrs. Neely said, eyes pinched with concern.

"Jaz is in the den," Patty told me, helping her father dry dishes. "You know the way . . ."

That, I did. Relieved to not have to answer any more questions, I left the Neelys in the kitchen and headed down the home's main artery, a long hallway lined with family photos. There were a few of me and Jaz over the years, including one at graduation last year. And a photo that made my heart clench: all four Wags, sitting on a dock with paper pirate hats when we were eight.

Steeling myself, I headed into the den, where we would watch movies on their home projector when we were kids. The room was empty, but I spotted movement outside a set of French doors. I took a moment to collect myself before stepping onto a wide balcony that looked out onto the marina.

It was easy to get seduced by the view. The soft marina lights. The lake to one side. Haven Beach lights to the other. But my focus was on Jazmine, who was sitting cross-legged in a big deck chair with her sprained arm in its sling, scrolling on her phone with her free hand. Her hair hung loose over her shoulders, creating a halo of curls around her face.

"Hey," I said in low voice.

She didn't look up. "Hey."

Okay . . . After a few moments of awkward silence, I dared to take a seat in another chair and noticed her phone screen before she quickly flipped it over on the arm of her chair.

She'd been texting with Benny.

"You're not surprised to see me," I said flatly. "Guessing that's because of Lulu?" I assumed the girl got in touch with Benny when I left Bean's, and he'd texted Jaz to warn her.

Jaz sighed. "Yeah. Lulu."

Another moment of quiet passed, then we both started talking at once.

"Paige, I don't even know what to say—"

"Were you really seeing Pretty Paul?"

She blinked at me. "Yeah. But not anymore."

It was true, then? My mouth hung open until I found my voice again.

"I don't even know where to start, Jaz. Paul Vanderburg is the enemy. He fractured the Wags and took Seb away from us!"

"I know."

"His father's the biggest fentanyl dealer in western Michigan."

"I know."

"And Paul is his right-hand man!"

"I *know.*"

"Okay, then. You're going to have to help me understand because those reasons alone should be enough to make any sane person run in the opposite direction. He's dangerous. He's put more people in the hospital than I can count on my hand. "

"I know, I know, *I know*!" Her head fell, and she covered her face with her hand.

"Then why, Jaz? And why hide it from me, of all people?"

She lifted her head, upset. "Of *course* I'd hide it from you—for the exact reasons you just listed! Do you think I was looking for this to happen? He's the last person in town I'd consider hooking up with—"

"But you did."

"Yeah, I did."

"Jesus, Jaz. How long has this been going on?"

It took a second to answer. "After you left for Cambridge, before the holidays. You won't believe me, but it . . . it hasn't been easy, since you've been gone."

"Me?"

She nodded. "After your nana died, you went straight to Harvard. It was like . . . I don't know. I felt like you were still in the middle of grieving, and I didn't know how to help you from here, and before I knew it, you didn't need me anymore. I felt really alone."

I tried to understand what she was telling me. "So you ran into Paul's arms? *Paul's?* Did you show up at one of his stupid bonfires, or something?"

"Trust me, I never intended any of this to happen. It started innocently. We were at the same party and ended up playing drunk Jenga together—"

I lifted a brow.

She shook her head. "It doesn't matter. I guess I just saw another side of him that night, and maybe he saw another side of me. He's . . . not what he seems."

"Does he secretly donate all his father's drug profits to a charity for underprivileged kids?"

She sighed. "Look, I'm not excusing his past behavior, but . . . I don't know. He's had it rough? His father is a horror-story villain, not even joking."

"Yeah. Big Burg's prepper compound is dangerous," I agreed. "Anything could happen to you out there."

"No, *nothing* can happen to me out there because Paul and I are no longer an item. I'll never go back out there again. Never."

"You don't have to convince me. I'm not judging you."

"Bullshit."

She had a point. I *was* judging her. But only because I expected better! Right . . . ?

"I get it," she said. "If I were in your shoes, I'd be judging you so hard right now. Paul ruined the Wags."

"And nearly ruined Seb in the process!"

"Yeah," she said, nodding slowly. "All of that's true, and I felt like a Judas the entire time I was seeing him. But for a while there, Paul was the only thing keeping me sane. This gap year? Huge mistake for me. I've done absolutely *nothing* this year, Paige. Nothing. Meantime, you lost Nana Malone and were still able to finish a year at Harvard." One shoulder lifted and fell. "I don't even know what I'm doing anymore. Am I waiting for something? Or trying to enjoy what little freedom I have left before I start my life?"

"You could've let me help you figure that stuff out if you'd just talked to me."

"And when should I have done that, Paige?" she said, a little fire behind her eyes. "Was I supposed to bitch and moan to you on a video call that I was feeling lost and lonely after you've broken down crying over Nana Malone?"

I didn't know how to answer that. I was definitely preoccupied last fall; she wasn't wrong about that. "So this is my fault because Nana died?"

She made a frustrated noise. "Of course not. I'm not comparing what I'm dealing with to what you've been dealing with."

"Good, because it's not a competition," I told her, trying to understand while feeling defensive about my own grief.

"I know that, but it still made it hard for me to communicate with you last fall because I didn't want to burden you with my petty shit. I was trying to spare your feelings."

"It's okay for best friends to burden each other," I said, looking out through the balcony railing at a boat coming into the marina with all its lights on. "Can you please just tell me what's been going on with you?"

A long moment went by before she began explaining. "After you left for Harvard, it felt like the start of big changes, with you gone, but I was okay with that. Excited, even? But . . . I don't know. The days began to blur, and I felt disconnected. Like everyone else was riding their own waves, and I was just stuck in the same town, with the same routines. Only, you weren't here. There were no Wag treasure hunts. Benny was off at school, and Seb had just gotten back to town—we hadn't totally reconnected at that point. I was just . . . alone."

Battling emotions tugged her facial features in several directions. She swallowed hard, trying to hold back tears.

"Jaz," I said.

She shook her head. "I know how dumb this sounds. Boo-hoo, I was alone. But it started slowly, like, one bad day, then another.

A good day, then back to bad. And before I knew it, Christmas rolled around, and all the days were bad. I mean, winter is never fun—"

Lake-effect snow was a real thing here, and we were often pummeled with blizzards. But it was the unending gray of winter that was so brutal. No real sun for weeks, sometimes months. And that was especially hard for someone like Jazmine, who needed to be on the water. Can't paddleboard when literal boulders of ice are washing up on shore and everything is covered with snow.

"I didn't realize how depressed I was," Jazmine said in a low voice. "It snuck up on me, and by that time, I was too weak to fight it. That's when I ended up hanging out with Paul at that party. When it all started."

Jesus. Now it all made more sense. "When did it end?"

She blew out a hard breath. "For good? Last week."

"Oh?"

"We had a big blowout in the parking lot of that old roller-skating rink east of town the day before you flew back. It was . . ." She shook her head and closed her eyes. "Messy. I'd just wanted to end things peacefully, but I didn't know how Paul would react. So when we agreed to meet, I asked Seb to take me there, sort of as backup."

"Swear to God, Jaz, if Paul *ever* lays a single finger on you—"

"He didn't." She held up a hand to make it clear. "And I don't think he ever would. But I didn't want to take any chances, so I brought Seb along. In hindsight, a huge mistake." She mimed punching her own eye.

"*That's* where Seb got the black eye?"

She nodded. "It's where we all got hurt. I was trying to keep Paul and Seb apart, slipped, and fell on this." She held up her sling.

Seriously? "Not showing off in front of your class on your board?"

She gave me an embarrassed look and scratched her nose. "Seb took me to the ER that night—which, by the way, was the worst ride of my life because his eye was swelling up, and he couldn't see to drive very well. Don't remember much except for that Rick Steves audiobook dude talking about the Black Forest over the Speed Buggy's speakers, and I remember being terrified we were going to die and thinking at that moment that I'd rather be riding in a car with Benny than Seb—"

I snorted. "That's saying a lot."

"Ye-a-a-ah. We flattened a stop sign a block away from Trinity Health."

"Jesus," I moaned.

"Don't be too hard on him. He's trying. He came back to town at my lowest point, and if it weren't for him, who knows what would've happened to me. This has pretty much been the worst year of my life."

"I'm so sorry," I told her, fighting past a lump in my throat. "You needed me, and I was oblivious. I'm a terrible friend."

"No, Paige." Two fat tears fell down her cheeks. "I'm a terrible friend for not telling you I needed you."

"No. I should've been here. I should've known without you having to tell me before you resorted to sleeping with the enemy."

She snorted softly. Then I did. We looked at each and smiled gently.

After a moment, I said, "Is Paul the reason you didn't pick me up from the airport?"

She groaned. "I'd only had my sling for a day, and I was freaked that you'd somehow be able to tell by looking at me . . . And then you'd be pissed that I hadn't told you about everything. It was irrational, but I just plain chickened out."

"For the record," I said, giving her a small smile. "I clearly had no idea about you and Paul. I thought maybe you'd just realized after a year apart that you didn't need me around anymore."

Jaz gasped dramatically. Then she reached out and offered me her pinkie finger. "I will always need you, Paige Malone. I just didn't realize how much until you left."

A swell of emotion crashed over me, and I smiled at her through bleary eyes while I hooked my own pinkie around hers.

"Forgive me?" she whispered.

"Wags always forgive." I pulled her into my arms before she could stop me and was enveloped by the familiar scent of her sweet almond lotion.

She embraced me back, clinging to me so hard that it hurt, and I had to complain through tears and laughter.

"Haven't lost your brutal hug power," I said, grinning as I wiped my cheeks. "*Spinebreaker*," I added in my best pro-wrestling-announcer voice.

"Ha! No one's called me that in a long time." She laughed a little, wiping her eyes on the hem of her T-shirt. Then she blinked at me and spoke in a soft voice. "Look. Not gonna lie, there are so many more messy details about this year I haven't told you yet. Don't know how much Seb has told you—"

"Seb? Almost nothing. You know him. He'll keep your secrets if you ask him to." I scratched the back of my neck. "At least, he used to. I'm still trying to figure him out. You trust him?"

"Daddy does, if that says anything. He claims Seb is a hard worker."

"Our Seb?"

She laughed softly. "Right? I guess he's sort of half our old Seb, half . . . something new. Something different from what he was becoming the past few years. Going away changed him."

"No surprise, considering what he endured at that Yooper boot camp."

Jazmine's eyes widened. "He told you stuff about it? He hasn't said but a couple words to Benny and me about his time up north, but we both suspected something bad happened there."

"He told me a little," I admitted.

"Huh."

Anxiety flared. "What is it?"

"Nothing." She hesitated. "I was just thinking it was funny he hadn't shared any of that, but that he had told me a little about . . . other things."

"What does that mean?"

She slowly arched a brow.

My stomach lurched with panic as my thoughts went in wild directions. "Oh my God, did he tell you about the cave grope?"

Jazmine's eyes widened. "Excuse me?"

Shit! "Forget I said that."

"Are you joking? I'll never forget that. Explain!"

"No, you first!" I said, terrified.

She hesitated again, making a strained face, then blew out a breath. "Okay, *fine*. Seb's low-key obsessed with you, which you probably already knew if you've been groping him."

"I haven't groped anything!"

"Jesus, did he grope *you*?"

"Forget the groping! It was accidental. What do you mean 'obsessed'?" A tremor went through me. "In what way?"

"What way do you think? He's all, 'Paige this, Paige that . . .'" Jazmine rolled her eyes. "Ugh, at first I thought it was kind of adorable, but it's getting annoying. And I'll tell you one thing. You're going to have to nip that shit in the bud before he embarrasses himself and gets hurt. He's an emotional wreck under all that swagger, you know."

I did know, but all my brain could think was:

Seb. Obsessed. Me?

My stomach dipped like it did when I was a ten-year-old kid riding the log flume down the big hill at the Little Dutch Boy waterpark north of town.

I was being ridiculous. Jazmine was probably wrong about this.

But what if she isn't?

I realized I'd been quiet for too long by the way her eyes squinted at my face. I regretted bringing up the cave grope. Did she suspect any of my feelings about Seb? How could she when I didn't understand them myself?

I wasn't sure I wanted to delve into them right now, either.

Deflect! Deflect!

"Very interesting," Jaz said in a teasing voice. "You know, I seem to remember sitting on this very balcony at the start of our senior year and you thanking the stars above that we'd both avoided dating another Wag."

"Oh yeah? Well, what about Benny?" I countered. "Come on, Jaz. It's clear to see that you've got some feelings for him that you didn't have before I left for school."

"Benny?" She squinted at me. "I don't think so."

Oh. Huh. She was being honest. "You were so angry about Lulu, I just assumed . . ."

"Lulu? Ugh, no. She's absolutely wrong for him, and I'd like to throw her down some rickety basement stairs, but only because I care about my friend."

"Fine, but only because I feel exactly the same way about her," I said, and we both chuckled good-naturedly.

"Hey, Paige?" Jazmine said, looking through the balcony railing to peer out over the dark marina. "Are . . . you and I really okay now? Because I need for us to be okay. I need . . . the gang back together. I know it sounds dumb, but I need it, Paige. I don't really care that much about actually finding the Golden Venus, but I want us all to feel normal again. Like we used to when the Wags were still Wags."

Water lapped against the docks below us while distant music played from the food truck court at the marina's entrance. When I looked at the person sitting in front of me, I saw a little of the pain she'd talked about, but I saw hope, too. With all my heart, I believed in the same truth that I'd known back when we were just those kids in paper pirate hats that now hung in her hallway:

Nothing could ever break our friendship apart.

Not permanently. I would always have her back, and I knew she'd always have mine. Benny, too. And sure, the past few years I'd given up on Seb, but maybe the boy we once knew really was still there.

I picked up Jazmine's hand and cradled it in mine. "You and I will always be okay, no matter what. Love you. Always."

"Love you, too," she whispered, and I knew by how her upper body suddenly relaxed that we were back to normal.

"Hey," I said. "It's still early. Want to—"

"Shit . . ." Jaz's eyes were fixed on the balcony door.

I squinted through the glass and saw a shadowy figure walking toward us. A man, not big enough and far too fair to be Jaz's father. "Umm . . . ?"

"Totally forgot," Jazmine said. "After Benny texted about you, I freaked and texted Seb. Do *not* tell him I told you about being obsessed with you!"

Oh God.

The door slid open a few inches, and Seb's upper body poked through. His gaze quickly evaluated Jazmine before flicking to my face. "Evenin', ladies. Is it safe to come out there, or do I need to arm myself?"

Chapter 13

Jazmine, Seb, and I settled into patio chairs and chatted like we did when we were all the best of friends, about nothing at all, silliness. Jokes and observations that made Jazmine's relationship with Pretty Paul fade into the background. *Look at us, just like old times.* There was nothing we couldn't overcome.

Well.

Maybe just one *teeny*, tiny thing.

When I was nine years old, a navy flight demonstration squadron came to town to perform some fancy flying at a public coast guard ceremony at the harbor. Three blue-and-yellow jets soared over our lighthouse to the delight of the crowds that had gathered to listen to a symphony performance in honor of several coast guard members—which included Seb's father—receiving service medals. During the air show, when one of the jets was demonstrating a roll, its engine cut out. At first, like everyone else, I thought this was part of the staged show. But the nosediving jet spiraled downward, falling faster and faster toward the harbor. Toward all of us watching. I was standing next to my nana, who shielded her eyes with her hand, looking up. When she gasped and covered her mouth in shock, I suddenly realized that the jet was in trouble.

In that dizzying moment, with the silent jet spiraling toward us, I'd never felt so small. Nothing I could do would stop the jet from falling. Nothing Nana could do. My world was about to end, and I was powerless.

At the last second, the jet's engine roared to life, and the pilot pulled up the nose. The crowd cheered. Everything was fine. Everything was good.

But those moments before? That head-rushing, dazed feeling of smallness?

I was experiencing that again, right now, watching Seb lounging in the patio chair next to mine, laughing like a maniac with Jazmine over something that I hadn't heard because all the blood had rushed to my head and I couldn't think straight.

There he was, my old friend, with his wavy blond mane and sun-kissed arms. With all that chaotic energy and charmed, buoyant attitude.

He's low-key obsessed with you.

True or not, I couldn't purge Jazmine's words from my thoughts. When Seb's eyes jumped to mine, even for a second, everything inside me went haywire, and I couldn't think straight.

Seb was the spiraling jet falling out of the sky, about to destroy my world, and I could do nothing to stop it.

Truth be told, I think I *wanted* him to crash into me.

It made no sense, but there it was. I could admit it to myself now, I supposed. But it didn't make me feel better because I was still wrestling with guilt over Jazmine's state of mind—I needed to be sure she was okay. I also knew if a jet named Seb ever *did* come crashing down, there was nothing I could do but watch my life explode into flames.

"Earth to Paige."

I blinked away those thoughts and looked at my friends. "What? Sorry, I missed that."

Jazmine's brow lifted, and she cleared her throat. "I *said*, do you have theories about the gold locket and those photos of Wyrd Jack and Mabel inside it?"

I stared at both of them blankly. *They're discussing the treasure hunt?* Jesus, how long had I been daydreaming? I had to pull myself together and focus, stat.

"I don't have any theories yet," I admitted.

"What about the Black Book?" Seb suggested. "Is it still in the cottage?"

The Black Book was my nana's ancient photo album. A real one, the cover bound in black silk. It was filled with old photos that went back several generations. There were even a handful of Wyrd Jack—original versions of several prints that now hung in the harbor museum.

"Can't remember anything quite like the ones in the locket," I said. "I haven't looked through it in years, though. Worth a try, I suppose."

They both nodded at me, and it felt as if something hung in the air between the three of us. Maybe some of it was just the drama of the evening, but a little drama never stopped the Wags from hunting treasure. Besides, Jazmine had said that she needed the gang.

"Hey," I said. "You guys can come over to the cottage and help me look, if you're up to it."

Seb's brows lifted. "Sure, I'm game. Jaz?"

"Yeah," she said, smiling. "I'd like that."

"Should we text Benny?" Seb asked, shooting us both a questioning look.

"Is there any way you can convince him to come alone? No offense, but I can't deal with Lulu again tonight," I told them.

"We'll call Benny if we find anything," Seb suggested. "Let's go."

I stood up from my patio chair. "I only have one request. There's a cold sausage roll stinking up my car right now, and I'd rather eat my own shoe than touch it at this point. Can we raid your fridge, Jaz?"

"Seconded," Seb said, opening the balcony door. "I haven't had dinner, and now I'm sort of regretting turning down your mom's offer for leftovers when I walked in."

"Same," I said, and he gave me a soft smile that turned all my insides to exploding confetti as he headed inside the house.

"Ruh-oh," Jazmine said teasingly behind my back as she followed us through the balcony door.

Ruh-oh was right.

We all took separate vehicles to Heron Cottage. The Corvair truly did stink with my discarded meaty hand pie, but it was a welcome distraction from my chaotic thoughts for the short drive. By the time I'd dumped it into my trash can, Jazmine and Seb were both parking behind me. And when I unlocked the front door, Punkin raced past me and headed straight for the bowl of water in the kitchen.

"What's going on with this?" Jazmine asked upon entering, gesturing toward Punkin. "My mom said she'd push that dog off our balcony if it ever came in our house again."

"No balconies here at the cottage," Seb said. "Paige said she could crash here sometimes, so I guess the only Punkin hater left is your mom. Your dad lets her lick his face."

Jazmine snorted. "You know very well that my mom hates her because she had to steam-clean her favorite rug. Besides, Benny's dad says she has fleas, so my mom's not the *only* hater. But I am surprised about you, Paige. We all know you and dogs don't mix."

"Yeah, well . . ." I opened the door to the basement and flipped on the lights. "Guess people change."

Jogging down old steps, I inhaled cool, dank air. The basement was small and crowded, built into the side of the land that made up the front yard, with a single window that looked out beneath the back porch. I'd always hated coming down to the basement when I was a kid and only did so now to wash and dry clothes. But last year, before I'd left for school, Jazmine and her parents helped me pack up most of Nana's personal things into giant plastic totes.

They stood together near the washer and dryer, a wall of memories that I didn't want to face.

As far as I could tell, the men who broke into the cottage never even made it to the basement. It remained just as I'd left it last year.

None of the plastic totes were labeled, but I had a vague recollection of packing the photo album away, so it didn't take me long to segregate four plastic totes—which were so big, they required two people to carry. Seb and Jaz helped me haul them upstairs, and after helping ourselves to leftover barbecued chicken and corn on the cob that almost made me weep with how good it was, we switched on Nana's old radio to a station out of Grand Rapids and proceeded to lounge on the living room rug and dig through the boxes we'd brought upstairs.

I was thankful they were both here to help. I didn't want to get swallowed by grief, sorting through all this stuff, and their presence was tempering, along with all the drama of the night that tumbled around inside my head while we opened boxes and talked.

Seb gave Jazmine a dramatic re-creation of our adventure on the *Devil's Revenge*. "And then we slipped inside the captain's quarters like this . . ." He demonstrated, hiding behind the boxes like he was trying to avoid getting shot by faux gunfire from the fictional FBI agents who were trailing us in his livened-up version of the events.

"Absolute foolishness," Jazmine said, shaking her head and laughing.

After that, we took our time going through nana's things, halting briefly to clean up our impromptu dinner and let Punkin outside to pee, and when we settled back down to continue our search, Seb sat on the rug next to me, and we unsnapped the lid of one of the big plastic totes and delved inside while Jaz answered a phone call from Patty.

As I finished sorting through a stack of books, Seb straightened out his leg and bumped into me.

"Sorry," he mumbled.

I glanced down, my gaze snagging on a shiny, triangular scar right above his knee. I knew that scar. It'd been there since he was ten and hadn't faded much over the years.

"Admiring your handiwork?" Seb asked, one side of his mouth lifting.

"It's not mine," I said.

He squinted at my face. "Are you screwing with me, Malone? This is absolutely your doing. You were pissed because I'd borrowed that fishing boat—"

"You *stole* one of Mr. William's boats."

"—and threw that net at me, and a J-hook jabbed into my flesh."

He wasn't wrong. I'd been shocked by the amount of blood. "I remember nearly passing out when you pulled out the hook."

"You and me both," he said, smiling.

I stared at the scar. "Your dad blamed me and got in a screaming match with Nana at the ER. He called me a jezebel, and I had no idea what that was, but I do remember him shouting that I was a bad influence on you. Talk about irony."

Seb's eyes slid toward mine. We both snickered, then he said, "Yeah, my mother had left us the year before, and Pops wasn't doing the best job dealing with it. He thought every female was trouble, no matter if it was you or Nana Malone, or the Virgin Mary. But you're missing the point. This scar? It's your handiwork."

"Fine, you're right. I did that, and I'm still sorry."

Seb set a pile of paperwork on the floor beside him. "I'm not. It's proof of life."

"Proof of life?"

He glanced up at Jazmine, who was pacing through the kitchen on her phone, and from what I could hear, trying to convince Patty that she hadn't lost a pair of shoes.

"Back at boot camp," Seb said, "when things were bad, it would sometimes feel like I was inside a nightmare—like, everything was surreal, and I couldn't figure out if it was really happening, or if I was just dreaming, or maybe even dead." He tapped his leg above the scar. "This told me I was alive. I would look at it and make myself remember everything that happened the day I got it. Stealing the boat, our fight, getting stitches . . . Proof of life."

Tender feelings softened my heart. I stared at the scar, and my hand lifted as if it had a will all its own. I hesitated, steadying a tremble, then reached until my fingertips touched the raised patch of skin above his knee. The air seemed to still around us, and I heard Seb's breathing catch . . . and then hold while I traced the pale triangle. Goose bumps spread across his thigh, and like magic, or maybe an infectious disease, they spread to my arms.

Seb shuddered softly.

"Sorry," I said, and tried to retreat into neutral territory.

But Seb quickly trapped my hand against his knee, and whispered, "I'm not."

My heart raced.

Everything was warm. His knee, his hand on mine. The air I raggedly breathed, making me feel dizzy and dumb. I felt trapped in amber, unable to summon enough bravery to look him in the eyes, so I just stared at our hands and tried to slow my rapid breathing while he watched me. His insistent grip on my hand relaxed, just barely, and his thumb stroked a slow pattern across the bones in my wrist. Pleasurable chills raced up my arm, followed by more luscious warmth. It rolled through me like the waves down the beach, and it felt like a drug.

Noise from the kitchen ripped me out of the moment. Seb and I jerked apart, and my heart pounded like I'd nearly been caught breaking into a bank.

"Ugh! Patty is going to drive me to murder," Jazmine complained loudly. "Should I let the dog back inside? She's whining at the back door."

"Ye-a-a-ah," he answered Jazmine, sounding dazed. "I mean, yes. Let her inside. If It's okay with Paige . . . ?"

"Yep, fine," I said, scooting an inch away from him, and then another, to put me out of the temptation zone. The way my heart raced, you'd think I'd been caught robbing a bank. I needed to cool down, and fast.

Jazmine cracked open the last plastic tote as I made an effort not to glance at Seb. When she moved the lid to the side, her face lit up. "Guys?"

"Did you find it?" Seb asked, craning his neck to peer around a stack of boxes.

Jazmine held up the old black photo album. "Boom! Let's take a little look inside, shall we?"

The three of us huddled around the coffee table, hovering over the faded black pages inside the album. I carefully flipped past black-and-white pictures that had been mounted with tiny cardboard corners. Photos of my great-great-great-uncle in Ireland. Of some of the Malones who immigrated to Michigan, standing in front of a shack on the family's former cherry farm. Standing in front of a Ford Model T that was built down the road in Detroit.

"There!" Seb said, tapping the page.

Three photos of Wyrd Jack, long before he got arrested. One showed him standing on his boat in the fog, looking ominous. Another was taken on the steps of some house. And the third photo was at a bar, him holding up a large mug of beer.

"No Mabel in any of these," I noted.

Jazmine turned the page. More relatives, but no Wyrd Jack. She flipped back and tilted her head, holding the page horizontally. "Huh. What's this?" Before I could ask what she'd seen, she slipped one long nail behind the photo of Wyrd Jack with his beer and picked carefully . . .

Until another photo came sliding out.

Two photos had been mounted together, one hidden behind the other.

We all leaned closer. The cottage fell silent.

The secret photo was upside down when she pulled it free. Familiar dots and dashes were scrawled across the backing. We stared at it for a moment before Jazmine flipped the old photograph over.

Wyrd Jack and Mabel, standing in front of a building.

"Oh shit," Jazmine whispered. "The faces in the locket . . . they came from this photo."

"Go get it!" he told me, jumping up.

And while I raced to our treasure-clue hiding spot, grabbing the shoebox that contained the gold locket, Seb snatched the framed copy of "Prison Poem" off the wall and quickly began deciphering the Morse code on the back of the secret photo Jazmine had found.

"It's numbers, just like before, sets of three to correspond with letters in the poem," he said, biting his bottom lip as he scrawled down his translations on the side of a catalog mailer. While he concentrated, I dug out the gold locket and opened it to the two photos inside before setting it on the coffee table.

Same as the secret photo Jazmine had found.

"Exact match," she said. "Must have had a duplicate copy printed. Someone cut out the faces and put them inside the locket."

We stared at the locket, then Jazmine flipped over the secret photo, briefly arguing with Seb when she interrupted his deciphering. "I'll give it right back, just let me see it for a second . . . Look. The happy couple is standing in front of a building. See that fancy stonework above the doorframe? I know that . . . don't I?"

Of course!

"It's Mabel's parlor downtown!" I said, nearly dumping the entire photo book on the floor out of excitement.

The reason Wyrd Jack was called "Wyrd" originated with Mabel and her interest in spiritualism and fortune-telling. For several years in the early 1920s, she held séances in the big Pink House, north of the river, until Wyrd Jack leased some space downtown for Mabel inside a three-story apartment building, where she read tarot and performed spirit-medium services for the locals.

"Mabel's old spirit parlor," Jaz whispered. "Holy shit. Is that right?"

Bean's Trading Post was quite literally a block away. I'd been so close today and hadn't had a clue. Surely that was a sign from the universe that we were on the right track.

"Okay, I think I've got it," Seb said, furiously scribbling the final letter. "'Hidden in deep corners.' That's what it says on the back of the photo."

"Shit," Jazmine said, scratching her cheek. "Deep corners? Guys, what if another clue is hidden inside the spirit parlor?"

"Easier to hide something on your own property than on a confiscated ship," I said, considering it. "But wouldn't anything hidden have been found already?"

After Wyrd Jack was arrested, Mabel's spirit parlor was abandoned—the townsfolk turned against her and her unborn child, my great-grandmother—and eventually the space was leased to another tenet. Over the years, it had been many things, but for the past decade, it had been occupied by another business.

"Pretty sure High Spirits Brewing owns the entire building," Seb said.

A local craft beer company. They ran a bustling taproom and restaurant on the first floor, and in the basement, brewed a popular sour-cherry IPA and several cannabis-infused drinks.

"It's one of the busiest places in town," Jazmine said. "We could go check it out, but there's no way we're getting in if they're carding at the door."

I asked, "Does anyone know anybody who works there? Dishwashers, hostesses . . . ? Maybe someone can let us take a tour?"

Jazmine and Seb both shook their heads.

"We don't even know if we're on the right track," Jazmine said.

"What if the spirit parlor behind them in the photo is a coincidence? Just a backdrop."

"Everything has been personal so far," I argued, pulling out other items from our box of clues. "The marriage license, the key leading to Wyrd Jack's ship, the locket. All of these things are centered around the two of them, so it makes sense that Mabel would hide something in her own place of business."

"Fair point," Seb said.

"Hidden in deep corners," Jaz contemplated. "Why 'deep'? Why not 'dark'?"

Great question. "Maybe in the basement? That would be deep . . ."

Seb tapped the secret photo. "I'm on board. We need to explore inside that building. Poke around in all the corners, try to figure out what she meant by 'deep.'"

"Right," Jazmine said, thinking. "When does High Spirits' taproom close? Midnight? Can't really do that without looking sus in front of tables of tourists chugging flights of pale ales."

"Then we figure out a way to explore the brewery after-hours," I said.

"I hear you, Paige, I really do," Seb said, scrunching up one side of his face. "But what you're suggesting is technically known in the real world as breaking and entering. That's pretty daring, even for the Wags."

Point taken. "I didn't say it would be easy. Maybe Benny can turn off the alarm system. You know . . . hack it?"

"Christ," Seb mumbled, scrubbing the back of his head. "That's a lot of pressure on a guy who just wants to dream up ways to shake down parents for babysitting money."

"He hacked the security system at school," I pointed out.

We all looked at one another, hesitant to make a group decision.

"Come on, guys. We don't even know for sure if these photos are pointing us to Mabel's old spirit parlor," Jazmine pointed out. "Are we really willing to go to jail for a hunch?"

"To be fair," Seb said, "I've gone to jail for a lot less. They *really* don't like me at the sheriff's station."

Jazmine was right. This was only a hunch. But the fact remained that someone put that locket inside Wyrd Jack's ship—the same person who'd put the skeleton key in the flooded cavern. If it really was Mabel who'd done that, was it so inconceivable to imagine she might hide another clue inside her own place of business?

We were on the brink of something—I could feel the shifting current in the air. The anticipation for something big. "Might as well call Benny," I said. "He can tell us if we've all gone off the deep end."

"Yeah, and if hacking into a commercial security system is above his pay grade," Seb said.

When he put it that way, it really did sound ridiculous. "Okay, fine. Maybe Benny's got better ideas about exploring that building."

Jazmine put a hand on Seb's shoulder. "Make that call, Jansen. I think we can all handle a little Lulu if it means we're finally on our way to finding that golden statue."

"Yes, ma'am," he murmured.

The way the two of them smiled at each other, like everything wrong in the past had been forgiven, and all that remained was friendship and an unwavering trust . . . Nothing made me happier.

Pulling out his phone, Seb toggled on speakerphone and dialed. While we all waited for Benny to answer, blue eyes flipped up to meet mine, practically crackling with electricity.

They seemed to say, *We're not finished.*

Or perhaps that was just my imagination. But my stomach fluttered wildly, regardless. It fluttered, flipped, and dropped like it anticipated big thrills . . . and big danger. As if my entire being was warning me, *Look up, you fool! Look up at the sky!*

A malfunctioning jet could fall down at any moment.

Maybe even the sky itself.

<h1 style="text-align:center">Chapter 14</h1>

Turns out that hacking into a brewery's security wasn't impossible. Just not ideal.

"If we get caught, we're all going to jail," Benny pointed out. "Probably not the best thing for you, when you're already battling the financial aid office. Don't think Harvard brags about making special accommodations for felons."

I didn't think so, either.

But even if I was just lost in the excitement when I formulated that plan, Benny and his cool, rational mind devised a better one that involved less jail time.

"Remember the Kumaras, who live across the street from me? The mom's an attorney; they have two boys?"

"The Sri Lankan family with the pool in their backyard?" Seb asked. "The younger brother was in the class ahead of us. What was his name, Amal?"

"Yep," Benny confirmed. "And the older brother is training to be a Cicerone at High Spirits' taproom," he reported over the speaker on Seb's phone.

Jazmine squinted. "What the hell is a . . . ?"

"Beer sommelier."

"Whelp, I've heard it all now," Seb said. "Maybe I've missed my calling."

"I'll talk to Amal and see what I can do," Benny told us before hanging up.

We didn't know how long it would take. Half an hour later, we'd repacked all the totes with Nana's things and hauled them back to the basement. As we headed back upstairs, Seb's phone buzzed with an incoming call from Benny.

"What's everyone doing around midnight?" his deep voice asked, a hint of victory and excitement beneath the monotone. "Our boy can give us a little tour before closing time, if you're game."

Oh, we were game, all right. Most definitely game . . .

"You're a genius, Ichabod," Seb told Benny. "A certified genius."

Boom, just like that, everything was forgotten but the treasure hunt. Jaz and Seb both had to work in the morning, but they were willing to sacrifice sleep for this chance.

At half past eleven, we left Punkin sleeping on the living room sofa and piled into the Bronco. As we headed downtown to meet up with Benny and Lulu, all of us were on edge. Personally, I was experiencing a nervous sort of eustress at a level I'd only previously felt on the Shivering Timbers wooden roller coaster when my car was climbing the track of the first hill.

An intoxicating mix of joyful anticipation and extreme dread.

We passed Bean's, which wasn't busy anymore. On a weekday at the beginning of summer, crowds dwindled by this time of night. So it was no surprise when we pulled up to High Spirits Brewing and found only a handful of people inside the taproom right before closing. That was probably a good thing. Fewer eyes on us.

"We're just going to take a little tour," Seb said under his breath as he hunted a parking space. "Just a little tour . . ."

We spotted Benny and Lulu waiting on the sidewalk as we pulled into a nearby spot. None of the Wags were legal yet, drinking-wise, so I doubted any of us had been inside the brewery much. A couple years ago, I picked up some donations for a school fundraiser from the bar. But I did have one dramatic visit here, when I was thirteen. Nana took me inside to protest the brewery's ghost tours. They claimed to be able to show patrons Mabel's wandering spirit. Nana said they were disrespecting our ancestors and went full-on righteous fury on the manager, threatening to sue the brewery.

They never hosted another ghost tour.

"Back in the day," Seb said as we exited the Bronco, "if you knocked on the service door around back after midnight and asked for Alex, they'd sell you growlers of their THC mocktails under the table. But Alex got fired, and the good times ended." He thumped his heart. "RIP to a real one."

"Maybe," Jazmine said, "you could've called up Alex and asked if he's seen anything weird in the deep corners of this place. How are we actually going to do this?"

With Lulu trailing behind him, Benny strolled up to us, hands deep in the pockets of his hoodie. He lifted his chin in greeting and said, "Got it all covered. Just follow my lead inside. Ready?"

"No time like the present," Seb said cheerfully, clapping Benny on the back good-naturedly, and we headed toward the entrance.

Big windows on either side of the front door glowed with warm light. We stepped beneath the sculptural frieze crowning the door—the detail in the secret photo that pointed us here in the first place. Once inside, we were greeted by muted indie music and the low din of the taproom. Steel columns, wood walls, and copper brewing vats dominated the space—sort of "industrial brewpub" meets "upcycled contemporary." A few college students and a smattering of tourists were placing orders for last call.

Two waiters casually leaned against the hostess podium, chatting aimlessly as they waited for the dregs of the night to tally their tips and leave. They didn't look eager to serve us when we approached and acted relieved when Benny asked for his friend's brother. A minute later, a young South Asian man appeared, dressed in chino shorts and Top-Siders, and sporting the most perfect pompadour I'd ever seen. He shook our hands enthusiastically.

"Hey, Amal said you'd be coming. I'm Dinesh," he said by way of introduction, looking us over with curiosity. "Which one of you is the Harvard student?"

Uhh . . . I glanced at Benny, whose eyes widened dramatically, as if to say, *Go on . . .*

"That would be me," I said.

He brightened and shot me double finger guns. "Terrific. Benny tells me you're doing research for a school project—local folklore? And that you're actually related to the building's original mistress, the Medium of Haven Beach." He waggled his brows and made spooky noises.

"Uh, yeah," I said, flicking a dirty look at Benny. *He could've at least prepared me, for the love of God.* "Mabel Malone is my ancestor."

"Wild! So cool to be a part of history, I really dig it," Dinesh said, nodding appreciatively. "Yeah, so, you're just wanting to take a look around? There's some pretty interesting old things in the brewhouse downstairs. Usually, when we give tours, to corporate groups or YouTubers with travel shows, or whatever, we take them downstairs. There's also Mabel's office upstairs—where they used to take people on the ghost tours a few years ago."

"I definitely want to see that," I said.

"No problem. It's basically just an empty room with a couple pieces of furniture, so fair warning not to get your hopes up. And, of course, you can't leave without taking a photo at 'Mabel's Table' . . ." He gestured with one arm, pointing toward a booth beneath one of the front windows, and a round table there. A brass plaque attached to the wall announced its history:

Original séance table, 1901–1929
Owned and used by
Mabel Malone, spirit medium and wife of Wyrd Jack

I'd seen this same table when Nana brought me in here to yell at the manager. There wasn't anything remarkable about it, other than its presence being documented in several framed black-and-white photos hanging nearby on a wall. The photographs showed Mabel sitting at the table, intensely staring at the camera with raccoon eyes while holding a crystal ball in her hands, tarot cards fanned out around her. Currently, a server was bent over Mabel's Table, wiping up ketchup and a basket of spilled fries.

Dinesh turned his head to one side and quietly spoke into an earpiece. Then he gave us an apologetic look. "Gotta step away for a moment. We're closing soon, so you can get started alone. I can't really let you roam through here after we're closed, so you'll need to make it quick."

Benny raised both hands. "Not a problem. We appreciate you accommodating us."

"Sure, man. A friend of my brother's is a friend of mine," he said, smiling. "Feel free to look and take pics for research. There's nothing much else to see in the taproom besides the table, and it's best to stay out of the kitchen at this time of night. Gets a little hectic, you know?"

"That's fine," Benny said.

"But you can go through that door back there and head to the brewhouse. Jeff's down there, so just tell him you're part of the Harvard tour group. Also, if you want to poke around upstairs, feel free. It's mostly just a couple banquet rooms, but Mabel's old office is up there, like I said. I'll have to get the key from the manager. So I'll meet back up with you in five."

He flashed us another pair of finger guns and dashed away, leaving us all feeling a little awkward as we stood around with patrons staring at us.

"Look," I said. "We should probably split up. The taproom closes in, like, fifteen minutes.

"No way we can explore every corner in fifteen minutes," Seb said.

Benny looked around. "Dude's probably right about the taproom. They basically stripped it back to studs when they remodeled in here. It's new paint and plaster, so we can eliminate all this, right off the bat."

"What are we even looking for? Deep corners?" Lulu said, still sporting the heart-shaped glasses atop her head that she'd been wearing when I ran into her at Bean's.

"Just like we discussed on the phone. Anything unusual. A mark, Morse code, secret panels . . ." Seb said. "Jaz, you take Benny and Lulu downstairs to the brewhouse. Paige and I will head upstairs. Text if you see anything."

Jazmine frowned at Seb, then at Lulu, and I started to protest, but Benny was already heading toward the door that led down to the brewhouse. I mouthed "sorry" to Jazmine as Lulu merrily linked arms with her, provoking the most epic side-eye I'd seen in a long time. God help Lulu. If Jazmine didn't kill her first, I might take a crack at her.

As Benny, Jazmine, and Lulu went downstairs, Seb and I headed up an iron staircase to the second floor, where the taproom's jangly music faded along with the chatter. A dark landing didn't hold much but a couple of potted palms and a couple of benches. It was quiet and still until a server emerged from a restroom, tucking her shirt into her pants. My heart sped, thinking we were about to be told that this was for employees only, but she just looked embarrassed.

"Sorry," she mumbled as she passed, jogging down the iron staircase.

"Christ," Seb whispered. "How come I feel like a criminal?"

"If you have to ask . . ."

"You're hilarious, Malone. Come on, let's see what's up here."

Beyond the restroom stood a few doors. The first two were clearly labeled ROOM A and ROOM B, and when we poked inside them, we found the banquet rooms. Nothing but stacks of chairs and tables, a small stage. We flipped on the lights and raced around the rooms to check the corners for anything suspicious, and found . . . nothing.

No wobbly boards.

No mismatched paint.

No elaborately carved secret panels.

Just a dry-erase board and some corporate packets leftover from a team-building meeting.

Seb made a beeline for the door at the far end of the landing. It had to be Mabel's old office; it was the last room left. Only, it wasn't locked—a shipping carton of bar napkins was keeping it from closing completely. And when Seb pushed the door open and moved the carton out of the way, we were able to flip on a single overhead light and look around.

An old wooden desk and a filing cabinet. A metal-framed single bed without linens. A fireplace.

"Mabel's office?" Seb said, glancing at a stack of boxes lined up against the wall—more bar napkins.

The furniture looked old, but it could've been brought in to make it feel more 1920s, to stage it for the brewery's discontinued ghost tour. Still, Seb and I quickly checked as many corners in the room as we could find—in the fireplace, the desk, and the very corners of the room itself.

Nothing.

"Why would Mabel have an office up here if her business was on the first floor?" I wondered. "The rest of the building was a hotel back then."

"The brewery could've just picked a random room up here and called it Mabel's."

Disappointment settled inside my chest. We only had a few more minutes before midnight. Maybe the rest of the Wags were having better luck in the basement.

Seb must've been thinking similar disappointed thoughts, because he sighed heavily and let his head loll backward as he stared up at the ceiling. Then his head tilted in curiosity. "Paige . . ."

I glanced at the ceiling. A few feet away from the overhead light was an access panel with a single piece of twine hanging down and two words stenciled.

Roof Access.

Before I could even open my mouth to speak, Seb was pulling the piece of twine. After a couple of tugs, the panel dropped and a wooden ladder unfolded from the ceiling. We stood at the bottom of the folding ladder and peered upward, into darkness.

Seb shook the ladder, testing. "Seems solid. I'll go first."

"Wait . . . oh, okay," I said as I stared at his butt ascending. He made it to the top, and his sneakers disappeared. A moment later, a string of curses floated back down the ladder. It was followed by some pounding noises and a grunt, and finally, the squeal of metal.

The light changed. Night air rushed down the ladder. "Roof hatch!" Seb called to me. "Come on!"

Blowing out a breath, I headed up the rickety ladder, following Seb's instructions—"Watch that third step!" And before I knew it, he was lifting me onto the roof of the building, where an iron hatch stood open to the stars.

"Holy shit," I said.

"Right?"

You could see half of Haven Beach from this vantage point. The higgledy-piggledy rooftops of downtown jutted around us. And farther away, the harbor was a sea of golden lights, with streets crisscrossing in every direction and red taillights streaking.

It was magical.

But we didn't have time to admire the view.

A cool night breeze ruffled Seb's hair and chilled my bare legs as he got out his phone and turned on the flashlight function to take a better look around. The roof itself was expansive and black as pitch, but it looked stable enough. We definitely weren't the first people since Mabel's time to be up here, as there were several modern structures—commercial HVAC units, satellite dish. We walked around them to check the literal corners of the building, where a low brick wall circled the entire roof. Being up here at the top of the brewery, no one would describe these corners as "deep," but I guess we were both just propelled by desperation at that point.

We had to step over some mechanical equipment to reach the last corner on the front of the building. The low wall forming the corner showed nothing unusual—no loose bricks, no suspicious mortar.

"Fuck," Seb said, sighing. "Not sure what else we can do up here, so I guess that's it for us. I'll text Benny."

"It can't be it. We just aren't looking hard enough. Have a little faith—I mean, back when we were kids and were losing hope in finding the treasure, wasn't it you who always said you'd never stop believing in it? That you had enough faith in it for all of us? Where's that faith now?"

"I'm all about chasing impossible dreams, Paige, but this one's going to need more time. Probably shouldn't have run out here tonight without thinking it all over first."

"Thought you were all about big-risk, no-thinking situations. I can remember when you went around the middle school cafeteria telling everyone that 'don't think' was your personal motto."

"Why in the world would you pay attention to any motto I've got?" he argued. "Hey, you can see the roof of Bean's from here. Come on, let me help you get back over this machinery . . ."

But I just wasn't ready to give up.

"Hidden in deep corners," I said, running my hand over the corner of the brick wall one more time. A metal gutter hung on the outside. I wondered if the gutters were original to the building. Water was deep. Water flowed through gutters . . . Okay, sure, I was clutching at straws, but if I just carefully leaned over the wall and stretched my arm down, I might reach the gutter . . .

"What're you doing?" Seb asked. "You'll kill yourself. Come on, Paige . . ."

Just a little farther . . .

Without warning, my ankle weakened—the one I'd hurt in the cave. It . . . gave out.

Mortar crumbled under my fingers. One second, I was trying to balance myself, and the next, it felt like the entire building was slipping away. Disoriented, I scrabbled for purchase and tried to pull myself up, but I continued sliding—until I suddenly felt a steely hand clasp my arm.

My body jerked backward.

"Jesus, Paige!" Seb shouted in my face as I wobbled on my feet, still unsure if I was safe.

"I—I slipped . . ." I said, heart thudding as adrenaline caused my body to tremble.

He clasped my upper arms in a death grip, still holding on to his phone, its flashlight beaming in his eyes every time I drew a breath. With an exasperated noise, he let go of me only long enough to shove the phone into his jacket pocket, breathing raggedly as he stared down at me.

"You scared the shit out of me, Paige. Especially after the flooded cavern. I thought that was a fluke, but now I'm wondering. *Do* you have a death wish?"

"M-me?" I stuttered. "That's rich. I think I asked you that a hundred times after you abandoned the Wags."

"I didn't abandon anything. You kicked me out."

"That's ridiculous."

"Then what did 'you're no longer welcome in the cave' mean? Or 'if I see your face again, I'll smash it with a brick.'"

Had I said that? All I remembered was the feeling of betrayal.

"Paige?"

"I heard you. I just . . . have different memories."

An ambulance siren bleated in the distance. Seb's hands still clutched my arms.

"Why did you keep my letter?"

I blinked up at his face. "What?"

"The letter I sent from boot camp . . . the one with the photo. You kept it. I know because I saw it in your dresser drawer when I was crashing in your room."

Several emotions rolled through me in succession. I felt insulted and resentful that he was baldly admitting to going through my things, even though it wasn't a surprise. And I was embarrassed that I'd kept the letter all this time and felt defensive.

"Why did *you* send *me* a letter? You didn't send one to Benny or Jazmine. Why me?"

The expression on Seb's face was so unguarded, so open . . . something inside me that was wavering under strain finally snapped. I didn't wait for his answer. I gave him my honesty instead.

"I kept your letter because you were my best friend," I said. "Even before Jaz, it was you and me. When we were kids, you were my entire world. But then you went away like everyone else—my mom, my dad, Nana. So I guess . . . I was mourning you, Seb. And maybe that takes longer than I thought it would."

When I dared to look at his face, I found pain and hurt there, along with a raw tenderness I hadn't seen in a long time.

"I'm still here, Paige," he whispered. "That's the difference. They're gone, but I'm not. I'm still here . . ."

Night air whipped across us. Here in the half dark of the rooftop, circled by downtown's lights below, I could make out the sharp planes of his face. He looked like he'd stepped out of an early-nineteenth-century painting, a windswept romantic poet on a moor, brooding and serious and epically handsome.

I was spellbound, unable to take my eyes off him but utterly lost for words. It didn't help that I was still a little shaky, still breathing heavy after nearly falling to my death.

So why did I feel so safe?

So calm?

So willing to do it again?

When he spoke, Seb's voice was so rough and low, I almost didn't hear him.

"Paige . . . ?" he said.

"Yes?"

"I . . ."

"Yes . . . ?"

"Fuck it," he whispered to himself, eyes fixed on mine. "Paige. Listen to me for a minute, okay? *Don't think.*"

"What?" I whispered back.

Adrenaline zipped through me. I didn't understand, not at first. Not until the hands gripping my arms loosened and slid over my shoulders, where he cradled the back of my head. I was so shocked by the intimacy of his touch that I froze, and he stared down at me with an intensity that felt electric.

"Don't think," he whispered again, his face inches from mine.

My heartbeat quickened inside my chest.

His gaze dropped to my lips, and I knew what was coming a second before it happened.

He kissed me.

My body was still frozen in place when his mouth came down on mine. It wasn't an erotic kiss, or even a tender one. His lips roughly pressed against my lips as if he were trying to take control or argue his point. And I . . . didn't kiss back.

Maybe I was in a state of shock. Maybe I was doing the thing he asked me not to do—

Thinking.

Whatever it was, he stopped kissing me and pulled back. Just a little. Centimeters. Our noses grazed. Breath intermingled. His fingers were in my hair, and it was hard to tell because of all the adrenaline racing through me, but I was almost positive his hands were shaking a little.

Shaking for me.

Unable to stop myself, I lifted my head and kissed his mouth. Once. Then again. I felt all the rigidity in his hands soften, and we met in the middle.

Soft lips opened to mine, and a thousand warm tingles rushed over my arms. For a moment, we were out of sync, testing each other. Then the kiss deepened, open-mouthed and hungry, and his hands slid down my back, pulling me closer. But it wasn't enough. I wrapped my arms around him like I had a hundred times, but now my breasts were pressed against his chest, and I could feel all of him pressing back against me.

All the boundaries we'd maintained over the years crumbled at once.

His tongue stroked inside my mouth, rolling with mine, and his hands were everywhere, running up my back, caressing my hips, leaving a trail of fire. Warmth flooded the center of me as a joyous vertigo spread. And before I realized what was happening, my knees buckled and bent like they were wet noodles.

For one dizzy moment, I felt like I was slipping off the side of the building again.

This . . . was a real thing? The kiss so good that it buckles your knees?

This was actually happening to me?

My God.

"Whoa," Seb murmured as I broke the kiss with my wobbling. He tightened an arm around my back and held me up.

"S-shit," I slurred, sounding like an old-timey TV drunkard. "My ankle?"

It was *not* my bad ankle. It was all my hormones conspiring against me to get me horizonal so that Seb could have his way with me. Or maybe so that I could have my way with him. Either way, my body wanted Seb's.

Quite a bit, actually.

But Seb clearly knew this, indicated by the low chuckle that reverberated through his chest into mine. That chuckle sounded like power—like he knew *every last thing* my body wanted, even if I didn't. Like he'd won some kind of victory.

Stupid, stupid body.

His shorts buzzed, and we both took a rapid step back, putting distance between us. Seb finally let me go when he fished out his phone, cussing the flashlight function, which was still on. When he managed to shut it off, I saw the text that had come through, from Benny:

Get outside now bad news

"Bad news," I said, still extremely turned on and not precisely stable on my feet. I didn't want to deal with any news, good or bad. I'd just had one of the best kisses in my life with someone I probably shouldn't be kissing but was not sorry about it whatsoever.

I mean, come on, universe. Could I not relish one single moment of euphoria?

But the moment Seb clicked off his phone, we both heard it.

A shouting match, outside the brewery. Seb hesitantly leaned over the wall where I'd nearly slipped earlier, and whatever he spotted on the sidewalk below, it wasn't good.

"Son of a bitch," he whispered. "He came after Jaz again? I'll fucking kill him."

That sobered me up pretty fast. "What?"

"Come on!"

I wiped the wet kiss off my lips as we struggled to clear the hurdle of the machinery, as if we both had concussions and forgot how to move right. Seb repeated "Jesus fucking Christ" over and over. But we finally managed it and raced toward the roof hatch.

"What's going on down there?" I asked.

"That's a porch-swing conversation. No time to explain, just hurry."

Ah, the sacred porch-swing conversation. That's what Nana called a serious talk—you did it out on the porch swing, where the lake air could keep your head clear. I chuckled internally at Seb's reference as we descended the rickety ladder into Mabel's office, but any humor I felt was fleeting. I was too worried about Jazmine to hold anything else in my head.

When we raced down the main stairs, I realized that the tap-room had closed—no customers, lights dimmed—and spotted a group of servers gawking through the front window, headed by the beer sommelier. His head turned when we jogged across the taproom floor, and I could tell he was pissed.

"Hey!" he called out. "Your buddies are causing a scene. If they don't break it up, we're calling the cops. I don't want to, for Benny's sake, but I can tell you this much. Tonight was the last time I do anyone any favors."

Seb snorted and pushed past the servers. "Well, there goes your Yelp review. I swear, no one cares about service these days . . ."

He shouted for someone to unlock the door, and when they did, we rushed outside.

And stopped short.

A small crowd had gathered on the sidewalk in front of the brewery, near a black Jeep with a padded roll bar and a custom paint job on the hood that depicted anguished skeletons crawling out of the ground. The DIY monster truck was crookedly parked across a couple spaces, its natural height boosted by giant tires.

I knew that Jeep. The owner was none other than Pretty Paul Vanderburg.

He was in the middle of a shouting match that was occurring between Benny, a stranger in the crowd, and Jazmine.

Oddly enough, Lulu stood a few feet away, arms crossed, with a funny look on her face. "Shrewd" is what I would've called that look on anyone else, but this was silly little Lulu. I wondered what that was all about.

"There he is," Paul called out when he spotted Seb. "My former brother-in-arms, come to rescue the damsel again. Looks to me like your eye has barely recovered from the last time we tangled. You sure you wanna come back for more? What, you and Benito going to gang up on me? Try to strengthen your odds?"

"No, Seb," Jazmine warned.

Seb pointed at Paul. "Touch her and you're dead, mother-fucker."

"No, Seb!" she pleaded again.

My pulse swished in my temples, adrenaline spiking. I absolutely didn't want Seb fighting. It was juvenile and dumb, and even though Seb was nothing but lean muscle, Paul was built like a brick shithouse. He'd fought boxing matches for money in Detroit. He could very well put Seb in the hospital.

"Let her go, you piece of shit," Benny warned, stepping up to Paul.

"STOP," Jazmine shouted, pushing her way between them. "No one is fighting tonight."

"Wrong," Seb said, stalking toward them.

I tried to grab his arm but missed.

Jazmine physically pushed Benny away with her good arm. "I said, stop it! Did I ask for your help? No, I fucking didn't!"

Benny stopped in his tracks, blinking at Jazmine with a stunned look on his face.

"See? The lady wants you to back the hell up," Paul said. "No one's holding anyone hostage, so stop yappin' that bullshit. I just want to talk with her, like I said."

Jazmine held up a firm hand to Seb. "Stop. I mean it."

"What the hell is going on?" I said, coming up behind Seb.

Paul's attention flicked to me. "Oh look, it's the Ivy League bitch, blessing us with her presence."

Now Jazmine shoved Paul. "Say it again and there won't be any more talks between us. Ever."

He held up both hands in surrender.

"Jaz," I begged.

Eyes filled with guilt and shame met mine, and that made me feel awful.

"I need everyone to back off," Jazmine said. "Please. I'm going to leave with Paul now—just to talk. And I don't want any of you following me."

"See?" Paul said. "The lady doesn't need rescuing."

"Shut the hell up," she angrily told him. "I'll go with you to talk, but only on my terms. I need a moment, Paul."

"Fine by me," he said, victory twinkling in his eyes. "I'll be in the car."

Paul strolled to the curb, speaking briefly to Benny and Seb as he passed. "Gentlemen. Nice to see you, as always."

"Swear to God," Seb started, but Jazmine grunted at him, and he shut his mouth.

She pushed past the boys and pulled me to the side. "I'm just going to talk, okay?"

I didn't want to judge her, not after everything she'd already told me, so I ignored the feeling of betrayal that was pricking at my heart and tried to remain neutral. "You're really going somewhere with him? Is it safe?" I whispered hotly, afraid that she might be in danger.

"It's safe, I promise," she whispered back. "We're going to park at the marina and talk. That's it. When we're done, I'll text you to let you know I'm okay, like we did in the old days. We'll talk later. I swear, okay?"

She quickly gave me a one-armed hug and kissed the side of my head, then, just like that, she was jogging off to jump in the passenger seat of Paul's ugly Jeep. Seb jogged over to Paul, and as anxiety swelled inside me, the two of them exchanged sharp words through Paul's open window. I heard Jazmine's voice join in, but I couldn't make out any of it. Seb finally held up his hands, surrendering to whatever she'd said, and backed away from them.

We all watched in various states of horror as the engine roared, and Jazmine rode away into the night with the devil of Haven Beach.

"What the actual fuck . . . ?" I said while the crowd dispersed.

Seb looked utterly defeated as he returned to me, but I needed to know.

"Is she safe, Seb? Or do we need to rescue her?"

Sad blue eyes looked at me. Then he nodded and dropped his gaze. "She's safe."

I let out a breath. His assurance didn't stop me worrying, but it did stop me from outright panicking.

Benny clasped his hands atop his head, pacing in a circle briefly before glancing at us. "Tell me you guys at least found something back in there?"

I shook my head. And if he was asking, that meant they hadn't found anything, either.

"Dammit!" Benny kicked the curb in frustration, shaking off Lulu's hand from his arm.

I didn't know what to say. The night was a bust. No new treasure clue. And Jazmine was off "talking" with the worst human being to set foot in our town.

Then there was just the small matter of me kissing Seb on the roof.

Minutes ago, confetti was exploding inside my chest, but now everything felt like a terrible mistake.

Seb said something to Benny in a low voice, and the two of them talked for a moment, but I didn't hear any of it. Benny just nodded, and they exchanged low-energy shoulder claps before Seb glanced at the brewery window on his way back to me.

"Let's go before the brewery calls the cops," he said. "And maybe you and I should talk about Jazmine. Porch-swing time."

Chapter 15

$\mathcal{B}$enny took Lulu back home with him. He asked me if I was okay when we had a moment to speak before the group disbanded for the night, and I told him the truth.

"I don't know anymore."

He seemed to understand. I was worried about Jazmine and confused about the details of her relationship with Paul. I should be thinking about the fact that we'd screwed up Mabel's clue and came away from the brewery empty-handed. But my stubborn brain only bounced back and forth between Jazmine's predicament and what happened on the roof.

Seb kissed me.

I kissed Seb.

What was I going to do about that? Was it a one-time thing, or would it happen again? Did I want it to? Did *he*? And why was I remembering Seb's hands roaming down my back when my friend was in trouble?

By the time Seb and I returned to the cottage, my thoughts were completely tangled around the night's events, and I couldn't make sense of anything. It was already one in the morning, and Punkin barked at us from inside until we'd unlocked the front door. That was a good thing, I figured. She made a decent guard dog.

"Do you have anything to drink?" Seb asked after we headed inside and turned on a lamp. "I'm dying of thirst."

In a haze, I got out two glasses from the kitchen cabinets and filled them with tap water. I handed one to Seb, and he tipped his head in thanks, then headed out the back door, letting Punkin run out with him.

Okay, then. He was taking the porch-swing conversation quite literally.

Nana's porch swing was built for her by an old woodworker who lived down the beach—probably the same guy who carved the Mr. Legs tree-trunk sculpture, but I never asked. More raft than swing, it was wide enough to take a good nap in, whether you were human or canine. The turquoise canvas pad that lined the bottom and backrest had always been there, and when Seb plopped down, it seemed he'd always been there, too.

Don't think about the kiss. I set my glass of water into a cup holder built into swing's wooden armrest and sat next to Seb, a respectable distance away.

"Last time I sat in the hot seat with Nana Malone," he mused, "she was cussing me out for stealing cigs from Mr. Hammond's trailer."

I snorted. "Yeah, I remember that. We must've been fourteen. Nana was hot for Mr. Hammond. You were harshing her love life."

"Found that out a little too late. She was so mad at me." He smiled to himself, and the dimples *almost* appeared. "I couldn't believe a trailer would have a security camera. Lesson learned—never assume."

Right. Maybe that was a lesson I needed to take to heart myself.

The swing didn't do much swinging. You could get it going if you really tried, but mostly, you just floated. And that's what Seb and I did, we slowly floated in the moonlight, staring at Punkin's dark form running around the beach.

"Talk to me," I told him, kicking off my sneakers to pull my feet onto the swing. "Tell me everything I don't know about Jazmine and Paul."

"Everything?"

"As much as you can. She's already told me some, but clearly not the whole story."

He nodded, scooting farther back, then he reached over the armrest on his side and patted around the underside of the swing. With a small noise of victory, he pulled out a purple disposable vape.

"What the hell?" I complained. "You're hiding weed around my property?"

"Not anymore. You tossed most of it. This has been here a couple months." He offered the vape to me, but I shook my head.

"Harvard made you prim and proper, huh?"

"Not really. This year has been tougher than anything I've ever done, academically, and I never have time for much else."

"See, I imagined you going to frat parties and dating one of those crew rowers who competes with Yale."

He'd imagined my life in Harvard? That surprised me. "You should've been imagining me sitting at the same library cubicle every day for nine months. I've never worked so hard in my entire life."

Seb clicked a button on the vape several times, and the digital screen lit up. Whatever it said made him groan, and he tossed it onto the swing cushion, muttering, "Useless." Then he kicked off his Converse and scooted farther back in the swing to lazily bend one knee. "I respect that, Paige. Seriously. I'm just giving you a hard time. Besides, can't tell a fib on the porch swing. Nana Malone said it, so it must be true." He slid his eyes toward mine and gave me a soft smile.

I smiled back, then exhaled a long breath. "Okay, so tell me about Jazmine and Paul."

He sighed and leaned an arm atop his bent knee. "She told me it started around Christmas. I was back in town, staying at Benny's place, out in the pool house. Benny was still at school in Kalamazoo, but he and Jaz had been staying in touch, and he started to get really worried about her about a month ago. So I . . . started tailing her."

"In secret?" I said.

He winced. "I know, but she wouldn't tell me anything, and Benny was right. She needed help. I tailed her to the fucking Vanderburg prepper compound outside town."

It was a farm, at least it used to be. The Vanderburgs sold off most of their land, and all the boys in the family had built homes there. The compound was surrounded by a ramshackle fence and KEEP OUT signs. I'd never been inside the fence.

It mildly terrified me that Jazmine had been.

"As you already know by now, Jaz was hooking up with Paul," Seb said. "No need to sugarcoat it. She'd told Benny it was just casual, purely for the sex, no emotions. She could have any guy in Haven Beach, so I have no idea what she was thinking . . ."

"Maybe she wasn't," I said quietly, as our roof kiss popped back into my head. *Don't think.*

"Anyway, she told me all this after she busted me tailing her. She was not happy about that, in case you couldn't guess. We had a fight, and she nearly broke my nose."

"Jesus."

"Couple weeks later, she called me crying from the compound and asked me to come get her, no questions asked. She was in a panic. So I parked off the highway near the compound and stealthed my way through the woods and through their dumb fence—which couldn't keep a rabbit out, much less the Feds. And I helped her escape Paul's house through the bathroom window."

"What the hell?" I said, sitting up straight. "Was he keeping her prisoner? You told me she was safe with him tonight!"

He held up a hand. "She is, and he was not holding her prisoner. Apparently, she met Paul's dad, Big Burg, and he freaked her out. You know they buy and sell illegal weapons, right? It's not just the fentanyl."

Everyone knew. They were eternally a week away from being raided. For the gun sales, for smuggling fentanyl and a host of illegal prescription drugs from Canada via the lakes. Paul's mother was in prison for tax evasion.

These were not fine, upstanding people.

"Well," he said. "That day when Jaz called me to come get her, Paul had left her in his house while he went on some urgent errand for Big Burg. Apparently, Jaz got bored, didn't stay put, walked through the compound, and stumbled upon Big Burg conducting a deal—guns or narcotics, not sure. But she saw more than she expected, and it scared her. She didn't have her car with her, and Paul wasn't answering his phone. She just freaked—and who can blame her? I saw so much bad shit when I was hanging with Paul, and the worst of it always started with Big Burg. That man is a psychopath."

"And Paul isn't?"

"He's no choirboy, but when he gives you his word, he honors it. He's very particular about his code, I guess you could say. And he promised me tonight that he won't touch a hair on her head."

"And you trust him?"

"I trust that much. And I trust Jaz when she says it's okay."

I hugged my knees, trying to figure out if *I* did, especially since she'd already told me about her mental state. When I added Pretty Paul into the mix, I could absolutely see why someone like him could be destabilizing. I thought back over everything both she and Seb had told me. "Jaz said she sprained her arm in a parking lot when you got the black eye."

"*Ye-e-eah*," he drawled. "That whole thing was a misunderstanding. Paul mistakenly got it in his head that Jaz had left him for me."

Hold on, *what*? "You and Jaz . . . ?" Confusion and worry rose.

"God no," he said, shaking his head emphatically. "It's just what Paul assumed."

The relief that flooded my chest was monumental. "Oh my God, *this* is what you meant when I asked if you'd stolen something of Paul's and you said 'maybe'? You stole *Jazmine*?"

"I took her out of a bad situation and gave her my protection. I'd do it for any of you."

The way he said this, eyes slanted and expression dead serious, anyone would believe he meant it. But I *knew* he did, after what he'd sacrificed for Benny.

"Thank you for helping her," I said.

He nodded, then settled against the back of the swing and stared at the dark horizon over the lake. "Anyway, for a while after I got Jaz out of the Vanderburg compound, I thought Paul just wanted revenge against me for fucking up his game. He challenged me to settle it at the bonfire . . . that's when you walked up."

"Right," I said, remembering Seb shirtless, about to get his ass handed to him.

"But after tonight, I'm thinking I miscalculated when I assumed that Paul was just out to get me because I helped Jaz get out of the compound. See, I thought he blamed me and not his own father for scaring Jaz away from a relationship after that day."

"But he didn't?"

"Paul's pissed at me, for sure. But from a couple things he said tonight, couple things he *didn't* . . . I'm starting to think what we're looking at here is that Paul's seriously hung up on Jaz. However things started between them, they must've been more serious than Jaz let on."

I thought about that for a moment and remembered Lulu saying that breakups were hard. "Paul has feelings for her?"

"Maybe. But I'll be damned if I know how she feels about him."

I wished I could've said differently, but I didn't know, either. She'd told me it was over. Guess it was a little more complicated. "What do we do? Jaz doesn't need this right now."

"One thing I've learned is that you can't tell people what they do and don't need, even if you're right. Like it or not, Jazmine is an adult. Even if it's hard not to think of her grinning down at you with pigtails and a missing tooth the first time she stood up on a paddleboard."

He wasn't wrong. I had that same image of her. But I suppose that none of us were those children anymore. I double-checked my phone to make sure Jaz hadn't texted, then I took a long drink of water and watched Punkin digging a hole in the sand in the dark. "Well, then. Guess there's nothing to do but wait for Jaz to let us know she's okay. Not sure how long that will be."

"Your guess is as good as mine."

"As for you, you're still on the hot seat," I pointed out. "While you're doing all this confessing, you might as well tell me about what's happened to you since boot camp . . ."

Chapter 16

Geb stretched out his long legs into my side of the swing, crossing his ankles. "Shoot, Malone. What do you want to know about me? I'm an open book."

"Okay," I said. "Guess I just want to know . . . what you did. There are entire chunks of your life I don't know about."

"I'll tell you mine if you tell me yours."

I nodded. "Fair warning, life outside of boot camp was pretty dull."

He snorted. "God, I would've taken dull any day. I don't know . . . where to start? I already told you a little about what it was like in that place."

"Was there anything good about it?"

"After you understood what they wanted from you, it was just a matter of putting your head down and doing the work. Rebellion wasn't worth it, so I just went into survival mode and kept going until I'd graduated."

I could definitely relate to that feeling. I'd done a lot of keep-calm-and-carry-on–ing since Nana died. "Did you have friends there?"

"There was a girl, Kaylee, whose older sister was a musher—has done the Iditarod sledding race in Alaska? Anyway, when her sister picked her up from boot camp, I was trying to figure out how to get home because, you know, my father didn't come. So I guess she felt sorry for me and let me ride with them."

I narrowed my eyes at him. "Hold on. You're saying Captain Jansen *left* you up in the Yoop? He didn't come get you after graduation?"

Seb shrugged. "We weren't speaking at the time."

"He must've paid a fortune to put you in there. You'd think he'd at least want to see a return on his investment, if nothing else."

"No, see. The investment for him was paying someone to take me off his hands. So he got what he wanted out of it."

I truly hated his father. Maybe almost as much as I hated mine.

My father . . . Without consciously thinking about it, I tapped on my phone screen to pull up my email as I had thousands of times before over the past couple of days, waiting for a response from the inquiry message I sent through his company website.

Nothing. As there never was.

"Everything okay?" Seb asked.

"Oh, um, no text from Jazmine yet," I said, putting my phone down and refocusing on him. "So what happened after you got a ride with the girl's sled-dog sister? The musher?"

"The musher had a camp in the Yoop between Marquette and the Wisconsin border, bunch of little log cabins. She and some other people had been practicing for the Iditarod there for the winter, like a dozen mushers. All the winter snow was melting, so they were packing things up to disband for the summer. I'd never seen so many Huskies at once."

I blinked at Seb. "That's where you got Punkin."

The lines on his face softened. "Yep. Punkin had hurt her leg, and she'd healed up but couldn't race with the other sled dogs anymore. They were going to send her to a rescue, but the two of us bonded instantly. So they let me adopt her, and Punkin and I were able to catch a ride with one of the mushers who was headed back home across the peninsula to Milwaukee. So that's where Punkin and I settled."

"Milwaukee?"

He nodded. "When I got my lifeguard certification back when we were kids, I remembered the YMCA had some rooms for temporary housing, you know? So it was the first place I went in Milwaukee. They were super cool, let me rent a room for cheap, and the manager was a dog person, so she let me keep Punkin, even though it was against the rules. We spent the summer there while I earned a little cash doing oil changes for a mom-and-pop garage."

"Auto repair?"

"No, boat. The garage was right on Lake Michigan. Did a good-enough job that the man I was working for, Mr. Legaspi, let me have the Speed Buggy for almost nothing—he buys lots of cars and boats damaged by storms on the side. He's the one who got me hooked on audiobooks. He immigrated here from the Philippines, and he used to listen to audiobooks to better understand American culture. He told me to pick something I liked and lean into it, learn everything I could about one subject. I've always wanted to travel, so I picked that."

"No fault found," I said, meaning it.

"Anyway, the deal I had with Mr. Legaspi was that I had to get the Bronco running myself, so I fixed it up in my spare time and drove back to Michigan last fall. And that's basically all there is to tell."

"Huh."

"Disappointed?"

I shook my head. If anything, it sounded like he used his post-graduation time to better himself. But somewhere inside, I was trying to extinguish a flicker of jealousy over this girl he mentioned. "I dunno, guess I sort of imagined you doing wild things up north, like meeting someone in boot camp and Bonny and Clyde–ing your way across the country. Not . . . adopting dogs. Are you still in touch with this . . . what did you say her name was?"

"Kaylee? God no."

"No Bonny and Clyde–ing with her, then, I guess."

"Kaylee and I weren't friends. Pretty sure she couldn't stand me, and to be honest, the feeling was mutual. Our relationship in boot camp only consisted of getting each other off to pass the time."

I turned up my nose. "Gee, romantic."

"Hey, she felt the same way about me."

And *that* was supposed to make me feel better? "You frequently have hate-sex with people you can't stand?"

"Only when the people I like are busy."

He was joking, but knowing this did nothing to assuage the petty jealousy that continued to prick at my heart. I frowned. "Why do you say stuff like that?"

"Like what? The truth?"

"Ugh, whatever." A little worry joined my jealousy. What if he wasn't being crass for "the likes?" Maybe this was just his overall attitude toward sex. Jokes, put-downs, casual apathy. I couldn't reconcile this with the memory of how he'd made me feel on the roof when his arms were wrapped around me.

"Still waiting for your witty retort, Malone."

"Don't have one. Too busy kicking myself for letting you kiss me."

The air between us changed immediately. Seb's head swiveled in my direction, and his sharp gaze fixed on mine, a defensive electricity crackling behind his eyes.

"You kissed me back!" he argued.

"And, what? You were just bored, like you were with this Kaylee girl?"

"I was not bored, and neither were you."

I felt my cheeks heat but couldn't do anything about it. I just knew that I'd made a huge faux pas, bringing up the kiss. I wasn't ready to talk about it with Seb. Best to try to steer the conversation into other pastures. "I guess our high school experiences were a little different, that's all."

"Right, sure. While I was up north, trying to make it out of boot camp without losing my mind, you were bumping uglies with Little Lord Fauntleroy at prom."

My stomach tightened. "How the hell do you know about me and Henry?"

It took him a moment to admit, "Benny. Guess your prom date kissed and told. I mean, you and Henry were the only two in the class to end up at Ivy Leagues, so you were both meant to be, I suppose."

I didn't know where to place my anger. At Benny, for talking about my love life behind my back? Or at Henry for telling everyone? "It was not 'meant to be.' It was a one-time thing—I haven't even seen Henry since graduation."

"You're in the hot seat, too, you know," he sat, patting the swing's cushion. "I told you my shame. You next."

"There's nothing to tell. I went to prom with Henry; it seemed like a good-enough time to lose my virginity, so I did. It wasn't great, wasn't a nightmare. It just . . . was." I shrugged as casually as I could. Though, now that I was thinking about it, Henry and I didn't really speak after that, so maybe the experience was worse than I remembered.

He snorted softly. "Leave it to you to calculate the right time to lose your virginity."

"Well, I wasn't going to wait until college . . ." What did he want me to say? "I literally could not think of Henry less. And why are you judging my decisions?"

"You judged mine."

"I . . ."

He was right, I had.

"The porch swing is a judgment-free space," I said, loosely quoting my nana. "Sorry."

"Apology accepted. Less judging, more hugging. We're all broken people."

Maybe we were.

My phone buzzed. I snatched it off the swing's cushion to find a photo of Jaz inside the front hall of the Neely house, looking exhausted. Her accompanying text was brief: Home safe. Everything okay. Will tell you the whole story tomorrow if you still want to hear. I'm sorry. Please don't hate me.

I blew out a hard breath and typed a quick response to thank her for letting me know. "She's okay. Guess you knew what you were talking about," I said, showing Seb the photo.

Seb breathed a sigh of relief, and then a silence stretched between us. I was thinking about Jazmine, wondering what she'd talked about with Paul, and whether they were . . . a concern. But I soon became increasingly aware of Seb's leg shaking next to mine. He was anxious. He could never sit still when something was bothering him.

I slowly reached out and put a gentle hand on his leg to settle the nervous shaking.

Big eyes blinked at me. "Sorry."

"Don't be, it's fine."

"No—" He squeezed his eyes shut. "Listen, Paige. I'm sorry for *everything*. For being a total prick when we were younger, and for ditching my friends for the likes of Pretty fucking Paul." His face was long and anguished as he struggled for words. "I'm . . . I'm sorry I couldn't fix things with my dad, because if I hadn't been a dick to him after the Ferrari incident, maybe he wouldn't have sent me away. And if I hadn't been sent away, then I would've been here when Nana Malone died."

He was upset. More than he should be.

"It's okay, really."

"It's not, but I want it to be. When I got back home after Milwaukee, I knew the first thing I had to do was own up to my mistakes, okay? I knew I'd fucked up with the Wags . . . like, years of fuckery. I was just so lost . . ." He shook his head. "When I got back, I went to Benny to apologize, then to Jaz. And I tried to come to you. I . . . drove out to Cambridge."

"What?" Everything felt hot inside. I had no idea what he meant. "No, you didn't."

He nodded. "Punkin and I. You'd been there only a couple weeks, so I guess it had been a month after the funeral. I found your dorm, and I saw you walking out of it with another girl. Looked like you were headed to class, in a deep discussion about something." He blinked several times. "You looked . . . like you were in the right place. You know, beautiful campus, surrounded by history and academia . . . It took my breath away, honestly, seeing you there."

"Seb . . ." I whispered, overwhelmed.

"I knew I didn't belong there," he argued. "Didn't probably even deserve to be standing on campus. I worried maybe I'd be making things worse, distracting you. I didn't know how you were coping, after the funeral, and maybe me showing up wouldn't be the best thing. So I just drove back home."

"You went all the way out there . . . ?"

He didn't reply, but his eyes were glossy with emotion, and we couldn't stop glancing at each other. Everything he'd told me tumbled around in my head, and I didn't know what to do with any of it. I felt guilty that he'd driven all the way out there for me while I'd been utterly oblivious. As if it were another example of how I wasn't paying attention to the people who needed me. Him. Jaz. Maybe even Benny, too.

But more than that, I couldn't stop thinking how Seb had been all over the place the past couple of years. Driving across states. Living in weird places. Surviving. The kid I'd known my whole life being forced to grow up faster than any of us, roaming the frozen northern wilds without family or friends. Being one step away from homelessness even now.

My heart squeezed.

We were quiet for a time as Punkin slowly nosed her way up the beach, back to the porch.

"Listen. You can crash here," I said in a low voice. "For the summer. You can have Nana's . . ." I blew out a breath. "You can take the second bedroom."

A jumble of emotions crossed his face. "Paige, whoa. I . . ."

"I know it's kind of weird, but we'll figure it out. Maybe agree on some house rules . . . ?" What those would be, I wasn't sure. I was riffing. "I mean, you were already staying here before I showed up, and you need to know where you're going to sleep every night—a place to eat and wash your clothes. You shouldn't have to play musical chairs. It's not healthy."

"It keeps me on my toes."

"You've got a freaking dog, Seb. You both need stability. Crash here for the summer and get your shit together. I don't know about after I go back to Harvard—if I even can go back."

"Hey! Don't put it out there in the universe. You're going back. I'll help you get in touch with your dad. You'll get what you need."

He sounded a lot surer than I felt. Even now, I desperately wanted to pick up my phone and check my email one more time for a message from my father.

"Regardless, we'll figure out something at the end of the summer. Just stay here for now."

"Nana would roll over in her grave if she knew her precious virginal granddaughter was cohabitating with some random criminal."

"One, you're a *known* criminal; that's different. And two, I'm not virginal, and Nana never treated me like a precious doll who had air for brains, so fuck right off with that."

"Paige, we can't live together," he scoffed, as if I'd asked him to turn a pumpkin into a carriage. Then a tiny line appeared in the middle of his forehead, and he murmured, "Can we?"

"I didn't invite you to sleep in my bed, I said you could *crash* here. As a friend. Or . . . a roommate. I mean, for the past year at Harvard I had a roommate I hated. At least you're good company." I gave him a soft smile.

"Roommates . . ." He blinked rapidly, trying to get his emotions under control. "I don't know. It's a generous offer. I'll think about it."

"Come on," I encouraged, scooting closer. "Nana would want you to. Stay and get your shit together . . . Help me find this goddamn treasure. I mean, if we found the Golden Venus, I wouldn't have to worry about getting my dad to sign a damn thing."

He blew out a long breath. "If we found that Venus, none of us would have to worry about anything ever again."

"Exactly!"

Timid eyes flicked to mine. He was thinking hard, I could see that. But he didn't say anything.

"Come on," I encouraged. "It's just us, the oldest of friends. If you're worried about what we did on the roof earlier tonight, don't be. Forget about it. It's all good. Mistakes were made, but we're adults."

I felt rather pleased about this idea of mine and settled against the back of the swing by his side, certain that I'd fixed everything—old friendships gone astray. War. Hunger. The rise of global fascism.

However, next to me, Seb had gone very still, very quiet. I feared I'd said something wrong. I just didn't know *what*.

"Seb—"

"It wasn't a mistake," he said in a low, grave voice that was defensive and a little hurt.

"I didn't mean . . ." *What?* I didn't mean *what?* I blinked at him while he stared at the lake for a moment.

"What we did on the roof wasn't a mistake, and I don't want to forget it," he told me, looking me directly in the eyes. "Do you . . . regret it?"

We stared at each other in the moonlight, knees touching on the porch swing as chaotic emotions zigzagged around my chest.

I shook my head slowly. "No."

He said something under his breath that sounded like "*Thank God,*" nodding as he exhaled a long breath. "Okay, all right. I'll think about your offer. But that's a start for now."

A start of *what*, exactly, I don't think either of us knew.

But the expression on his face turned tender as he studied me. "Tired?"

I nodded. I hadn't realized until he said it, but I felt like an empty husk. It was past two in the morning.

"Paige?"

"Yes?"

"Can I hold you?"

Frantic flutters gripped my chest. I wasn't just experiencing a case of butterflies; I had an entire trained army of them living inside me, and they were about to riot.

"No funny business," he assured me, blue eyes glinting in the moonlight as he held out his hand. "Please. C'mere."

Hesitant, heart racing, I slid closer, and we stretched out sideways together on the swing, halfway sitting, halfway lying down. The weight of his arm curled around my shoulders and tucked me tightly against his body. It felt so natural, the way I slipped my arm around his back and easily fit into the crook of his arm. The way he gathered me closer. The way my head rested against his shoulder.

He was right. We couldn't be roommates. I mean, come on. *What had I even been thinking?*

Fact was, I wanted him, simple as that.

Complicated as that, too.

Punkin jumped onto the swing and turned in a circle, settling into the corner and draping herself over our feet. Seb and I held each other, drowsily watching the moonlit lake as sleep began to pull me under.

"Just this," he whispered, running gentle fingers down my hair.

And I knew exactly what he meant. *Just this*. Calm. Safe. Together. Possibilities stretching out in front of us as far as we could see. Not friction, not uncertainty, not loneliness.

Just this.

Just us.

I'd give anything for it, too.

Chapter 17

*D*azzling sunlight woke me on the porch swing the next morning. Punkin lay beside me. Seb did not. After bolting up, spotting a couple taking a leisurely morning walk along the shore, I rushed inside with the dog on my heels and found the cottage empty. A note scribbled in the messiest lettering known to mankind was tucked under a pizza magnet on the fridge:

Off at noon today. Wags meeting at Benny's this afternoon? Can swim and brainstorm about the cipher. Will pick you up. —S

P.S. Best porch nap I ever took

My stomach fluttered. Good Lord. *I slept with Seb.* It was only sleeping, but still. And it was nice. Really nice.

I checked the driveway but his car was gone. He'd used the shower—it was still wet, and a damp towel hung. Another note sat atop my razor and toothbrush: *Had to use these, sorry.* He'd used my toothbrush? That felt wildly intimate. As I was looking over the rest of the bathroom, Punkin nudged my leg with a cold, wet nose.

"Oh, I guess you're hungry? Come on, sled dog, let's find you some vittles . . ."

After filling up the husky's bowl with an amount of kibble that I had to guess, I showered and dressed—cutoffs, T-shirt, black one-piece swimsuit underneath—then I made toast. I considered texting Jazmine, but before I could, she texted me to confirm that I was going to Benny's this afternoon and promised to spill the beans then.

Eager to pass the time before our get-together, I busied myself with domestic chores and took the Corvair to the grocery store for a few necessities. When I got back, I checked my email for the first time and nearly had a heart attack when I spotted the subject line *R. Lee and Associates*.

I couldn't click on it fast enough.

My eyes scanned a form letter that had been sent from a generic email box: "Thank you for contacting R. Lee and Associates. If you'd like to make an in-office appointment to discuss commercial real estate with one of our brokers, please call us Monday through Friday . . ."

Disappointment collected in my chest, followed quickly by anger. Did anyone even read my email, or was this sent by some kind of automated AI assistant? Did I not identify myself as his former daughter? What kind of person sends a thoughtless, callous response to a clearly personal message? *My father, that's who.*

I let the disappointment burn through me for a minute, then I typed a brand-new message into the Contact form of his brokerage website:

Dear Mr. Lee,

Please contact me about a legal matter as soon as possible.

Thank you,
Paige Malone

There. Short and simple. Maybe this one wouldn't get a form reply.

But what if it does . . . ? I scrolled to the top of the webpage and stared at the telephone number listed for several anxious moments before tapping it. When the number started ringing, I nearly hung up in a panic. But before I could even make a decision, fight or flight, a recorded voice blared through my phone's speaker:

"You've reached R. Lee and Associates. Sorry we missed your call, but if you leave your name and number at the tone, someone will return your call just as soon as we're back at our desk . . ."

Fuck! I was unprepared but tried to be professional. "Um, yes, hello. This is, uh, Paige Malone? I'm trying to get in touch with Mr. Lee, and it's sort of urgent? I've sent two messages on your site, but I don't know if anyone's read them. So if someone could get back in touch with me at your earliest convenience, you can reach me at . . ."

After reciting my telephone number, I couldn't end the call fast enough. My heart raced like I'd been running a marathon, but hey: I'd done it! I'd initiated contact. Now I just had to wait for a reply. I'd give it a couple days, but that was my limit. And I supposed if he wasn't going to respond to messages and a voicemail, I'd be forced to drive there in person.

My gut twisted at the thought.

To put it all out of my mind and stop myself from worrying,

I started cleaning up the living room. Halfway through, my eyes fell upon something in the middle of a bookshelf lined with old books.

Sunshine and Smuggling: An Early History of Haven Beach.

Several books were written about our town, some better than others. I remembered thumbing through this one when I was a kid because it had a lot of historical photos of the town. It even had a section about the downtown area and early local businesses. I pulled the book off the shelf, made a pitcher of lemonade, and leisurely browsed the pages while lounging on the sofa.

By the time I heard Seb's Bronco pulling into the driveway, I was knee-deep in a passage about downtown Haven Beach and was genuinely startled it was past noon. I rushed to grab sunglasses and my keys, and hopped to the door as I tugged on an old pair of flip-flops. When I swung the door open, Seb stood outside in shorts and a marina T-shirt, poised to knock.

"Hi there," he said, face open and curious. His energy was high, and he anxiously tapped his fingers on the side of his leg. "Got my note about Benny's?"

I pointed to my swimsuit strap and gave him a thumbs-up. "Ready when you are."

"All right, then—" He started to turn around but his brow furrowed. "What's going on with you?"

"Got a little disappointing news. I emailed my father's real estate brokerage to try to schedule a time to meet with him and got a form email that basically told me to call the office if I needed an appointment."

"Did you say who you were?"

I nodded. "Yep, identified myself as his former daughter. I don't think anyone read it."

"Ugh, sorry, Paige. I told you I'd help you track him down, and I meant it."

"Appreciate that. I sent a second message, so I'll wait for a response again, but yeah. Might take you up on that offer. Might need some moral support."

"Absolutely. Count on me."

"Thanks. Really mean that."

"Of course." He studied me again. "But there's something else, isn't there?"

"Is there?"

"Why do you look like a chipmunk with a secret? What's that you got there?"

"Oh, you mean this . . . ?" I dramatically held up the local history book I'd been reading, barely able to contain my excitement. "I've just been reading up on a little place called Three Corners."

He squinted. "What?"

"Downtown used to be called Three Corners in the late nineteenth century. It was 'downtown' by the time Wyrd Jack was in operation, but locals still called it 'the Corners' for decades."

Seb's eyes widened. "Well, shit. I didn't know that."

"Me either, but it's a good direction for brainstorming about the locket clue, don't you think?" Was I talking too fast? Out of nowhere, I suddenly felt self-conscious about our porch-swing conversation last night. Why had I asked him to stay here? *Ugh.* Now it felt like an invisible wall had been erected between us while I waited for his final answer. "Punkin inside or out? Or are you taking her to Benny's? I fed her this morning, by the way."

He frowned at his dog. "Punkin, you conned her into feeding you a second breakfast? Guess I can't let you pass up a chance to swim in the river, so you're coming with us. Everyone told me huskies hate water, but not this one, buddy."

"I'm sorry! She begged me," I argued, worried I might have made her sick, but Seb didn't seem concerned.

"She'll be bloated and gassy. Serves her right." He directed her out to the Bronco, where she jumped in the back seat, after which the three of us promptly left for Benny's.

For once, I was more than happy to listen to Seb's gentle travel writer talk about hiking in Sweden during our drive across town. Seb and I briefly discussed what I'd found in the book, but I didn't really have any more to share. The sun was warm, and the lake looked stunning, clear and blue. Hard to concentrate when the day was so pleasant. And then there was Seb himself, who gave me glances that I could practically feel on my skin.

But that was all he gave me.

He didn't bring up the kiss, my offer for him to stay at the cottage, or the fact that we'd slept in each other's arms the night before.

To be fair, I suppose he'd mentioned it in that note he left on the fridge. But I guess . . . that was that? I certainly wasn't going to bring it up and come off as needy. So I just pretended everything was normal and tried to ignore the mild anxiety that was lurking in the pit of my stomach.

When we got to Benny's, Jaz's Volkswagen was sitting in the driveway, and dark electropop thumped from the backyard. Punkin took off, and we followed her around the side of the house to the double-decker dock at the riverbank, where Benny and Lulu were opening boxes of food delivery atop a long outdoor dining table on the lower deck.

"The crew is all here," Lulu announced jubilantly, wearing

a yellow SpongeBob SquarePants swimsuit that made me do a double take. "Hope you're hungry. I ordered from three different places."

"Sup," Benny said, leaning down to scratch Punkin behind the ear. Questioning eyes flicked from Seb's face to mine. "Everything okay?"

"Yup," Seb confirmed, inhaling warm steam from the food as he hiked a leg over the long bench on the far side of the table. "Are those containers from Pete's Vegan?"

Pete's Vegan was everyone's favorite restaurant in town, meat eaters and tree huggers alike. I'm not sure what they put in their food—jokes abounded—but everything on their menu was a home run.

"Did you get those potato wedges with that coconut sauce?" Seb asked. "I could inhale all of this, I'm so hungry . . ."

I was, too. And it was nice to be out here on a day like this. I'd forgotten how sweet Benny's double-decker dock was, strung with lights and boasting a wicked stereo system and an outdoor kitchen that was far nicer than the one inside the cottage. A stone trail led from the dock to the back patio of the house, where I spotted Jazmine in her red bikini top and shorts, backing out of French doors while juggling two additional bags of food with one good arm. I jogged over to her, causing her to jump when she turned around and spotted me.

"Good God," she said. "Scared the crap out of me."

"Sorry. Need some help?"

She gave me a smile and nodded, handing me one of the bags. "This just got delivered. Lulu seems to think we're all one step away from starvation. Or maybe it's that she went nuts with Benny's American Express card."

"I've known him all my life and he's never once let me use it."

Jazmine snorted. "*You* don't have a cartoon swimsuit."

"Right?" I said, looking over my shoulder. "I can't figure out why it bothers me so much. I guess she's wearing it ironically, but it makes her look . . ."

"Like a ding-dong?"

"Old."

When Jazmine raised a brow, I said, "Like someone who's trying to look younger."

We both glanced at her. Maybe I was wrong and just needed to accept that Lulu was in Benny's life now, cartoon swimsuits and all.

"Hey," Jaz said in a low voice, setting down her bag of food. "So, this isn't the most ideal place to talk about last night . . ."

"Thank you for texting me that you were safe."

She nodded. "Thank *you* for not freaking out."

"Oh, I freaked out, trust me. But I'm trying to keep an open mind. And fair warning, Seb already told me about breaking you out of the Vanderburg compound and the confrontation with Paul in the parking lot that got him that black eye."

"Ah," she said, squinching up her mouth. "So you're up to speed."

"*Am* I?"

An awkward moment passed, then we both started talking at the same time.

"Look—"

"Hey—"

We chuckled nervously, then I said, "You first."

She blew out a hard breath. "Okay, so if you talked to Seb, I guess you know that I haven't really been able to sit down and have a polite conversation with Paul since Seb got me out of the compound that day. There's only been shouting and black eyes. So I felt like I owed him an explanation about what I saw that day at the compound, and why I ended . . . our relationship."

Heck, *I* wanted an explanation about what she saw that day, but she didn't volunteer any information.

"So, anyway," she said, lashes blinking. "We talked. I told him my side of the story, and he listened. And hopefully we both got a little closure. Hard to know because it's just so messy, this thing between us. And when everything's on the table, I just can't see any kind of future with him—"

Thank God!

"But," she continued, "I dunno. Maybe we can be friends when all the emotional wreckage gets sorted."

I studied her face and saw anxiety and lack of sleep. "Are you okay?"

"Yeah." She hesitated, then nodded firmly and repeated, "Yeah, I'll be fine. Just not sure if I'm ready to face all my problems yet. I know that sounds immature—"

"Hey, avoidance can be a legit coping mechanism. I mean, it's basically how I got through first semester. I couldn't deal with Nana's death, so I didn't. I blocked everything out. Avoidance is happiness."

One brow slowly arched. "*Is* it happiness, or just being unhealthy as hell?"

"Is there a difference?"

She snorted a light laugh. "Look, the bottom line is that I'm okay. Mostly? But yeah, I honestly don't want to even *think* about Paul today, so maybe there's something to your avoidance thing. Would much rather focus on a treasure hunt."

"Hey, no argument with that. Treasure hunt it is."

"Thanks, Paige." She looked relieved and smiled at me. "Come on. This food smells good. Let's go see how many egg rolls the boys can eat before they puke."

We hauled the bags to the dock, where Lulu was fooling with the music while Seb and Benny were huddled over a mason jar filled with weed. Benny was rolling some kind of mutant joint involving multiple papers pieced together with some impressive origami skills.

"Jesus, Benny," I said. "Are you making a voodoo doll?"

"Tulip," he said, looking smug. He held up a ridiculously fat joint that vaguely resembled the flower after which it was named.

Jazmine took a seat on the bench across the table from the boys. "Is that the hashish from the dispensary north of town? Remember what happened the last time you rolled one of those."

"What happened?" I asked, sitting next to Jaz.

Lulu plopped next to me. "I found Benny asleep in the next-door neighbor's gazebo the next morning."

"Worth it," he said, smiling to himself. "Besides, the Wags have never really partied together, have we?"

"Not unless you count beer and cooking sherry when we were fifteen," Seb said. "What better time to start than now, though? We've got a Mabel clue to crack, and I personally don't have work tomorrow."

"Me neither. It's Friday, no paddleboard classes," Jazmine said.

"Free as a bird," Lulu agreed.

"Paige?" Seb asked, raising a brow. "You sticking with prim and proper? Or are you going to get in the mud with us?"

Everyone looked at me.

"Jesus with the peer pressure," I complained.

"Look, this is how I see it. Yesterday sucked," Benny pointed out. "For many reasons, not looking at you, Jaz—"

She lifted her good arm. "I'm sorry. I have no idea how Paul found us at the brewery—he wouldn't tell me. But we hadn't been in contact, so it wasn't me. I'll take the blame for making the choice last fall to hang with him instead of telling him to get lost. But hasn't every one of us done dumb things?"

"Facts," Seb said appreciatively, clapping a couple times. "I dub thee forgiven, Jazmine Elizabeth Neely."

She flipped him off good-naturedly.

"If everyone is forgiven, can we all just chill today?" Benny asked. "No drama. Buena onda."

"Fine," I said. "Buena onda."

"Woo-hoo!" Lulu shouted while Jazmine grinned at me. Across the table, Seb gave me a tiny, mischievous smile and said, "Well, all right, then. I say we call this Wags meeting to order properly. Benito, light 'er up!"

Benny happily complied, and we all took turns puffing off his monstrous origami creation, coughing and teasing one another. When it got passed to me a third time, I could already feel it warming me from the inside out and slowing my thoughts. Seb must've noticed, because his foot nudged mine under the table.

"Hey. Should probably take it easy to start. Always more later."

I was a little embarrassed that everyone might be thinking I couldn't keep up with them, which is how I'd felt at every party I attended back in Cambridge—all two of them. But none of the Wags gave me a hard time, and when the tulip was ash, I felt lovely and relaxed. My previous worries receded to the background, and soon we were all digging into the spread of food Lulu had ordered, laughing and retelling old stories. Gossiping about the town. Even teasing Jazmine about Paul. I forgot about everything else. It was just us, old friends, and not even Lulu's presence could put a damper on that.

Strangely enough, she was the one who got us all talking about the treasure hunt again.

Chapter 18

So, about that whole brewery fiasco," Lulu said, moving half-eaten food containers aside. "Obviously found nothing. But is it worth going back?"

"Paige may be onto a new trail," Seb said. "Show them what you found."

I pulled the book about Haven Beach from my bag and leafed through it until I found the right place, then laid it on the table for everyone to see. "Downtown was once called Three Corners. Check it out . . ."

Everyone bent over the book, but it was Benny who pulled it closer. "I've heard old people in Bean's calling it 'the Corners'—but I always thought they meant that roundabout intersection by the brewery."

Seb grunted. "They do. Look. Here it is in 1918," he tapped on a historical photo printed on the page. It was where Main Street crossed Tembly Avenue, one of the other big streets that ran through town and stopped at the river next to the brewery. At that intersection was Haven Beach's one and only roundabout. In the center of the roundabout's grassy median stood an American flag, and at the base of the flagpole was a plaque embedded into the grass. The flag and plaque were still there today.

"What's that memorial for?" Lulu asked.

"It's not a memorial," Benny said. "It's a time capsule."

"Cornerstone of Haven Beach," Jaz elaborated. "Something the town erected when they went from a township to an incorporated town."

"In 1930," I confirmed, telling them what I'd learned in the book. "First we were Three Corners in the 1800s—barely a village. Then we were Haven Corners. Then Haven Beach."

"If that time capsule was buried in 1930, Wyrd Jack was in prison most of that year," Seb said.

I nodded. "He died at the end of the year."

"If Mabel was the one who hid the Golden Venus and the clues to find it," Seb mused, "she might've been doing it in early 1930. The stock market had already crashed, and people were coming out of the woodwork to harass her for locations to Wyrd Jack's smuggling hauls."

"Shit!" Benny tapped on his phone screen. He pulled up the secret photo of Mabel and Wyrd Jack that Jaz had found in the Black Book—we'd texted it to him when he was arranging for us to get into the brewery—and pinched the screen to blow it up. "I remember spotting this when you sent it, Seb. Look." He held out his phone to show us what he'd blown up in the corner of the photo—in the distance was the flagpole that stood over the time capsule plaque. "Literally in the corner of the photo."

"Shit!"

Jaz tossed her sunglasses on the table. "I don't know, guys. Sounds to me like something buried in the ground might be considered 'deep.'"

"Deep in the Three Corners," I said.

We all looked around the table at one another, smiles popping up.

"Wow!" Lulu said. "You really think we'll find something there? Let's go dig it up!"

Benny shook his head. "We'd all be arrested on the spot, Lu. You can't destroy a public memorial in broad daylight."

"Gotta be stealthy about it," Seb agreed.

"This might be another midnight job," I said, excitement coming over me. "We'll need shovels and probably something else to get under that plaque. Anyone got digging tools?"

"It's really out in the open, guys," Benny pointed out. "Even at four a.m. there's still the occasional car passing through. If we decide to pursue this, we're going to need some kind of cover."

What that was, we didn't know.

But after some further excited discussion, we ended up temporarily putting the plan on the back burner while folks stripped down to bathing suits and raced for the water.

We were all water people: swimming would give us clarity.

At least, my hazy head sure thought so, until Seb took off his shoes and marina T-shirt. I knew I stared too long at his chest. I couldn't help it. I felt I'd been trapped in a convent all year and this was the first bare male flesh I'd seen. And as I tugged off my own clothes, I felt self-conscious, worrying about my bathing suit choice. I mean, it wasn't SpongeBob, thank God, but it wasn't a two-piece, either, because I hated how the bottoms always looked on me. As I scolded myself for even caring, I set to work smearing myself with waterproof sunblock and glanced up just in time to catch Seb's gaze roving down my legs. When his eyes flicked to mine, he immediately looked away. No teasing comment, no wink, no nothing.

Huh. I didn't know what to do with that. But as I turned to head to the edge of the dock, I spotted Lulu watching us. Had she noticed me gawking over Seb's body?

Maybe I was paranoid.

Just forget it and have a good time.

Jumping off Benny's dock into the Little River was something I must've done a thousand times over the years. But the dive I took that afternoon felt better than any of them. It was hot enough outside to warm the water to a near-perfect temperature, and this section of the river was unpolluted and clear. Tall trees hung over the riverbanks, creating a dappled patchwork of light that was calming and peaceful. And there was no one else around. All the other neighboring docks were empty while their owners were at work.

Almost better than swimming in the lake.

Almost.

Benny threw out a couple of inner tubes, which we fought over, whooping and laughing. The girls decided Jaz deserved one on account of her arm, but we just couldn't hoist her up on it without multiple attacks of the giggles.

It didn't take long for the boys to dare each other to dive off the top deck of the dock—something that was illegal in our town after a kid died doing it in the nineties. But that never stopped Seb or Benny before, and it didn't now. It was way too far up, and I refused, but it was exciting to watch Seb and his feline, muscled body leap into the air like a daredevil and crash into the water below, covering the back half of the dock in spray.

Glorious. All of it. I hadn't laughed so hard in a long time.

After a time, the group splintered, with Lulu and Jaz settling on chaise longues on the upper deck, and Benny and Seb playing fetch with Punkin, throwing sticks into the river that she happily retrieved. I watched them for a while, laughing, until someone Benny knew from down the block showed up to chat, and he didn't go to school with us, so I didn't know him. So as Benny and his friend climbed to the top dock to sit with the girls, I hung back in the water.

Where Seb had gone to, I didn't know. The fact that we hadn't really said much to each other the past hour or so made me anxious. *You're being silly* . . . Maybe I should just focus on the fact that we might have a new lead for Mabel's clue and stop thinking about him. Besides, maybe I should just head up to the top deck with the others; my arms and legs ached because I hadn't really used any of these muscles this year at school. I swam around to a side ladder on the dock and started to climb when I spotted the rope hammock.

Benny's father installed it years ago: a knotted rope hammock that hung between the dock and a round post that had been driven into the riverbed. The hammock itself hung taut, *just* over the water, so when you got inside it and stretched out, your weight took it *just under* the water. Your body floated in and out of the river while you lazily stared at the tree tops swaying in the breeze above.

Absolute pleasure.

I climbed into the hammock and lay back, letting the river gently flow over me, closing my eyes to bright, warm sun on my face. Music still blared from the lower deck of the dock, and I could occasionally hear distant laughter from the group lounging up top, but I couldn't see them.

A nearby splash jerked my eyes open. Seb swam through the water and disappeared underneath the surface. I tracked him for a bit, then he disappeared.

Only to emerge right next to the hammock.

"Jesus!" I complained, secretly thrilled to see him.

"Boo." He ducked his head underwater to slick back his hair, holding on to the edge of the hammock. "Remember when we found a soggy diaper caught in the rope?"

"I hadn't, no. Thanks for ruining a good thing. You aren't up there trading stories with Brad, or whoever that guy is?"

"No, thanks. He said he'd be taking off soon, good riddance." He settled his arms on the edge of the hammock and peered down at me, his gaze roaming over my black bathing suit.

"You're going to capsize me if you keep pulling on it."

His eyes sparkled mischievously. For a moment, I went rigid because I expected him to try to tip me into the river. Instead, he stopped paddling with his legs and let himself float on his stomach, then he glided up and over the edge of the hammock, grabbing rope near my head to aid him. In one fluid movement, he hoisted himself atop me.

"What are you doing?" I said in a panic, glancing around his head to see if anyone on the upper deck was watching. They weren't. We were alone for the moment.

"Oh, lookie here," Seb said, dripping water in my face. "I've caught me a real, live mermaid in a net."

"If you don't want anyone to know what we've been doing, this is not the way," I said, taking another glance at the dock.

"I never said I didn't want anyone to know." He shifted his position, and water lapped between us. My torso was almost all the way below the surface. "Wait. Know *what*, exactly?"

I didn't answer.

One corner of his mouth curled up.

"Interesting," he said, and with a grunt, he pushed himself off the hammock and dove under the water.

I moved around to track his movements and spotted him

swimming below the hammock as I felt his hand deliberately trail over the backs of my thighs. I squealed and covered my mouth, glancing up nervously at the top deck. But Seb turned in the water and returned. This time, when he mounted the hammock, he held himself above me, breathing heavy and laughing.

"Hey," he said, face glistening. "Maybe we should just go try the time capsule by ourselves tonight. More people attract more attention."

"Maybe," I said, a little overwhelmed to have him so close. "You've been ignoring me today, so I don't know."

"Funny, because earlier, when we were stripping down for the river, I could've sworn you caught me *not ignoring* you when I was *not ignoring* you."

I chuckled. Seb chuckled. And just like that, all my anxieties from the afternoon floated away. I liked seeing Seb happy. The dimples, the white teeth of his big smile. Slits for eyes. His blond hair glittering in the sun. Miles and miles of bronzed skin.

"So," he said, as his legs floated against mine. "I've been thinking about your indecent proposal."

"Staying at the cottage? It wasn't indecent, and—" *And I take it back!* Why was he torturing me? I had a moment of weakness last night, and that's all there was to it.

"You mentioned the possibility of house rules. What kind of rules?"

Oh wow. Okay, so he was actually considering moving in?

"Um, not sure," I hadn't thought it through. "I guess I was thinking about rules to ensure we're both satisfied with the arrangement. Division of labor, that kind of thing."

"Sleeping arrangements."

"And that." My pulse picked up speed.

He shifted his arm above my head, leaning on it for support while his other hand reached out to touch the chain around my neck, shifting my vintage Blackbeard decoder ring around. "You still have it," he said softly.

"So do you. I saw it on your keys."

"Nana Malone said they were magic. Who am I to disagree?" He bit his bottom lip, staring at my ring for a moment longer before he glanced at the top dock. "So, this division of labor in the cottage . . . what did you have in mind? You need me to give you like twenty orgasms a day or you'll find another roommate?"

Hearing the word "orgasm" come from Seb's mouth threw my brain off-balance, but I recovered quickly, laughing. "I doubt I'd find any roommate who could keep that up. Obviously we need to address this . . . topic. I mean, if you were really considering my offer. Probably easiest for us to just to say no and avoid it altogether."

"No sex," he said, a dark, teasing humor behind his eyes.

"No sex," I agreed.

"Is that rule just for me, or did you have it with your roomie back at Harvard?"

"It was pretty much understood," I said, smiling up at him.

He sighed, smiling back at me as he let his head drop next to mine. "So, no sex. I take out the garbage, and neither of us bring home hookups," he said near my ear.

"It'll be a struggle, but sure."

"The no-sex, or the no-bringing-home-hookups?" he asked.

"The garbage part."

His laugh reverberated through me. I looked up at the dock again. Still safe.

"What else do I need to know about this potential living situation?" he asked, nuzzling the column of my neck under my ear.

I shivered. He *definitely* noticed. The weight of his hips slowly sank against mine. "Do I need to pay rent? Cover half the utilities?"

It was hard to think when he was basically lying on top of me. I gave up trying to hold myself away from him and dared to slide my hand around his back, feeling his warm, wet skin. "No rent. Yes to utilities. Pitch in for food."

"Seems fair," he said, opening his mouth like a vampire on my neck. But he didn't bite me. He just breathed me in deeply and sighed against me. "You smell so good."

"SPF sixty sunblock."

He chuckled. "I don't think that's it . . ." His hips slipped into the valley between my legs, and his erection was shockingly warm in the water. I was unable to stop my legs from winding around his.

That's when he bit my neck.

Not hard. Just enough that my hips rose against him in answer. I couldn't control my body. It was doing its own thing, and not listening to the panicky thoughts in my head about being caught. We shouldn't have been doing this out in the open, in front of all the mansions lining the riverbanks and the occasional boat. It was lewd. Obscenity laws were probably being broken. I was hot all over, molten between my legs . . .

Jesus. He hadn't even kissed me.

I wrapped him in my arms. Water rose around us as we both fully sank into the hammock. He pulled back from my neck and lifted his face out of the water, droplets falling over my face. I wanted him. Badly. I don't think I'd ever been so turned on. Not in public, that's for sure.

"What are we doing, Paige?" he whispered. "You think we can really be . . . just roommates?"

Just roommates? Whose dumb idea was that? I didn't even know if I could make it off this hammock without tearing off my swimsuit and begging him to give me those twenty orgasms.

I glanced up one last time at the dock. Lulu was standing on the top deck, peering down over the rail at us with the strangest look on her face . . .

"Oh shit!" I said, shoving Seb off me.

Lulu's face disappeared. I had no idea how long she was up there, but she *definitely* saw us messing around—I mean, if that's what we were even doing. Much like Seb, I had no idea.

I had less of an idea after we scrambled off the hammock and swam to the dock ladder. But it felt like I was the only one freaking out when Seb held the ladder and encouraged me to go first.

"Gonna need a second," he said.

I was too freaked out to even respond to that. I just whispered, "I don't trust Lulu! She's going to tell everyone."

"It's fine. I'll take care of it," he assured me.

How?

Dread awaited me at the top of the ladder. Music thumped as I crested the top and wrung out my wet hair, glancing around. Punkin was asleep on a chaise longue. The guy from down the block who was visiting was gone. Benny and Jazmine were playing paper football on a lounge table, flicking a triangle of folded paper through a series of empty beer bottles. Lulu was trying to get their attention.

Dammit!

Seb emerged from behind me, shaking himself off like a dog. Before I could think of what to do—what to say—he grabbed a beach towel off a table and began drying his hair as he walked toward the other Wags.

"Hey," he called out.

Lulu froze. Jazmine and Benny both looked up from their tabletop game.

"There you are," Jazmine said. "We were about to go looking for you. Benny and I have news . . ."

"Me first," Seb said, scrubbing his hair with the towel. "Just so everyone knows, I'm going to be moving in with Paige for a while. She's got an extra room, and there was that break-in when she first got back in town. You know. Safety in numbers."

"And you're offering . . . what? Your protection services . . . ?" Benny asked, skeptical.

I honestly wouldn't mind another person in the cottage for that very reason, but Seb and I had never discussed it. Obviously he'd been thinking about it.

Seb shrugged. "Besides, I'm a third wheel here. It will give you guys more space."

Holy shit. I couldn't believe he'd just announced that, like we'd been considering it for weeks and finally come to a decision. We hadn't agreed on anything! We were just joking around down there in the hammock. *Weren't we?*

"Paige?" Jazmine said, face concerned. "Is this for real? You're moving in together?"

"Just roommates!" I added a little too quickly. "Totally platonic."

Everyone squinted at us like they didn't believe a word out of our mouths.

That was fair. I wasn't sure if I believed us, either.

"So anyway," Seb said, as if it were business as usual, nothing to see here. "That's our news. What's yours?"

Jazmine held a paper football between two fingers and leaned back in her chair, looking pleased with herself. "Benny and I may have just figured out how we can dig up the time capsule."

"How?" Seb and I both asked.

A slow smile grew across Benny's face as he turned his phone around to show us a screen with a poster that advertised the upcoming Cherry Festival. "Like Mabel's other clue said—right under their noses."

<h1 style="text-align:center">Chapter 19</h1>

If you wanted to do something secretly in public, like dig up a time capsule in the middle of your hometown, you could wait until four in the morning. But as Benny had said, you might have to avoid the occasional car, and of course if you're unfortunate enough for a cop to drive past, you're a sitting duck.

You could try your luck at that.

The Wags, however, had come up with a different approach. The guy who'd stopped by to visit was working a booth at Haven Beach's annual Cherry Festival . . . the same festival at which I'd won Little Miss Cherry Princess when I was a kid. It was always held downtown in June, a couple weeks before Traverse City's Cherry Festival—the bigger draw in our state—to try to nab potential attendees.

This year, the festival was being held this week. In two short days, downtown would be blocked off to traffic, and both tourists and locals alike would gather in the street. Thousands of people. And with a little luck, not a single one of them would be paying any attention to the four of us Wags.

Plus Lulu.

Ugh. I suppose even *I* could tolerate Mrs. SquarePants coming with us if she'd keep her nose out of my personal business. So as the day turned to night, we sat around Benny's party deck, making plans to dig up the capsule. And thankfully, everyone was more interested in figuring out how to accomplish this task than Seb's announcement to move into the cottage.

Since he'd already promised Jazmine's dad that he'd drive an hour down the coast tomorrow afternoon to inspect a boat for repair, Seb thought it would be easier for everyone if he continued staying at Benny's for the next couple nights before moving his things into the cottage with me.

"After the Cherry Festival," I confirmed.

He smiled. "Looks like you and I have a plan, Malone."

Yep, Seb and I had a plan; the Wags had a plan . . . It was plan central, and that made me happy. Only plan I needed to make now was to track down my father in Grand Rapids.

Unless we find the golden statue. Then I'll never need to lay eyes on him again.

Wouldn't that be nice?

The action at Benny's died down around midnight. Once we'd sobered up, Jazmine gave me a ride home, but not without grilling me during the car ride about Seb moving in.

"Have you lost your mind? It's a terrible idea. Didn't I tell you he was obsessed with you?" she said. "If you string him along, playing at roommates, he's going to get hurt."

She was concerned about him. *Him!*

"We'll be fine," I assured her. "It's just a living situation for the summer. No one is going to get hurt."

But as the next couple days passed, the anticipation I was feeling about him moving in continued ratcheting up, and Jazmine's words haunted me. I didn't want to screw this up with Seb, whatever it was. And I convinced myself that I'd made a terrible error in judgment, that we'd never be able to live together without burning the cottage to the ground, and our friendship would once again end up in tears.

Maybe I needed to discuss it with Seb again before he brought all his stuff over here.

By the time the Cherry Festival rolled around, however, I'd quelled most of my doubts. I hadn't seen Seb in person, but we texted a few times, with him asking various questions about what to bring—sheets? Towels? Definitely more towels, we decided. He seemed fully committed to moving in, and everything was normal and good between us.

The next time I saw him was the morning of the Cherry Festival. It was already sunny and hot when Jazmine picked me up at the cottage. We drove into town until traffic started piling up due to the festival parking, so we had to take an alternative route, looping around the stretch of downtown that had been blocked off to traffic. It was nine and already filling with people, so we met up with the others a couple blocks away from the festival area, in the parking lot of Dear Heart Donuts—who made the best glazed doughnuts, period.

As Jaz pulled into a parking spot next to the Speed Buggy, I spotted Seb's white-blond head ducking out of the shop, and my nerves staged a coup.

He strolled toward us with a box of doughnuts, a faded navy baseball cap with a Red Wings logo sitting backward on his head. When his eyes connected with mine, the sweetest smile lifted his cheeks. I smiled back without thinking. It felt as if someone had suddenly come along, reached inside the darkness of my body, and flipped on a million lights.

"Mornin', Wags," he said, opening up the box of doughnuts on top of the Bronco for us. "They're out of the festival crullers already, but the plain glazed is on point today. And I had them throw in a couple fancy ones, in case words like 'cranberry mimosa' rev your engine."

I stuck with the glazed. And while Jazmine gathered our purses to lock them in her trunk, I had a small moment alone with Seb.

He squinted into bright sunlight and spoke in a low voice. "So, is Jaz giving you a hard time about our living arrangement?"

"A little. What about Benny?" I licked crackled sugar off my finger. "Did Lulu tell him she saw us in the hammock?"

"Oh, she did," he said, tugging his cap down more tightly. "I told Benny she must've been wasted because we were just goofing around."

"He believed you?"

"Everything is hunky-wunky," he said, making an okay sign with his thumb and index finger.

"It's hunky-*dory*, dumbass."

"Hunky-wunky sounds best," he said, giving me a little wink. "Anyway, guess the hammock is still our little secret."

Jazmine returned from the trunk as Benny's car drove up and parked next to us.

Lulu waved from the open window, sunglasses up. "Hey, everyone!"

"Hey," Jaz and I said flatly.

"Yo, I got it," Benny told Seb as he closed the driver's door.

"Yes! Excellent!"

"What did you get?" I asked.

Benny waved us behind his Land Rover, where he lifted the back to reveal three shovels, a pry bar, chain, and a long metal tool with a handlebar with the words "Big Red."

"Perfect," Seb said.

"What is that thing?" Jazmine asked. "Some kind of mutant car jack?"

"Hi-Lift jack," Seb said. "This is the extra muscle we need. You can use them off-road, like, if you're stuck in the mud. Or you can use it like a winch to lift heavy objects." He showed us how you could attach a chain to it and pump its handle to lift. "See? A Hi-Lift can pull concrete posts out of the ground, so I figure it can pull out a little, ol' time capsule that's been buried in concrete."

"My dad calls it a farm jack," Lulu said.

We all looked at her. "Is your dad a farmer?" I asked.

"Oh, God no. He's a bookie."

All righty, then. Next time I needed to place a bet on a horse race, I'd know who to call.

"I scoped things out, early this morning on foot," Seb said. "Where they're setting up the festival, and everything."

"How was the time capsule spot looking?" I asked. "Are we still good to go?"

"Exactly as we anticipated." Seb checked the time on his phone screen. "Speaking of, live music starts in an hour. We should probably sugar up and get a move on."

Benny pulled out a small cardboard box from behind the Big Red jack. Inside were five intensely red T-shirts printed with the festival's double-cherry graphic and, in big white letters, *STAFF*.

"Compliments of Brad," he said.

Guess we were really doing this. I blew out a long breath to calm my jangly nerves as Benny handed out shirts. Jazmine and I just put ours on top of our own clothes, but Lulu insisted on running into the doughnut shop bathroom to change. Once we were all decked out like actual festival staff, we loaded the shovels and jack into an old wheelbarrow that Seb had brought in the back of his Bronco, and we covered them with a painter's drop cloth.

"Remember, Wags," he said, taking the handles of the wheelbarrow. "If we're approached by any real staff who ask what we're doing, we—"

"Offer them a glazed doughnut," I said, gesturing toward the box.

Jaz crossed her arms. "Then we change the subject to politics and start spewing conspiracy theories."

Benny waved his hand mystically. "No, we just say, 'These aren't the droids you're looking for.'"

Seb shook his head slowly and picked up the wheelbarrow. "When we're all sitting in front of the judge, I'm going to remind you that you made that joke."

"What's a droid?" Lulu asked.

While Benny tried to explain the plot of *Star Wars* to Lulu, I walked alongside Seb while he pushed the wheelbarrow. The walk to the festival area took about fifteen minutes, which doesn't seem long unless you're pushing a bunch of metal tools up inclining sidewalks. So we took turns with the wheelbarrow until we began to hear sunny, 1960s Motown hits being blasted over speakers—that's about when the crowds on the sidewalks started to thicken. Seb took over the rest of the way, and we formed a line behind him, smiling at people as we made our way to the center of downtown.

A dizzying array of food scents swirled in the air. Moms and dads pushed strollers. Kids carried cherry balloons: red balloons tied to green plastic "stems." Street performers staged magic tricks. Artists created chalk drawings in the middle of the street.

Not a single person asked what we were doing.

Not when we passed a couple of food vendors who were rolling a commercial barbecue grill, and not even when a toddler with a cone of pink cotton candy meandered up to us and asked what we were hauling—his mother merely snatched him away and apologized.

So by the time we turned onto Main Street at the intersection with the time capsule, we were all feeling more positive than I anticipated. Especially when we saw what Seb had already scoped out earlier.

The live music stage was set up on the grassy median in the middle of the roundabout, bisecting it. The front of the stage faced the final three blocks of Main Street, and the back of the stage faced the flagpole that stood over the time capsule. A small trailer was parked between the flagpole and the back of the stage, at the edge of the roundabout—the door marked PRIVATE, PERFORMERS ONLY—and several portable barriers with black mesh screening had been erected around it to cordon off the backstage area and block it from public view.

The time capsule spot was wedged between these black barriers and a fire truck that had been parked across the road to block it off from traffic.

"Oh my God, are we are really doing this?" Jazmine whispered upon seeing it all. And I didn't blame her. Inside my head, I was trying to keep a panic attack at bay.

The stage basically marked one end of the festival. Three blocks toward the harbor, a roped-off beer garden marked the other end.

"No cold feet," Seb warned. "We're here to get what Mabel hid in 'deep corners.' In and out. We're part of the festival crew, and we're supposed to be here."

"It's our job, and we're getting paid to do it," I said, settling into my role as I tried to pump myself up, exhaling long breaths.

"If we get caught, I'll take the fall this time," Benny told Seb.

"Over my dead body." Jazmine shot Benny a dark look.

"Christ, stop it with that negative talk," Seb said. "You guys are messing with my vibe."

The bulk of the crowd were out of sight from back here. Most festivalgoers were in the three blocks on the other side of the stage, browsing long rows of booths filled with cherry-themed art, food, and tchotchkes. Yet stragglers were continually strolling past this part of the roundabout. The fire truck helped to block the area—it sat empty and unguarded—but the time capsule wasn't as shielded from view as I would've preferred. However, when I glanced around to survey the area, I spotted something that would help.

"Look! There's a couple extra of those black barrier screens leaning against the trailer," I said. "Jaz and Lulu, help me."

The girls rallied to lift the barriers, and we walked them toward the time capsule while Seb turned the wheelbarrow around to lug it over the roundabout's curb with Benny's help. All the while, I told myself that everything would be okay—*We belong here*—while my pulse raced faster and faster. Somehow, we managed to set up the barriers around the time capsule, making a "V" shape around the flagpole that blocked our activities from both passersby who milled around back here *and* the backstage area.

Well, *mostly* blocked. But it was the best we could do, and every second we stood on the green seemed to count.

"Everyone cool?" Seb asked, handing out shovels. "All we have to do is dig a trench around the plaque, deep enough to wrap the chain around it. Then we can hook up Big Red and pull it out."

It seemed to make sense, and I trusted that Seb knew what he was talking about. There weren't enough shovels to go around, so Lulu played lookout while the four of us stuck in and got to work, digging.

When my shovel first broke ground, I had a moment of indecision because it felt as if I were destroying the town like some kind of hoodlum. A pang went through my heart. Nana would not approve of this one bit. *I'm sorry*, I told her inside my head as I dug. *But I need to find this in order to stay in school, please forgive me . . .*

Despite my angst, I continued digging around the time capsule's plaque with the others, making a channel around it. When Benny's shovel clanked against something hard, we stopped for a minute.

"Concrete," he informed us while he and Seb squatted over the hole. "Looks like they built some kind of concrete shaft to hold the capsule. Was probably meant to be unbolted at the plaque, then you could reach into the shaft and pull out the capsule."

We'd already considered trying to unbolt the plaque, but Seb thought it would take some industrial equipment we couldn't get our hands on. Our only option was to dig out as much dirt around the concrete shaft as we could, so that's what we continued doing. How deep could it be, anyway? A foot? A yard? I didn't know, so I just dug, dug, dug, then wiped away sweat and peered through the black barrier to make sure no one was noticing us. Then back to dig, dig, digging. I just kept my head down and repeated these actions, trying not think about what would happen to us if we got caught.

Until I heard a small voice behind us.

"What are you doing?"

Chapter 20

We all stopped digging and swung around to see a small boy blinking at us. He couldn't have been more than five or six and wore a double-cherry temporary tattoo stuck to his cheek. Curious, he peered around the barrier with big eyes.

Just a kid, I told myself as my heart raced out of control and visions of prison filled my head. *Calm down.*

"Uh, hey, little buddy," Seb said. "We're doing dangerous work. Where are your parents?"

The kid shrugged a moment before a woman's hand grabbed the back of his shirt. "I told you to hold your sister's hand and stay close, Carl! What's wrong with you?"

Carl gave us a desperate look before disappearing in the crowd with his mother.

"Holy shit," Benny said, clutching his chest. "For a hot moment, there, I was sure the FBI was coming to haul us away."

"You and me both," Seb said.

"Let's refocus, okay?" Jazmine said. "Can't be too much more to dig. How far down does this concrete go?"

Seb stuck his shovel into the channel we'd been digging and made a noise. "It goes to here, like another inch down. Let's—"

Before he could finish, a stack of speakers on the stage crackled to life, and someone from the mayor's office walked onstage to applause as the canned music was turned down. From where we were, if we put our faces close to the black barrier, we could see through to the back of the stage, framed in bright lights, and the back of a woman with big hair and the same T-shirt we were all wearing.

"Good morning, Haven Beach!" she called into the microphone. "Welcome to the fifty-third annual Cherry Festival. We've got a tremendous lineup of performers for you throughout the day. But right now, we wanted to kick off the festival with a local favorite, former Atlantic recording artist and two-time Michigan Music Award winner for best doo-wop group . . . put your hands together for the Haven Beach Smugglers!"

Seb pretended to cheer and scream in excitement while Jazmine mimed sticking something sharp in her ear.

"Hey, I like the Smugglers," Lulu said, pouting.

I started to ask where she'd heard them before—I mean, they played county fairs and the Fourth of July fireworks display, but other than that, they were retirees with bad hips who couldn't do a lot of synchronized dancing anymore. But they could get a crowd going with "Big Girls Don't Cry," which they tore into to start their morning set, cutting off any conversation I considered having.

Bass and drums thumped beneath our feet as the crowd cheered on the Smugglers. It was hard to hear anything over the music, so the Wags used hand signals to communicate. We'd dug far enough to give up the shovels and switch to the tool that would pull the concrete shaft out of the ground.

Time for Big Red.

Seb and Benny seemed to know what they were doing. They set up the tool on the edge of the hole we'd dug. Benny stabilized it and wrapped a chain around the concrete shaft below the plaque. Once the chain was secured, Seb began pumping Big Red's handle while we all held our breath and stared at the concrete. Each pump of the handle lifted the chain by a sliver, at best, and it took strength to use the tool.

It was slow work. Too slow.

As the Smugglers ended an original tune to sweeping applause, Benny switched with Seb to pump the handle. And it's possible that I was distracted when I peered through the black barrier screen for a hot minute because I could've sworn I spotted the back of Pretty Paul's buzz cut creeping around the backstage trailer. But while I was trying to tell if it was actually him or just some army recruit enjoying the lake before being shipped overseas, I didn't notice the security officer walk into our little hiding spot. *Why isn't Lulu doing her job? She's supposed to be lookout!*

"Whoa, what's happening here?" A ginger-haired man in his twenties frowned at the hole we'd dug around the time capsule. Dressed in an unmarked black uniform and wearing a walkie-talkie, he was definitely a rent-a-cop that the festival hired for security. Only problem was that I recognized his flaming orange hair and beady, suspicious eyes.

Off-duty cop!

Chaos erupted inside my head. I forgot everything we'd rehearsed. Visions of my life being ruined filled my head. Losing Harvard, going to jail . . .

"Mornin'," Seb said brightly, wiping sweat from his brow. "Just digging up the time capsule for Miss Betty."

Miss Betty was how the town referred to our mayor.

The security guard cocked his head. "The mayor is digging up the town time capsule?"

"For the award ceremony this afternoon? They announced it yesterday. They're going to open up the capsule onstage."

Good God. Seb sounded utterly convincing. No one could lie like he could. The security guard wore a pinched face for a moment, then he seemed to buy it.

Maybe . . .

"No one said anything about a time capsule in the morning meeting. Who told you to do this?"

"Mrs. Hawsley," Benny said, referring to the mayor's assistant who'd announced the Smugglers onstage. "We've got about half an hour to get it out so that the capsule team can get it ready."

Capsule *team*? Lord, the lies were flying fast and loose.

"I'm going to need to check with her," the off-duty cop said. "No one gave me notice."

Seb shrugged, chest heaving. His reply was cut off by the band onstage starting "Runaround Sue"—a crowd favorite— and once the drums kicked in, no one could hear a thing. The security officer gestured toward the trailer, and Seb gave him a thumbs-up.

The officer slipped around the black barrier and disappeared.

All of us shouted, "Fuck!" to one another but we still couldn't hear anything. All I knew was that if the security guard found Mrs. Hawsley, we were toast. Was she in the backstage trailer? I didn't know. But by the way Seb and Benny started pumping the Hi-Lift jack, I was pretty sure they also were worried that we had mere minutes to get this thing out of the ground.

All at once, the concrete suddenly gave way and came loose. It must have been a couple feet deep and a foot or so in diameter. On Seb's signal, we all pitched in to pull it up—*Why is concrete so heavy?*—but when we hoisted, it slipped sideways and knocked against Big Red, punching a hole into the old concrete, which crumbled and fell apart to reveal a glimpse of silver inside.

The time capsule!

Seb had seen it, too. As the crowd sang in unison beyond the stage, he picked up his shovel and struck the concrete, again and again, until the hole widened and a spherical tube about the size of a yarn skein fell out.

No markings. Old. Definitely the time capsule.

Joy raced through me. *We got it!*

But our triumph was short-lived. Lulu waved and flapped her arms, and when we looked up, she pointed toward the other side of the black barriers, where the security officer was emerging from the backstage trailer with a serious-looking man and woman.

Shit!

We didn't have time for anything, just up and left it all—Big Red, the shovels, and the wheelbarrow. I grabbed the time capsule, and we took off like wild things, racing through the crowd and weaving around couples and kids with cherry-flavored slush drinks. I could feel something dinging against the side of the time capsule with every step, and that freaked me out. I lost the group for a minute when I ducked behind a frozen lemonade truck to see if the security guard was chasing us. Then someone grabbed my shirt.

"Come on!" Seb shouted.

I kicked into gear and raced down the sidewalk with him until we spotted the others and followed Benny, who cut through a narrow side passage between two buildings. We all ran through it, and when we came out the other side, we all stopped to catch our breath.

"Are we safe?" Jazmine asked.

"Maybe for a second," I said, peering down the side passage to make sure we weren't followed.

"Fuck me," Seb said, face red with exertion as he rested against the brick of a nearby building. "People saw us."

"Of course they saw us," Jazmine said. "We ran out of there like a nuclear bomb was headed this way. Did you not hear me shouting, 'Don't run, idiots'?"

I hadn't, honestly. I just panicked.

"Hope they can't trace Big Red back to where you got it," Seb said.

Benny shook his head. "I ended up buying it at that little pawnshop near Paw Paw Lake. I doubt any detective in Haven Beach has the time or interest to drive around to all the regional pawnshops to grill the owners."

"So we just gotta hope no one recognized any of us back there," I said, glancing in the direction of the festival.

"If we get taken down by that little kid with the cherry decal on his cheek, I swear to God . . ." Jazmine said.

"Seb's right. Let's not poison the well with negativity," Benny said. "We might've barely scraped by back there, but come on, Wags. We just had a win."

Huh. I guess we did. Everyone stared at the time capsule, and I felt the same pull to get it open. Double-checking the side passage one last time and finding it empty, I examined the lid of the time capsule. It wasn't even sealed properly, not really. It had a wire lightning-closure mechanism on the lid that was similar to Nana's old canning jars, with a rubber ring around the edge. Just pull up the rusty wire, and . . .

The seal popped. The lid swung open. We stared into the cylinder's darkness.

"Empty?" Seb whispered in disbelief.

It couldn't be! I'd felt something rattling around when I was running. I turned the time capsule upside down and something small fell onto the sidewalk. Seb crouched and grabbed it before I could get a look.

"What is it?" Jazmine asked as we all stood in a circle to see what he'd picked up.

Seb held it out in the palm of his hand, a shocked look on his face. I soon realized why.

It was a single penny. Dated 1930, so probably had been put in there by the people who originally buried the capsule. But that was it. There was nothing. No memorabilia. No newspaper to show current events. No photographs or artifacts.

Just the penny.

Distraught, we all investigated it, inspecting it from every angle in the sunlight, in case it contained another set of Morse clues. We found nothing.

"A penny?" Benny finally said. "We just risked everything for . . . a penny?"

I wasn't sure if I wanted to scream or sob. Had someone else dug it up before us and taken the clue out? Or had we got "deep corners" completely wrong? If so, then why was there nothing left in the capsule?

The Wags fussed and fought about it, desperate to make sense of what we'd dug up. But the fact of the matter was that if there was no clue in here, then we had no idea where to go next.

Had our hunt for the Golden Venus just hit a brick wall?

Chapter 21

*D*enial is a funny thing when you're desperate. Needing to believe that the Wags hadn't just come to the end of our treasure hunt, I told myself that we weren't wrong about the time capsule or its leering penny. No other treasure hunters had emptied it before us. Mabel was the last one inside it, and she wanted us to find the penny. We just hadn't cracked what it meant.

Given time, we would.

I had to believe that. I wasn't sure how or when it'd happened, but I'd come to hope that the hunt was a legitimate path to keeping my place at Harvard and avoiding my father. And I wasn't ready to give up on that.

So after the Wags disbanded with heavy hearts, and I was back inside Heron Cottage with nothing but my thoughts, I did my best to keep hope alive. But as the afternoon wore on, it became more and more difficult to hold my chin up. Paranoid that we'd be identified, I scanned socials, hunting for any mention of the festival and the time capsule, and even when I didn't see anything, I still worried that the shoe was going to drop eventually.

And even if it didn't, I knew I'd have to face that the treasure hunt had just been a diversion. Fun, sure, but it was not a practical way to earn the money I needed to keep my head above water.

The only way I was keeping my place at Harvard this fall was through the man whose biological matter just happened to bring me into this world. *You've got to face him. Just bite the bullet and do it. No more excuses.*

The only thing keeping me from spiraling into a deeper depression was the knowledge that Seb was still moving in the following day. I clung to the thought as if it were a life raft.

After dark, I sat by the lake until midnight, watching the reflected moonlight and talking to Nana in my head. *Was I foolish, believing in the Golden Venus? Why couldn't you have just told me the truth about it, instead of stringing me along with all this hope? Please, if the treasure exists and is possible to find, give me a sign . . .*

I waited, watching the lake. The night sky. The dark beach. Repeating my question like a mantra that would provide illumination. But the dead don't answer, no matter how many times you ask.

The next day, I was still a little depressed when I woke, but my mood brightened when Seb texted to confirm move-in day. Vigor temporarily revitalized, I spent the rest of the morning getting both the cottage and myself ready, eager to see him and discuss what to do about the treasure hunt.

But after lunch, when I heard the Bronco rumbling up the cottage's driveway, panic reared its head, and all of Jazmine's concerns about Seb and I moving in together went haywire in my mind.

My heart raced when a knock sounded on the front door. I jogged to open it, and Seb stood in the doorway with dark shades on and a vertical army duffel bag slung over one shoulder. "Afternoon, miss. Heard you've got a room for rent."

"Sorry, already gave it to another tenant who promised . . . what was it? Thirty orgasms?"

He grinned and made a fist at the sky. "Dammit! I knew I should have offered thirty instead of twenty."

Punkin panted up at me, and when I tugged a thumb, signaling for her to come inside, she brushed by me without hesitation, heading to the water bowl in the kitchen.

"I'll help you bring your stuff in," I told Seb.

"No need, this is it," he said, plonking his giant duffel bag on the floor. "Other than an inflatable paddleboard and my old surfboard, which are in the back of the Speed Buggy. When you're a road scholar, you travel light."

Wow, okay. I carried more with me to Harvard. But I reckoned half his stuff was over here already, all the clothes and various things I found when I first cleaned up. My eyes fell on something sticking out of one of the outer pockets of his duffel. "What the hell is that?"

His eyes dropped to the bag. "Oh, this? It's a prop gun." He pulled out what looked to me like a sawed-off shotgun. "I call it Calico Jack because it's nice and flashy."

I frowned. "Come on, Seb. That's no prop."

"Have a little faith."

"You're the one with all the faith. No guns in this house. Period. The police might be after us for the time capsule—last thing we need is them finding an illegal weapon in here."

"Benny's been monitoring the news. Only one post online about the time capsule, and it's making fun of the festival security. I'm thinking we got lucky."

Thank God. This instantly reduced my stress levels.

"And secondly," Seb continued, "this isn't a gun. It's a replica. Doesn't fire real ammo. Doesn't fire at all." He showed me what he meant. "It came from the Wyrd Jack museum—back when they redid the gangster room about the Valentine's Day Massacre and Bugs Moran. They tossed this in the dumpster along with a couple of prop machine guns."

"Seriously?" I took a closer look. "Huh. Not historical, is it?"

"Nope. Pretty much valueless. Weighs nothing, which gives it away, but it *looks* real, and that's the important part. Sometimes all you need is a little flash to convince people that they'd be wise not to break into your house. That's what this baby is for, flashy ol' Calico Jack."

I had my doubts that Calico Jack would convince a would-be burglar, but as long as it wasn't real, it could stay, I supposed. I wasn't all that happy about it, though.

"How's it going here?" he asked, tossing the prop gun aside. "Have you been wallowing like we have at Benny's?"

It honestly made me feel better to know that he'd been depressed, too. "I'm trying to claw back some hope. If there's any to be had."

"The time capsule was just a little road bump," he said, sounding as if he were trying to convince himself, too. "We're going to find the Golden Venus this time. We aren't kids. We'll figure this out, okay?"

Foolish to even dream that was possible, I knew. But how could I not? I was just relieved that we both still cared about it after all these years.

Seb glanced at the open door of the empty second bedroom. Not totally empty: Nana's bed and mattress were still there, as well as a chest of drawers and a lamp. I'd walked through it several times today already, dusting, making sure I wasn't going to freak out when Seb showed up. It was hard, letting go of memories I had in that room . . . and feeling guilty that I was somehow dishonoring Nana by not making a shrine out of it. But I knew that wasn't true. She was one of the most generous people in town and, more than likely, would be more upset with me if I just wasted the space and didn't use it.

"Hey," he said. "I was thinking, maybe it would be better if we rearrange the room. You know, move the bed to a different spot. That way it will be . . . I don't know. Fresh."

I nodded enthusiastically. "It's a good idea. Let's do that."

We headed into the sunny room and tackled the chest of drawers first. It wasn't all that heavy, but it was old—from the 1950s—and we tried to be gentle with it. Last year, when the Neelys came over to help me pack everything up, we emptied the drawers and separated out clothes to give to Goodwill.

"It's still a nice piece of furniture," I told Seb. "Plenty of room for your stuff."

"I haven't put clothes in drawers since I was a kid," he said. "This is four-star luxury."

We argued about where the double bed should go. Only two choices, so Seb finally relented to my suggestion and we began pulling the heavy wooden headboard away from the wall— something that had never been moved. Not in my lifetime, anyway.

"Holy shit, this is heavier than it looks," Seb marveled. "What's this carved out of?"

"It's called wood. You might've heard of it. Humans made furniture out of it before the age of plastic. Ugh—Jesus! Maybe we should just leave it."

But we'd already pulled it out from the wall, so we figured we might as well finish. Both of us wiggled into the space between the wall and the headboard as Punkin looked on from the doorway with a *These folks are nuts* expression. But once we'd wedged ourselves back there and readied ourselves to push, my eyes lit on a yellowed piece of paper affixed to the back of the headboard.

"What in the world . . . ? Are those nails holding it in?"

"Think they're old tacks. Maybe it's the warranty, or something?"

"On a bed?"

We looked at each other for all of two seconds, then Seb grunted and used his shoulder to shove the bed farther out from the wall so he had space to remove the tacks. He couldn't get them out without ripping the paper, so I got a butter knife from the kitchen and we carefully pried them out.

The paper was folded like a letter, and when I opened it, the bottom third of the paper broke off along the fold line. "Oh shit."

Seb grabbed it out of the air and took the pieces around to the mattress and laid them out, unfolding the top piece carefully.

"Whoa, it's a genuine handwritten letter," Seb said with wonder in his voice.

A very old one, written in a beautiful cursive hand and addressed to "Elsie." The name signed at the bottom was none other than Mabel herself.

"Who's Elsie?" Seb asked.

"That's . . ."

"Oh shit, is that Nana Malone's mother? That photo of her looking like Rosie the Riveter over the fireplace."

Indeed, my great-grandmother. Elsie was Mabel's daughter, the one with whom she was pregnant when Wyrd Jack went to prison. I spotted Nana's name in the text, too—Kitty—and that made my pulse race.

We perched on the bed and read it together:

June 7, 1949

My sweetest Elsie,

If you are reading this, our attorney has given it to you. That means I've passed through the veil and am no longer with you. Please do not mourn me for too long, my dear. Do me that favor?

I'm leaving everything to you in my will, but this letter concerns things that I cannot declare in any legal paperwork: the Golden Venus. Your father never wanted to part with it, and if you'd seen it, you'd understand why. If it ever were to be sold, it would surely bring in wealth beyond belief. But I have tried to ensure you will never need to do so. Greedy strangers who want it are coming out of the woodwork, circling like hyenas. They already believe your father's poem will lead them to one of his hidden smuggling caches. So I've devised a game to keep these covetous hunters occupied and have hidden a series of clues based on the poem that lead to nowhere. However, if you ever find yourself needing to retrieve the sculpture, know that I have placed it in the smuggler's hole your father built near the beach cottage. I showed you how to open it using both rings as keys. I've buried those in a grave at the foot of the stone tower south of Sleeping Bear Dunes. I know you'll remember when I took you there to see your father's old hideout. Hire a boat to take you up the river to the war camp with the tower. The grave is behind the tower, marked with a simple cross.

It is my hope that you'll never need to retrieve the sculpture and will pass along its location to Kitty. Knowledge of its hiding spot is a blessing but also a heavy burden. Perhaps it will be less of one when Kitty is old enough to understand her family's history.

Know that I will always be with you, even past the grave.

All my love,
Mama

"Son of a bitch," Seb whispered, sounding as shocked as I felt.

I blinked at the letter, eyes flicking over the lines again. "We've been following a treasure hunt to nowhere?"

"Jumped in that hole in the cave for no goddamn reason."

"The stupid time capsule!"

"It really was just a fucking generic penny?"

"Jesus." I pushed off the bed and paced the floor around it. "I've been anxiously checking for news that the cops are looking for us since we left the festival. What if we'd gotten in trouble? It was a wild-goose chase the entire time."

I'm not sure why this smarted, but it did. Maybe it was because this treasure hunt had made me feel like my life was opening up again over the wash-rinse-repeat of this past year, that I was finally letting go of the unending grief.

My stomach felt sick. What an utter fool I'd been. "Why didn't Nana tell me about this?"

"Maybe she didn't know."

"The wedding certificate was hidden behind one of *her* paintings."

Seb's face twisted. "Right."

"Besides, she had to know." I pointed at the letter. "Mabel told her daughter, Elsie, and I assume Elsie eventually told Nana because she's mentioned by name—Kitty."

"Maybe she'd planned on telling you or leaving you a note like this. She definitely didn't expect to have a heart attack."

None of us did.

Seb held up his arm to stop my pacing. "You're focusing on the wrong thing. Fuck the time capsule and the rest of it. We can just go straight to the grave she mentions. A tower near Sleeping Bear Dunes . . . ?"

Sleeping Bear was a few hours up the coast. It had been designated a national shoreline—one of a handful in the country—and the park included a couple of islands and adjacent coastline on the mainland. Lots of sand. Really beautiful.

"Paige, listen to me. We can find this grave, I just know we can."

"What if someone already found it? Nana's mother, or even Nana herself. The instructions for finding it are right here."

"No way. Nana Malone was *always* clear that the Venus had never been found. She wouldn't lie to us about that."

He was right. She wouldn't.

"But hey," he said. "What about this smuggler's hole? Mabel wrote that it's near the cottage. Did Mabel and Jack own this cottage?"

I shook my head. "I don't really know, to be honest. Nana inherited it from her mother—from Elsie, but Nana never mentioned it being passed down from Mabel. And I've never seen mention of any cottage in all the books that have been written about them."

"If I were a betting man, I'd say this is Mabel's cottage. Which means the smuggler's hole she mentions is near here."

I couldn't imagine where. There was the cottage and the garage, a couple of trees, and a little grass that still needed mowing. Beyond that was sand and water.

"You know what I think?" Seb said.

"Please."

"I think we have everything we need to find the treasure in this letter. We just have to put our minds to it and figure out a few details."

"A few? How are we in any better position to find the statue now?"

He whistled at me. "You're spinning out. Take a breath."

Was I? He used to tell me that when we were young and I was freaking out about something. I stopped pacing and stood in front of him, exhaling a shaky breath. "I'm okay."

He nodded. "There you go, see? We were on Treasure Hunt 1.0, and it led us to this. All we need to do now is a little research for Treasure Hunt 2.0, and we're back in business."

"Do you really think so?"

"Don't you?"

Oh, I absolutely did. This was the break I'd been hoping for. Or maybe it was even the answer from Nana that I was hoping for last night on the beach. I said a thank-you in my head, just in case. "We can get started after you unpack . . . unless you have other plans."

"No plans are a match for the Golden Venus." Seb fell back on the bare mattress and sighed. "Besides, with all these roomie rules we've both agreed to, we're going to need something big to distract us from putting our hands on each other again."

The way he looked at me from the bed, blue eyes glittering with mischief, we were going to need a lot more than Treasure Hunt 2.0.

Chapter 22

Hard to believe, but Seb and I cohabited without incident for a couple weeks. We went out and bought new sheets for his room. Found an old rug in the basement that was in good shape and hauled it upstairs. Installed a video doorbell camera at the front and a dog door at the back that only unlocked with Punkin's microchip. Ate takeout together on the porch swing. Got high. Watched bad TV. Laughed.

And we researched.

However, that was *all* we did, and I could thank myself and all those dim-witted "roommate" rules I imposed on both of us. Seb worked at the marina all day, so I had the cottage to myself until five or six. A couple of days, I had things to take care of, like a meeting with the family attorney to discuss how much was left in the estate trust—not nearly as much as I thought.

When I found that out, I counted back how many days it had been since I'd left that voicemail at my father's brokerage (too many) and called his office again, hoping to catch a receptionist, or anyone, really. Three times I called, at various times of the day, and three times I got the same, old voice recording. The fourth time, I left a more forceful voice message. I both desired and dreaded a response.

When I wasn't dreading, I spent time reading art history books to get a leg up on my classes for the upcoming school year. Every night after Seb came back to the cottage, showered, and we ate, we'd go into treasure research mode. We'd pull out the laptop, maps, and books, looking for information about any towers near Sleeping Bear Dunes. And we found a lot of interesting things, most of them too obvious, like a lighthouse on a nearby island.

Nothing we found fit Mabel's description.

But while we huddled together over maps, unwilling to give up, Seb didn't once try to kiss me. Or touch me. Or tease me. He called us "roomies" and frequently made comments about following the house rules. So many comments the first week, I thought he was trying to push my buttons. But nothing happened. Not then. Not the second week. And not when the Wags all gathered at the cottage on the beach for Fourth of July to watch distant fireworks over the harbor. It was just a normal celebration with friends.

Horribly, horribly normal.

I only had myself to blame. The whole platonic, no-sex rule was mine, after all, and Seb was just doing what I asked. Maybe I needed to clear the air and find out what he was thinking. Or maybe I needed to figure out why I was getting cold feet about even bringing it up.

He slept in only his bed the first couple nights. After that, he fell asleep in increasingly back-aching positions on the sofa. I was worried that he was weirded out over sleeping in Nana's old room but too afraid to ask him because I was beginning to think that us becoming roommates was a terrible mistake. At least, when it came to our relationship. Our friendship? Getting stronger every day. And I knew I was doing the right thing by giving Seb a place to stay.

But sometimes the right thing and the thing you want aren't the same.

After too many nights of takeout, I tried to do something nice and roasted a chicken in the oven. But an hour later, it was still raw, and I realized the heating element was trashed. Embarrassed, I had to toss the bird when he walked in the door, but we ended up just eating the sides and he acted like it was great. It was not, but he was polite about it. Maybe that's because he'd made a research breakthrough.

"I think I may have found it," he told me.

"Wait, seriously? How? Where?"

"One of the yacht owners who uses the marina is a huge military history buff. While I was getting his boat ready to launch, he got to talking about the War of 1812, and some of the skirmishes in northern Michigan . . . He says there's a ruined 1800s military encampment in the woods. Here."

On an old paper map of Michigan, he pointed to a body of water: a tiny lake, several miles inland from the coastal dunes, with a short river leading there. No roads around for several miles. Backcountry.

"They built a stone lookout tower," he told me. "He doesn't know if it's still standing. It was in ruins when he toured the site twenty years ago. But this has to be it, Paige. Right?"

Mabel's tower.

Could this really be it?

After poking around miliary history forums online, we dug up a little more information. Seb's tower was, indeed, erected around the time of the War of 1812, when Michigan soldiers needed to survey the surrounding land and waters for the British. After the war, the military encampment was abandoned. Now the state owned the land.

"Sleeping Bear Dunes is just three hours up the coast from us,"

Seb pointed out, full of energy and excitement. "We can drive there and back in day. But we don't know exactly what we'll find when we get there. Might be smarter to take tents and camp for the night."

"Camping?"

"Why not. Easiest way to navigate through the backcountry. Don't have to worry about chasing daylight, cheaper than a motel room."

A zip of excitement went through me.

The Wags hadn't been camping since we were twelve.

I was totally onboard. After speaking to Jazmine and Benny, we agreed to give it a go. We could take Benny's canoes with us. Jazmine still had a tent. And so did I, we discovered, when Seb poked around the garage and found it stored in the rafters with old holiday decorations. We even found an old cooler and a box of sleeping bags, both kids and adult varieties.

The next day the Wags all met up at the food truck court outside the marina to discuss strategy. There were two nice surprises. The first was that Lulu wasn't with Benny. The second was Jazmine. She walked up to the table slowly with her head down, looking depressed, then suddenly pulled her arm out the sling and lifted it in the air victoriously.

We all cheered.

"Got the all clear from my doctor this morning," she said, smiling big.

"That'll make a trip through the woods a little easier," Benny said, congratulating her. "Now we won't be a paddle down."

"And when I come back, all the dumb kids in my paddleboard class will have to eat shit for calling me the One-Armed Bandit."

We all laughed, then the topic turned to something Seb and I had discussed in private.

"You've got to convince Lulu that she can't come," Seb told Benny. "I know she's your girl, and I don't hate her, or anything, but this is a Wags-only trip. Please, man. It's only one night away from her."

"She's not going to be happy," Benny said, scratching his beard. "Sometimes I think she's more into finding treasure than we are."

That was what worried me. "I haven't spent time with you without her since I got back," I argued. "We need you, Benny. *Just* you."

"Please," Jaz pleaded.

He looked at her and nodded. "Okay."

We didn't expect Benny to agree so fast. Maybe he was getting tired of her, too. He phoned her right there, even fibbed and told Lulu he was going on a boys-only camping trip with Seb and some other guys. Jazmine and I gave each other secret fist bumps under the table.

And just like that, everything was back. The Wags. The hunt for the Golden Venus. Heck, even Jazmine's arm getting out of the sling. It was all coming together.

Everything . . . except me and Seb.

But even that showed signs of changing a couple days later, when we left for the dunes. The Wags all gathered at the cottage at lunchtime, carting camping supplies and treasure-hunting necessities that Benny bought for the trip: brand-new flashlights, a couple collapsible shovels—seeing as how we ditched all the other shovels with Big Red downtown. Benny even bought a special hiking GPS that would ensure we didn't get lost in the backcountry if we couldn't get a phone signal. Seb oohed and aahed over the new gear while I quietly ogled how nice his arms looked in the sleeveless tee with which he was torturing me today.

Jazmine and Benny stacked my paddleboard on Jaz's—both strapped to the top of Benny's big black Land Rover—the vehicle we'd be taking up the coast. They'd packed two additional inflatable boards in the back. Seb helped me load up the tent we found in the garage and the sleeping bags. Jaz and Benny already had three other tents loaded, so we each had one.

In a grand mood, Seb checked to see that we were alone and said in a low voice near my ear, "An entire night outside the cottage where roomie rules don't apply . . . Anything could happen, don't you think?"

I elbowed him lightly in the ribs, having heard a variation of this teasing for weeks. "So you keep saying. Show me the money, Jansen."

When he didn't reply, I turned to glance at him and our gazes connected. And *oh*. The way he looked at me, like he was willing to throw everything away for another kiss. Maybe I was projecting, seeing what I wanted to see. But the hope that sparked in my chest could have started a forest fire.

It was sunny and warm, not a cloud in the sky over the lake. A perfect summer day. We piled into the Land Rover, boys in front, girls in back with Punkin. As Benny started up the car, Jazmine was the first to say what I was thinking. "I swear to God, if you drive this thing into the harbor with me in it, I will never get in another car with you again, Benny Morales."

"Already did the harbor. I don't wreck in the same place twice."

"Oh, you're like lightning now, are you?"

"Lightning McQueen," I teased.

"Ka-chow, motherfucker," he said, flipping me off with the smallest of smiles, and we were on our way.

The drive up the coast was pretty grand once we got out of a tourist traffic jam in Haven Beach. The lake was a dazzling bright blue. With the windows down and the wind blowing through our hair, Jazmine and I sang along to pop songs at the tops of our lungs, and Seb pretended to stab his ears and begged us to put on "real music."

It was around five when we finally made it to the Sleeping Bear area, where we pulled off the highway into Happy Rest Campgrounds and paid the twenty-dollar fee for one night. The grounds were pretty, mostly tent camping with a few RV spots, and a nice pavilion building in the middle with showers, a TV lounge, and a snack bar.

Seb had reserved us a spot alongside a small creek. It even had its own firepit.

"You did good," Jazmine told him as we unloaded our stuff onto a wooden picnic table.

"I've spent a *whole* lotta time sleeping on the ground," Seb said, hauling out one of the tents. "Guess that makes me a camping expert."

"Was this the 'camping' you did last fall when you got back?" she asked. "Hate to break it to you, Jansen, but there's a difference between camping and being homeless."

"Nothing you can say will put me in a bad mood today," he informed her. "We're on the road to Shambala, baby. By tomorrow, we could be driving back with Mabel's rings—that's one step closer to riches beyond our wildest dreams."

Benny pulled out the other tent and dropped it on the grass.

"What if our wildest dreams are to live forever? Money can't buy you that."

Seb huffed out a laugh. "Good thing your dream is to buy a castle high in the mountains of Transylvania, which will get you pretty close to that forever wish, if you can just convince Vlad to bite you."

"Well, at least my dream isn't to live in an RV," Benny said.

"Not that again," Jazmine complained. "I told you, tiny homes are great in theory, but you're a walking dead man during storms."

I picked up a bag of metal tent stakes and glanced at Seb, thinking about all the travel audiobooks he listened to in his car. "Is that really your dream?"

The expression on his face was so open, just for a second, that I knew the answer was yes before he even said it. "Nice vintage camper would do. See, I figure instead of a storm chaser, I'd be a gold chaser, wandering the country, seeing all the sights. If things go south, you can always pick up and go to a new town." He cocked his head. "Why are you looking at me like that?"

I shrugged. "You used to want to travel abroad. Kinda assumed you might still since you're listening to all those travel audiobooks. Flying to Cambodia to investigate temple ruins is a little different than driving a camper through Nebraska."

"Well, sure. That's the goal. But an RV seems doable in the short-term. Besides, travel of any kind is freedom, isn't it? And considering everything I've been through, any freedom sounds like paradise to me."

Did it? I wasn't so sure. But I gave him a sympathetic look, reached out, and squeezed his arm.

"What about you?" he asked, flicking a glance to my face.

I shrugged. "Guess I'm already living my dream at Harvard."

The geek in me had always wanted to go to a good university, and I'd sacrificed so much to be there. It was difficult to think of any other future but that one.

"Liar," Jazmine said, tying her curls back with a wide scarf. "You always wanted to be a female Indiana Jones."

"I believe the term is Indiana *Jane*," Benny said.

I shook my head. "Nope. Bzzt. Wrong. I wanted to be Indie's cool girlfriend, Marion Ravenwood. She owned a bar in Nepal and could keep up with all the men." We'd all seen *Raiders of the Lost Ark* a hundred times. Pretty much every treasure-hunting and pirate movie.

"Should've gone for an archaeology degree," Seb said. "Then you could own the bar in Nepal *and* get the treasure."

"*You* were supposed to get the archaeology degree," I reminded him.

"That's what audiobooks are for," he said, tapping his temple. "All my education is free. Hell, I've even listened to a book about climate change by one of your fancy professors—what do you think of that?"

None of my art history professors had written books about climate change, but I could tell when Seb was getting defensive, and I wasn't interested in fighting. So I just said, "I think it's great."

He gave me an odd look, then shut his mouth and started laying out one of the tents.

"Hey," Jaz said. "Weren't there four tents? I only see two. Did we forget a couple?"

Benny stuck his head inside the back of the Land Rover. "Holy shit, you're right. There's only two. Who loaded up the tents?"

"We did," I said, as confused as they were. "I could've sworn we loaded all four."

"Guess we didn't," Seb said, sounding a little annoyed. "It's fine. We can just double up, girls in one tent, boys in the other."

We could, and it *was* fine. But it was also odd because I really didn't understand where the other tents went.

On top of that, I didn't understand his plummeting mood. Which was funny, because now that we were "roomies," I understood him less and less. One minute he was whispering about no rules, and the next, he was erecting invisible walls around himself.

I tried not to let it bother me, to just allow myself to be in the moment and have a good time with my friends. We erected both tents and got the rest of the campsite set up. Walked around the camping grounds and inspected the showering facilities—mostly clean. When dusk fell, we got a big fire going and roasted hot dogs that Jazmine had nabbed from Patty's food truck. And we planned exactly where we'd drop in our paddleboards along the river so that we could travel down it to the old military ruins in the morning.

After we realized we needed more ice for the cooler, Seb left the camp to drive the Land Rover to buy a bag at a nearby gas station because they were out at the pavilion. While he was gone, I was goofing around with Jaz near the creek behind our campsite and the ankle I hurt in the flooded cave earlier this month gave out on me, causing me to fall and get muddy. At first, I thought I'd reinjured myself, but the ankle was okay; it was just my pride that was injured, looking like a klutz. Which put me in sour mood.

It only worsened when Seb returned from the ice run. He seemed to be avoiding my eyes and even got up and moved to the other side of the picnic table when I sat next to him. I didn't understand, and it made me feel powerless and anxious. I couldn't handle how hot and cold he was.

When I could walk without ankle weakness again, I left the Wags making up silly ghost stories around the fire and hiked toward the campers' pavilion to wash dried mud off my legs.

A couple of people were inside the lounge, watching TV, but the showers were empty. I grabbed a few paper towels from the dispenser on the wall and took them into one of the shower stalls. There was a button inside that you had to push every thirty seconds to keep the water on—I assumed to conserve water consumption. I balled up the towels and wet them and made a washrag and stuck my legs under the spray of water to wipe away the mud.

When I finished, I washed my hands and headed back through the TV lounge, only to find Seb sitting in one of the seats near the entrance to the showers, scrolling on his phone. He looked up at me with big eyes when I approached.

"What are you doing here?" I asked. "Where's Punkin?"

"At camp." He stood up and glanced back at one of the other two people in the lounge, a grim-looking teenager. "I left my wallet in the Land Rover and saw you come in here. So I'm just making sure you didn't get kidnapped by some Ted Bundy wannabe."

"Chivalrous," I told him, and walked outside the pavilion.

The door opened and closed behind me as I walked down the steps. Seb caught up with me. "What's eating you?"

"Nothing. You didn't need to rescue me from potential serial killers. I can take care of myself, you know. I've been doing just fine for the last year."

"Don't doubt that," he said, matching his stride to mine as we headed down the lit path through the trees that led past the RV spots to the tent section of the camping grounds. "But it doesn't explain why you're being a jerk."

"I'm not being a jerk."

"Okay . . . ?"

I stopped in the path near a tree and turned on him. "Okay, fine. I'm being a jerk because you're ignoring me and I don't understand why."

"I'm not ignoring you. We're talking right now. And we live together, hello? See each other every day."

"Right," I said tartly, struggling to control a storm of dark emotions. "Sure."

"What the hell does that mean?"

I didn't answer him, just turned my back and kept walking to a fork in the path marked by a bench. The left fork would take me to our campsite. But Seb stopped me when I rounded the bench, coming around me to step into the middle of the path with his arms out like a roadblock.

"Stop," he said firmly. "I can't read your thoughts, Paige. Or maybe I'm just dumb. Because I can't understand where any of this is coming from. Did you hit your head when you fell in the creek?"

"Fuck you."

"Fuck *you*! What the hell is wrong with you?"

"Me? *Me?* One minute you're kissing me like we're the last two people on earth, and the next you're cold as ice. Ever since you moved in, you've been acting weird."

"We're fucking roommates, Paige."

"Stop saying that!"

"Why? It's what you wanted. You made these rules, not me. And I could say the same thing about you, by the way. You've been acting weird ever since Lulu caught us in the hammock, like being caught with me is the worst thing that could happen to your reputation."

"That's absolutely not true."

"You move around me in the cottage like I've got a disease!"

"What am I supposed to do? Every time I look at you, you look away!"

"Oh, *excuse me* for trying to be a gentleman and not ogle my childhood friend."

Maybe I wanted to be ogled . . . ? But the way he said this, it made me feel like I was the bad person. Like I was depraved, and he was virtuous.

"Is this all just a big game to you? Lead me on with all the flirting and kissing, then sit back and watch me squirm when you pretend it didn't happen? Is that what gets you off?"

"Oh, you've *really* lost it, now, Malone!"

"Fuck you!"

"Fuck *you*!"

If I could've been granted one wish in that moment, it would've been to push him away and head back to the camp. But I just couldn't reel in my emotions. Like a fish that had bitten a hook, they went wild, floundering and flapping around to get free. My control slipped, and the worst possible thing happened.

I began crying.

All the fight left Seb at once. His eyes went wide, and inside them flickered a mix of concern and *oh no a girl is crying* uncomfortable.

His reaction sobered me up pretty fast. Feeling like a trapped rabbit, I desperately wanted to bolt away. Put some space between us. Recover my lost dignity.

"Paige," he said in a different voice, one that seemed to be struggling to stay in control as he tentatively reached out a hand to me.

I swatted it away and backed up. "Nothing's changed. I've been such a fool to hope there was something real between us . . ."

"Wait!"

"Leave me alone!"

Wild emotion contorted Seb's face. "For fuck's sake, Paige! I'm in love with you."

Chapter 23

I froze. Stopped breathing. Insects chirped in the trees, and noise from a television trickled from somewhere among the nearby RV spots.

Seb's expression was raw and defenseless. He looked a little shocked, like he couldn't believe those words just came out of his own mouth. And I knew right there, in that moment, that he'd meant it.

His gaze fell to the ground, and his shoulders dropped. His Adam's apple bobbed as he swallowed hard and explained, "Think I have been for years. Before Paul and I started hanging out. I left the Wags because I was trying to juggle all these feelings about you that you clearly didn't share. I was miserable being so close to you—it was agony."

"That was . . . we were just kids."

"Felt real enough. Still does."

Tears flowed freely down my cheeks again. I angrily swiped at them, trying to understand what he was telling me. Love?

Love?

"I guess when we were young, I suspected that's how I felt. Later on, I tried not to think about you at all. But no matter how hard I tried to forget about it . . ." He shook his head lightly, and glossy eyes full of emotion flicked up to meet mine. "Then you came back. I saw you on the beach at the bonfire, and I just knew. I just . . . knew."

He was wrong. He meant he had a crush on me, like I had on him. He wasn't in love with me. I would've known. I would've known how he felt. How *I* felt.

Wouldn't I?

Oh God. *Oh God, oh God, oh God . . .*

"You don't have to say anything," he told me, shaking his head like the weight of the world was on his shoulders. "I know, trust me. It's why I didn't talk to you when I drove out to Harvard last year. We're in different worlds. You've got a megawatt-bright future, and I have nothing."

"Seb—" I said, voice cracking.

"You're headed for the stars, and I'm deadweight. I *will* hold you back, and that can't happen. You're probably going to end up with some high-paying professor gig at another Ivy League, or some important museum job, and what the fuck can I add to that? Nothing of value."

I shook my head rapidly. "I don't believe that."

"No? Well, it gets worse when you *really* get to know me. I haven't told you everything. I've done bad shit, Paige. *Really* bad shit. If you knew, you wouldn't even speak to me, much less let me crash in your house."

"That can't be true," I whispered.

"Well, it is."

He was *so angry*. It scared me a little, just for a second. My heart had a long memory and was still wary of how much emotional pain he could inflict if he wanted. But when I squinted at his face I saw through the mask to the pain underneath. Very real pain that I could almost physically feel radiating from him.

"When we were in high school, I went out collecting with Paul," he said gruffly.

I didn't know what that meant and shook my head.

"It's for Big Burg. When people don't pay up, he sends collectors. We had to get the money by any means. Beat the shit out of them, steal it . . ." He shook his head and shivered like someone had walked over his grave. "There are people around town I still can't face because of what I did to them years ago. I'm ashamed, Paige. I'm fucking ashamed, and if I could take back all that time I spent running around with Paul, I would do it in a heartbeat."

"Oh, Seb," I whispered, wiping away fat tears that just wouldn't stop.

He shrugged loosely, looking broken. "So that's why I know it could never really happen between us. I know you deserve so much more than I can ever give you. I know all that, okay? I knew it when I agreed to move in, and I should've told you no. But I couldn't because I'm weak, and I'm a fuckup, and . . . I wanted you, even when I knew I couldn't have you. Jesus, Paige. When we were going to bring four tents, all I could think about was how I could get you into mine because I'm a selfish fuck."

"*You* removed the two tents from the Land Rover," I said, flabbergasted.

"I can't even trust myself, Paige. How can I ask you to?"

I didn't know how to respond to that.

"So *there*. There it all is, the ugly truth." He held up his arms like he'd just been caught shoplifting. "You didn't force me into moving in. I moved in, knowing all this—knowing that you didn't feel the same way, that we weren't really on the same page. Knowing I *shouldn't*. But I did it anyway, and if you hate me now, I understand. I'll move out."

I was trembling so hard, it felt like an earthquake was erupting inside my body. My brain struggled to process what it'd just heard. How could I think properly when there was a firework display exploding inside my chest?

"Sebastian Jansen, if you say one more word about what you think I deserve or how different we are, I will punch you right in your beautiful face."

"Listen to me—"

"No, you listen to me. What if we *are* on the same page? Huh? What if we are? Does that change anything?"

He stared at me with wild eyes, a fight-or-flight expression contorting his face. I could almost see wheels turning inside his head.

"What do you mean, Paige? Say what you mean because I think I'm misunderstanding . . ."

Without another thought, I erased the distance between us and craned my neck to kiss him. Hard. It probably felt like an attack. I just needed him to understand.

To kiss me in return.

But he wouldn't. He pulled back, putting several inches between our faces. Far enough to pin me with an unblinking, intense stare. And he spoke in a low, taut voice. "Say it, Paige. You have to say it, or it's not real. What page are we both on?"

My breath was coming too fast. But if I didn't say it now, I never would.

"What if I'm in love with you, too?" I whispered.

Seb inhaled sharply.

For a moment, I didn't know how to read his reaction, but then he reached for me and pulled me into his arms, and we collapsed against each other.

We slowly dropped to the bench, pulling apart a little but still clutching each other.

He wiped tears from both my cheeks, blinking with dewy lashes as he studied my face. "Paige? What about all the other stuff?"

"There is no other stuff. We'll figure it out. The past never has to dictate the future."

"Are you sure?" he asked in a broken voice. "When we were kids and I fucked up, you didn't want anything to do with me and now . . ."

"I'm sure," I said, and with a start, realized I meant it.

"You're *sure* sure?"

I nodded rapidly, absolutely certain.

For a moment, he looked so dazed, I thought he might pass out. Maybe I would, too. Then a slow smile lifted his cheeks. He cupped my face with his hands, looking at me like he'd just won the lottery. And he kissed me.

Tenderly.

The softest of lips nuzzled mine. I opened my mouth to him, and we kissed like we both meant it. Like we were explorers who discovered a secret door to Shangri-la, and nothing but bliss was in our future.

Like we forgave each other for all the hurt in the past.

It was almost too much for me to handle. When we pulled apart for air, chests heaving, unable to stop smiling, he said, "Sort of forgot we were in public."

"Wish we weren't," I said, fisting the front of his shirt.

"Yeah?" Oh, the delight in his eyes. "Gotta figure out some-place, because some asshole got rid of two tents."

"If you don't take me somewhere and touch me, I'm going to lose my mind."

"You have no idea how long I've dreamed of you saying that." He held my face in his hands and gave me several quick kisses. Then he grinned at me, dimples on display before looking around the dark campground. "But where? Pavilion?"

"With the dirty showers and that awful lounge?"

"Nope. Well, what else? Going out in the woods at night in a public campground seems like a bad idea for so many reasons."

"So bad," I agreed.

His brows lifted. "Land Rover?" Instead of being parked at our campsite like it was earlier, it sat in a parking space near the pavilion after Seb's ice run, due to an RV temporarily blocking the road to our campsite. "Not ideal, but . . ."

He didn't have to convince me further. I grabbed his hand, and we raced to the pavilion's parking lot like we were bank robbers, running from the cops and looking for a place to hide. Seb clicked off the car alarm, and we slipped into the back seat and shut the door. The Land Rover's black windows blocked out the parking lot light, leaving us in darkness as we shoved things Jaz and I had left back here on the floorboards. I could barely see anything, only the whites of his eyes.

"I feel like I'm in high school again," he said.

"Just don't think about what Benny and Lulu have been doing back here."

Seb laughed. Then he tugged my arm, urging me closer. "Are you still cool?"

Was I? My nerves felt like they were being jolted with a cattle prod. It was one thing to be in the moment and quite another to find one's way back to that moment. I blurted out, "I'm on the pill. I mean, just so you know."

He made a surprised noise in the back of his throat and choked out, "Good, good. Pretty sure there are condoms inside the armrest."

"Good, good," I repeated, probably sounding as nervous as I felt.

"Maybe we should just take it slow and see what happens," he suggested. "I have no expectations."

"Okay."

"C'mere."

He pulled me into his arms, and we were back on. He dispelled my nervous quivers by kissing a slow, erotic trail up my neck that lingered on my earlobe, making me shudder while goose bumps raced over me.

"So soft," he marveled. "How are you so soft? I wish I could see you."

"Wish I could see you, too."

Seb shifted away for a moment and flipped on the interior light. I squeezed my eyes closed for a second, eyes adapting to the golden light, and we both chuckled.

"Well, hello there," he murmured, curling both arms around me.

"Hello . . ." My hands dared to slip under the front of his T-shirt and trace the muscled planes of his chest, making him shiver briefly.

Our kisses turned frantic as our hands wandered freely over each other's bodies, in and out of each other's clothes. I fell back on the seat as his hands roamed under my shirt. He kissed his way from my belly button upward, and when he pulled down a cup of my bra and licked my nipple, I nearly died of pleasure.

My fingers struggled to undo the button on the front of his shorts, and we both halted our explorations briefly, chuckling and whispering as we shifted around on the back seat to maximize the space, with our legs dangling onto the floorboards. And that's when I heard it.

A dog barking.

The sound barely registered in my head, it was so muffled and distant, so far away from our erotic cave in the back of the car. Then I recognized the bark at the same moment Seb did.

Punkin.

Seb jerked up his head. We both listened intensely while my pulse thumped in my temples. It wasn't just Punkin we heard. *Someone was outside the car.*

Why did we turn on the interior light? Now I felt *extremely* exposed.

That was my last thought before I felt Seb roughly jerking down my shirt to cover me up, and the door near our heads suddenly opened to the most terrible, blinding light. Was it a UFO? Or the cops, and we being arrested for indecency? *What in God's name is happening?*

The blinding light dropped to the pavement, and there stood Jazmine and Benny, staring into the back seat of the Land Rover with their mouths open and dueling looks of horror on their faces.

"Knew it!" Jazmine said. "You fucking little liars!"

Chapter 24

The walk of shame back to the campsite was mildly humiliating. Thank God it wasn't far because Jazmine was giving us so much grief, despite Seb's insistence that we never intended to keep this from them (we absolutely did) and that it was none of their business (it truly wasn't) and that we knew what we were doing (nope).

Jazmine imitated talking with her hand to show him how little she believed him. And as I ducked into the girls' tent, I gave Seb a look that said, *I have to deal with this,* and he gave me one back that said, *Good luck.* It was the last thing I wanted to do—my body was still hoping all of this would blow over so that we could get back to it—but I needed to make sure Jaz was okay with this. I didn't *think* she was genuinely upset with us, but the guilt made it hard for me to know for sure. She sat on her sleeping bag, pretending to look menacing, with her arms crossed while I zipped up the door.

"Got anything to say for yourself?" she asked in a low voice.

I lifted my shoulders slowly, gritting my teeth. "Oops?"

Jazmine snorted a soft laugh. "Just fell on top of him, did ya?"

"Oh God."

Her laugh was bigger this time. "Go on, confess."

I sighed deeply and crawled to my sleeping bag, flipping onto my back to stare at the camping lantern that hung from a hook in the top of the tent. "Okay, so I didn't plan for any of this happen."

"Mm-hmm."

"We have strictly been roommates this entire time."

"Mm-*hmm*."

"No, really! It's as much of a surprise to me."

"But see, it's *not* a surprise to me. I told you he was obsessed with you."

I closed my eyes and grinned like a Cheshire cat.

"Paige!" she whispered hotly, poking me through my sleeping bag with her foot.

"I can't help it. I'm so happy."

"Holy shit, you really are. I don't understand . . ."

I flipped onto my side and propped myself up. "I need you to be okay with this. We're doing this, me and him."

She raised a brow. "Looks like you already got started."

I shook my head to emphasize that we had not done the deed. "This is all new, and we have no idea what we're doing. But I've never wanted anything more, and I hope you can be happy for us."

"I'm not a monster, Paige. I'm your best friend. I would never not be happy for you when you're happy."

I smiled. "Same."

"Besides," she said, running her fingers through her curls. "Who am I to throw stones when I'm living in a glass house? But why didn't you tell me when I fessed up about Paul? You were asking me if I had a thing for Benny, and I remember thinking that was such an odd question. But now I get it. You were secretly hoping you weren't the only Wag."

"Maybe I was just confused and didn't understand my own feelings."

"And you do now?"

I nodded. A small part of me wanted to share everything he'd told me that night. But it wasn't as big as the part of me that wanted to keep it just for me and Seb. There had to be some balance between honesty among the Wags and our own private business. I knew Jazmine would understand that because of Paul.

Sometimes you just need a little space to make mistakes.

And maybe Seb and I needed more space than others.

Hushed voices filtered in through the thin tent walls. Seb was talking to Benny, and it sounded like an argument. My stomach tensed as I tried to make out what was being said. Were they fighting? Jazmine made a face that said she was thinking the same.

But just when I was starting to worry, I heard Benny's deep laugh, and then Seb's. More light laughter followed, and it sounded like they were okay. I released the breath I'd been holding.

Jazmine's eyes softened. "Our very first Wags couple. Guess it was bound to happen sooner or later."

"Really sorry for not telling you," I whispered.

She shook her head, dismissive. "I suspected. His emotions have been all over the place since you got back. All I ask is that you guys try not to have a terrible breakup that destroys the Wags all over again."

"We've barely even kissed. Give us a chance to screw it up first, okay?"

She snorted a laugh. "Fine. But I'm going to need all the filthy details before you do."

"Deal."

We talked about it a little more, but Jazmine was tired. After we shut off the lantern, I lay awake in my sleeping bag, replaying everything in my head, when my phone buzzed. The screen lit up the small tent when I touched it, so I ducked into the sleeping bag to read the text I'd received from Seb: Everything okay over there?

I sent a quick response: Hunky-wunky. How bout there?

He replied:

> Also hunky-wunky. Haven't changed your mind yet, have you?

I quickly typed: Not a chance.

He didn't text back right away. I waited and waited for him to reply, getting nervous when it seemed like he could be hesitating. Just when I began to wonder if I should amend my reply, his response appeared on my screen:

> When we get back home, new rule. No clothes inside the cottage.

A thrill went through me. I texted: Being naked all the time might be cold.

This time, his response was swift:

> I'll keep you warm, don't worry.

I grinned at the screen, but before I could reply, Benny's deep voice came from the boys' tent. "Can you two save the sexting for tomorrow? Some of us are trying to sleep on hard ground, and if those fucking screens don't stop lighting up the tents, I swear to God . . ."

Jaz snorted a laugh and called back in the dark, "Thank you, Benny."

"Fine. Good night, everyone," Seb's voice said.

I shouldn't have doubted Benny's and Jazmine's reactions to Seb and I. Whatever happened in the future, I knew that night that the Wags were going to be okay.

***

WHEN I WOKE the next morning to a chilly tent, Jazmine was already sitting up in her sleeping bag. Judging from the silence in the boys' tent, we were the first ones up. I retrieved a change of clothes and some toiletries, and Jaz and I shuffled off to the pavilion to shower. By the time we got back to the campsite, Benny texted they'd already showered and gone to move the Land Rover back to the site so we could load up. Jazmine and I broke down the tents, and when we'd gotten most of the site packed, the boys drove up.

Seb jumped out of the Land Rover wearing cargo shorts and a long-sleeve red T-shirt that read *World's Sexiest Grandpa*. When his eyes met mine, everything melted inside. We smiled at each other like absolute fools.

"Mornin'," he said, holding up a bag of food. "Luke-warm breakfast muffin, anyone?"

"Is this an apology muffin?" Jazmine asked, snatching the bag from him. "Because I'm hungry enough that it actually might work."

"Definitely the sorriest muffin I've ever eaten," Benny said with a little humor. "Eat up, Wags. We've got to drive to the spot, blow up two paddleboards, and make sure the coordinates are right."

"Chop-chop," Seb said, clapping his hands twice before pulling down his sunglasses over his eyes. "Let's find Mabel's rings so we can get back home."

I couldn't agree more.

When we ate and got everything loaded, Benny took a quiet county road that curved through the woods until they opened up to flat marshland farther east. The place we wanted to drop into the river was halfway between Sleeping Bear Dunes and Traverse City, and the Land Rover's GPS turned glitchy. Too rural, I supposed. But we had Benny's portable GPS, and after twenty minutes of driving, we found a tiny dirt road that dead-ended at our river.

"Holy shit, this is where backwoods killers dump their bodies," Seb remarked when we parked in some underbrush. "Look, tire tracks. Fairly fresh ones. Hope we're alone out here. Punkin, I'm counting on your warning bark, girl."

Benny inspected the tracks and dismissed them. No way of knowing exactly how fresh they were, really, and more likely that they were made by people wanting to fish than any *Deliverance* types. So Seb and Jaz divided the gear we'd be needing into a couple of backpacks. Then we pulled out the hard paddleboards and inflated the others. When we were all ready, Seb found a break in the underbrush with better access to the river. One by one, we put our boards on the shore, stepped onto them, leashed up, and pushed away from the bank, with Punkin joining Seb on the back of his board.

The river wasn't wide, but it was fairly slow-moving. When I stepped on my board, it took me a second to get my balance. I hadn't been boarding in a year, and it showed, unlike Jazmine, who was so happy to be back in the water, both arms functioning, that she whooped out a joyous call, loud enough to scare up birds along the riverbanks.

"I'm back, universe!" she shouted. "Let's do this!"

I pushed off with my paddle and did a quick pivot to get myself going in the right direction, sharing Jazmine's good mood as air rushed over me. It felt *so* good to be moving. I quickly forgot about the chill on my bare legs. And once we were properly on the river, it turned gorgeous, with a canopy of trees bending over the water and dappled morning light coming through. The four of us streaked across the water's surface, laughing and breathless as we tried to race one another, navigating around rocks and wayward tree branches. Seb and I couldn't stop grinning at each other like fools. He breezed past me, holding out his arm to grab my ass, and I nearly knocked him with my paddle.

The GPS coordinates of the old military camp were about a mile and a half away. We made good time when the river was straight, but then hit a lot of twists and turns that Jazmine navigated breezily, but the rest of us had to slow down. All in all, it took us about half an hour, and once we rounded one final turn in the river, I spotted the stone tower.

"Look!" I shouted.

"Stone tower, check," Seb said. "And completely deserted."

Benny pointed. "Look, on the bank."

The perfect sandy spot to stop and get off our boards. Lots of tracks here that looked like they could've been made by canoes or kayaks. "Who comes out here? I wonder. Military history buffs?"

"Who knows," Jazmine said. "Might just be a spot local kids like to explore."

"Hope they haven't explored any graves," Seb said, gliding

up to the bank with the nose of his board and stepping off after Punkin.

We all followed suit, pulling our boards onto shore. Then we took a look around. White pines circled an open area that was overgrown with creeping vines and tangled underbrush. I spotted the remnants of a few structures—old bricks, and what might have been a log cabin at one time but was now just half a wall. If you squinted, you could see how it would've made the ideal spot for a snug encampment at one point in time. But now it was nothing but blight and ruin.

The ruined stone lookout stood tall in the center of it all. It was crudely built from mismatched hunks of stone, and when it was still intact, it probably stood four stories high. Now, the back half of the tower was missing. Definitely not climbable unless you wanted to feel what it was like to have a building collapse around you and get buried in stone.

"Bastards!" Seb said, slapping his neck. "These mosquitoes out here are no joke."

We had insect repellant. I got him to turn around so I could retrieve it from the front pocket of his backpack, and when we'd all doused ourselves with it, we explored the encampment. The good thing was that there wasn't much to look through but what we'd already seen when we paddled up. The bad thing was that the wild grass was to our waists, so it was difficult to see anything on the ground.

Seb and Jazmine got out the collapsible shovels and extended their handles so they could use them to swat at the grass. "Where's a machete when you need one?" Seb asked.

"Let's focus, shall we?" Jazmine said. "Tell us what the letter said again so we know where to look."

"Behind the tower," I remembered. "Mabel said it was behind the tower marked with a cross. So, over there . . ."

Where an entire wall of the tower had collapsed into rubble.

"What if the grave is under all this stone?" Benny asked. "No way we can move all this, even if we did it all day."

He wasn't wrong, and I shared his worry. But we carried on, splitting up and combing the grounds around the rubble, swatting at the high grass, searching for anything. After slapping my millionth mosquito and nearly reinjuring my weak ankle on a loose rock, I stopped to take a breath. A dark shape caught my eyes in the nearby woods. I cautiously took a few steps into the trees.

It was a cemetery.

A ruined one, covered in moss and juniper shrub. I quickly counted seven simple gravestones that all seemed to be made from the same rock used to build the tower.

"Guys!" I called over my shoulder. "Come here, quick!"

I pulled aside foliage to make my way closer to the graves while the gang ran up behind me.

"Oh. My. God," Jazmine said, letting her mouth drop open.

"It makes sense," I said, excited. "Why would they bury soldiers right next to the lookout tower? Off here in the woods is more ideal."

"Are they solider graves?" Seb asked while Punkin sniffed around.

None of them had names. One of them had a date of 1811. "That's my guess. How could this be left out here, forgotten like this? It's so sad. That guy who talked to you about this place—had he seen these?" I asked Seb.

He shrugged. "Didn't mention them. But I didn't tell him I

was looking for a grave, either. Wait, do any of these have crosses, or are they all these plain stones?"

Benny crouched and brushed away a blanket of decomposing leaves.

There it was. A flat cross made up of several pieces of stone was embedded in the forest floor.

"Holy shit."

"Is that the only one?" I asked. "Check around before we start digging."

We ran around the graveyard, buzzing with excitement as we searched.

"Nothing," Benny said. "This is it. Has to be."

We'd take turns digging, starting with Jaz and Seb. It wouldn't be easy, I knew that much after digging up the time capsule. In movies, people always dig graves in minutes when it would really take hours with a shovel. And when Seb's and Jazmine's arms grew weary—harder to dig with these little camping shovels than the full-sized ones we used before—we were about to trade off.

But Seb thrust his shovel into the ground, and went very still.

"What was that noise?" Benny asked. "Sounded like metal."

"Hit something. Not rock. Oh shit, hold on."

"Can't be a coffin," I said. "It's not deep enough."

He threw the shovel aside and began scooping out dirt with his hands, working frantically as we all crouched around the grave. Then I saw it under his fingers as he wiggled it free.

A tin container with a lid. Orange and black. When Seb wiped away dirt, we all saw vintage artwork and the words: "Sir Walter Raleigh Smoking Tobacco." Seb's face was wide with anticipation when he looked up at me just for a moment, then he cracked open the lid.

Inside was a piece of muslin cloth that was tattered and falling apart, half-eaten by bugs. But when I reached inside to pick it up, the material fell apart in my fingers to reveal what it had been hiding.

Two gold wedding bands held together by a piece of twine. Initials were engraved inside the bands: "R.T.M." and "M.E.S."

"It's Jack's and Mabel's wedding bands," I said, absolutely floored.

"Oh shit," Jaz whispered.

"WOO-HOO!" Seb shouted.

"Hell yeah!"

"Is this real?" Benny asked. "These are really what we need to finally get the treasure?"

"I think so," I answered, feeling stunned. Like I'd been punched in the solar plexus.

But before I could think too hard again about a mystery lock near the cottage that these rings might somehow open, noise farther inside the forest caught my attention. Not just mine: Punkin started barking a loud warning.

We all looked up to see two figures emerging from shadow, one big and one very small.

"Digging up graves is such a bitch, isn't it?" the big one said, pointing a handgun in our direction.

Pretty Paul.

Somehow the disconnect of seeing his scarred face all the way out here didn't surprise me as much as the small figure who stepped to his side.

"Lulu?" Benny said, standing up and looking dazed.

"Hi, Benny," she said, sounding slightly less perky than usual. "Really sorry it came to this."

My heart pounded fiercely. I didn't know what was going on, but I knew it wasn't good. As fast as I could, I dropped the rings inside the tobacco tin and shoved the lid back on.

Punkin barked enough to wake the dead. Paul kicked out his foot at her, but she just jumped back and kept barking.

"Shut your mutt up or I will," he told Seb, who shouted at the dog to get behind him. She sort of obeyed.

"What the hell, Paul?" Jazmine shouted, standing up from the grave. "Have you lost your mind? Put that thing down."

"Why are you here?" Benny asked Lulu, a look of growing horror on his face.

Paul laughed without humor. "Shit, Benito. They say you're as smart as little Ivy League, over there, but I'm not so sure. Lulu's my cousin, you fucking idiot. No one suspects sweet, little Lulu. She's been playing you all summer."

Holy shit! I *knew* something was off about her.

"You rancid little bitch!" Jazmine shouted, and for a second, I thought she was going to jump on Lulu. But she didn't get a chance.

With an angry shout, Benny went berserk, rushing Paul like a linebacker.

He stopped short when Paul lifted the muzzle to Benny's forehead.

"Back off right now," Paul said, "or we're going to need that hole you just dug."

Benny slowly raised his hands with hatred burning in his eyes, and we all stood in place, chests heaving, waiting for a pin to drop. Everyone except Punkin, who'd backed away but still barked. And Seb, who sighed deeply and crossed his arms over his chest.

"Come on, Paul," he said. "You think that piece of plastic in your hand is going to fool me? You taught me that trick, jackass. It's not a real gun."

Paul's head slowly swiveled to look at Seb with curiosity. Then he smiled and aimed the gun at the open hole of the grave. A bullet ripped through the air and hit the dirt a few feet in front of me. A cloud of debris exploded. Punkin lurched away, finally cowering behind Seb.

"Jesus!"

"For fuck's sake!"

"What the hell, Paul?"

Paul's face stared back through the falling dust, eyes fixed on Seb. "Guess you don't know everything, do you? Big Burg sent Lulu out to Kalamazoo for recon after that gold brick turned up in the sewer. Didn't expect you'd just invite her to move into Morales Manor, Benito. Talk about a gift . . ."

"What the hell?" Benny mumbled, shock lining his face.

"Personally," Paul said, "I told my daddy no way in hell a twenty-six-year-old barmaid could pass for a college student, but the girl is good."

Lulu gritted her teeth and made an apologetic face. "Really sorry, Benny. I had fun. I truly did."

Benny's face crumbled. My heart hurt for him.

Paul tapped the side of the gun with his index finger several times. "Knew you weirdo Wags were really onto something when you wouldn't invite Lulu to this grave-digging party. What'd you find? The pair of ring keys? Don't act so surprised. It's pretty easy to learn someone's phone passcode when you're sleeping with them. We've seen your texts, Benny." He craned his neck toward me. "And yeah, I see you trying to hide what you just found, Malone. Go on, hand it over to Lu."

He pressed the muzzle of the gun against Benny's head to emphasize his command.

Punkin began barking again.

What could I do? I handed the antique tin to Lulu when she reached for it, and told her, "Please, don't do this. These rings belong in my family. They're part of history."

"Sorry," she said. "It's not personal."

How could it not be personal? She was living with Benny, hanging out with all of us. I'd been betrayed by so many people in my life—my own father, even Seb—but you never got used to the empty feeling.

"Check to see what's in there," Paul told Lulu.

She complied and held up the rings. "Bingo."

"Beautiful. Big Burg will be happy," he said, instructing Lulu to put them back in the tin for safekeeping. Then he shoved Benny in the chest, forcing him to back up with the rest of us before he trained his sights on Seb. "Now, if you'll do me one last favor, old buddy of mine, old pal. We know there's a lock these fit into near that old beach cottage. Wanna tell us where that is?"

"You could try sticking them up your asshole, see what that unlocks," Seb said.

Paul sighed heavily and pointed the gun at me. "Lulu says you got a little thing going with your old flame here. Maybe you don't want to see her head explode. I wouldn't."

I wouldn't, either, but Seb's face showed no worry. "We don't know where the rings go, you prick. Haven't figured that out yet. See, if you and Lulu had been a little smarter, you would've waited for us to suss that out before you charged in like a blind bull, stomping all over this pitiful spy operation you set up with

Lulu," Seb said. "But you didn't, and now all you've got are a couple of old wedding bands worth diddly shit."

Paul squinted at Seb like he was trying to figure out if we were holding out on him. Then he lifted his head toward Jazmine. "Is he telling the truth?"

"Is *that* what you want to ask me?" Jazmine said. "Think really hard before you answer, because the minute you walk out of these woods, you and I? We will never speak to each other again. Not as friends, not as enemies, not as *anything*."

He blinked furiously and clicked his jaw to one side. "We'll see."

"We'll see nothing," she said. "You just declared war against us."

"I couldn't care less about this hidden treasure shit," he said, defensive. "This is my dad's deal. Like every idiot in this stupid town, he's chased it since he was a kid. So if you want to fight a war, you're going to have to go toe-to-toe with Big Burg. I'm just the messenger."

"You are who you're aligned with," I said. "Can't have it both ways."

"Can't change your family," he said. "You should know that better than any of us."

I glared at him.

He chuckled darkly. "Yeah, Big Burg says your old man used to run with him now and then, back in the day. By the way, is Hound Dog Lee still spending your dead mama's fortune? He had the right idea—didn't run around town, digging up old graves to hunt for treasure. He just married the treasure."

My face heated. I hadn't heard anyone call my father "Hound Dog Lee" since I was a kid. "Keep my mother's name out of your mouth," I warned him.

"Right. Well, how 'bout this. You tell me where the lock is that these rings unlock, and I'll never speak of old Hound Dog or your old lady again. RIP."

"We don't know, shit stain. We *don't know*," Benny shouted.

Paul cocked a brow. "All right, already. Calm your ass down, Benito. I believe you. Treasure hunting is hard. That's why we're letting you do the legwork. Here's what I'm going to do. Lulu and I are going to hold on to these rings for safekeeping. Meantime, your little Nathan Drake gang will do whatever it is you do and figure out where these gold bands go. You can't open a lock without the keys, so now we need one another."

"Absolutely not," Seb said. "Give us back the rings and we'll cut you in."

Paul laughed. It almost made him look like a normal human being. "Nice try, bruh, but I'm not falling for the biggest liar in town. *We* keep the rings. *You* find the lock. If we don't hear back from you in, say, a week, I might be forced to take more extreme measures. That beach cottage looks awfully flammable, wouldn't you say? Or maybe the Moraleses' mansion. Or—wait, inspiration is hitting. How about Neely's Marina . . . ?"

"Not funny," Jazmine gritted out.

He looked at her, and something like hurt crossed his eyes. He blinked it away and told her in a softer voice, "Not laughing."

"If you think you can threaten my friends and family like this and walk away, you are *so much dumber* than I ever imagined," Jaz said, sounding fierce but vaguely heartbroken. "That was a hard line you just crossed. Can't uncross it. So I guess we are really and truly over."

"You and I? We never started," Paul told her bluntly. "So there's nothing to be over. We're just back to being enemies now, like the good old days."

Fucking hell. I tried to quickly think of some other way to bargain with Paul, but he was already whistling for Lulu to head back into the woods with him. "One week," he said, pointing his gun at us while he backed up. "Be seeing you."

Then he turned around, stuck his gun in the back of his waistband, and disappeared into the trees with Lulu.

Chapter 25

The Wags were all in various states of shock after Pretty Paul left us standing around the dug-up grave, empty-handed and depressed. Seb blamed himself for befriending Paul all those years ago. Jazmine was trying to hide it, but she was clearly wounded by Paul's betrayal and swore to us that she never once mentioned the treasure hunt to him.

"I talked about treasure hunting back in the day, when we were kids," she told us. "But I never said a word about this hunt."

She didn't have to, not when Lulu was doing all the work. I knew Jaz was reeling over Paul's betrayal, but she wasn't the only one. Benny let a stranger into his life, and she manipulated, lied, and tricked him at every turn. He wasn't some gregarious, open guy who dated on the regular. He must've really liked her.

"How could I have been so blind?" he said as we tried to console him. I couldn't imagine how it felt to be in his shoes, all I knew was that I was furious on his behalf.

Furious for all of us.

Treasure or no treasure, those rings belonged to me. My family. *My* history. And I would get them back by any means necessary. Easiest would be to track Paul and Lulu and surprise them before they left the area, get the gun away from him without getting anyone hurt. I briefly tried to follow their tracks into the woods, to see where they'd come from. No nearby roads, so they must've hiked for a good bit.

"How did they even find us out here?" I asked, stunned.

No one said anything, then Benny groaned, fishing out his phone. His fingers quickly flashed over the screen, then he squeezed his eyes shut. "Fuck. She must've flipped on location-sharing on my phone."

"Can you still see her location?" Seb asked.

He showed us. The blip on the map was moving at a pretty good clip away from the war encampment. She wasn't walking anymore, she was inside a vehicle. Seb and I hiked a little farther in their general direction with Punkin and found an unmarked dirt road with fresh tire tracks.

"Son of bitch," he said under his breath. "These are motorcycle tires. Skinny ones. Maybe motocross."

I blinked at him. Where had I recently heard about a pair of motorcycles . . . ?

Oh God. "Paul and Lulu," I said. "They were the ones who broke into the cottage and trashed it!"

Seb lifted his head to the tree canopy and let out a frustrated yowl. "When is he going to stop fucking me over?"

"He fucked *us* over," I pointed out. "All of us Wags! That was his mistake. We won't catch up with him today, but he's a dead man walking, as far as I'm concerned. I don't know how, yet, but we're getting those rings back."

It was one thing to believe that in a moment of fury and hurt. Another thing to keep believing it when you're stuck in a Land Rover for hours on the ride back home, scratching mosquito bites, and everyone's mental states are sinking. I think we all blazed through several stages of grief during the return trip, each for our own reasons. And when our perfect summer day took a turn for the worse, and dark clouds formed over Lake Michigan, it was the cherry on top of the whole shit sundae.

We dropped off Jazmine at the marina first. Her mom met us at the Land Rover and helped Jazmine carry her stuff inside. When she asked what was wrong with all of us, Seb said, "You're looking at a crew of fools right now, Mrs. Neely. Once we get over the feeling of being duped, we'll be okay."

"Well, can you get over it by tomorrow? We're having our first Sunday brunch of the summer. I want you all there, okay?"

Sunday brunch was an honored Neely tradition. Anyone who was important in town had showed up for mimosas and eggs over the years. What could we say but yes?

I hugged Jazmine hard and repeated Seb's assurance that everything would turn out all right eventually. But at the moment, we were all going through the motions.

Benny dropped off Seb and me at the cottage next, and he was so down, I begged him to stay with us instead of going back to an empty house. But he declined. "I'm terrible company right now," he told me. "Let me lick my wounds."

After unloading our stuff, Seb and I watched Benny pull out of the driveaway right as the darkening skies lit up with lightning. A summer storm was here. Nothing to do but round up Punkin after she took a long pee on Mr. Legs and hunker down inside.

Seb dropped our bags in the middle of the living room floor as rain began falling against the roof. "Welp. This was not the homecoming I fantasized about," he said.

"Same." I dragged the cooler into the kitchen and unloaded the remnants of our food into the fridge. "Never in a million years would I have thought I'd have a gun pointed at me."

"Unfortunately, I've already had the pleasure on more than one occasion. Not a good feeling. I'm sorry, Paige. I know I keep saying it, but Christ."

"And I'll keep saying that it's not your fault. You can't control another person's behavior. Paul chose to be dick."

"It's his fucking father. Paul would be a different person if it weren't for Big Burg."

I closed the refrigerator door. "Paul's in his twenties. He can make decisions for himself. You grew up. Why can't he?"

Seb puffed out his cheeks and exhaled heavily, crossing his arms behind his head as he leaned back on the sofa. "Don't know the answer to that, but I can only see one solution to this problem right now, and that's breaking into Big Burg's compound and stealing the rings back."

I slammed the refrigerator door. "Absolutely not. And if you do try to sneak off and do that, and you get yourself killed, I will be furious at you for the rest of my life."

"Damn, Paige," he said. "You look a little furious now."

"Aren't you?"

"I'm just sad, I guess. The past forty-eight hours have been a roller coaster."

He wasn't wrong. I closed the cooler. There was still a lot of mostly melted ice inside, but it was too big to dump in the sink.

Thunder struck near the cottage. It was really coming down out there.

"What a mess," Seb said, looking out the window as Punkin settled herself on the rug in front of the fireplace. "Guess our no-clothes rule is going to have to wait."

I hesitated at the kitchen island, pretending to look through the mail as a wild thrill zipped through me. "Does it?"

I couldn't see his face from where I stood. But something in the air between us shifted radically, and the cottage suddenly felt a lot smaller.

A floorboard creaked behind me. "I suppose, on one hand," his voice said, a little closer than it had been, "it feels disrespectful to be thinking selfish thoughts when Jaz and Benny are sitting home alone, depressed."

"Invite them over, then."

Another step. "Eh, I'm all for experimentation, but I'm a one-woman kind of guy."

I smiled to myself and straightened the bills. "You said, 'On one hand it feels disrespectful.' What's on the other?"

"Well," he said behind me, very close now. "On the other hand, maybe getting naked would cheer us both up. You know, like being on an airplane when you're about to crash—everyone knows you don't help others until you put an oxygen mask on yourself."

"Sure, yep. That's logical," I said as my stomach took a nervous dip.

"The logical thing to do," he agreed, breath tickling the hair on the back of my head. "Practically our sacred duty, don't you think?"

"Can't ignore a sacred duty." I dropped the bills and turned around as my heart hammered. We both looked at each other and chuckled nervously.

After a rumble of thunder, he reached for my face, fingers gently trailing down the hair that framed my face, tucking a tendril behind my ear with a trembling hand.

"Hey," he said softly. "Stop thinking, analyzing, and second-guessing. It's just us."

"Just us," I whispered in agreement. His face was so close. Our breath intermingled. "Don't think."

"That's right. Don't think . . ."

His hands cupped the back of my head as his mouth came down on mine. His kiss was soft and gentle, achingly slow. Pleasure rippled through me, and an unbidden moan escaped. Seb's hands tugged at the hem of my shirt, questioning, and before I could think—or *not think*—I lifted my arms above my head and allowed him to take it off.

His heavy-hooded gaze roamed all over my skin. My heart hammered wildly against my rib cage when he lightly traced his finger down the valley between my breasts. Barely a touch at all, but it caused battalions of goose bumps and made me shiver.

"So beautiful," he murmured, letting his hand fall away while he licked his lip and blinked for a moment. Then he reached over his shoulder and pulled his T-shirt over his head, tossing it aside. His bronzed chest lifted and fell hypnotically under my gaze.

With increasing urgency, we stripped off the rest of our clothes. Shoes, shorts, underwear . . . it was as if the very fabric was burning our skin, forcing us to get rid of them as fast as humanly possible.

There. Both of us naked. Once I kicked away my shorts and got over the shock of it, I couldn't take my eyes off him. Difficult not to. His erection proudly jutted out between us.

"Jesus," I mumbled.

"Is that a *good* Jesus or a *bad* Jesus?"

"You're practically a work of art," I said appreciatively.

His low chuckle sent a rush of pleasurable chills over my skin. "Well, then. High compliment, coming from you." He slid an arm around me to pull me in closer, and I felt his heavy length pressing against my stomach.

So much warm skin . . . I faintly smelled remnants of the day, soil and mosquito spray, and, underneath it, just Seb. I was going to lose my mind.

He held me against him and looked down at me, a halo of wild, blond waves floating around his face. "It's always been you, *always*," he whispered. "Tell me you want this, too. Tell me you're mine."

"I'm yours," I whispered desperately.

He groaned, then his mouth captured mine again, possessive and reckless. He kissed me like he was worried all of this could disappear without warning, like I might get washed away with the deluge of rain that poured against the cottage windows. He pressed me up against the archway separating the living room from the kitchen, hands exploring everywhere. The curve of my waist. My hips. My breasts.

When he slipped his hand to stroke between my legs, I gasped so loud, I startled him. But it felt too good to waste time being embarrassed. So I reached between us and wrapped my hand around him, hot and hard and velvety, and he groaned with pleasure. At least for a moment.

"Stop, stop," he begged. "This is going to be over before it even starts."

I released him reluctantly, a little drunk with power, but that was quickly eclipsed by the same desperation that I'd felt in his kiss. "Please. I'm dying."

He slung an arm around my back and lifted me off the floor like I weighed nothing. My legs automatically curled around his hips, and for a moment, I didn't know if this was how it was going to happen, up against the wall. Some feral part of me wanted that. But he grunted and carried me several steps away, into my bedroom, nearly running us into the chest of drawers when he struggled to turn on my bedroom lamp while I kissed his ear.

"Jesus," he repeated several times.

He set me on the bed. I lay back as he kissed his way up my legs, pausing at my knees to look me dead in the eyes. Did he want my permission? He slipped a hand between my knees, and my legs fell apart to accommodate him. Then his tongue roved between my thighs, and my body arched against his mouth, desperately trying to get closer as every flick sent jolts of pleasure through me.

It was both overwhelming and not enough, and I wound my fingers in his hair and tugged him upward. "Need you. Now. Please."

He crawled above me, every muscle flexing, and briefly sucked one of my nipples into his mouth as he headed northward, making me gasp. My legs wound around his hips, inviting. And when his lips found mine, tasting me, he pushed my hands over my head and held me in place as his weight came down on me.

One moment, I felt the pulsing heat of him urging against me, and the next, he pushed inside me.

We both sucked in sharp breaths and held them. He didn't move again—not right away. And I was so thankful, because it was overwhelming. He was too big, or I was too small, or maybe I just wasn't good at this and needed an instruction manual. Everything inside me seized, and I needed a moment, which he somehow intuitively understood. Both of us peered into the dark space between us to see where we were joined, as if we could hardly believe it.

"*Goddamn*," he said reverently, pulling back to look at my face with slitted eyes.

In response, my body finally relaxed and fully accommodated him. I urged him on with my hips, and slowly, deliberately, he moved inside me, testing . . . and then a little faster. We settled into a rhythm, and he surprised me by continuing to talk, whispering a string of sentiments. Instructions. Questions. Filthy things. *So beautiful. Jesus Christ. Touch me here. Tell me you want this. Does it feel good? Tell me you like me fucking you.*

Yes, yes, and *dear God, yes.*

Everything felt good. Every part of me. Every part of him. Pleasure rocketed through me as I listened to his running commentary, reveling in the intimacy of every whispered word.

Delighted by it.

My head fell back against the bed while he continued pinning my arms down, his thrusts quickening. His commentary soon became desperate and clipped. I knew he was on the verge. He knew it, too, and released one of my arms so that he could slip his hand between us and stroke me while he plunged into me with increasing gusto.

A new-to-me experience.

My body went haywire.

"Oh God," I whispered, and that was all the warning I could give him.

"Not yet," he said desperately, thrusting faster.

But it was like stopping a moving train. I just couldn't do it.

Didn't want to.

My body began shaking as I strained against him. The orgasm crept over me like a mile-high wave of rising pleasure, threatening to obliterate me, him, and possibly the entire solar system. Right as it was hitting, I opened my eyes to Seb. Every muscle tensed and heaved; his body was a machine, and I was astounded by all of it. By him. By us.

One moment, he was begging me to wait for him. The next, his head was rearing back, eyes squeezed closed, straining. And as the building pleasure crested and exploded inside me, he joined in, his entire body rigid, and we cried out together.

He collapsed on top of me like he'd been shot, murmuring, "Jesus Christ" over and over. I didn't mind his weight. It was heavy and comforting, like a sexy weighted blanket. I could feel his heartbeat pounding in time with mine, fierce and insistent, and then slowing down.

But Seb became overly concerned about squishing me, and after a few more ragged breaths, he rolled me over along with him until he was on his back. My legs remained wrapped tightly around him to hold him inside me, a losing battle.

"Not yet," I told him. I wanted to remain connected, that's all.

But he said, "Give me five minutes."

"Really?"

"Maybe four."

I chuckled and finally shifted my hips away from him, letting him slip out. We both groaned, then I laid my head down on his chest and exhaled. Our breathing was still labored, and my head lifted and fell along with his chest.

"Are you okay?"

"Okay does not *even* begin to describe it." I looked up at him, unable to stop myself from smiling when I saw him grinning down at me with heavily slitted eyes.

"Yeah?"

"One hundred percent yes."

"Thank God," he whispered.

"You?"

"Oh, me? Well . . ." He tucked one arm behind his head. "I can die happy now. There's nothing more I want from this world."

I chuckled and sighed, still tingling with pleasure. "I feel like we just accomplished the most important task in the history of humanity and basically just saved the world."

Seb laughed, and I felt it echo inside his chest. "Damn right we did. We deserve awards."

"Sex heroes."

"Best undressed."

We both chuckled, then he gently pushed my hair away from my face and settled me more snuggly into the crook of his arm. "What if after all this, we didn't click in bed? I don't think I could go on."

I kissed his chest. "Honestly, I think this might be one of the best days of my life."

Blue eyes blinked down at me, sparkling with delight. "You're going to make me have a heart attack if you keep saying stuff like that."

"I can't remember the last time I was this happy. And that's the truth." I hesitated, thinking of everything that had happened before we got home. "In some ways, this has also been one of the *worst* days of my life. I mean, I never thought anyone would pull a gun on me and my friends."

"Yeah, not a great feeling. We're going to find the Golden Venus, Paige. I don't know how, but we will. It's our calling."

"Is it?"

He rolled us until we were both on our sides, and scooted around until we were face-to-face. "Of course it is. Our families have always been connected. If anyone is going to find Wyrd Jack's treasure, it's us. Right? We're not going to just stand by while the fucking Vanderburgs find it—you already know what will happen."

"They'll rule the fucking town."

Seb nodded. "Yep. They'll get all the credit, all the news reports, and people will start treating them different, thinking they're the new town heroes—and the worst part is that they don't even care about the Venus, or Wyrd Jack. That statue might as well be a fat stack of cash, for all they care. Now tell me, are you and I going to let that happen, after all we've been through? Just roll over and give the Vanderburgs *our* treasure? *Our* sacred duty?"

"Sacred" might be going overboard, but I agreed with the sentiment fully, getting a little fired up about it, too.

"You better shut your mouth, Seb Jansen, talking that trash."

One brow arched slowly, and he pulled me closer. "Why don't you shut it for me?"

Gladly. I pressed a fierce kiss to his lips, feeling far less depressed about the treasure hunt than I had been, and delighted we were both on the same page.

About everything.

Chapter 26

If there was ever such a thing as too much sex, Seb and I surely came close to achieving it that night. We did it in my bed. In the shower. On the living-room rug, on our hands and knees. God help me, we even did it on the kitchen island.

When we finally shut our eyes in the wee hours of the morning, I was not expecting to want to do it *ever* again. Especially when I woke up around 10:00 a.m., rolled over, and discovered that not only was I unexpectedly sore, every muscle screaming in protest, I was also covered in small bruises, bite marks, and had possibly dislocated my jaw at some point.

"Holy shit," I complained hoarsely when I opened my mouth and my jaw cracked. "Think I've been pancaked by a semitruck and then backed over several times."

"Same," Seb said, sounding like his voice was coming from a deep well. "Um . . . is my back bleeding?"

I glanced at several ugly scratches. "Did I do that?"

"Those fingernails are deadly weapons," he said, wincing as he tried to touch the scratches. "Ugh. We're going to need to wash these sheets today. It looks like a crime scene."

"What's wrong with us? Is this normal?"

"*Nothing* is normal about this. I think I pulled a muscle in my ass—is that even possible?"

I was going to need a long, hot soak in the tub and a handful of Tylenol.

"What's today?" I asked.

"Sunday, all day. Which means I only have to work at the marina for a few hours in the afternoon. We can sleep in till noon. Two more hours." He tugged me closer, spooning me.

"No, we can't. Sunday brunch."

"*N-o-o-o-o*," he whispered into my hair, pretending to cry. "Did we agree to that?"

"Unfortunately. It's in an hour." I wanted to make sure Jazmine and Benny were okay, so it wasn't all bad. I just didn't want to face real people while I was in this state. "Jesus, I smell awful. How is that possible? We already showered."

"How am I hard again?" he mused. "This is ridiculous. I think I've got friction burns."

He wasn't the only one. We resisted the urge to touch each other, and both crawled out of bed like we were ninety years old and had drunk an entire bottle of Scotch the night before. I ran a hot bath, and we both sank into it with a sigh of pleasure, hurting too much to do anything but lounge against each other and bathe.

We waited until the last possible moment to leave. I threw on a sundress that I'd worn to several minor events at Harvard, and Seb wore khakis and a nice short-sleeve button up. Not having time for coffee, we downed two energy drinks, and drove like demons to the marina, where the Neelys' personal parking spaces were filled with a couple of cars I didn't recognize and Benny's Land Rover.

"Last people here," I bemoaned as we walked up the steps to the Neelys' front door.

"Last in, first out," he quipped, flashing me dimples. "Let's get this over with so we can get back to defiling the cottage. I'm starting to get my mojo back."

"Keep that mojo in your pants during brunch," I said, smiling back at him as I knocked on the door.

It opened almost immediately. I tilted my head back and looked up into Benny's sad eyes.

"Hi." He kissed me on the cheek in greeting.

"Hi," I answered, kissing him back. "How are you?"

His eyes flicked from my face to Seb's. "Not as good as the two of you, I'd wager."

I gritted my teeth, embarrassed. But Seb slung an arm around my shoulders. "You'd wager right, my friend. I know it's hard, but try to be happy for us."

Benny snorted. "I'll do my best. Did you get my text this morning?"

"Got it, but only saw it when we were on our way here, sorry," Seb said, looking around him through the doorway to make sure we were alone. Laughter and music floated through from somewhere inside. "Were you saying what I thought you were saying?"

He nodded and pulled out his phone, and we circled around it, staring at a map of Haven Beach. A red blinking circle marked some place outside of town.

"That's Paul," Benny explained. "It was pure luck that I spotted that shitty Jeep of his parked at Bean's last night. I bought the tracker last year to help with a project for class—it doesn't matter. I sped back home and got it. Thought I'd never make it back before he left, but I got the tracker on his car just in time. He didn't see me."

I shook my head, trying to clear my thoughts. "Wait. You've put a tracker on Paul's car? You can see where he goes?"

"All day, all night," he confirmed.

"Holy shit, B," Seb said, grinning from ear to ear. "You fucking legend, you!"

Benny pocketed his phone. "May not lead us to where he's stashed the rings. He might've already handed them over to Big Burg. But it won't hurt to keep track of him. I'm building a script to analyze his movements, but it's going to take a little time to collect enough data. At least he won't be able to surprise us again."

Jazmine's curls appeared behind Benny's shoulders. "Did you show them the tracker? If we wanted, we could wait until he's parked somewhere and set his fucking Jeep on fire like he threatened to do to us."

"No car fires," I said. "We're not maniacs. We're smarter. Just keeping tabs on his comings and goings is the best idea any of us have had so far."

"Fine," Jazmine said, pouting. Then she looked at me and Seb. "Mother of God. You two look like you've just been involved in a hostage trade."

My cheeks heated, but Seb just smiled.

"New rule. Don't show up at Heron Cottage unannounced ever again unless you want to see things you've only dreamed about."

"You smug little bastard," Benny said.

"My friend, you have *no* idea—"

I covered Seb's mouth with my hand. "Just get inside, for the love of God. This isn't brunch conversation."

He was all smiles as we headed through the doorway, laughing. Jazmine hugged me from the side as we walked into the entry hall. I inhaled good-food smells that instantly made me glad we'd come.

"Are you okay?" I whispered.

"Managing," she answered as we headed into the kitchen and dining area. "Now you're about to have to do the same with your boy. I'm sorry. I just found out when they walked in a few minutes ago."

I had no idea what she was talking about, until I nearly ran right into Seb, who stood motionless in the middle of the Neelys' kitchen.

Big flowers and fine china covered the length of the big dining table, and several people I recognized chatted with drinks in their hands. Jazmine's sister, Patty, and her wife, Emily, who waved at me from across the room. Mr. and Mrs. Neely's best friends, a couple who owned a yacht and liked to do a lot of fishing in the lake.

But it was the conservatively dressed, middle-aged man next to them that snagged my attention. Someone I hadn't seen since Nana's funeral.

Captain Jansen of the US Coast Guard.

Seb's father.

Looking like a deer in headlights, Captain Jansen stood alongside a woman about his age. I was stunned to see him. Seb, too. It felt like we'd been hoodwinked.

Mrs. Neely jogged over in kitten heels and a flowing floral caftan, calling out to us, "Kids! So happy you're here. I see you've already noticed our surprise guests this morning. I ran into Katie in town and insisted they come."

I didn't know this Katie person but remembered Seb mentioning that his dad had his hands full these days. Guess the captain finally worked through his wife's abandonment and was now on a second-chance romance. The two of them looked nervous. Easy to understand why. It felt like I was walking into the movie set of some Western and had stumbled upon a good, old-fashioned standoff.

"Good morning, Sebastian," Captain Jansen said stiffly. He was fit for a man his age, but impossibly rigid. Crew cut that was more gray than blond. Permanent frown on his long face.

"What are you doing here?" Seb asked in a low voice.

"Enjoying my Sunday, seeing my son," he answered formally. "You don't come by the house anymore, so I had to come to you."

"Just giving the two of you space," Seb said gruffly. "Like you asked."

Captain Jansen looked at me and cleared his throat. "Hello, Paige. It's good to see you back from college. I'd like to introduce you to my fiancée, Katie Yoshida. Katie, this is another of Seb's childhood friends, Paige Malone."

A middle-aged Japanese American woman with short hair and a sweet face canted her head at me, pushing glasses farther up her nose. "The Harvard girl," she said.

I nodded. "Nice to meet you."

"Katie teaches out at a middle school north of town," Captain Jansen informed me.

Huh. Another teacher. Seb's mother had been a teacher, too: our first-grade teacher, in fact. Maybe Seb was thinking the same thing, by the way he anxiously tapped his fingers against his side. But how could I blame Katie for that? Not her fault. I smiled at her. "What subject do you teach?"

"Art," she said cheerfully.

"Oh! I'm studying art history."

"They told me. I'd love to hear more about that." Katie brightened considerably, eager to share our mutual area of interest. And maybe I relaxed a little, feeling the same, because that's the only reason I could think as to why I didn't consciously realize I'd slipped my arm around Seb's waist. Not until Captain Jansen's eyes squinted suspiciously at me.

Seb and I hadn't talked about this. Were we going totally public with our relationship? Should I be keeping it secret until we were certain? *Weren't* we certain?

Regardless, this was Seb's father, and there was a lot of baggage between our families. Captain Jansen and Nana hated each other, in the end. She called him Captain Deadbeat Dad all over town. He threatened to get a restraining order against her. It was . . . complicated.

I tried to stealthily remove my arm from Seb's waist.

Seb stopped me. He put his arm around my shoulders and pulled me toward him.

Captain Jansen's face twisted with surprise. He didn't know what to say, I suppose, because when Mr. Neely strolled over a moment later, the captain looked relieved.

"Would you look at this?" Mr. Neely said, opening his arms wide. "All our babies in one place. It's a Wags reunion. We've got to get a picture of this. We should dig out the old pirate hats and do one of those photo re-creations—pose you in the same way as that photo in the hall, when you were just little bitty things. Look at you now."

Benny audibly groaned. I almost laughed.

"Nope," Jazmine said. "No one's doing any now-and-then homage photos."

"Maybe after a few mimosas," Seb said, waggling his brows at Mr. Neely, who laughed and escorted Seb away.

I didn't need to worry about Captain Jansen. No man alive

could have a bigger stick up his butt, and he wasn't about to start any kind of awkward conversation with me. Or *any* conversation.

His fiancée, however, was more than happy to chat, and I soon found myself with a mimosa in hand, looking at all the artwork in the Neelys' entry hall with Katie and Mrs. Neely.

"And this one, the bird," she said when we were halfway down the hall. "It feels different than the others."

"That's my heron. It's priceless," Mrs. Neely said, picking up my hand. "This young lady's grandmother painted it, and we miss her every single day. Don't we?"

I smiled at up Mrs. Neely as she squeezed my hand. "Yes, we do."

"Such an unusual color palette," Katie remarked. "The eyes really jump out at you with those orange irises. They look as if they're on fire."

"That's Mr. Legs," I told her. "He's an old tree-trunk sculpture in our yard."

Mrs. Neely admired the painting. "I promised Kitty this would never leave our hallway as long as I lived. Oh, looks like the buffet is coming out. Let's get our brunch on, ladies!"

We walked into the dining room, where silver buffet trays were steaming with wonderful scents—some kind of asparagus dish, a strata casserole. Hashbrowns cooked into little nests. More bacon than should be legal, and so much fruit. We helped ourselves to plates and made a line around a buffet table. I stood behind Seb and touched his hand when no one was paying attention, mouthing, "Are you okay?"

He nodded once, leaning back to plant a kiss on my forehead before hooking two fingers around mine.

Patty wolf-whistled from across the room, and some light laughter followed.

Seb just flashed his dimples and shrugged.

Fine. Guess we *were* doing this in public, which made my heart flutter. When I glanced at serious-faced Captain Jansen, I hoped Seb wasn't just trying to shove our relationship into his dad's face to piss him off.

We all filled our plates while Sun Ra's cosmic jazz played on the stereo. I was actually starving, having skipped dinner last night in favor of stale Doritos and gallons of water to replenish the metric ton of fluids we lost. Seb must've been hungry, as well, judging from his heaped plate when he sat down at the big table to my right, with Benny and Jaz to my left. And for most of brunch, everything was fine. Conversation flowed. The food was delicious. We had another mimosa. Benny left the table briefly and returned high as hell, making funny little comments under his breath that made Jazmine and I giggle.

Which was nice, honestly. I worried losing Lulu might make him sink into some mental quicksand—the same worry I had for Jazmine. They both seemed okay, all things considered.

All was well around the brunch table, until someone brought up the police in Haven Beach, and the topic of police reform rose. Not great brunch conversation when there's multiple opinions at the table.

"Look," Mr. Neely said when things started to get heated. "I know the sheriff, and he's a good guy. I think he's willing to usher *some* changes. I'm just saying that there need to be *big* changes. Their budget should be reevaluated, for one."

"They need more money, not less," Captain Jansen said, speaking up for the first time from the foot of the big table. "More police to round up all the scum on the streets around here. This town has changed, and it's not for the better. We have real criminals living here who kill, steal, assault people. There shouldn't be a dime taken away from the police department until the entire Vanderburg family is behind bars."

Oh shit. He was talking about Big Burg. All the Wags glanced at one another and fell silent.

Mr. Neely waved a dismissive hand. "Personally, I think US Marshals need to take care of Big Burg. That whole mess involves drug sales across state lines and into Canada, if rumors are true. It's above the Haven Beach PD's pay grade."

"Can't blame my father for feeling that way," Seb told Mr. Neely. "He sees himself as a lake cop, so when you talk about slashing budgets, he gets defensive about his own job security."

Flames sparked behind Captain Janson's eyes. "And does *your* job security depend on Mr. Neely feeling sorry for you? Still haven't gotten around to growing up, have you?"

"Whoa," Mr. Neely warned lightly. "Let's keep it cool. Brunch is for loving, not fighting."

But that didn't quash anything.

"Mr. Neely," Seb's father said. "Respectfully, you shouldn't be giving the boy handouts like this marina job. It's undoing everything I tried to teach him about responsibility and everything he learned at boot camp, and I don't appreciate it, if you want to know the truth."

Angry lines tightened Seb's face. Mr. Neely's teddy bear demeanor fell away. He stared at Captain Jansen like he was about to flip over the dining table. His wife put a steadying hand on his arm.

You could feel electricity in the air. It was going to go real bad, real fast.

I knew one thing: if Nana were alive, she wouldn't just sit here and stay silent. Guess all I could do was try to honor that.

"No," I told his father, pointing a finger. "*That* crossed the line. You don't get a say about Seb's choices. You abandoned your child when the going got rough, and now he's grown up without you. He belongs to us now. *We're* his family. You forfeited that right."

The captain looked stunned.

Seb's eyes slid to my face, but he stayed quiet.

Mr. Neely hid a little smile.

"I did not abandon my child," Captain Jansen finally bit out.

"It's cool, Dad," Seb said. "I've had a lot of time to think about it, and you've actually set a good example for me to follow. Because I know one day in the future, when I become a father, and I'm unsure about what to do? I'll think, 'What would my father have done?' And then I'll do the exact opposite."

Captain Jansen blanched. He glanced around the table, then he blinked at me and Seb with a look of revulsion. He asked his son in a low, indignant voice, "Have you gotten this girl pregnant?"

"*What?*"

Seb stood up from the table. "Nobody's pregnant, for the love of God. But I'll tell you this much. One day I'm going to marry this girl, and we're going to have a dozen happy kids that you'll never lay eyes on. Maybe then you'll finally wake up and realize you're an even bigger fuckup than I am."

I sat back, stunned. "Um," I said under my breath, looking up at him. "Maybe let me finish my degree first before we start repopulating the planet?"

Benny snickered. Someone across the table muttered lasciviously. But Seb just looked down at me, all his quick anger fading as a look of wonder began filling his face, as if he really *had* just popped the question, and I'd really just said yes.

He held out his hand to me. I wiped my mouth on my napkin and stood up with him.

"Mr. and Mrs. Neely," he said. "I'm sorry if this spoiled your brunch. It was delicious, and I appreciate you inviting us. Katie, you seem like a nice woman, and I'm sorry you had to witness all this drama." He slid his arm around me, placing his hand on the small of my back. "Anyway, I do have a shift that starts in less than hour, and I need to get back home and change. Probably best that we go."

"Us, too," Benny said, giving Captain Jansen a dark look as he stood up. "Right, Jaz?"

Jazmine threw her napkin down next to her plate. "Probably best, Mama. Daddy, I'll help you and Patty clean up later."

A little chaos broke out at the table, with everyone talking at once. The Neelys assured Seb that all was well, and Patty tried to argue in favor of us staying. Even Katie looked upset and was trying to smooth things over. But it was too late.

Captain Jansen sat at the foot of the table with a blank expression on his face, as if someone had just informed him of a tragic death in the family.

In a way, maybe that wasn't too far off from reality.

Chapter 27

A dozen babies?" Benny said, howling with laughter when the four Wags were standing in the private parking lot down the stairs from the Neelys' front door. "Sounds like the title of a horror movie."

Seb groaned and glanced down at me with regret. "I don't know why I said any of that shit, Paige. I'm sorry I embarrassed you."

I shrugged as if I understood completely. "I mean, haven't we all made a shocking declaration about marriage and kids in front of our families, only to regret it later?"

"He just gets me so worked up!" Seb argued. "I can't think straight when he's scowling at me. Why was that fucker even here?"

Jazmine held up both hands. "Swear to God, I didn't know he was coming. I would've warned you—you know that."

He nodded. "I know. But damn . . . What was your mom thinking?"

Mr. Neely strolled up to us, catching us off guard. "She was thinking that with the captain getting serious about Katie, it might make him sentimental and want to repair things with you, Seb. I'm sorry he wasn't ready. But you shouldn't let that slow you down. You've done good, and the job isn't a handout. Sure, maybe I gave you a chance when Jaz begged, but you've proven yourself, and I honestly need you here at the marina."

Seb swallowed hard and nodded rapidly. "Thank you, sir. I'm sorry about all that back there. Honestly some of it's my fault. I let him get to me and can't keep my mouth shut. We're just oil and water, you know?"

"I know," Mr. Neely said with a little smile. "Now y'all better clear out because he's coming down. Seb, just take the afternoon off. Raj came in today, so we've got extra coverage. And I'd rather have you working on the motor of that pontoon tomorrow. Go home and rest . . . or whatever it is that y'all have been doing over there." He muttered under his breath, "Both look like you've been wrestling wildcats."

"Daddy," Jazmine groaned.

He raised his hands in the air. "See you tomorrow bright and early, Jansen."

"You're a real human being, Mr. Neely," Seb told him. "A real human being."

* * *

IT WAS EASY to forget about Pretty Paul's impending threat against the Wags when you were too busy being blissfully happy. And for a few days, Seb and I were exactly that.

In a state of bliss.

Everything was new and surprising. The sex. Shopping for groceries together. Teaching Punkin to fetch. Sneaking down to the beach at night and swimming naked in the dark water.

I didn't know life could be simple and happy. It was like a revelation, and I wished it could stay that simple forever.

Four perfect summer days after the brunch-gone-wrong at the Neelys, Seb went to work at the marina in the morning, and I was planning to drop off some signed paperwork at the family attorney when I got a call from Benny.

"The tracker alerted me to a location outside of Paul's normal routine," he told me.

"Oh yeah? Where?"

Benny hesitated. "In Grand Rapids."

"Okay . . . ?"

"I looked up the address. I think it might be your father's house."

My head emptied of all thought, and a chill raced through my veins. With everything that had happened—the time capsule fiasco, Seb moving in, finding and losing Mabel's rings to Paul—I'd pushed the business with my father to the back burner. I hadn't wanted to face him, but I suppose I knew it was only a matter of time.

"Paige?"

"I heard you. I just . . . Are you sure?"

He read off an address to me. "Tax records show the owner is Rufus A. Lee. Bought last year for two-point-four mil. Five bedrooms, one-point-three acre lot, panoramic views, four-car garage."

Definitely sounded like my father. I asked him to repeat the address and scribbled it down. "What the hell is Paul doing out there?"

"Dunno, but Paul mentioned your father when he was holding that gun on us at the military encampment, remember? Maybe he's trying to squeeze your father for information."

Or maybe they were working together. Though, I couldn't see the how or why of it. My father had everything he wanted, didn't he? All the money that had been passed down, generation to generation. All his now. Why would he need the Golden Venus? It felt too base, too messy for someone who was living an entirely new life, popping champagne with the other movers and shakers in the city.

"Is Paul there now?" I asked Benny.

"No, this was last night. He was there for only fifteen minutes, then he drove back to Haven Beach. Sorry, I missed the alert while I was asleep."

Probably for the best. I didn't want to run into him.

I thanked Benny, feeling dazed and anxious. When I hung up, anger began simmering. I mean, what the hell was Paul doing at my father's, anyway? Meanwhile, I'd been sending emails to his brokerage and not getting any response . . .

Thoughts darkening, I stormed into the kitchen and dug out the financial aid form for Harvard. Then I left Punkin sleeping on the porch swing, got in the Corvair, and I drove the hour to Grand Rapids, fueled by gas fumes and fury.

Treasure or no treasure, I wasn't going to let my father take away Harvard from me. I had to get him to sign this form. No ifs, ands, or buts. After I did that, I'd find out what the hell he'd been doing with the Vanderburgs.

The address Benny gave me was in a picturesque, quiet neighborhood around Reeds Lake—lots of trees, lots of mansions, lots of black Mercedes parked in long driveways. Nicer than Benny's neighborhood, and twice the price. I spotted my father's house when the GPS on my phone alerted me that I was approaching my destination.

Two stories tall, and made of stone and cedar shake, it looked pristine, standing in a manicured yard with a winding drive that was blocked with a big black gate, like he was some kind of

Hollywood star who needed protection from clamoring fans. It made me more furious than I already was.

I drove into the mouth of the driveway, pulling up to a small keypad that stood sentry outside the gate and pressing the call button. "Um, hello? I'm here to see Mr. Lee. I'm his daughter."

There wasn't a video screen. I couldn't tell if anyone had even heard me. But the black gate *clicked* and started opening, so I supposed someone had. I drove through and headed up the drive to park near the entrance. No other cars here. Guess they were all tucked inside the four-car garage. After grabbing my Harvard form and taking a deep breath, I got out of my car and quickly approached the front door before I lost my nerve.

I didn't have a chance to knock. The door swung open, and a fortysomething white man in tailored khakis and a pale blue button-up stood barefoot on the other side, loosely holding a beveled lowball of whiskey by the tips of his fingers. Graying, overlong hair curled around his ears, and his five-o'clock shadow was moving into six-o'clock territory.

"Paige," he said in a voice that sounded like a pack of cigarettes. Instantly, I remembered it from childhood. Rough and boisterous, a big laugh that turned heads. "It really is you, isn't it?"

"Hello, Mr. Lee."

"I can't believe it," he said, leaning against the doorway casually as he looked me over from head to foot several times. "Last time I saw you, you were . . ." He held out his whiskey glass, measuring the air at a point near his waist. "This high."

I could remember the last couple times I'd seen him. Once was at the lawyer's office, a year after my mother had died. Then, when I was sixteen, after Seb left the Wags: Jazmine and I found Rufus's old home address in Nana's things, drove there, and parked outside until I spotted him exiting. I didn't try to talk to him then, just drove away. And I couldn't say why I did it, only that it felt like my life was falling apart.

Seeing him then didn't help. I doubted seeing him now would, either.

He gestured toward me. "Look at you, now, grown into a beautiful young woman. How wild is this? But where are my manners? Come inside, please."

I stepped into a foyer with granite slab floors and tasteful but boring decor, like a Four Seasons hotel lobby. A big, modern chandelier hung near the balcony at the top of the staircase, where there was a perfect view of the lake through a tall window facing his backyard. *Of course* he had a pool. The lake wasn't enough, apparently.

He led me into a small sitting room that had some seating anchored around a contemporary fireplace. He sat on a love seat, and I took a wingback chair across from him, perching on the edge like a flighty bird.

I couldn't feel any less comfortable. Sweat blossomed over my brow.

"Been a few years," he said, leaning back with both arms spread across the tops of the back cushions. "Talk to me. I take it you did the work to find me for a reason. Clearly weren't in the neighborhood."

"Clearly." I fished through my purse for the form I'd brought. "Mr. Lee—"

"Come on, Paige. Call me Rufus."

"How about I call you Hound Dog?"

He chuckled. "Haven't heard that in a long time. Folks still call me that around Haven Beach?"

I didn't answer. I wasn't going to feed his ego. "Rufus," I said, trying to be as professional as possible. "Perhaps your office has informed you about my messages and voicemails? I've been trying to get in touch with you for weeks."

"Really? I had no idea, sorry," he said, shrugging casually. "Why?"

"I'm going to school out east—"

"Nice. Which one?"

"Harvard."

"Look at you," he said, lifting his glass. "Very nice, indeed. You always were a bright little thing. I work with a man from Harvard at the brokerage. A lot of our clients have Ivy League degrees."

Bully for him. I wished I could punch him right in his puffed-up chest.

A dark-haired housekeeper appeared in the doorway, dressed in a black polo shirt and matching pants. "Mr. Lee, can I get you anything?"

He raised a dismissive hand. "Not now, Ester."

"What about the lady?" Ester lifted her brows in my direction. "Coffee or tea?"

"No, thank you," I answered. Absolutely not. I just wanted to get this over with. When the housekeeper nodded and backed out of the room, I resumed our conversation. "So, as I was saying, Harvard's financial aid office needs you to sign this form stating that you claim no financial responsibility for me."

His head tilted to one side inquisitively. "Why would they need that?"

Ugh. "Guess they somehow got wind that you're worth millions. If you had financial responsibility for me, then I'd have to pay full tuition, room, and board because people who have money don't need help. As you know, the Malones are worth nothing. So unless you want to cough up about $250,000 to finish paying for my education for the next three years, then you can sign this form."

He studied me quietly while absolute mayhem was going on inside my chest. If he didn't say anything soon, I might bolt. Being in the same room as my family's own personal monster was not something I was well equipped to do.

Just when I thought he was going to drill me some more about Harvard, he smiled at me and shrugged. "Okay. Sure."

I blinked. "Really?"

He held his arm out and gestured with his fingers. "Give it here. I don't mind, really."

I lifted out of my seat and reached to hand him the paper. "The sections you need to fill out are at the bottom—name, address, social security . . ."

"Goodness, they want it all, don't they?" He took the paper to a nearby desk, found a pen, and began scribbling on it. Then he padded across the rug in his bare feet and handed it to me, withholding it when I reached. "This is really it? This is why you came out here?"

I nodded. "It means a lot. I really appreciate it."

He made a surprised noise in the back of his throat and dropped the paper into my hands.

Here is it, I thought, as a little joy peeked through my anxiety. My entire summer's plans were wrecked over this. I could've lost everything. Then again, if I hadn't come home, I would've never reconnected with the Wags.

I wouldn't have found Seb.

"Thank you so much, Mr. Lee," I said, meaning it.

"Of course, it's no problem. Least I can do to help out . . ."

He couldn't say "my daughter." That wasn't a surprise.

"To help out *you*," he finished. "What are you studying out there? Law?"

"God no. Art history."

He laughed, and I felt embarrassed for a moment. "Oh, I'm sorry, sugar. I just didn't expect it. You know, my wife likes art. We've got a few nice pieces in the house. Let me show you, come on."

I didn't want to see them, I wanted to get the hell out of there. But as I folded up the signed paper, I felt some twinge of responsibility to placate him. The least I could do, I supposed, and maybe it would give me the opportunity to quiz him about why Pretty Paul had visited him out here last night.

I followed him back into the foyer, where he took me to a boring Ellsworth Kelly knockoff. "I think she paid around ten for this one," he said. "We had it appraised last year for fifteen."

"It's . . ."

"A good example of early-eighties minimalism—that's what my wife says. I know nothing about art." He smiled and gave me an odd look that I couldn't interpret. Then his face widened. "Oh! I've got an even better one you need to see, the crown jewel of my wife's collection. Real quick, you'll be impressed, I promise. Up here."

He headed to the staircase and jogged upstairs, but I didn't want to follow. I just wanted to leave.

But I *was* curious to find out why Paul was here.

Reluctantly I looped my cross-body purse strap across my torso and climbed the stairs, taking out my phone halfway up to check my messages. One from Seb an hour ago: *Where are you?* And several missed calls from both him and Benny. *Crap.* I should've told

Seb where I was going and not just run out like that, but luckily everything worked out fine. As soon as I got back to the Corvair, I'd phone Seb and tell him the whole thing.

"Down the hall, this way," my father called back at me.

He was walking fast, and his mood was a little hyper. Maybe he was always like this. I followed him past palm trees and several open bedroom doors to a room at the end of the hall.

"In here," he motioned. "I just know you're going to appreciate this . . ."

Cautious, I stepped into a bedroom with sparse contemporary furniture. Maybe a guest room, considering how soulless and clean it was. The only good thing about it was a balcony on the back wall with French doors. The balcony overlooked the pool in the backyard, and beyond it, Reeds Lake.

"Here it is," my father said, standing in front of a textured beach landscape that looked as if it had been painted by someone with double vision. Two suns. Two women lying on the sand. Two palm trees. "A Brazilian painter did it, he's supposed to be a big deal. What do you think?"

"Interesting brushwork. What's the name of the artist?"

"Hmm, can't remember . . ." He squinted at the messy signature in the corner of the painting. "Can never read these things, can you? But I can look it up really fast. Do you mind, can I see your phone for just a sec?"

My phone? I still held it in my hand and wish I could've hidden it, especially the way my pulse was swishing rapidly inside my temples. But he just reached out and took it out of my fingers like it was nothing. Like we were oh so close and borrowed phones all day long.

"Hey—"

"Before we look up the artist, here's a question for you," he said, cutting me off.

A fresh layer of panic built up inside me when he smiled and held the phone away from me as if he were dangling a carrot. "You hear about that gold bar that was found downtown?"

My heart raced inside my chest. I swallowed hard and asked, "Is that why Paul Vanderburg showed up here yesterday?"

"Paul Vanderburg? Now that's a name I haven't heard in a while."

Absolute liar. "Oh, really?"

He fisted my phone and held up both arms to sidle around me and move past the bed. "Just one sec . . ."

He was . . . leaving the room?

"Hold up. Where are you going with that?" I asked as he headed out the door, pocketing my phone. "Wait! What—"

I raced to the door, but he slammed it in my face.

The lock snicked.

"You just stay put for a little while," he told me through the door. "I promise nothing will happen to you. But I need to make some calls. Then we'll talk again. Sorry, Paige, but I've got a feeling you're keeping something from me."

"Fuck you, you maniac! Let me out!" I rattled the handle, but it was no use. "You can't do this!"

But I supposed he could whatever he wanted in his own house.

And what he wanted, by all appearances, was to kidnap his own daughter.

<h1 style="text-align:center">Chapter 28</h1>

I raged at the door, screaming for help. Someone had to hear me. I'd seen that housekeeper downstairs, Ester. Surely, he had to have other staff. Gardeners, pool boys . . . When I stopped screaming, I heard raised voices—*downstairs?* Was he talking to Ester? I couldn't tell, and after the voices quieted for a long time, I resumed screaming. When I paused to listen again, I heard nothing.

"Dammit!" I kicked the door in frustration and tried to calm down so I could think. My father had taken my phone, so I couldn't call Seb. He'd be worried about me when he got off work, if he wasn't already, judging by that last text he sent. Worried and pissed as hell, probably. Hard to blame him. This was shaping up to be one of the dumbest things I'd ever done, coming out here alone.

Then again, no one expects to be kidnapped.

Maybe I *should* have.

"Is this about the Golden Venus?" I finally called out with a hoarse voice, heart racing.

No response. Could he even hear me up here? I was all the way at the end of the upstairs hall. After a while, I gave up at the door and tried across the room, where the French doors led out to the balcony. Locked, naturally, but not one I could just flip open.

There was a keyhole. *Who locks their damn balcony with a key?* Was this a rich-people thing I didn't know about, or had he locked other people in this room?

"Help!" I banged on the glass and looked outside. The neighbors weren't visible; trees surrounded the property right up to the edge of Reeds Lake. Even if I could open the door, it was too far above the ground. I'd probably break both my legs on the concrete that surrounded the pool. Only thing I could do was call for help. Someone had to hear eventually. We were in a residential neighborhood, for the love of God!

Maybe I could find something in the room to help me escape. A key to the balcony or a screwdriver. Something! But the room was devoid of humanity. The bedside tables had no drawers. The only thing that did was a bureau, but it was empty. Nothing in the closet but an extra pillow. But when I bent to look under the bed, I heard a voice coming from inside the heating vent in the nearby wall.

I put my ear next to the vent and strained to hear.

"—up your phone when I call, got it? Just shut up and listen to me. We've got a change of plans. I've got her here. Well, that's your problem, now, isn't it?"

Who was my father talking to? He went quiet, listening to the person on the other end of the phone. I waited for him to speak again.

"Fine, I don't care, but I'm not bringing her to that cesspit you call a compound."

Holy mother of God, it was Big Burg. Panic surged inside my chest.

"Just send Paul back out here," my father's voice said from inside the vent. "But he can't park that truck in my drive. Draws too much attention. Tell him to park it down the street. I'll leave the gate open for him."

He must've hung up because I heard nothing else, even after I camped out on the floor and waited to see if he made any other calls but it was silent.

None of this was good. Now I worried my father might be planning to hand me off to Paul, a prospect that made my stomach sick. I tried to consider less-awful hypotheticals that might play out but just couldn't see how my father would let me go without some assurance I wouldn't head straight to the police.

No possible scenario would end with him handing me back my phone and opening the front door. This wasn't an *Oops, my bad* situation. It was a felony. And I didn't know enough about the true nature of my father's character to make assumptions about his reasoning. All I knew was that he'd manipulated legal loopholes to rob my family blind, and when it came to him accepting guardianship of me, his only child, he'd tossed me aside like a broken doll.

What else would he do?

What else had he done already?

I emptied my purse onto the bed, searching for something to pick a lock. Granted, I had no idea *how to*, but if I stuck something small inside the keyhole for long enough, maybe I'd get lucky. While I was searching, a knock on the door made me jump and scatter my things.

"Paige?" my father's voice said behind the door.

"Let me out!" I shouted, racing to the door and slamming against it with my shoulder.

Bad idea. Not sure how that always worked in movies, but

the pain that rocketed down my arm was almost unbearable. The door didn't budge.

"Stop wearing yourself out," my father said in a muffled voice beyond the door. "No one can hear you through these walls but me, and it's getting a little annoying."

Jesus fucking Christ. Who even *was* this monster? How did I share any DNA with this man?

"I knew you were up to something with Paul," I said.

"Is that why you brought that form for me to sign? Was that just a rouse?"

I wasn't giving him the satisfaction of knowing it wasn't. The form was on the bed with all the scattered contents of my purse. I snatched it up and quickly folded it into a small square and stuck it in the coin pocket of my shorts in case he tried to take it back.

"You know," his voice said outside the door. "When Big Burg called me up last month after that gold bar resurfaced, I hadn't heard from him in a few years. I'm sure your grandmother has told you by now, but we use to run together, back in the day. Never knew my daddy, and my mom was a boozer who couldn't even hold a job cleaning toilets. But Big Burg and his daddy took me in—they were good to me. Showed me the way of the world. We chased treasure, just like you and your friends are doing now."

"You are nothing like us."

"Maybe. But we were the OG treasure hunters. I heard about the Golden Venus from the Vanderburgs, long before I met your mother."

"Did the two of you plan to steal from her?"

"Oh, Paige. You know nothing about any of that. All we did was take control of an account that belonged to your mother—not to Kitty. Your mother knew about it. Why do you think she left it all to me in the will?"

"She didn't! You took it!"

"Remember that Kitty poisoned your mind to me," he said. "So if I were you, I wouldn't trust anything she's told you about me, your mom, or the Venus. Kitty just wanted to horde it—she even kept its location from your mother. Big Burg was the one who figured that out and opened my eyes to it. What kind of mother keeps things from their child?"

"What kind of father ditches their child for cash? Did Big Burg inspire that, too?"

"Say what you will about Big Burg. If it weren't for him, I might be dead in a ditch."

"I wish you were."

"Now, now. I know you're sore about the family money. But you should know that I wanted to take you with me. I tried. My lawyer tried. But Kitty was relentless." He chuckled darkly. "Sorry to speak ill of the dead, but your grandmother was a selfish bitch."

My blood boiled.

Whatever leeway I'd given him for being my flesh and blood vanished.

"Listen to me, Paige," he said. "You may have memories of your mama; I don't know. But you don't have a full picture of her. The one thing she wanted in life was to find the Golden Venus. I'm going to honor that wish."

"Bullshit!"

"When it's finally uncovered, I don't need you and your friends taking it to Haven Pawnshop and selling it for a fraction of what it's worth. Let the adults take care of it, darling."

"I'm not your darling or your daughter, you sick bastard! I'm the person who's going to cut out your heart and feed it to my dog if you don't let me out of here right now!"

"Keep screaming at me, and I'll call the police and say I caught you breaking in here, trying to steal valuable artwork from me. I'm one of their biggest donors in town, so I'm sure they'll be happy to take you in and lock you up. One way or another, we're going to have a chat about those rings you dug up, and you're going to tell me where the lock is that they fit."

Jesus. He knew *that* much about our treasure hunt?

"When you do," he finished, "you have my word that I'll cut you in for some of the profit, under the table—Big Burg doesn't have to know. I'll pay for Harvard, if that's what you need. You think about it, and see if we can come to an understanding before Paul gets here with the rings."

I listened to his footfalls retreating down the hallway before he called out for his housekeeper and headed downstairs. Shock held me at the door a little longer. I just couldn't wrap my head around everything he'd just told me, couldn't wrangle all the wild emotions that were filling up my chest.

Stumbling to the bed, I fell apart, crying into the mattress so he couldn't hear me.

Until I was empty.

There wasn't a clock in the room, and I didn't have my phone, so I had trouble gauging how much time had passed since he'd locked me in here. But I could tell by the light that it was no longer morning. My throat hurt from all the screaming. I stared at my father's dumb double-vision beach painting for God only knows how long, until the two suns in its swirling sky started to look like the eyes of some sky god, peering back at me.

I needed to pull myself together and figure out how to escape before Paul got here. Because the last time I saw him was when he was pointing that gun in our faces, and I didn't know what he'd do this time. Or what my father was capable of doing under pressure. All I knew was that Nana had been right to hate him, and if he was telling the truth about trying to keep custody of me, then I owed Nana everything for preventing that from happening.

After taking a moment to breathe, I tried to focus on getting past either of the locked doors. I picked through everything I'd dumped on the bed and shoved it back in my purse. The only thing I had that might pick a lock was an old ballpoint pen with a chewed cap. I took it apart and tried to use various pieces of it to open the lock on the bedroom door. But I just ended up getting ink all over my fingers.

MacGyver I was not.

More time passed. I was starving, so it was well past lunch. I paced the room, combing every inch of it. Crouched near the vent to try to hear more conversations. Trying to figure out how long I had until Paul got there. *It was only an hour away. Shouldn't he be here by now?* I'd been trapped in here for hours, surely. I finally sat down in the farthest corner from the bedroom door, so that I could watch it, stroking the Blackbeard ring around my neck like prayer beads.

Until I heard something . . .

Chapter 29

At first, I assumed the sound was inside the vent—another phone conversation, maybe. But it wasn't a voice I'd heard, and it wasn't coming from inside the house.

It came from outside. Somewhere outside those locked French doors . . .

Anxiety flaring, I stood up and walked to the balcony doors to scan the backyard. That housekeeper, Ester, was down by the pool, straightening chaise longues. I guess that's what I heard— the sound of metal scraping across concrete. At first I thought she was just doing her job, but she was craning her neck, peering into the trees that flanked the yard. *What the hell is going on . . . ?* I watched her pull out her phone and talk into it as she swiveled and searched around the pool. Then she nodded and left the backyard.

As she entered the home's back door, just below the balcony, I slammed my fist against the glass, trying to get her attention, but she disappeared into the house without looking back.

Frustrated and scared, I wilted against the balcony doors.

Until I heard the sound again.

*What *was* that . . . ?*

Some kind of heavy scraping. Of stone? Was there construction work being done on the outside of the home? Plastering, maybe?

It gave me hope that I might be able to flag a builder or contractor down, so I scanned the pool again. The housekeeper hadn't returned, and the chaise lounges sat neatly in a row, so they weren't the source of the noise. Not really a scraping noise. Not really a noise at all. I put my hand against the glass and *felt* something. It felt like . . . scrabbling.

Out of the corner of my eye, I spotted movement between the wrought iron rails that lined the balcony. Was it a bird or something? Hard to see anything past the massive monstera plant. Taller than me, the big-leaved plant sat outside the French doors in an enormous steel planter, blocking my view of that side of the balcony.

But I *had* seen something out there. *Wait. What is that . . . ?*

A hand.

I jerked away from the doors, backing up a step as my heart thudded wildly against my ribcage. Someone was climbing onto the balcony!

The hand was soon followed by another, and then a dark silhouette lurched over the balcony railing, landing behind the monstera plant. The silhouette darted to one side, out of sight, then it moved like a shadow around the potted plant to peer into the French doors.

Holy shit.

"Seb . . . ?"

A chaotic tangle of blond waves blew in the breeze, and two blue eyes squinted into the balcony doors, his hand blocking late-afternoon sun so that he could see inside.

"SEB!" I whispered loudly, putting my face and both palms against the glass. Unbridled joy washed over me. I'd never been so happy to see anyone.

His eyes snapped to mine, and a look of supreme relief fell over his face.

Tears brimmed. I just couldn't help it. "I can't get out!"

He jiggled the door and mouthed, *"Fuck."*

"I've tried everything," I told him miserably, remembering that my father claimed this room was soundproofed. Could Seb even hear me?

He was still wearing his marina T-shirt, and it had engine grease streaked on it. His eyes flicked around the balcony until they stopped on the big monstera plant. He looked at me and held up one finger then shooed me away from the doors.

"No," I whispered, shaking my head. But I backed away when he bent over, muscles flexing, and picked up the giant plant. And when he swung its big steel planter back to get leverage, I knew he meant business, so I rapidly doubled back once more and moved out of the way.

Half throwing, half swinging it, Seb launched the monstera at the French doors. With a terrible crash, glass exploded inward, and the wood framing splintered. He hadn't smashed the entire set of double doors, only one side—and the monstera planter was half-stuck in the broken glass. But when he kicked the planter farther into the room, he was able to knock away glass with one of the monstera branches and quickly stepped through behind it, white Adidas crunching the shrapnel.

"Seb!" I cried out, flying into his arms.

He squeezed me tightly. "Did he hurt you? Are you okay?"

"He fucking kidnapped me!" I said, and then exhaled. "But I'm not hurt."

"Thank God." He released me quickly and glanced at the bedroom door, saying, "Someone would've heard that."

"How did you find me?" I asked, still stunned.

"Benny called. We figured you came out here, but Jaz still has your location enabled, so that confirmed it."

Jaz and I never thought to turn off location sharing when I left for Harvard, thank God.

"We saw you on her phone just in time, too. Like, less than a minute later, your phone turned off while we were looking at the location. I knew it couldn't be dead because I put it on the charger last night."

He had, indeed. Who could ask for a better roommate?

"You never turn off your phone. So *that* told me you were in trouble. Only tricky part was trying to figure out where you were in the house, especially after we didn't see you in any of the first-floor windows."

Panic flared. "Jaz and Benny are here? My father's insane. I don't know what he'll do if he catches them."

"Don't worry about them. Let's take care of us first," he said matter-of-factly. He'd always been good at staying calm in tricky situations. I was *so* grateful he was here. I should've known I could count on him. Why did I ever doubt it?

A bright, warm sensation bloomed in my chest, obliterating all the panic and fear. It felt like I was on the threshold of a door that might lead to a brave, new world if I was willing to take a chance. But once I stepped through, I could never return.

"I need to tell you something important!" I said, grabbing the front of his shirt.

"Paige—"

"Sebastian Jansen, I fucking love you. We have to figure out a way to be together when I go back to school because I can't lose you again."

His eyes went glossy as he blinked at me.

He brought my face to his and kissed me roughly. Just for a moment. Then he pulled back and said, "I fucking love you, too, Paige Malone. But if we're going to have any future outside these walls, we need to hustle, okay? So come on!"

But we didn't have time to escape.

Heavy footfalls rushed toward the bedroom door.

A moment later, it clicked and swung open.

My father looked around the room, breathing like he'd just run a marathon. He took in the broken balcony door, the glass . . . and Seb.

"Did you just break my door? Who the hell do you think you are?"

Seb got in front of me and reached for something that stuck out of the back of the khaki shorts he was wearing.

Oh no. *Oh no, no, no* . . .

Seb pointed a sawed-off shotgun at my father with such aplomb, even *I* forgot it was a prop for a split second. "That's a question I should be asking *you*, motherfucker."

Sometimes all you need is a little flash.

Most definitely a move the real-life Calico Jack would've appreciated.

My father's hands went up in the air slowly. His eyes narrowed. "Is that Frank Jansen's kid? Christ. Okay, listen. I can see we're all emotional right now, so why don't we take it down a notch—"

"Back the fuck up," Seb said.

My father raised his hands higher. "Look, I get it. Everyone wants a piece of the Golden Venus. But seriously, what would you do if you actually got your hands on it? Do you know who to sell it to? How to protect it and yourself? Because you know once the world knows you have it, bad people will try to take it from you."

"Bad people like you?" I asked.

He lowered his hands a little. "Come on, Paige. I'm not the bad guy here."

"You're *literally* the bad guy!" I shouted. "Look around! You've been holding me hostage—good people don't do that!"

"This is hardly a prison cell. That mattress alone is worth more than that beach cottage you've been holing up inside."

"Goody for you," I said darkly.

"That cottage was never meant to be occupied in the winter, you know. It was just a summer house. Kitty spent the last of her cash getting it insulated after your mom died. I could never understand why—not even a valuable piece of lakefront."

It sounded like he knew a lot more about me than I did about him. And where was he going with this?

"I can help you with that," my father said. "Get you into a real house. Something in Haven Beach, or if you're going back to Harvard, I'll buy you something out there. I'll even go downstairs and write you a check right now—to show you that I'm speaking in good faith."

"So generous," Seb said. "Can't imagine there'd be a catch to that."

"No catch," my father insisted. "Just let me help you retrieve the Golden Venus. I'll get the rings from the Vanderburgs, and we'll ride out together. You just say where, and I'll drop everything I'm doing today and go with you. We'll do it together—we can be a family again, Paige. This statue was meant to stay in the family, so let's honor that, okay, baby?"

He couldn't sound less convincing if he tried. And to be honest,

I wasn't sure he really was. No way in hell he actually thought it would convince me.

I held out my hand. "Why don't you start this little show of good faith by giving me my phone back."

His hands dropped to his pants pockets, which he patted, giving me a sheepish look. "Sorry, I must've put it down somewhere. We can go find it together, if you'd just ask your friend to put the gun down. Come on, Paige. This is silly. We're family."

A female voice called out distantly from somewhere in the house. "Mr. Lee? I have the key. Do you want me to release them?"

Something like a smile came over my father's face. He shouted behind him, "Go on, Ester. Let's see if Thing One and Thing Two can make these two kids start thinking more reasonably."

He stuck his fingers in his mouth and whistled loudly.

"Hey!" Seb warned, pointing Calico Jack more firmly at my father. "Don't move, or—"

I, too, wanted to know what Seb was going to say after that "or," but he didn't get a chance. My father turned on his heel and raced out the bedroom door.

"Son of a bitch!" Seb said.

The good thing was that he'd left the bedroom door open.

The bad thing was that something big was galloping down the hallway toward us. A pair of them. I caught a glimpse through the open doorway of two sleek Dobermans with studded collars running hell-for-leather toward us.

Thing One and Thing Two.

My blood turned to ice as a little whimper escaped my lips.

Why did it have to be Dobermans . . . ?

"Shit!" Seb said, abandoning the prop gun on the bed to grab my hand. "Out the balcony!"

We raced toward it, shoes crunching on the broken glass, and ducked through the broken door, onto the balcony.

If I'd thought I was too far up when I first evaluated the balcony from inside the room, being out here now made me realize I'd been wrong.

It was *much* farther down than I'd imagined.

How had Seb climbed up here? Ornamental trees grew below. I could see a path from the trees to a drainpipe, to a small ledge that connected to the balcony. But the dogs were baring down on us. I could feel their galloping under my feet.

"No time," Seb shouted when I looked toward the area he'd used to climb up here.

The dogs burst into the room behind us. They barked like demons from the pit of hell, and a terrible, old fear came over me, irrational and urgent. I froze in place as if they'd turned me to stone with their shiny, black demon eyes.

They lurched into the room but stopped midway through when one of them stepped on glass and made a high-pitched whine. The dog frantically bit at its paw while the other backed away a step, wary. But then it held its ground, barking so loud it made me shudder.

"PAIGE!"

I shook myself and became aware of Seb tugging me toward the railing. He began climbing, and that's when it hit me . . . what he intended for us to do.

"N-no," I said, shaking my head.

"No choice. Just like Benny's dock. You've done it a thousand times."

Wrong. *He'd* done it a thousand times; this was as high up as the top deck on Benny's river dock, and I'd *never* jumped from there. The pool felt impossibly far away, and it wasn't below us. It was several feet away.

The dogs barked behind us, and past them, through the open doorway, I could see movement coming up the stairs.

Dammit.

Seb was right. No choice now.

It's just like a paddleboard, I told myself. *You can do this . . .* I climbed onto the railing next to him, wobbling precariously on my bad ankle, and used every ounce of my leg strength to slowly push myself up and stand.

Sweat bloomed.

The pool below swayed in my vision.

I could feel Seb's weight shift on the railing next to me, but I didn't dare turn my head. Didn't look directly down at the concrete or the chaise lounges lined up neatly by Ester. I just took a deep breath—

"One," Seb counted from my side. "Two . . ."

He grabbed my hand.

"Three!"

And we jumped.

Chapter 30

Part of me wouldn't have been surprised if our lives had ended there, two bloody splats by the side of the pool. When we hit the surface of the water, I still wasn't convinced we weren't dead. The shock of entering the water blinded me, and for a moment it felt like I was back down in Pinemoon's flooded cavern. Only this time, I hit the bottom.

Nonsensically, as columns of bubbles clouded my vision, the only thing inside my head was the painted pair of double-vision suns from my father's Brazilian beach landscape, back upstairs in the room. Those painted suns reminded me of something I couldn't quite remember. But then, for the smallest sliver of time, Mabel's wedding bands glittered inside my head—so real, I could almost reach through the water and touch them.

The suns. The rings. And something that was on the tip of my tongue . . .

A holy vision caused by all the pool chemicals? Or just a meltdown from stress?

We pushed off the bottom of the pool and cut through the surface, my thoughts turned to more important things, like survival. And air. And Seb, who bobbed next to me, blinking away pool water.

We swam to the side of the pool and pulled ourselves out. I

barely had time to suck in a breath before Seb was pushing me into the nearby bushes, getting us out of sight from the home's windows. We crouched together in the grass, breathing heavy while he pulled out his phone and shook water from it, making a happy noise when the screen turned on. "Still works," he said, quickly typing a text message and then glancing around nervously as he waited for a reply. "Come on, come on . . ."

At least he had a phone. Would I ever see mine again? That was another expense I hadn't planned for.

"Finally!" He pocketed his phone. "Come on. Benny and Jaz are over this way. We're going to have to sneak around the side here where there aren't any cameras. Follow me."

We ducked past the bushes and bent low to make our way through the outskirts of a rose garden, sneaking past the windows. We were both soaked to the bone, and chlorine stung my eyes as we pushed aside wisteria and headed around a screened-in patio—

Where we ran into Jaz and Benny, squatting near the patio door.

"Oh my God!" Jaz said. "Are you okay?"

"He fucking had her locked up," Seb said.

"This is what you meant by 'exited via pool route'?" Benny said, blinking at our wet clothes. "You absolute legends."

"We'll take our award later," Seb said, pushing damp hair out of his eyes. "Let's make a break for the side gate where we came in. Paige, it's over there, behind that little brick wall. See it?"

I nodded. Running there would take us in full view of the front of the house and the driveway. The Corvair was still parked there, and the gate I'd driven through was cracked open.

I'll leave the gate open for him.

I looked around wildly, trying to spot Paul Vanderburg, but the front yard was quiet and still. Even the road outside the gate was quiet.

"Ready?" Jazmine asked.

When we nodded, she signaled, and we all took off like we were running from the devil. Maybe we were. This entire hellish estate was nearly as bad as the Vanderburg compound, just with a fancier wrapper. I raced across the lawn with the other Wags, wet shoes squishing in the grass, heading straight for a waist-high brick wall, which partially hid a little curving path from our view until we got right up on it. But there was the path, and there was the little side gate in the property fence that Seb mentioned.

There was also Pretty Paul and Lulu, walking through the side gate.

We all skidded in the grass as Lulu closed the gate. Paul glanced up with a genuine look of surprise.

"Shit," Benny mumbled.

"Front gate!" Seb said, and we all doubled back, scrambling to put some distance between us while Lulu shouted, "It's them!"

Did Paul have his gun? I couldn't tell. When I glanced over my shoulder, he was booking it toward us. But he wasn't the only one.

Black lightning streaked across the front lawn toward us. Thing One or Thing Two, I didn't know. Didn't care, either. We were almost at the front gate, and there was just enough space for us to get out. Behind us, I vaguely heard my father shouting along with his housekeeper. Heard Lulu's Mickey Mouse voice. But we were there. We were going to make it!

One. Two. Three. Four. All Wags slipped through the crack in the gate.

And ran right into two Grand Rapids police officers.

"Whoa, whoa!" the first officer said, a middle-aged man with short gray hair, who put his hand on his holster while his partner, a young officer who didn't look much older than us, held up both his hands to block us.

All I could think was how my father had bragged about bribing the Grand Rapids police. Had he called them? I didn't get an answer to that right away because the Doberman lurched against the gate, barking his head off. The officers moved back, wary, but my father ran up and grabbed the dog by its studded collar.

"All right, now," he shouted at the dog. "Stand down. Stand down!"

The dog obeyed, but you could tell it would rather eat our faces off. A reluctant Ester raced up behind with a chain leash, which my father used to control the dog. "So sorry about that, Officers," he said, breathless. "She's normally better behaved."

"Whoa!" the younger cop warned, looking behind my father. He quickly took out his gun but held it pointed down at his side. "Who's that, now?"

Paul and Lulu were trying to sneak out and leave the yard the same way they came out.

"Oh," my father said. "They're with me. It's fine. They weren't involved in this, so you can just let them go."

"Excuse me?" the older cop said, and then called out to Paul and Lulu, "Grand Rapids PD. Get over here, now, before my partner has to shoot a hole in your leg."

The younger cop trained his gun on Paul, who looked like he was cussing us under his breath, but after a moment, both he and Lulu slowly walked over to the gate. The younger cop herded them outside with us. We gave them dirty looks as they stood on one side of the gate, Wags on the other.

"Everyone stay put," the young officer said.

"Sir," the older cop called out to my father, "I don't know what in God's green earth is going on here, but we got a call from the Haven Beach sheriff that something might be amiss."

Haven Beach . . . I glanced at the other Wags. Jazmine's father was good friends with the sheriff. Was this his doing? Jaz nodded once, and it made me feel a little better. Certainly wouldn't stop them from siding with my father. But maybe there was some hope.

"So what am I looking at here? Do we have a domestic in progress?" the older officer asked. "Or is this a break-in? Someone start talking and enlighten me."

Past the gate, my father's eyes snapped to mine, and they weren't filled with concern. They were furious. And that fury came with a sharp warning: *Keep your mouth shut.*

If he wanted any hope of that, he shouldn't have called my nana a bitch.

"That man with the dog is Mr. Lee. He's the homeowner. I came here to ask him to sign some paperwork for my college—"

"She goes to Harvard," Seb interjected, as if that gave my testimony more gravitas. Maybe it did. I'd take any advantage I could against my father.

"Which he did, and then he locked me in a room for hours against my will and stole my phone so I couldn't call for help," I told the officers, praying they weren't in my father's back pocket.

Praying they weren't as incompetent as the cops in my town.

"O-*kay*, uh-huh . . ." the cop mumbled slowly, eyeing my wet clothes. When my father tried to speak up, he said. "Wait your turn, sir. Go on, young lady . . ."

"My friends had to drive all the way from Haven Beach to come rescue me." I gestured toward the Wags. "My boyfriend destroyed the door to the room I was locked inside in order to get me free."

Seb looked like the cat who'd eaten the canary. "Boyfriend," he murmured.

Well? What else was I going to call him? It was nearly impossible not to return his pleased-as-punch smile, but I forced myself to shake it off and focus. "Oh, and Mr. Lee sicced his dogs on us, too."

"Officer," my father called out from the other side of the fence. "The only thing right about her statement is destruction of property. That blond hoodlum destroyed one of my doors. *And* he threatened me with a gun. Look!" He held up Seb's sawed-off shotgun, surprising all of us. I suppose he'd found it up in the bedroom. "When someone points something like this at me, I'm well within my rights to stand my ground."

The younger officer still had his gun out. "All right, sounds like we've got issues. Hands up, all of you."

We all complied. Some of us more slowly than others, namely Paul.

The cop's older partner kept one hand on his holster and gestured toward my father. "Let's put that sawed-off on the ground, sir. Yep, right there. Put it down and step away. Get that dog put up, too, while you're at it."

As Ester gripped the chain of the Doberman, urging it away from the front gate, my father tossed the sawed-off onto the driveway. The officer moved it farther away with his foot, instructing my father to back up, and he started to radio something into the speaker that was strapped to the shoulder of his uniform until Seb spoke.

"That's a prop gun, Officer."

The man cocked a brow at him in disbelief. "Pardon?"

"That's mine, but it's a prop. Replica. Came from a museum. Doesn't shoot."

The officer picked up the sawed-off and immediately chuckled, weighing it in his hand. "Almost fooled me. Feels like a kids' toy." He checked the gun, making sure it didn't have ammo, then squinted at Seb. "Any real weapons on you?"

"Just my good looks," Seb said, smiling.

The officer shook his head. "Let's pat them all down. Everyone sit your asses on the lawn, and we're going to figure out what's happened here today."

"What's happened here today is that these kids broke into my house and destroyed my property," my father said, looking aggrieved. "I want to press charges against all of them. Those two are with me, my friend's kid." He pointed toward Paul and Lulu. "They're innocent. It's these four you need to arrest."

Jesus. That wasn't going to work, was it? Part of me was terrified it would. His word against ours.

"Sir," Benny said to the older police officer. "You might want to check his security footage. I didn't get a chance to look it over too well, but you can access it right here . . ."

Benny held up his phone slowly, and offered to show the officer.

"How've you got his cameras on your phone?" the man asked.

"His security system isn't secure. Any phone using the Wi-Fi can access his home security system through the app, and his Wi-Fi doesn't have a password," Benny said casually, unlocking his screen. "Here you go. See, he's got cameras inside and out, a good dozen or more of them, so it shouldn't be too hard to prove that he locked her in the room. You can access the controls to that footage there and rewind it."

Was all of this true? Camera footage was a heck of a lot better than someone's word. I could kiss Benny right now.

The officer kept his hand on his holster as he looked at the footage Benny offered up, making faces at the screen until he lifted his eyes and stared at my father. "Well, now. This is getting interesting . . ."

My father shook his head. "Whatever you're seeing, they're twisting things. I didn't lock her that room."

"Sir, I'm going to need you to put your hands up where I can see them," the older officer said, flicking open his holster. "Don't make me take this out."

My father held up his hands, and hope rose inside me. If the Wags could just get out of this mess without being arrested, I'd be relieved. But if I could take my father down and avenge my family in the process . . . ?

I'd be happier than a bird with a french fry.

Seb pointed at Paul. "While you're at it, Officer, *that* guy is helping his father try to rob my girlfriend, here"—Seb's eyes flicked toward mine—"but his father is on house arrest, and he's on probation himself, so he shouldn't be in possession of a weapon. You might want to frisk him. Last time we saw him he pulled a handgun on us—a real one, in case that wasn't clear . . ."

"Fuck you, Jansen," Paul said. "You're dead."

The officer's brow lifted again. He glanced at Jazmine. "What about you? You got anything to say?"

She shrugged. "My daddy called the Haven Beach sheriff to ask y'all to come out here because we were all afraid Mr. Lee might do something bad to her."

"Mr. Lee thinks we know where some priceless treasure is," Benny added. "Maybe you've heard of Wyrd Jack, and the pirate museum in Haven Beach? *That* treasure."

"And *do* you know where this 'treasure' is?" the police officer asked, almost amused.

"Nope," Seb said. "We do not. But Paul and Lulu there are working with Mr. Lee to try to find it. They've robbed us, threatened us, and kidnapped one of us—"

"She's my daughter," my father called out. "Why would I kidnap my own daughter?"

"He robbed all the money out of my mother's bank account when she died," I said. "So he's basically a piece of trash, and I hope he spends the rest of his life in a jail cell."

The older cop couldn't look more discombobulated if he tried. He handed Benny's phone back to him, looking dazedly at both him and Jazmine, then at Paul and Lulu . . . then at me and Seb in our wet clothing. Finally, he squinted at my father and sighed deeply. He mumbled something into his shoulder speaker that started with his badge number and ended with "requesting backup."

"Want me to cuff any of them, Sarge?" the younger cop asked.

The older officer glanced toward the house and said, "You might want to start with him."

We all turned to see my father running as fast as he could across the lawn, until the sprinkler came on, and his bare feet slipped in the grass. He landed flat on his back and didn't move until the younger officer came to cuff him.

"Dreams really do come true," Seb said, eyes twinkling. "All hail Calico Jack."

"All hail Benny for hacking into the security system," Jaz said under her breath.

"All hail Mr. Neely for listening when his daughter said this was a five-alarm emergency," Benny added.

All hail the Wags, the best friends anyone could ever ask for.

Chapter 31

We spent hours at the police station in Grand Rapids giving our statements. It was nearly dusk by the time we got back into town, all of us climbing out of the Land Rover in my driveway like we'd been sapped of our vital life energy.

"Food," Jazmine said. "Any food. I could demolish an apple right now."

"Weed first," Benny said. "Then apple."

"My stash is depleted," Seb told him.

"Backup stash?"

"Yeah, that's possible, if we can find it . . ." Seb turned his key in the cottage's front door and pushed it open. Punkin darted outside and circled us, tail wagging in greeting.

Inside, the cottage was warm, but not warm enough for the air conditioner, so I opened up the windows and the back door to the porch while the boys ransacked the basement for Seb's backup stash. Our clothes were pretty dry after sitting in the police station for hours, but I could still smell the chlorine. So I quickly changed into fresh shorts and a top, and strolled into the kitchen to find Jaz invading the fridge.

"Gotta let Daddy know we're back," she said. "He's going to want us all to come over there."

"Then give it a few before you call," I said. "I think we all deserve to sit down for a minute. Stress melted my brain. I need to reset."

"I hear you," Jaz said. "Where's your orange juice?"

I pointed to the side door and watched her down half the juice container, not bothering to get a glass. "Hey, Jaz? You okay? I mean, Paul-wise."

One of the first things that happened when we all got to the police station was Paul getting booked for violating his parole. Which was glorious to see—at least for most of us. But almost as sweet was watching what happened to Lulu: she had a bench warrant for her arrest issued by a judge back in Kalamazoo—failing to appear in court for shoplifting charges—and got booked alongside Paul. The last we saw of them both was them being hauled off to different parts of the station in cuffs.

Benny snapped a pic for posterity.

"Does it hurt that someone I opened up to could betray me so easily?" Jazmine mused. "Yeah, it does. But it's been over for a while. This was just the universe making sure I wouldn't be tempted to go back to him."

"Not tempted, then?"

"Not tempted," she confirmed, taking another slug of orange juice while the boys cheered triumphantly from somewhere in the basement, presumably having found what they were looking for. Jaz looked toward the door, smiling to herself. "Benny was pretty amazing with the security system hack, huh? I watched him do it, and you've never seen fingers type so fast. It was impressive."

If Benny hadn't done it, we might not be standing here. My father had kitted out his entire house in cameras like he was some kind of international arms dealer. Those trust issues came back to bite him in the ass, though, because they were able to pull all the footage—of me showing up at the house, of him signing the paperwork, and him locking me in the bedroom.

Now he faced aggravated kidnapping charges and extortion, and had to post nearly half a million in bail. Right now, he was locked in a jail cell—at least, until he could get the funds together. He might be millions on paper, but we overheard the police laughing about his cash flow.

Anyway, in the morning I had a meeting scheduled with an attorney. I had no idea how hard it was going to be make charges stick, or how much testimony I'd need to provide. I didn't even know if I'd be safe once he made bail.

Would he come after me? Would Big Burg send Paul after they let him out?

I didn't know.

But there were a couple of small bright spots. I still had the Harvard paperwork that he'd signed before he went psycho on me—it was damp from the pool but still legible. And the police had recovered my phone; I'd get that back tomorrow, hopefully. If not, I'd brick it and get a new one.

And on top of that, we were all safe. At least, for now. And that was enough.

"Want to chill out back? Grab a soda for me, will ya?" Seb asked as the boys headed out to the porch. "Benny's ordering Pete's Vegan."

"Thank God," Jazmine said as we followed them outside.

The horizon above the lake was streaked with magenta as the sun fell. Everything felt magical at this time of day—past golden hour, not quite night. The painted sky. The quiet surf rolling in from the lake. I crossed the back porch, where Benny lounged on the porch swing. Jaz joined him, taking over his phone so she could pick out what food to order. And I took a seat on the porch steps, hugging my knees as I watched Seb throwing a gnarled frisbee to Punkin.

Everyone content, at least for the moment. And a perfect picture, if I'd ever seen one.

Nana sure would've loved to see this, that's for sure.

"Yo," Benny said from the porch swing. "I know we just got back, but we're going to need to figure out what to do now. Because even if we don't run into any more trouble from Lulu and Paul—"

"*If?*" Jaz said. "That's being generous. I'd say we're on borrowed time."

Benny frowned at her. "I'm just saying, no matter what happens, our treasure hunt is pretty much at a standstill because they've still got Mabel's rings."

Right. That pesky little detail. I'd forgotten all about the rings today. Well. Mostly. There was that moment when I was having a mental breakdown and on the verge of death, diving into my father's pool from a second-story balcony. Something still niggled about that. I'd forgotten something. What was it . . . ?

"Can't open a lock if you don't have a key," Benny pointed out.

"True," Jazmine said. "Especially hard when you don't know where the lock is."

"Maybe we should put the treasure hunt on the back burner," Benny said. "Just until we find out what's going to happen with Paul and Lulu. Because I don't think any of us need to even consider trying to get the rings back."

"No one's going back in that compound." Jazmine then shouted toward the beach, "You hear me, Jansen? That means you."

Seb looked up and jogged back to the porch with Punkin trailing. When they were almost to me, Punkin stopped near Mr. Legs and peed.

"Again?" Seb asked. "That's about five times since we got home. How much water did you drink while we were gone?"

The dog looked up at him, red Frisbee firmly held between her gnarled front teeth, and for a moment, the last rays of the sun beamed over the beach, lighting up both Punkin and Mr. Legs with the most spectacular shade of orange.

It almost looked like they were on fire.

What had that woman Katie said, when we were in the Neelys' hallway, looking at Nana's painting?

The eyes really jump out at you with those orange irises.

It felt like being hit with lightning.

As close as I'd probably ever come, anyway.

"My God!" I said as Seb stopped in front of me, chest heaving from running around the beach with Punkin. "MY GOD!"

"Yes? I'm here, my child," he joked. "What does thou needest from thy Lord?"

"Mr. Legs!" I said, standing up. "It's Mr. Legs!"

He squinted. "Huh?"

I scrambled toward the old tree-trunk sculpture, nearly tripping over the bottom step, and then again when Punkin veered in my way. Seb followed, and then the other two Wags.

I stood at the base of the sculpture, looking up at it in the dazzling, fleeting light that shimmered as the sun dropped into the lake.

Mr. Legs' eyes looked like they were on fire, just like Nana's painting.

They were carved deeply, the circular ruts that defined the heron's eyes.

The perfect size to fit a pair of rings.

"The eyes!" I said as everyone ran up behind me. "The rings go inside the eyes!"

We stared up at the heron, and one by one, everyone made noises of surprise.

"Is it possible?"

"How would it work?"

"Are you sure?"

Seb put a hand on Mr. Legs. "Only one way to find out. Move."

Before we could stop him, Seb grabbed the base of the sculpture—the part that was still an old tree truck—and hoisted himself up, climbing it like a monkey trying to get a coconut.

"Be careful!" I called up to him.

"Fucking splinters," he complained, but he made it to the head of the heron.

We stared up at him. "What do you see?" I asked. "Is it just the sculptor's style choice, or . . . ?"

He shifted his grip and peered into the bird's eyes. "Holy shit! You guys—she's right! Something fits inside the eyes!"

Our combined cheer echoed around the beach. I looked behind us, paranoid that Paul and Lulu might show up out of the blue. But we were still alone. *Thank God.*

"If we only had Mabel's rings," Jazmine lamented.

Right. Can't open a lock without a key. A little disappointment weighted my chest as the reality of this truth brought me back down to earth. As close as we kept getting to the treasure, it remained eternally out of reach.

Maybe that was just the nature of treasure. It was the pot of gold at the end of the rainbow that you could never quite get to, even if you believed with your entire heart that it existed.

"Come on down," I told Seb. But he continued peering at the eyes and muttering to himself. He fished around in his pocket and pulled out something that he fiddled with for several moments, cursing under his breath.

"What's going on up there?" Benny asked.

I called up, "Hey! We're talking to you! Yoo-hoo!"

"Um, guys?" Seb said as if he hadn't heard us. "I think we were wrong about Mabel's rings."

What? "No!" I whined.

"You just said—" Jazmine started.

But Seb cut her off. "Paige! Tell me you've got your decoder ring."

Decoder ring . . . ? My hand flew to my neck, where the old Blackbeard decoder ring hung on its chain. I couldn't make sense of how our rings could unlock the heron. They were from the 1940s. Wyrd Jack was long dead.

But Mabel wasn't. And as we'd learned this summer, Mabel was the one who hid her husband's smuggled treasures.

"We had the real rings the whole time!" Seb gripped the sculpture with both arms and looked down at me "Throw yours up here! Fast as you can!"

I didn't think about it. I just unhooked the clasp, slid the ring off, and . . . well. No way could I throw it to him and not miss, so I gave it to Jazmine. She underhanded it, aiming at Seb's open hand.

He snagged it out of the air, nearly losing his grip in the process. But he shifted on the heron, foot straining for purchase on the carved wing of the bird. And we watched as he pushed the ring into the left iris.

No one breathed.

We just waited. Watched.

Seb pressed his fingers into the heron's eyes, making a happy noise when he finally got them into place. A dull metallic click sounded from somewhere within the sculpture's base.

"Get down!" Benny called.

Seb didn't climb down gracefully. He stepped off the wing and dove for the sand, landing with a thud. His head snapped toward the heron just in time to see what we were all witnessing.

As if it were a king on a giant chessboard, Mr. Legs slowly moved backward to reveal a small trapdoor hidden under his base. It was a minor shock to me that the sculpture moved freely after being told all my life that it had been carved from a tree trunk that grew on the property.

If Mabel's letter to her daughter was right, this was the smuggler's hole.

"Open it!" Seb said, scrambling across the sand toward us.

Heart speeding like a moving train, I glanced around the beach again, utterly paranoid, and was relieved to see that we were still alone. We dropped to our knees in front of Mr. Legs, brushing sand away from stonework and a crude wooden door that had been sunk inside. A single iron ring was affixed to it, and when Benny pulled it, the door creaked and complained, but it finally swung open like the trunk of a car.

We all stared inside the hole.

Benny was the first to turn on his phone's flashlight. And when he did, we could better see the size of it—maybe three or four feet in diameter, a straight shaft going down into the earth. And inside the shaft was the top of wooden crate.

"We gotta pull that out," Seb said excitedly. "Get that side of it, Benny!"

The boys reached into the hole and grabbed the sides of the crate. But try as they did, all they managed to do was grunt in frustration.

"What the fuck is in this crate?" Seb complained. "Either it weighs a ton, or it's wedged in there too tight."

"Shovel?" Jazmine suggested.

My mind flew to the tools in the garage. "Crowbar?"

Seb pointed at me. I raced around the cottage and retrieved both a shovel and an old crowbar from the garage, and when I raced back to the hole, Seb and Jazmine took turns trying to crack open the crate. It didn't seem to want to budge . . . and then wood splintered.

"There!" Jazmine said, lifting the shovel out of the hole. "Put the crowbar right there!"

Seb stuck the crowbar inside, and with the edge of the hole as a fulcrum, used all his weight to pry the top off the crate. Rusted nails lined the inner lid, but we avoided them and got the rest of the lid off, and Benny shined his phone's flashlight inside.

Packed tight as sardines in neat rows, gold bars glittered in the old wooden crate. Dozens of them. I reached inside and picked one up, only to be shocked by the weight of it.

"Jesus! This is . . ." Seb couldn't even finish. One by one, everyone picked up a gold bar, murmuring in amazement. "Holy shit, guys. Are you seeing this?"

I was seeing it. I just wasn't believing it. Not until Seb desperately pulled out more bars, trying to see how far down they went and quickly counting. "There must be . . . fifty gold bars, easy. Maybe more."

"The gold bar that was found downtown!" Jazmine said.

"Shit!" Benny said, his face lit up like Christmas with the biggest smile I'd ever seen on him. "The news said that bar was worth thirty thousand. Fifty times thirty thousand . . ."

"Wags," Seb said, looking around at all our faces. "There's more than a million inside here. We're fucking millionaires!"

Nervous laughter erupted, as well as dismissals of Seb's claim. *It can't be. This isn't happening. It must be fake, another one of Mabel's tricks.*

But as we all worked together to pull out all the gold bars, loading them into a wheelbarrow and hauling them toward the back deck, where we stacked them into some plastic totes that were left over from when I packed up Nana's stuff. All in all, there were forty gold bars, potentially worth more than a million.

Even splitting it four ways, it was more money than I could fathom.

When we'd removed all the gold, Seb and Benny pulled out the wooden crate that had held the bars. It was so old and damaged from being inside the hole that the sides were rotted and crumbled in their hands. But once they'd retrieved the bottom of the crate, we peered down in the hole to see another crate below it.

"What the hell . . . ?" Jazmine said, joy dancing in her eyes.

Like the sides of the gold-bar crate, this wood was rotten, so we made quick work of its nailed-on lid. Once it was torn off, we peered at something wrapped in burlap. Something that was about the size of a lamp, maybe a couple feet high. And as Seb lifted it out with a strained grunt, Benny helping him get it over the edge of the hole, it was clear that we'd reached the bottom of the smuggler's hole.

Seb dropped the heavy burlap sack on the nearby sand. And as my heart thudded wildly I my chest, I tore at the rotting fabric to reveal what lay inside.

The glittering figure of a nude woman stared back at me, carved marble covered in flaking gold. Unlike the larger, armless Venus de Milo sculpture, this little lady had all her appendages, and stood on a small hill made of seashells.

The Golden Venus.

Mabel was right. Once you'd seen it, you understood why it was so precious. All of us were lost for words. We just sat around the gilded statue, amazed and dumbfounded.

After all these years. And everything we'd been through this summer. It felt like a dream.

I couldn't breathe.

The statue literally stole my breath away.

"She's beautiful," Jaz whispered.

"Unbelievable," Benny said.

"Is it real?" I whispered, clutching my chest. "We really found her? This isn't a dream . . . ?"

"It's real," Benny said reverently. "It's very, very real."

"Nana Malone wanted us to find it when she gave us those Blackbeard rings," Seb said, looking at me with happy tears shining in his eyes.

The realization was a potent one. Nana had trusted us, even as kids, not to lose the vintage Blackbeard rings, just like she trusted the Neelys to look after her painting of Mr. Legs. Maybe she'd inherited Mabel's spirit-medium talents.

Or maybe she was just a sucker for a good treasure hunt like the rest of us.

"We didn't let her down," I said as Seb wrapped me up in his arms and tears of joy streamed down my cheeks. "I can't believe it. I just can't believe it . . ."

"Oh, *I* can," Seb murmured into my hair as Jazmine's and Benny's shouts of victory sailed over the darkening lake behind us. "Told you a million times, Paige. I've got enough faith for both of us."

Chapter 32

Cambridge, Massachusetts, three months later . . .

A chilly autumn breeze lifted my hair off my shoulders as I strolled toward Lowell House's front entrance. I'd been in classes and meetings all day, so it was a relief to be heading back to my dorm, even if I couldn't relax yet. I'd just finished my last class of the day—dating ancient and medieval art—which was held in the art museum's study hall. The small digital device I used to record lectures stopped working halfway through my class, and I was worried that I'd missed some of the discussion around ceramics that would be on the midterm test.

"Paige!" a male voice called as I jogged up a couple steps.

I glanced behind me to see one of the other art history majors—Cal Hodgkins, a junior, one year ahead of me—waving to flag me down. I paused at the top of the steps so he could catch up. "Hey, Cal. How was that architecture class?"

"Brutal," he said, pausing at the bottom of the steps to adjust his backpack. Dark-headed Cal was smart and good-looking, one of the friendlier juniors who often invited a few of us sophomores to parties around campus. He was one of those generational legacy students whose father and grandfather had attended Harvard.

A good person to know, especially for those of us who could never get the hang of all the weird social traditions around campus.

He set a foot on the bottom step and looked up at me. "It's Tuesday, in case you forgot."

I stared at him, a little confused. "Tuesday . . ."

"Poemical night," he said, giving me a big smile.

Right. Completely forgot. Harvard had twelve houses, and I'd been assigned to this one, Lowell House, along with four hundred other students. Lowell had a lot going for it: some historic Russian bells, home to the longest running opera company in New England, Thursday tea in the faculty deans' residence, a Bacchanalia in the spring, and a big yule party in the winter.

It also hosted the Poemical Society. Every Tuesday night, the poet in residence gathered students to read and listen to poetry. To be perfectly honest, the spoken word wasn't my thing. Maybe that's why I'd forgotten about being invited.

"Crap," I told Cal. "Is that tonight? Is Mary still coming with us?"

"She bowed out. But you and I can grab something to eat beforehand, if you're hungry," he said. "You might even call it a date . . ." He gave me a soft smile, both brows lifting hopefully.

I winced internally. "Oh, Cal. I'm sorry, I thought you knew. I have a boyfriend back home."

"Of course you do," he said, looking a little disappointed. "Really doesn't surprise me. Back in Michigan, right?"

"Yep." I nodded.

"Long way away. Doing the long-distance thing, huh?"

We were. I'd been back in Cambridge two months, and he'd visited twice. It was going to cost us an arm and leg to fly back and forth every month.

"Is it serious, or . . . ?" he asked, crossing his fingers.

"Very serious," I confirmed. "And sorry to keep disappointing, but I really need to study tonight, so I'm going to have to bail. Maybe next time, though?"

He looked a little bummed. "Damn, all right. Well, perhaps you'll consider going with me next Tuesday? Can't blame a guy for trying to get a pretty girl to love poetry."

"You actually *could* blame a guy for trying," a voice said behind me. "But I'm feeling generous today, so I'm going to let it slide, Robert Frost."

I whipped around on the front steps to see Seb standing against a white column, arms crossed over his chest. I let out a little cry of joy and threw my arms around him. "What are you doing here? Your flight's not supposed to be here until Friday!"

"Surprise," he said, dropping three quick kisses on my lips, cheek, and forehead. "Missed you like crazy."

"Missed you more," I whispered before I remembered Cal. "Oh, sorry." Clearing my throat, I twisted around in Seb's embrace and gestured loosely. "Seb, this is Cal—we're both Lowell House. Cal, this is my boyfriend, Seb."

Cal held up both hands. "Sorry, bruh. I really wasn't trying to overstep."

"All good, *bruh*," Seb imitated, cocking a brow. "Just don't make her turn you down again, or we're going to have a problem."

Jesus. Before Cal could answer, I tugged on Seb's shirtsleeve to get him to back down while I told Cal, "I'll see you around campus."

"Yeah, later," he said glumly, jogging up the steps to pass by us.

I linked elbows with Seb. "You didn't have to do that. He's not competition."

He tapped his temple with one finger. "Paige, up here, everyone is competition. But if you ever did decide to leave me, all I ask is that it's for someone a little cooler than a smarmy poet laureate wannabe in a preppy shirt."

"Deal," I said, standing on tip toes to kiss him, feeling giddy to have him here a few days early. If he couldn't fly out here regularly, I didn't know what I'd do. The cash we got for the gold bars had come in handy already, that's for sure. Split four ways, we each ended up with around three hundred thousand, give or take. A small fortune to us.

"Better leave the good stuff till we're alone," Seb said against my lips. "I've got a big surprise for you."

"Oh yeah? How big?"

"Thirty-five feet."

I choked out a laugh. "*What* now?"

"You'll see. Can I assume you're done for the day if you're being invited to poetry slams? If so, I'd like to show you what I'm talking about."

"I've got to study later, just for a couple hours. But I'm all yours right now."

He grinned. "Never get tired of you saying that. Come on, Professor Malone. Our chariot awaits." He gestured toward the long curb at the front of Lowell House, where I spotted the Speed Buggy parked in a no-parking zone.

I did a double take. "Wait, how . . . ? What's the Bronco doing here? Didn't you fly?"

Punkin's ugly head poked out of the back window. She gave me a little bark as we approached, and I unlinked my arm from Seb's to scratch her head. "What in the world? Hey, girl! You drove all the way out here to see me? What a good dog!"

"Don't let her fool you," Seb said, taking my backpack away from me to toss it inside the Bronco next to Punkin. "She's a terrible driver and nearly got us killed on the interstate."

I gave her a good scratch, happy to see her wagging tail, then I got into the front of the Bronco with Seb. "This is nuts," I told him. "Why didn't you tell me you were planning a major road trip? How long did it take you to get out here?"

"Two days," Seb said. "Seven hours the first day, then we spent the night in Rochester. We got up early this morning and made it here before noon."

I squinted at him. "That was hours ago."

"We've been busy," he said, barely able to contain a smile that told me he was up to no good. "Now hold on while I input a route into the GPS. Traffic on campus is a nightmare . . ."

He wouldn't let me see where he was taking me, but it didn't matter. I was just ecstatic to see him. His early arrival threw my study schedule off a little, but that was fine. I'd been working ahead in my classes to ensure that we had the entire weekend to ourselves, no distractions. The last time he visited, three weeks ago, we never left the hotel room.

We headed south, off campus, and took a road that hugged the Charles River, talking nonstop about every little thing . . . His trip here. Punkin's new flea medication. How Jazmine was adjusting to the University of Michigan in Ann Arbor and her snagging a spot on the women's water polo team. And, of course, the app Benny was building in his spare time between classes back in Kalamazoo.

"I truly don't understand why he thinks he's going to make a killing from babysitting," I said. "Babysitters aren't raking in big cash . . . are they? What kind of cut does he think he can take?"

"Let him have this," Seb argued. "He deserves it after dealing with Lulu again last week."

Benny got a long, handwritten letter from Lulu that she wrote from a women's correctional facility near Kalamazoo, where she was serving three months for shoplifting clothes when she first met Benny on campus, posing as a college student. I hadn't personally read Lulu's letter from jail, but Seb had, and he reported that she'd used the word "sorry" eighteen times while begging for his forgiveness. Benny hadn't forgiven her, though, and I'm not sure Lulu's attempt at a prison poem was going to repair the damage she'd done.

"No word from Paul?" I asked as Punkin stuck her head over the front seat and panted in my face.

"Still awaiting trial. But I don't think there's a lawyer in the state who can get him off."

Felony firearm offenses came with mandatory jail time in Michigan. Two years. His dad still had about six months left on his own house arrest. We were all still waiting for the shoe to drop on that, but nothing had happened with Big Burg. He didn't send anyone after us, didn't burn down anyone's house. Maybe he was waiting for the outcome of Paul's trial.

Or maybe he was waiting to find out what was going to happen with my father.

It took my father nearly two weeks to get bailed out after that horrible day I went to his house. When his new wife finally came up with the bail money, the cops caught him trying to charter a plane to South America, so he earned himself the flight-risk label. Now he was sitting in a cell, awaiting trial, which was due to start in November, around the time of my Thanksgiving break.

I'd already notified my professors about taking time off to testify and had flight tickets booked to return for the trial. Everyone had been kind about it. Ironically, because of all this mess, I had no problem convincing the financial aid office that my father was, indeed, not financially responsible for me: making the news for being kidnapped by the biggest commercial real estate agent in Grand Rapids really helped drive that point home.

It also made the Wags realize that we couldn't tell anyone about what we found. Not the gold, and not the Venus. If we announced anything, it would be all over the news, and if I thought I was worried about the cottage being broken into before all this, well. Let's just say that Mabel was right to be paranoid, back when she was responsible for it. And now that we were its guardians, we decided jointly that the best way to do that was to hang on to its secrets. For now, at least.

Seb drove us into Boston proper, where traffic was even worse until we got to Boston Harbor. I surveyed all the sailboats bobbing in the water from my window alongside Punkin, who eagerly sniffed the briny harbor air as if it were made of beef jerky.

"Seriously, Seb," I said. "Where the hell are you taking me?"

"I barely know myself," he said, taking a turn toward the harbor. And that's when I saw a sign that identified our destination: CHARLESTOWN MARINA. "When I tell you that I made a large deposit on something, sight unseen a month ago, I feel like you're going to get mad and yell at me."

Uh-oh. "Sight unseen . . . ?"

"But," he argued, flicking a sheepish look in my direction. "I think it all turned out okay, so maybe you'll fall in love with it like me and Punkin did."

"You're making me nervous."

"I'm making myself nervous," he muttered under his breath as we drove through a small parking lot that bordered some of the slips in the marina. "Oh shit, this is us." He whipped the Bronco into a parking space and shut off the engine. Punkin got excited.

"Seb . . . ?"

"Just come see it before you say no. Please?"

I had no idea what I saying yes or no to until I climbed out of the Bronco and watched Seb jog across a narrow strip of grass that separated the docks from the parking lot. He stepped onto the dock and stood in front of a white-and-brown trawler—one that was clearly being used as a houseboat.

I stopped in front of him, head cocked. "What am I looking at?"

"Madame, you are looking at a custom-built houseboat—a real, working boat, not just a floating barge. It's seaworthy. Slow, but seaworthy."

"Um . . . ? Huh?"

He stepped onto the boat's main deck from where it was moored to the dock. "A lot of houseboats aren't real, working boats. The guy who built it is totally legit. He spent like three hundred thousand renovating an old fishing trawler into this. Let me show you . . ."

Seb offered me his hand and tugged me onto the boat with him. Punkin jumped on as if she'd done it a thousand times. The trawler had some nice seating on the main deck, a windowed wheelhouse on a small level above, behind which was a second covered seating area under a canvas Bimini top.

"Look!" he said. "You get inside it proper through here," he said, inviting me inside to a cozy cabin with seating, a TV, and a two-person dining table. "And through here, there's a sweet galley. That means kitchen, Paige."

I knew what a ship's galley was, but he was so excited, I let it go. This galley was super tiny and you had to step down to get to it. But I was surprised how nice it was. Nicer than the kitchen in the cottage.

We headed through it, into a narrow hallway with storage and a couple of doorways.

"Main bedroom is here," he said, showing me. "Queen-sized bed, baby! Bigger than the cottage! Lots of little nooks for storage. And the bathroom isn't ridiculously small—look. Fancy shower. Oh, and there's a tiny room back here with two extra fold-down sleeping berths and a little desk. See . . . ?"

"Seb," I said, trying to get a word in edgewise as he bounced around the boat. "What is all this?"

He stopped in the open doorway that separated the galley from a short flight of stairs leading to the main deck and spread his arms wide, waggling his blond eyebrows. "*This* is *Queen Anne's Revenge.*"

I tilted my head. "Blackbeard's ship?"

"Exactly!" he said, excited. "Technically, it's just *Queen* Ann's *Revenge*, without the 'E,' because the owner's wife is named Ann. But come on! When I saw the name, I knew it was meant to be."

I put a hand on my chest. "Seb. You just said this was a custom three-hundred-thousand-dollar boat. You don't have that kind of money."

"Nope. I rented it."

"Oh." Huh.

He was practically exhilarated. "The owner built it to cruise the Great Loop when it was just him and his wife—"

"I have no idea what that is."

"Great Loop—you cruise through the Great Lakes, Mississippi, Gulf of Mexico, and up the East Coast into the New York and Canadian canals. Takes six weeks if you're speeding through it, but people sometimes take years to do it. Anyway, the guy who built this is a Looper—he's done the Loop a couple times. But now he's got kids and needs something bigger. So he's renting this out while he builds a new one."

"And you now have this one because . . . ?"

"I got it for us," he explained. "You said to figure out a way for us to be together while you go to school."

I had.

"So I'm moving here to be with you," he said, shrugging. "If you want to stay in the dorms, that's fine. I know you work hard and don't need distractions. But if you want to live in here with me, there's a tiny extra room back there that we can turn into your study room. And it's only twenty minutes from campus, even in shitty traffic, as you just saw. Plus, the views from these windows are pretty excellent . . ."

I looked around at all the warm wood and steel inside the belly of the trawler. It was pleasant in here, I had to admit. And he wasn't kidding about the views. Nothing but water and boats. My favorite.

"What about your job with Mr. Neely back in Haven Beach?"

"He was disappointed but I gave him notice. He hired my replacement last week."

"Jaz and Benny know?"

He nodded. "I asked them to keep it secret. I wanted to surprise you?" He didn't sound very sure about that. "I rented this slip here at the marina until next summer. It's a little pricier than Neely's Marina, lemme just say . . ."

"This isn't an RV," I said, remembering his ultimate dream of life on the road.

"It's way better. I mean, Jazmine's right—if a hurricane comes, we're going to need to go to a shelter, but otherwise, it's perfect. You go to school and get your art history degree while I go to this tech institute up the road and get my ASE certification to become a mechanic in a year."

I shook my head, astounded. "You signed up for school here?"

"I start after the New Year. Registered and everything. I can always find work as a mechanic, and certification will get me better pay."

Punkin trotted through the cabin, sniffing every corner. I watched her, a little overwhelmed. "What about the cottage?"

Seb reached for my waist and tugged me closer. "The cottage will always be home base. We can still spend summers there. And now that Benny and I reinforced the smuggler's hole under Mr. Legs, the Golden Venus will be safe until we're ready to bring her out."

We put her back into the smuggler's hole. She needed to be authenticated, and there was the matter of cultural reappropriation because technically, she'd been smuggled out of ancient Rome. I was making contacts at Harvard who could help, but I wasn't ready to trust anyone yet.

Mabel was right to worry about literal gold diggers who'd do anything to get their hands on treasure. We didn't want the local news celebrating our discovery of the statue or the gold bars, didn't want our faces and names plastered everywhere. I mean, the town was *still* talking about the single gold bar that was found in the downtown sewer. If people knew how many other bars we'd uncovered, we'd be fighting people back with pitchforks and fire.

Best to keep it down low. So we all agreed that our discovery was Wag business, no one else's. Not until we were ready.

"Venus will be fine," he told me, encircling me with his arms. "No one knows her resting spot but us, and we have the keys to open Mr. Legs. Not even Paul can get to her."

"You're right."

"And like I said, you don't have to live here with me if you think it's distracting, but I can't do long distance. Not with you. It's been three weeks since we last saw each other, and I can't take it."

I slipped my arms around his back. He felt so nice, warm and solid.

He felt like mine.

"I can't take it, either," I told him. "Having two homes is too hard."

He kissed me softly on the top of my head. "Then you and I are lucky, because we can make our home wherever we want. It could be in an RV, or a beach cottage, or this unbelievably dope boat. It doesn't matter. You know why?"

"Why?"

He pulled back to look into my face. "You and I don't really need walls. All we need is each other. As long as we're together, that's home. In fact, we're home right now. Doesn't it feel good to be here?"

My eyes brimmed with happy tears. "Oh, Seb, I don't know what to say."

"Say you'll make a home with me here, and that you're not mad that I did this."

"If you'd *bought* the boat, I'd be mad. But you did good. Maybe we could make this work . . . ?"

"This is a try-it situation, Paige. We could hate the boat. But we might just love it. And, bonus, it just so happens that Benny discovered chatter on some treasure-hunting message boards about a series of buried gold caches along the Great Loop left by some Canadian fur traders around the Revolutionary War."

"Seb . . ." I warned.

"Just saying, this summer, if we decided we wanted to take this baby through the Great Lakes, we could renew the rental and ride it through the countryside. It sleeps four. So Jaz and Benny could join us, and we could just take a little peek at those Revolutionary War gold caches—"

"A *little* peek?"

"The littlest!"

"Seb?"

He made a face and braced himself. "Yes . . . ?"

"You can help me move my stuff out of the dorm tomorrow."

His eyes lit up. "Yeah? Roomies again?"

I nodded, ridiculously happy. "We *just* need to agree on a few rules . . ."

"Nope, nope, and *hell nope*," Seb said. "We only need one rule this time. The golden rule . . ."

"Do unto others?"

He shook his head slowly then flashed me his dimples. "Never leave home."

About the Author

Jenn Bennett is the critically acclaimed author of several young adult books, including *Alex, Approximately*; *Starry Eyes*; and *Chasing Lucky*. She also writes romance and fantasy for adults. Her books have been Goodreads Choice Award nominees, translated into a dozen languages, earned multiple starred reviews, and included on annual Best Book lists for both *Kirkus Reviews* and *Publishers Weekly*. She lives near Birmingham with one husband and two good dogs.